ANGELS AT ARTHUR'S

James H. White

Heyward House Publishing, Charleston, SC.
Heywardhousepublishing.com

Visit James H. White at *angelsatarthurs.com*

Angels at Arthur's: A Novel

Edited by Danielle M. Walters, M.F.A, and Joseph Gartrell, MA.

Scripture quotations are taken from the King James Edition of the Holy
Bible and the New American Standard Bible.

Library of Congress Cataloging-in-Publications Data

Angels at Arthur's: a novel/James H. White

Heyward House Publishing

ISBN-13: 9780692242780
ISBN-10: 0692242783

ACKNOWLEDGEMENTS

Accomplished writer was never among my vocational aspirations or natural abilities. Wanting to avoid any undo presumption to the contrary let me classify myself a storyteller at best. I claim a measure of Godly inspiration, loads of pigheaded persistence, and much assistance writing this story.

First, I must thank my wife, Charlotte, for her divine forbearance over these last seven years, for her suggestion that the original amateur stage drama could become a novel, for her incredible ideas, each moving the story forward, and for her reads and rereads until she could no longer endure reading my writing and had wearied of my wordiness.

Unfortunately, this occurred at about the same time I also could no longer tolerate reading my work and was beginning to realize why my affliction of verbosity was indeed her perfect storm. It was mine too.

I give great thanks to my daughter, Dorathy Angelin Beers, the idyllic romanticist, who consistently shredded and refined my rambling story, bleeding the text like succoring leeches from red to read, and always sharply moving the adventure forward.

I must also thank my granddaughter, Mackenzie Claire Cruce, who, while studying for her B.A. and M.A. degrees in English at Clemson University and The Citadel, took time to read my proletarian manuscript and shared with me many creative writing tricks of the trade.

I had feedback from Eleanor Gunther, my former coworker and friend for over forty years, who likely feeling an obligation more than anything else, read the story and gave me her unbiased opinion—as she'd done over many years in business. I must also thank her daughter-in-law, Leeann Gunther, for giving the story a read through and critique as well. I extend my special thanks to Pastor Scott Kinney and his wife Megan Kinney of Seacoast Church, Mount Pleasant, South Carolina, for their diligent reading of the proof copy, for their constructive and helpful comments, for checking me on any potential heretical lapses or scriptural inaccuracies and for their enthusiastic support of the story.

I especially thank my talented Story Editor, Danielle M. Walters, M.A. English, M.F.A. Creative Writing, who is a professional writer, editor and teacher of English and Creative Writing at Charleston Southern University. Were it not for her honest assessments and repeated candid critiques of the manuscript through several evaluations and rewrites over more than two years, *Angels at Arthur's* would have remained scrambled chaos as it appeared when she first appraised the story.

And finally I'm deeply indebted to Joseph Gartrell, a very talented writer and professional editor in Charleston, who diligently critiqued each chapter of the story content and copy edited the final version of text. I am grateful for his meticulous efforts.

James H. White

PS: Charlotte just read this acknowledgment. Yes, you guessed it, "too many words."

Dedicated

Master David Taylor Korman
Born unto the Angels
June 21, 2003

Master Milo Cooper McDaniel
Born unto the Angels
December 13, 2014

INTRODUCTION

I believe angels are real. God's angels, like the unseen wind whispering through the trees, reveal a gentle, sometimes blustery and occasionally even gusty footprint if we but observe. I know beyond doubt that God's heavenly hosts surround us every day. I have no idea how many times God's angels have kept my wife, our daughters, our sons-in-law, our grandchildren and me. But they surely have!

I've heard accounts of many folks who have prematurely experienced Heaven and returned to this life to tell of Heaven's marvelous glory and multitudes of angels.

I've never seen an angel, but my son-in-law, Jeffrey Cruce, had the experience up close and personal. He can describe the angel's appearance as if the incident was yesterday. It was an event he clearly will never forget and one that indeed helped inspire this story.

Nonetheless, I'm quite certain I've experienced angelic presence countless times during my thousands of flying hours, first as a pilot, then as a passenger and businessman. I know God's heavenly hosts watched over me in my travels as I flew to the ends of this earth, as I visited hundreds of factories in dozens of foreign countries, some in sorely distressed parts of this world, as well as when I was home with my family.

I know they were with me in times when I was scared absolutely spitless, running for my life through the fire and into the valley of the shadow of death, and finding my Exodus only because of God's magnificent grace and the protection of His angels.

Hallelujah! He lives. God's angels are indeed among us.

Psalm 91

[10] No evil shall befall you,
Nor shall any plague come near your dwelling;
[11] For God shall give His angels charge over you, To keep you in all
your ways.
[12] In their hands they shall bear you up,
Lest you dash your foot against a stone.

1

KING STREET ROCKET

"Heads up, yanks!" someone yelled from behind them in a distinctly British brogue. "Rocket arse biker streaking in fast and low. Barney Rubble double trouble comin' to ya," he continued as the chill of the wintry morning air seemed to amplify his frantic but colorful warning.

Thomas instinctively grabbed Codi, pulling her toward him just as a speeding biker weaved out of traffic and onto the sidewalk. The biker flashed by Codi, almost taking off her left arm, his rubber handle bar grip catching the sleeve of her fleece jacket.

"Codi, you okay?" Thomas asked. He sounded panicked as he held her tight to his side. "That was seriously close."

"I'm okay, but he could have really hurt someone." Codi pulled at the small rip in the left arm of her jacket. "The jerk's got some severe mental health problems or he's really blazed on something."

They watched the guy stand, perched high on his sprocket pedals. He jumped his bike as he bobbed and weaved, nearly pummeling others on the sidewalk, forcing some to scatter into the street. He sped on toward the intersection of King and Queen.

His fenderless two-wheeler was far from the latest hybrid-racing bike and had seen better days. The paint was badly weathered and carried only a hint of its former fire engine red brilliance. He wasn't wearing a pointy-headed cyclist helmet, but a faded blue baseball cap, its bill fitted sideways in an effort to show some degree of social belligerence. He wasn't attired in the latest spandex cyclist touring tights, but ragged faded jeans and a dingy gray hoodie. His stringy shoulder length blond hair was coursing in the breeze as he gyrated onward.

Then, as if replaying video of a bad dream in slow motion, Thomas and Codi watched as the certifiable wacko ignored the red light and attempted to outrun a four door Ford Fusion speeding across King headed west on Queen.

The biker didn't make it. He peddled full speed pounding head on into the side of the white Fusion, upending his bike and flinging both biker and bike over the top of the sedan. Both tumbled onto the sidewalk.

"Call 911, Codi. The guy's got to be hurt real bad," Thomas cried as he ran toward the downed biker.

The driver of the Fusion screeched to a quick stop, exited his car, and observed a huge dent in his front right door and broken passenger side window. Codi quickly dialed 911.

"Come on. Pick up," Codi said. As she waited for the operator to answer, her fingers trembled.

"Charleston County 911. What's your emergency?"

"A biker just ran into a car at the intersection of King and Queen. He seems to be hurt badly."

"Is the victim breathing? How seriously is he hurt?"

"I don't know."

The driver watched as Thomas tried to help the stunned victim. He could see no blood, but the guy was obviously out cold. The driver guarded his remarks so as not to say something callous that those in the crowd might hear. Everyone could see he was incredibly pissed, but recognizing the circumstances, remained controllably irate.

At about the same time, Codi pushed through the small crowd gathering on the sidewalk. She tried to reach Thomas and the victim.

Then, to everyone's astonishment, especially the owner of the damaged Fusion, the not-so-injured cyclist sat up. He stumbled to his feet, mounted his damaged bike, and wobbled off down King Street as fast as the bent front wheel would shimmy and shake forward. It all happened so fast that no one in the crowd could grasp what had just taken place.

Codi, still on the line with 911, quickly said, "Ma'am, you're not going to believe this, but the injured guy ... well, maybe he was not so injured after all. He just got on his bike and rode off down King Street."

"Someone stop him!" the vehicle owner yelled to the crowd. "He damaged my car! Someone call the police." He dialed 911 to summon the police himself.

"Did anyone get a photo of the guy with a cell phone?" he questioned the crowd, but they all shook their heads no.

"Watch where he's going!" cried the vehicle owner.

The errant biker vanished out of sight, disappearing down one of the narrow cobblestone side streets south of Broad.

The excitement and rush of the moment over, Thomas took Codi's hand.

"Come on, Codi. We'll be late for court," he said as they walked on down King Street toward Broad. When they turned east on Broad, Codi pointed to Arthur's on King where their inextricable journey began on a foggy Thursday night late in February almost a year earlier.

Rachael Coedinger Joseph, Codi to her friends, was a North Carolina girl raised in a respectable family in Raleigh. She was a former, and very creative, recreational drug event planner, specializing in cocaine, pot, and other illicit frivolities. She plied her trade only to the rich and famous. Squeaky clean and never arrested, she had been well known from DC south among the party set.

Thomas Houston Stirk, a Charleston native and former notorious street punk and pothead, had met Codi completely by accident or, as law enforcement would say, because of "fate driven by common criminal wrongdoing." Whatever their unfortunate criminal past, Codi and Thomas were happily together now. Totally inseparable!

"Arthur's on King. How paradoxical," Codi quipped. "It seems like a lifetime ago but it's only a year. How ironic that today we're attending a trial to hopefully witness the end to the ill-fated journey we began at Arthur's."

"How could I ever forget?" Thomas added. "Awesome stress, riveting terror, gut-wrenching fear, all accentuated by moments of sheer panic! But hey! We've also been rewarded. How about that? Maybe a fair trade under the circumstances. Wouldn't you agree?"

"Totally," Codi quickly responded, "and that lunatic biker was out-of-his-mind stoked, all right. He was so lit up, he could've seriously injured someone. But his totally stoned bad was zero-nada bad compared to Aristide or Pinella and their drug cartel thugs. Were it not for Almighty God and you, Thomas ... well ... like ... I mean." Codi stumbled for words. "I'm sure ... you know ... I totally wouldn't have made it. I'd be dead now. I'm certain of that. It scares me to think about it." She raised her index finger and pointed toward heaven.

"God delivered and blessed us Codi," Thomas affirmed. "Blessings I know I certainly never deserved. Total redemption. Complete salvation. God's free gift! He covered us with His blood just as He protected the Israelites by the blood of the Lamb at the Passover. Little could I have imagined a year ago how God would guard and shield us," Thomas concluded as he pulled open the heavy mahogany door at the Federal District Courthouse, one of the foundational pillars at Charleston's historic Four Corners of Law.

2

FEDERAL DISTRICT COURT

"All rise," the bailiff announced as the judge mounted the bench. Codi and Thomas stood in the next to last row of spectators. The warmth of being inside, not to mention the heated rhetoric of the trial, had tempered the chill in the air on this wintry February morning.

The Federal District Courthouse, built in 1896 and anchoring the southwest corner of Broad and Meeting, was one of the most popular tourist sights in Charleston, but on this day, it was also the scene of one of the most notorious international drug cartel trials in US history.

The bailiff continued, "Hear ye, hear ye, Judge Horace H. Falcon presiding over this honorable court in the matter of The United States of America versus Jose Molina Vargus, and the State of Colombia, South America, in absentia."

Horace Falcon, his craggy face complementing his northeastern accent, could have easily been mistaken for a veteran fishing boat Captain or a New England lobsterman as he spoke his "good-mornin-to-ya." He looked worn and wrinkled but savvy. His stern expression shouted absolute control over his courtroom.

Judge Falcon took his seat, adjusted his reading glasses and glanced at the court docket in front of him. It became clear why his closest friends called him "Hawk."

His steel blue eyes laser focused on the bailiff as he instructed, "Will the US Marshal seat the defendant, please?" A side door opened and a guard escorted Jose Molina Vargus to the defendant's table as the court resolutely began the last day of the second week of deliberations. Vargus anxiously conversed with his Colombian attorney and his cadre of three American lawyers from Halley & Barton PA, Washington, DC. It was purportedly the best defense money could buy.

Vargus, a wealthy South American and resident of Cartagena, had been vacationing with his wife and six children in Lake Tahoe, when his 248-foot yacht, Hocus Pocus, exploded in Charleston harbor eleven months earlier. The explosion exposed a South American drug smuggling-cartel allegedly operating from on board his yacht.

Vargus owned World Quest Limited, a Colombian based travel agency specializing in luxury vacations and cruises, mostly in the Caribbean and South America. Unwittingly, his company had leased the Hocus Pocus and its crew of twelve to an alleged drug cartel.

Vargus testified his company had leased the yacht to diplomats from Haiti and Colombia through the Haitian Consulate in Colombia. Claude Pierre Aristide, Undersecretary from the Haitian Embassy in Colombia, and Fidel Rojas Pinella, a minor Undersecretary, Colombian Consulate in Miami, had both signed the lease and transferred funds from a bank account belonging to the Haitian Consulate.

Vargus claimed to have never met Pinella or Aristide and strongly asserted he had no knowledge of any drug cartel. He'd plead not guilty to all twenty-one counts in the indictment, including the nineteen counts of murder.

The explosion was terribly ill-fated for Vargus since his crew of twelve, who had been on the Hocus Pocus since her christening, and the additional seven on board, were all killed. It left no one to testify in his favor or to provide hope for a plausible eyewitness defense.

But for the grace of God, Codi and Thomas had barely escaped certain death in the explosion and both had testified in the initial days of the trial, which was now laboring through its last hours of testimony before the jury was charged and began deliberations.

The Justice Department was determined that Vargus would become the first "cartel boss" convicted in the United States in their quest to stop the massive trafficking of drugs from South America.

The circumstantial case against Vargus was strong, but the prosecutor had no direct evidence linking him with the cartel. Although Vargus was an unlikely candidate for criminal prosecution with no record of drug dealing or fraud of any kind, he was nonetheless a rich businessman. The prosecution knew he was vulnerable and could likely get a conviction. His political connection with former US Senator Tobias Edwardson did not help his case. Justice would not be served and he could likely spend the rest of his days behind bars.

The trial was now really all about Federal Prosecutor Houghton's quest for glory. It was obvious to the insiders he was shamelessly committed to climbing the promotion ladder at the price of justice. He was counting on accolades from winning this case pushing him up a rung or two.

Codi was thankful she'd not been called as a witness for the prosecution. Even more, she was thankful former Senator Tobias Edwardson was not on trial. Houghton had called Codi to explain her kidnapping and imprisonment aboard the Hocus Pocus. Codi had been on the stand for a full day as Houghton questioned her. He hammered her on whether she had ever met Vargus, which she truthfully denied.

Houghton never asked Codi about her relationship with Edwardson, and Edwardson had never been questioned regarding Codi's drug dealings. Their relationship was never obvious. Codi had dodged a speeding bullet and she knew it.

Concentrating on political connections to win the case against Vargus, Houghton never realized he was missing the Edwardson piece of the cartel puzzle. If he did know what was missing, he was unable to find facts supporting the truth.

Thomas watched day after day as Jose Molina Vargus sat at the defense counsel's table. Vargus appeared to be a fine, upstanding fellow, well groomed and sophisticated—not someone capable of sending nineteen men to their deaths. Thomas knew were it not for the grace of God, he and Codi would have also died aboard the Hocus Pocus.

"He's got to be the unluckiest man on earth," Thomas thought, immediately reflecting on his own wretched past.

If Vargus was the unluckiest man on earth, Thomas knew he had to be the luckiest. He'd been arrested twenty-three times by the time he was in his mid-twenties. By all rights, he should have been serving a ten-year sentence under the repeat offender statute. But he was a free man. So in some small way, he understood the plight of Jose Vargus and felt sorry for his family.

Thomas had driven his mother almost mad with his abhorrent behavior. She'd tried to raise him right but his constant delinquency had been almost impossible for her handle. His multiple arrests for drugs, DUI, possession, larceny and theft were well known by the Charleston Police. He'd been busted so many times he knew the drill by heart.

Mentally, he struggled to erase recollections of years of rebellious behavior and the mountains of unnecessary grief he'd piled on his mom.

Thomas particularly recalled being arrested for DUI just days before his eighteenth birthday when his mom bailed him out and once again tried to help him understand the root of his problems. Her best efforts were never enough then, but he clearly got it now. He was sure he could never forget her bitter plight and how the father he'd never known abandoned them both.

It hurt Thomas to recall hearing his mom speak of her desperation and anxiety when she was younger. He remembered his anguish hearing her tell of her fear and apprehension after she became pregnant and how her suffering was compounded when his father threw her out after she refused his demand of an abortion.

Thomas was fully repentant now and understood his mom's painful past. He would never forget the agonizing grief she'd described. He would see that she would never be thrown out again.

3

THROWN OUT

"The puppy! They threw him out!" Years ago, Thomas's mother, Mary Stirk, had screamed at her dad in horror as the car in front of them slowed almost to a stop, flung open the back door and chucked the furry little ball into the ditch. She couldn't believe anyone could throw out such a defenseless little animal. Her mom and dad saw too, but it didn't matter. Her dad drove on amid the painful yelps of the little black and white puppy. She never forgot the yowling, which seemed oddly loud coming from such a tiny puppy.

"Please, Dad. Please can we get it? It might drown in the ditch or get run over by a car." Mary begged as she leaned into the front seat, tearfully pleading for mercy.

"Hush, Mary!"

"But Dad, please. The puppy might die. Please, Daddy! I'll take good care of him. I'm old enough to take care of a puppy. It won't be any trouble for you and Mom. I promise. Please, Daddy?"

"Mary, we're already late. I've got to change my work clothes. Deacon's meeting is tonight. Can't be late. We don't have time for some mutt dog anyway, and we sure don't need another mouth to feed around the house. There are stray dogs everywhere in this world. We can't take them all in."

Then, screeching tires from two or three cars back and an awful *thrump thrump*. She and her mother refused to look back and covered their ears, trying to muffle the fading whine of the defenseless pup.

She was thirteen and in seventh grade, she told her son, tears streaming down her cheeks as she painfully recalled her father's callous response to the accident that ended that small pup's life so many years ago.

Thomas saw her pain as the afternoon sun, pouring through the blinds, lined her face like ruled notebook paper. He had never wanted a dog, but he knew that if he'd asked his mom, she would have gotten him one.

Earlier that day, Mary Stirk had posted $5,000 bond for Thomas's second DUI arrest. Confronted with daily anarchy trying to raise a rebellious son, she did what any dedicated single mom would have done. She called a well-respected local attorney who once again appeared at her son's bond hearing, convincing the magistrate, against his better judgment, to allow Thomas to make bail one more time. The judge knew Thomas Houston Stirk and was well aware of his alcoholism and many previous arrests.

Mary knew her son was addicted and needed professional counseling, but she nonetheless sat him down and once again trying to bang some sense into his thick skull. This time, she told him she'd finally had enough.

"Thomas you're almost eighteen. It's time you grow up, son. Learn to be responsible! Stop the drinking or next time they'll lock you up and I won't be able to get you out!"

Thomas always politely listened but rarely heard anything his mother said.

"I'm ashamed of you, Thomas," she rebuked him, still sobbing from the heartbreaking story of the abandoned black and white puppy. "I know you feel thrown out—discarded by a father you've never known—who was never there for you."

His absentee father had always been a convenient crutch for his conduct. It was easy, after all, since he always reasoned that if his father had been around, he wouldn't be so totally screwed up.

Thomas hoped that someday his mom would tell him about his dad. She'd always been reluctant to unlock the secrets of the past. He knew almost nothing about him. He wondered if his dad loved him. Why did he desert them? Who was his dad? Where did he live? Did he have brothers and sisters? He was desperate to know.

He wanted to open the lockbox, find his buried roots. He didn't know exactly what he might find but he wanted to know about his dad. He wanted the truth. Little did Thomas realize, when his mom finally did open up about his dad, he would get to know her too.

"Mom, just don't say anymore about my fantasy father. I don't have a dad!"

He whacked the chair down, slamming its back on the floor as he angrily got up from the kitchen table.

"I've really had it about him," Thomas continued. "You can't believe how I hate it. Just shut up about him. I hate him. He hates both of us, Mom!"

Thomas stormed out of the kitchen, slamming the door behind him with such ferocity it rattled the china in the cabinets. Mary followed him into the living room, sitting in the wingback chair across from him, tears continuing to stream down her face.

"Thomas, you're not to blame. I understand how you feel."

"Mom, you can't understand. You've never understood. Everyone I grew up with had a dad. But not me! I couldn't tell anyone anything about my dad. When I filled out questionnaires at school, I would leave the space for *father's name* blank and the teachers would always come around telling me I needed to include him. I soon learned to fill in a name. Just write in something, anything, so the teachers wouldn't ask me again for a name I didn't have—for a father I didn't know."

"I understand much more than you realize, Thomas," she said as she cradled her head in her hands, continuing to sob.

Mary knew the day would come. Her silent secret would one day have to be revealed. But not today. Not now. She knew she could never divulge all she had buried so deep for so long. She was aggravated at Thomas's insistence, but what was she to do?

"No way could you understand, Mom. At least you knew your father," he said, scowling.

"Thomas, I've never gotten over seeing that little puppy dumped out and run over so many years ago. That's why I told you the story. I can still hear the little thing yelping." Tears welled up in her eyes again. "I wanted someone to take him and love him. He didn't deserve to die in the middle of that road, just a bloody spot on the asphalt. Every time we drove down that road and passed that ditch I could never look."

She looked away from Thomas and wiped the tears from her cheeks.

"Mom, I've always known he hurt you. You never told me, but I knew. I could feel it. He totally destroyed your life, and he's trashing my life too. I hate him, Mom."

Bad-mouthing his dad always made Thomas feel better. He knew it was wrong but it relieved his pain. It was routine now.

"Thomas, you couldn't know, but I was wounded. I was hurt. I was thrown out and run over too. I felt just like that unwanted puppy."

She looked up at her son, hoping he could see her grief, feel her anguish. Prompted by his mom's story about the puppy, Thomas dejectedly recalled his equally miserable and painful seventh grade experience. He'd been so lonely then. He had hated being thirteen and in middle school. His thoughts were suddenly overwhelmed by the agonizing memories.

4

BEST FRIENDS

It was a frog-strangler of a rainy morning in September when Thomas first met Stacy Howard. They were both in seventh-grade at Charleston Middle School and gym class had been moved indoors. Thomas hated gym, especially when it was indoors and he couldn't casually wander off to sneak a smoke behind the dumpster.

In seventh grade, size was everything. The tallest guys soon began organizing a pickup basketball game. They started choosing sides and Thomas and another kid, both of whom were a good six inches shorter than the rest, were part of the inadequate few. They were flagged short-load rejects, relegated to the bleachers where size didn't matter much.

"I hate pickup games," Thomas half mumbled to the kid sitting next to him. "I never get picked. Everyone watching can see what a scrunty runt ass you are. Hey, what's your name?"

"Stacy. Stacy Howard. What's yours?"

"Thomas Stirk. Who's your homeroom teacher?"

"Mrs. Echols, but she's never there. Always some substitute—usually one of the bus drivers none of us even know.

"You're lucky she's never there. Homeroom teachers aren't good for nothing except sending you to the Principal's Office for smoking or something. I've been sent to Mrs. Tesling's office a bunch of times. I've lost count."

"Yeah, I've been sent there too."

"PE really sucks," Thomas winced. "It's no fun always being a scrunt."

"Yeah, I know. I hate it too."

"So you've been sent to her office too?"

"Yeah, she really chewed me out. Got into a lot of trouble. Real trouble. I was suspended for two days last month for smoking," Stacy said as he cut his eyes away from Thomas.

"Come on. No way. What happened?"

"My mom and dad had given me a new camera for Christmas. A Canon 350, with a telephoto lens and tripod. It's a really cool outfit. Anyway, I was leaving school one day with my mom and I was taking some shots of the school with the telephoto lens. One of the shots caught Mrs. Tesling standing outside the cafeteria next to the dumpster in the loading zone smoking big as hell. Got a really good close-up of her exhaling a smokestack you wouldn't believe. She had two butts going, one in each hand. She was really stoking the nicotine."

"Dude, you've gotta text that to me. Let's post it on online. Might go viral or something."

"Would be big time trouble for me. Can't do that. When she caught me smoking, I got sent home. They called my parents and told them to bring me and meet with Mrs. Tesling the next day. My folks didn't know but I came prepared. I had the close up of her smoking in my pocket."

"Wow! Unbelievable. Did you show it to her?"

"When she told my parents that I was suspended for a week, I showed the photo to my dad then slid it onto her desk. Her face turned white as Casper's ghost-ass peeing his pants."

"I'd give a grand to have been there and seen that," Thomas replied, almost laughing himself off the bleachers.

"It wasn't all that funny at the time. She exploded at my dad and told him I was suspended for two weeks instead. My dad was furious and demanded to know why. She totally dissed him. She wouldn't give him an answer, so he threatened to go to the school board. She dared him to just try it."

"Did he?"

"Yep, he went to the board, picture and all."

"Well, she's still here. Too bad they didn't fire her or something. That's the way things always are—never fair." Thomas frowned as they watched the basketball game, now in full speed, racing up and down the court.

"I was okay with it. I got to see her squirm. She'd really lost it, and the school board reduced my suspension to two days," as Stacy swatted an errant basketball that was about to hit Thomas.

From that rainy day on, Thomas and Stacy were best friends. They were inseparable. They did almost everything together and were about the only friends either of them had.

When they got to high school, they weren't exactly part of the in crowd either. They were both friendly but never outgoing. They never sought other friends. They just weren't interested.

5

HIGH SCHOOL DAZE

By the time they were seniors, they had gracefully accepted their fate. They were both okay they'd never be voted Most Popular or Most Handsome. They comfortably resided in the fringe.

Actually, Thomas would have just been content with not being voted Mr. Pothead or Most Popular Stoner. His bad reputation had preceded him to high school.

Shy, bashful, and introverted, neither Stacy nor Thomas ever had the courage to ask a girl out on a date. They were isolated in the land of the outsiders. They told each other they would go together to the prom when they were seniors, but they knew they never would.

Thomas and Stacy had long since agreed, at least silently, that their high school experience had more to do with fate, size, and testosterone than anything else. They never caught the growth spurt most late bloomers experienced. They were both seniors and their faces were just budding peach fuzz, expectantly awaiting a slather of shave cream and a sharp razor. High school was almost over and they'd not moved from losers sitting in the bleachers to contenders on the court.

"Stacy, after you graduate, are you going to college?" Thomas asked as they walked home from school in the bright spring sunshine.

"I have no idea, but for sure I'm sick of school. I've been watching the Marine Corps story on the History Channel. I think I'd like that. It's tough but exciting," Stacy replied, pulling his book bag up over his shoulder.

"Really tough. Macho strong man," Thomas replied. "I could never do that, man. I mean with boot camp and all. I've seen those pictures of Marine boot camp at Parris Island. Those grunts go through hell. Sure you want to do that, man?"

"I know. It's totally like mean-ass survival tough. But I want something that matters. You know, accomplish something other than scrunting in the bleachers. If I could make it, I'd feel good about myself."

"Like, I mean, I got no idea what I'm going to do. It hurts to think about it," Thomas said. "Hey man, want to smoke a joint at my house? Got some really heavy ganja weed."

"No way! Stuff stays in your system for months. If I join the Marines, they drug test for marijuana and other stuff. Not for me anymore. I've been telling you to get off that weed and booze. It's bad stuff. Totally trashes your body."

"I hear you, man, but it takes me so high. Like I'm totally mindless. Totally soaring!"

Thomas spread his arms flying a 360, his mostly empty book bag airborne behind him.

"Stop thinking about the stuff. You've got to stop all that crap. If cops arrest you again, you could get some jail time. Not worth it. So kick it before it's too late."

"So when did you become so piss prudish? Yeah man, too goodie for the stuff now? I mean you use to burn it all the time with me."

"Hey! Prom's next weekend and we promised last year we'd go. So what about it?" Stacy asked, already knowing Thomas's response.

"Not me. No way—all those girls gawking at me and their football jocks punking me! They'd all be looking at me like a mini scrunt asking who gave me permission to climb out of my crib. Or worse, one of those fee-fi-fo-fum jocks might grind my bones or something," Thomas replied as he and Stacy adroitly maneuvered between two oncoming cars while they crossed against the red light.

"I got an idea. Remember when I told you I found that school key in the hallway when I was a freshman and tried to find the teacher and give it back?"

"Yeah. I remember," Thomas looked at Stacy, puzzled anticipation spreading across his face.

"Well, I never found her to give it back, so I just kept it. I tested it the other day after school. You wouldn't believe it. The key fits all the side hall door locks. It opens them from the outside."

"Cool! So what does that do for us?"

They sat down on Thomas's front stoop steps.

"My mom and dad have these friends in Holly Hill," Stacy continued. "They got this pig farm just off I-26. They raise lots of pigs. Like it's one of those really stinky hog farms. You can smell the odor from their front gate if the wind is right."

"What's up with pigs, man?"

"Like I said, I got this idea. On Thursday before the prom, I can get my mom's car. We can drive up to the farm and buy a couple of pet piglets. You know, small ones, say around thirty pounds. They're selling them for about $25 each. I say we buy two. We can keep them overnight in your garage. It's important we don't feed them for twenty-four hours."

"Wild! But I don't need any pets. Where'd you come up with that? We've got to feed them. It would be animal cruelty or something if we didn't, right?" Thomas questioned, looking upward as if the idea had come from some naughty clairvoyant deep in the mystic universe. "Piglets? My mom would kill me if she found pigs in her garage."

"They'd only be there one night. My idea is to use the pigs in a gigantic prank at the school. We do our dirty work while everyone is at the prom Friday night. It will be the scam of all scams. Really cool!" Stacy said with a wry grin spreading wide.

"Totally cooler! Tell me more," Thomas said, his interest now perked.

"Around 11:00 p.m., just during the peak of the prom, I want to take the piglets to the school, let ourselves in the side door with my key, and place the feed troughs in front of Mr. Seithel's office."

"That's wild! Then what?"

"We take the piglets to the school each wrapped in a blanket. We hang name tags around their necks, call them *Piggy Number One* and *Piggy Number Three*. We also take three giant plastic storage containers and attach big name tags to them—*Piggy Number One, Piggy Number Two* and *Piggy Number Three*—and then fill the feeding troughs with fifty pounds of pig feed. We'll also fill up a gigantically huge tub of water, enough to last the weekend."

"Yeah, but I thought we got only two piglets?" Thomas asked, somewhat perplexed.

"Hey, that's what makes it cool. Monday morning, Mr. Seithel will be looking for three little pigs but will find only two. If I'm right, it'll drive him loony trying to find the third piglet." Stacy was greatly satisfied with his plan.

"Oh, wow! Totally insane, dude … like seriously perverted!"

"We'll spike the hog feed with several boxes of chocolate Ex Lax. Should make the odor fragrant on Monday. Then we'll take a can of Crisco and grease the piglets just before we leave. They won't have eaten for twenty-four hours so they'll feast on the pig feed and Ex-Lax all weekend. Pigs can eat half their body weight or more every couple of days. I'd give my left nut to see Mr. Seithel try and catch the greased little squealers. They'll be so scared they'll be squirting crap everywhere as they run."

"Ex Lax, hog feed, and piglets. I'm all in, man. Can hardly wait," Thomas answered, a wicked smile on his face. "We're on for tomorrow to get those piglets."

Thomas and Stacy carried out their plan around midnight Friday to the glow of the dim red nightlights in the school hallways. The piglets were docile and quiet while they were wrapped in blankets, but after they were slathered in Crisco and released, they squealed and headed directly for the feeding troughs.

When the students arrived for class Monday morning, the hallway in front of Mr. Seithel's office was covered with slick brown pig shit. It was everywhere. The piglets had wandered the hallways, pissing and crapping all weekend. Students were unable to walk without looking carefully before each step. The smell was pigsty aromatic, hanging in the air like the malodorous flatulence of a leviathan.

Almost immediately, Mr. Seithel came on the public address system advising students of the problem and suggesting they remain in the gym or outside the cafeteria until the hallways were cleaned.

"Animal control has been called and is on its way," he angrily blared. "It seems there is one pig missing. You are requested to report the little porker if you see it. We will leave the hallway doors propped open to air out the building. Maintenance has been called to clean up the mess."

His announcement was met with total contempt as the students laughed and cheered. They began to chant louder and louder, "Go little piggy go! Go little piggy go!" The cheerleaders even began to do their routines leading the pig cheers.

Things quickly got worse and by 9:30 Mr. Seithel was on the PA system again.

"You seniors may think this three little pig deal is clever, but you should know it's costing the district a lot of money to clean up the mess, not to speak of missing classes. You can take your YouTube plans and stuff them. Your classes will be made up on a Saturday. So just plan on it," he gleefully announced to the outrageous profanities of the collective student roar as they cheered for the piglets.

"Listen up, seniors," Mr. Seithel's voice continued quivering and openly hostile. "Hear me! I would suggest *you find your missing little swine, or don't you graduate on time!*" He then dismissed school and sent everyone home for the day.

Thomas and Stacy were elated when they saw the entire student population strongly support the pigs. Finally, they had some influence. They were in the game, on the court and off the bleachers. Brains over brawn! Even though they were the only two who would ever know, it gave them great satisfaction that at least partially erased their high school angst.

"Freaking awesome," Thomas said as he high-fived Stacy.

"Totally agree, bro," Stacy replied as they walked home laughing and joking about their conquest. "We make a good team and we got the last laugh!"

The school year, it seemed, dragged on and on. Thomas and Stacy thought graduation would never come. But it did. And immediately after, Stacy enlisted in the Marine Corps. Thomas had tried to discourage him, but Stacy was determined. They stayed in touch for a while but communicating even by email became more difficult when Stacy was deployed to Iraq. Thomas missed his best friend. Nothing would ever replace their friendship and camaraderie. Nothing.

If Stacy had only been around, Thomas thought, things might have been much different. Thomas could not erase those indelible images of that fiery explosion as his memories drifted back to that ominous Thursday night in February of last year when events at Arthur's on King began charting his and Codi Joseph's threatening and frightful journey, eventually and inexorably joining their paths toward Godly redemption.

6

ARTHUR'S ON KING

Last February, the weather had been almost balmy as Codi drove into Charleston. Mist speckled Codi's windshield, the aftermath of a late evening thunderstorm. As the wiper blades swished away the fine droplets, her GPS guided her through the maze of streets on the Charleston peninsula and toward Arthur's Pub where she was to meet her clients at 11:00 sharp.

Codi left Charlotte around 6:00, but rain squalls snarled traffic and now she would be fortunate to arrive on time. She had hoped to scope out the city since she had never visited historic Charleston, but she was late, almost 10:30. Being a Thursday night, Arthur's wouldn't be too crowded, she thought as she turned onto another street not mapped in her GPS. Would she ever find King Street?

Her clients were local Charleston attorneys. Beau Ravenel was from a long line of Ravenel barristers, dating all the way back to Kings Court, Birmingham, England, 1725. They hit the mother load of tobacco settlements several years back and now mostly diddled in politics, staying well connected in Washington. J. Rosin Daniels had inherited his formidable wealth from his real estate rich father and, thus far, had managed not to lose most of it. Daniels spent much of his time writing about the Great War for Southern Independence and had published several books on the Uncivil War, as he termed America's tragic nineteenth century war against the South.

Ravenel and Daniels had been classmates at the University of South Carolina School of Law and graduated together in 1979 at the top of their class. They were both middle aged, single, wealthy, and very well connected. Rumor around town speculated closet kin perhaps since they were both eligible bachelors and never seen with the ladies.

Tobias Edwardson, the recently elected Junior US Senator from North Carolina and close friend of Rosin Daniels, had connected Daniels with Codi. When Daniels called her to arrange the evening's party, he'd additionally provided some unsolicited but interesting history about Arthur's on King and the city of Charleston.

"Arthur's on King," Daniels began in his heavy Southern drawl, "is legendary around Charleston. It was established in 1849 and is purported to be the oldest continuous operating pub in the South. Some even claim Arthur's hosted the first organizational meetings of the Confederate secessionist movement. I must say I do believe that to be true."

"Sounds like you're quite an authority on Charleston."

"I pride myself on a command of Confederate history, especially as it impacted Charleston," he answered smugly. "Some, including myself, have speculated Arthur's had to be the most popular watering hole for Confederate soldiers until the troops abandoned Charleston in February 1865."

"Arthur's is famous then?"

"Oh, yes! But more than anything else, Miss Joseph, it survived. Arthur's Pub, along with several seventeenth century churches on King Street, never suffered any direct hits from Union cannon in a city almost totally leveled by bombardment during the Great War for Southern Independence."

"Sounds amazing, Mr. Daniels."

"Please call me JR, Miss Joseph, if you don't mind. Makes me feel a bit younger these days, don't you see?"

"Okay, if you'll call me Codi. Got my family name, 'Coedinger' from my dad's side of the family. Everyone calls me Codi."

"But back to Arthur's Pub for a moment," Daniels continued. "Without doubt, the pub is most famous because General William Sherman, when he arrived in Charleston in May of 1865, met with local dignitaries at Arthur's since it was one of the few buildings still standing. Sherman, it is said at that meeting, declared Charleston in *total ruination* thus sparing the city his fiery fury."

His lecture had been much more than Codi wanted to hear, but he was, after all, a paying client and listening was part of the gig.

It was 10:45 and she wasn't sure she was even close. She had reset the GPS, but it was giving her erroneous readings among all the short streets in downtown Charleston. Suddenly, she came to a dead end. She had no choice but to turn right or left and then there it was. King Street. She gambled, turned left and was pleasantly surprised to almost immediately see a weathered but handsome shingle hanging over the sidewalk that read, "Arthur's Pub Established 1849." She'd gotten lucky. Her clients had suggested the small parking lot across the street. She turned into the entrance, paid the attendant, and pulled into a parking space. She was relieved. She wouldn't be late.

Codi casually crossed King Street and entered the less than sizeable front door at Arthur's. The tobacco stench and sickly sweet odor of spilled spirits saturating the heart pine floor left no doubt of Arthur's long history. The massive mahogany bar and its well-worn brass foot rail was only surpassed by the dented but brightly polished brass spittoons along the floor. They looked their age.

The slightly distorted images reflecting from the wavy antique mirror behind the bar seemed to push the walls, making the tavern seem twice its size. A chain-wound clock, itself at least 100 years old, hung above the rows of liquor bottles and lent a sense of modernity to the nineteenth-century decor.

Codi was pleased it wasn't too crowded. She spotted three empty stools near the far end of the bar.

It didn't take long for the patrons to notice her curvy figure and below-the-shoulder blond hair. Everyone at Arthur's turned and gawked as she sauntered down the bar.

She was wearing a striking raspberry red skirt, V-neck matching blouse and a red newsboy hat slightly cocked to one side. She was stunning. There wasn't a guy in the place who didn't silently whistle, "You gotta be kidding me! And she's alone?"

Codi walked the length of the bar, her resolute look signaling to everyone she could take care of herself. She pulled herself up to the bar in the last of the three empty stools, saving the other two for her clients. The antique clock pealed 11:00, its tone slightly off key, much as a fractured brass bell in an old church belfry might sound.

As Codi waited for her clients to show up and identify themselves, she turned to the guy seated to her right who had his back toward her.

"Pardon me. Are you local, sir?" Codi asked as she tapped him on the back.

She realized too late the guy was very drunk. He was sitting with two thuggish looking, flashily dressed men. They were all drinking Jack Daniels on the rocks.

Thomas Houston Stirk, a well known local cokehead and alcoholic, turned toward Codi and rudely responded, "Hey man, don't touch the bod, man. Okay?"

As he turned, his view coming full circle, he was blown away by her beauty.

"No way, man! Can't be. You're a really foxy chick, man," Thomas slurred. He realized his intoxicated guffaw and wanted to undo the damage. It was already too late.

"W-aaay, pal. You're totally sloshed," Codi curtly replied and turned back in disgust.

Thomas's two sleazy friends quickly ordered another round of Jack Daniels. One of them helped Thomas find his sea legs as he excused himself and stumbled off to the men's room.

Codi was smart, shrewd, and sophisticated. She knew she was attractive and used her good looks to enhance her resume. Her slightly cocked hat was her ultimate MBA exclamation, qualifying her for pole position on race day. Everyone could tell she never finished second.

She'd learned her trade quickly during the past twelve months. She'd organized many parties for clients now and understood what they wanted for a good time. She made sure her clients always got more than they paid for. Her reputation had spread quickly among the sophisticated snow heads.

Her clients were too discriminating and paid too much to be offered street-grade stuff. She provided only the finest blow, premium grass, and uncut scripts. She was always discreet and meticulously vetted her clients, invariably loaded swingers in the high-society crowd. She took zero chances.

As Codi surveyed the scene at Arthur's, her thoughts drifted back to her ex-boyfriend, Tracy Poole, a guy she dated briefly during her senior year at UNC Charlotte. He wasn't exactly handsome but acceptably good looking. Like most guys, he thought himself sexier than he was. At about six feet, he was clean cut, polite, and an all around nice guy. He was fun to be with.

Codi was shocked when Tracy, on their second date boasted of having paid his way through school selling dime bags of Marijuana and half-ounce baggies of coke. He was no junkie and said he never used. He just bought and sold. His admission scared Codi. She dumped him the very next day.

Later on that year, Codi came to the stark realization that she hadn't exactly landed her dream job. Despite earning a double major in media management and public relations and placing over a hundred resumes, she had no prospects. Companies were not hiring.

Faced with her $70,000 student loan debt and with not even one meaningful job offer in sight, she was frantic. She was determined not to dump her student loans in the lap of her parents. Her dad was in the real estate business and had been financially struggling the last few years. Codi, if nothing else, was determined and entrepreneurial, both traits she inherited from her dad.

She became convinced she would never find a decent paying job. About a month after this sad realization, she became so desperate she called Tracy Poole, who agreed to a luncheon meeting at a downtown Charlotte bistro. Tracy was dutifully on time and delighted for the opportunity to see Codi again. Codi told him about the discouraging job market. Tracy shared he'd applied for law school at UNCC and had been accepted.

After ten or fifteen minutes of small talk, her cheeks flushed. Clearing her throat several times, Codi reluctantly asked, "Are you still selling dime bags and, you know, all that other stuff you told me about?"

Tracy frowned, recalling why he'd been dumped. "Every day just payin' my way. I thought you hated me for that."

"Wow! And you've never been arrested!"

"I'm not a druggie, Codi. I never use. Like I told you, I only buy and sell the stuff."

"Tracy. I need to pay off my student loans," she blurted. "I need something that will pay me some big money."

He became somber. His brow wrinkled a deadly serious concern. "That's the last thing I expected to hear from you, Codi. I'm shocked."

"I know. I can't believe I just said all that, but I'm desperate. I've got to do something fast. I need your help, Tracy. Please."

"First," Tracy whispered, "you never sell to strangers and never to anyone on the street. You must know your clients. If you work this gig, it will have to be sophisticated like one of those New York call-girl services. Those gals only deal with the high-end big rollers. They're the ones with the big bucks. There's always room at the top, Codi, and you can make mega bucks easy if that's what you really want to do. There's a huge demand and an unbelievably vast market."

Codi's hesitant blush had turned to a look of calm anticipation as Tracy explained the greatest danger—to be successful, he told her, she could never use.

"If you use even one time, you're dead. You've got to understand that!"

Codi nodded convincingly.

"You don't use now and there is no reason to ever begin.
It must be only business. Only about paying off your student
loans. You only do private parties for upper-deck clients.
Clients you've checked out. Just candy cane. Just give them
the fun stuff."

Tracy relaxed a bit and so did Codi. Over the next two
hours, he explained everything in great detail. Codi was a
quick study. She missed nothing.

As their lunch ended, Tracy agreed to put Codi in touch
with a discreet supplier and maybe even send a customer or
two her way.

"Just promise me you won't forget what I said; you can
never use," he cautioned. "Not even one time. You've got to
swear to me, Codi. Okay?"

Codi swore an oath to Tracy that afternoon and she meant it.

The bartender interrupted her thoughts. "What can I get
for you tonight, miss?"

"Nothing yet. I'm waiting on a couple of friends. They
should be here any time now. We'll order when they arrive.
Thanks."

"Name's Solo, miss. Just give me a shout."

7

ANGELS AT ARTHUR'S

W hen Thomas wandered back to the bar from the men's room, he was feeling no pain. His eyes were spacey from the line of cocaine he'd just snorted. He'd barely managed to mount his stool as his new friends lined up another round of drinks.

Unnoticed by Thomas were the two guys in pinstripes who had joined Codi while he'd escaped to boogered-up-land, blitzed out of his mind. Beau Ravenel and Rosin Daniels loosened their ties and quickly knocked back two vodka martinis. They had just flown in from DC on Daniel's Gulfstream IV after two days of intense lobbying for the South Carolina State Port Authority's efforts to obtain federal funding for dredging Charleston's harbor. They were tired, mentally spent, and ready to party.

Just as Thomas steadied himself on his stool, Codi, her back to him, tossed her hair over her shoulder and accidentally brushed against him. He turned quickly only to observe the back of Codi's neck and a triangular birthmark behind her right ear. He was so stoned, he paid little attention to the incident and turned back to his bar buddies.

Stirk's friends were nervous. Fidgety. One of them was constantly scoping the crowd. Occasionally, they spoke to one another in Spanish. The taller of the two was dressed in a bright orange and yellow flower-print shirt beneath a distasteful powder blue sports coat. Even worse, he smelled of citrus spice cologne. The aroma was so heady, so powerfully lemony sweet, it seemed to stick to everyone's clothes.

The other guy had a lighter complexion and was shorter. He was a suave Spanish looking guy—wealthy slime ball was written all over him. He was wearing an expensive cream linen sports jacket and a powder blue silk shirt unbuttoned halfway down his chest, exposing his greasy black chest hair.

So ostentatious were these two guys, they would have stood out at any crowded craps table in Vegas, much less at Arthur's tonight.

Codi's clients had paid six grand up front for the night's festivities and the finest candy cane money could buy. Codi had given them enough coke for two lines. But before she could stop them, they'd stroked a line on the mahogany bar. Solo, the bartender, caught sight of the impending debacle and covered the line with a plate before they could snort anything.

He discreetly remonstrated, "Take it to the men's room guys. Okay?" He then accommodated them with a free round of drinks.

Unseen by the patrons at Arthur's was a trio of angels from God's multitudes of archangels. They were seated around an empty table near the back of the pub. Invisible to all but themselves, the angels were watching Thomas and Codi with great interest. They had no idea until tonight that God's latest assignment for them would be shepherding a sophisticated good-looking drug dealer chick and an alcoholic drug punk junkie. But then God's Heavenly Hosts were accustomed to God's amazing surprises and unending grace.

Tony B, leader of the trio, reminded his partners, "God always said we gotta go where the sinners are and I must say it looks like we hit the jackpot tonight."

JJ and Scribbee nodded in agreement. "Like Jesus always said, lots of opportunity for angels in Heaven to rejoice tonight," Scribbee quipped.

"Heaven's full of these formerly smashed out of their minds repentant sinner types," JJ chimed in.

Protruding from each of the angel's upper arms were remnants of wings, vestiges from winged grandeur of past millennia. Full size wings had been long abandoned as much too cumbersome and far too slow in God's modern, high-speed Archangel universe.

The remnants, seven or eight inches long and a few inches high, spread from just below their shoulders to just above their elbows. The feathers were ivory white and fluttered when they stood. Since angels rarely cry, their wings quivered or flitted about at great sadness or joy, a proxy for tears.

The wings neatly protruded through slits in their upper garments. If the patrons at Arthur's had been able to see the angels, they would have concluded the small wings provided the trio a touch of celestial sophistication.

Anthony Cloutus Bartholomew, or Tony B, as the other angels nicknamed him, was the tallest of the three. About six foot two, he was a lean two hundred pounds. His bushy white hair hinted at his seventy-plus earth years, but his body defied his age. His poorly trimmed sideburns, their wiry white strands almost covering his ears, announced his lack of concern regarding personal appearance. He was, after all, a professor and a Heavenly renowned Hebrew scholar. He had deep blue eyes that penetrated like two steel-tipped spears. On the surface, he seemed hard as nails. At first glance, anyone could see he was in charge of the trio.

Jeremiah Jacob Israeli, or JJ, as his friends called him, was the youngest of the trio. JJ looked about forty-five and was muscular and short at five foot eight. His blonde flattop complemented his sometimes brusque drill sergeant demeanor. JJ was solid, built like Man Mountain, his muscular shoulders stretching the lapels of his one size too small blue linen sports coat, his biceps almost bursting the seams of his sleeves. He looked as if he'd been lifting weights since birth. His blue green eyes hinted at a hospitality that sometimes betrayed his tough guy posturing. He was obviously the enforcer in the group, not one to scuffle with.

Esther Beulah Scribner, or Scribbee, as God had nicknamed His slightly stout, gray-haired matriarch and Chief Heavenly Scribe, had seen it all from Adam and Eve to Codi and Thomas, from Eden's splendor to Arthur's Pub. She and her staff dutifully recorded every event on earth in the great Book of Heavenly Records, and she could, to this day, recall most of the details without referencing her notes. She was the oldest of the trio. Her African complexion and blue gray hair seemed to reinforce her gentle spirit. Her British accent lent confidence to her stature and quiet leadership.

Scribbee, watching the patrons at Arthur's, suddenly looked at Tony B and JJ. "I haven't had this much fun since my namesake cousin Esther went in to the King," she said, her wings briefly fluttering a sense of excitement.

"Now Scribbee," Tony B said, wrinkling his brow, "the evening is just getting started. We've probably got a long way to go tonight so don't get too worked up. Okay?"

"Oh, don't be such a prudy-tanical, Tony B. Nothing says we can't enjoy ourselves."

"Well, I must say you certainly dressed the part, Scribbee—knee-length leather boots? Not exactly our dress code, is it?"

"We were told to fit in, Anthony. Relax. I know saloons aren't our favorite venues."

"Scribbee, pay no mind to Tony B," JJ bolstered. "I want to know where you got those incredible digs."

"Probably all knock offs. I ordered over the Internet. The boots are Veleda. Italian! Well over five hundred bucks if you bought them retail. I paid only $99.95 for the pair," Scribbee said and hiked her leg to show her stippled leather boots to JJ.

"Good looking. Don't believe I've ever seen an archangel sporting knee-length boots. First time for everything," JJ exclaimed as Scribbee set her boot on the floor and straightened her skirt.

"Waste of good God bucks, I'd say. Everyone knows angels don't make scratch," Tony B again reproved.

"Lighten up, Tony B. I think she looks really sexy. Most of the time humans can't see us anyway. If they could, some guy might be asking who is that good looking senior doll back there with the white cabbie hat. She looks like an angel. One of those young Turks at the bar might just step back here and offer to buy her a drink," JJ jokingly spoofed with Tony B.

"My skirt and blouse are from Anthropologie, which I also bought online. Made in China. I was surprised at the dirt-cheap price." She straightened her collar. "Only paid $89.95 for both."

"Well, then I guess I owe you an apologie, Scribbee."

"Totally lame joke. Surely you can do better," Scribbee chided.

"It's just I hate a crowd like this. All these folks are looking in all the wrong places for all the wrong things. God's heart aches for them. Satan's alcohol is the first fiend of such extraordinary evil behavior," Tony B said, his lips pursed with concern.

"I don't like this duty either," Scribbee sympathized, "but I must say Anthony Cloutus Bartholomew, you're looking right spiffy yourself, all decked out in those tan slacks and white cotton pullover. With your brass buttoned navy blue blazer, you'd fit in right well with all those sanctimonious senior professors at Harvard Divinity School."

JJ laughed and responded, "Touché!"

"Okay, guys. I had that coming," Tony B apologized.

JJ pushed his chair back from the table as he stretched his enormous biceps and looked about the room. "Nothing but a bunch of cokehead lushes looks like to me. Nobody asked, but I think God might want to consider reelin' in some line on these folks before they hurt somebody." His tiny wings flitted inward, folding against his arm.

The clock over the bar chimed 2:00 a.m. Many of the patrons had already left, but Codi and her clients were still bellied up to the bar and Codi was still passing out baggies of coke. Her clients had progressed passed intoxicated. They were soaring toward stoner's promised land.

Thomas Stirk was passed out with his smashed face on the bar. His two foreign friends picked him up, draped his arms over their shoulders and began walking him out of the bar.

As they passed Codi, they asked her, "Hey missy? Por favor. Save seats. Okay? We take him to sleep it off. We come back. Okay?"

Codi, somewhat puzzled and mostly disgusted that these two thuggish looking strangers had the nerve to ask her to save their seats, reluctantly nodded okay, not wishing to seem rude.

The two thuggish looking guys mostly carried a stumbling Stirk to a black SUV in the parking lot across the street. They loaded him in the back seat, draped his legs down off the seat and fastened the center seat belt around his waist. They closed the door and returned to their seats at Arthur's.

8

PURSUIT

About 4:15, Codi asked Solo to tally her tab. Her clients were fully juiced. One of them had passed out on the bar. Their party was over. It was time to go and Codi had to drive back to Raleigh to meet her mom for their usual Friday lunch at Oliver's. She felt confident she would make it in plenty of time, but she couldn't leave until she'd gotten her clients safely in a cab.

Strangely, Antonio Reyes, Codi's supplier whom she'd never met in person, never showed up to introduce himself as promised. Codi had brought the eight grand she owed him. What Reyes had told Codi about Arthur's was right on; it was indeed one of those protected hangouts for the wealthiest and most politically connected in the city. After 9:00 p.m., the police obviously put Arthur's off limits. It was a great place for the sophisticated, beautiful crowd to snort their nose candy without fear of being arrested.

When Tony B, JJ, and Scribbee noticed Codi and her clients leaving, they all three stood, their tiny wings flitting nervously as if stretching their arms. They didn't know where things were headed but were pleased their observations for the evening were soon to be over. They watched intently as Codi and her clients exited the bar.

Codi thanked Solo for a great evening and asked him to call a cab. He assured her it was already waiting at the front door.

The two foreigners, still seated at the bar, abruptly paid their tab, leaving three C-notes under a shot glass. They quickly walked out, hesitating briefly on the sidewalk in front of Arthur's before disappearing into the dark parking lot across the street.

The cab pulled away as Codi's clients incoherently muttered their thanks. Feeling tired but happy with another successful gig, Codi walked across the street to the parking lot. As she approached her Denali, a shadowy figure behind a black Ford Expedition parked next to her SUV rounded the front of her vehicle. The disgusting guy in the powder blue sports coat met her at the driver's door, his citrus spice cologne permeating the heavy night air.

"Missy, Antonio Reyes, where he is tonight?" he demanded.

Codi, surprised and frightened, rushed toward her driver's door. The interrogator blocked her way.

"Out of my way, jerk!" she screamed.

"Where is Reyes, missy?"

Codi suddenly realized her situation was perilous and she had to do something. Without hesitation, as if she'd trained for this moment all her life, she grabbed the thug by his shoulders, pulled him toward her and, with Olympic expertise, kneed him in the groin with all the force her five foot seven, one hundred thirty five pounds could generate.

It was enough. She scored a double-jeweled bull's eye from below and straight on. He collapsed on the pavement, pulling his body into a fetal position. Only his partner understood the Spanish profanities he was screaming as he lay writhing in pain next to Codi's driver's door.

Tony B, JJ, and Scribbee were all casually standing just behind Codi's black Denali. They all smiled as the attacker went down. JJ gave an enthusiastic, if slightly subdued, twisted fist pump as Rachael Joseph showed her stuff.

"Yes! Excellent! Would you believe that?" Scribbee excitedly exclaimed. "She took him down."

"Incredible! Genuine David and Goliath moment," Tony B said. "You don't see that often."

"She's got guts," JJ agreed. He cringed as they watched the other thug draw his weapon and approach Codi.

Codi quickly stepped over the writhing mugger. She got into her vehicle, locked the doors and started the engine just as the other guy rounded the front of her SUV waving a very large handgun.

Codi floored it and her vehicle shot forward, its right front fender striking the lighter skinned goon, knocking him off his feet, his weapon skidding harmlessly under another vehicle.

Codi never thought about stopping. She drove over the hedge barrier at the edge of the parking lot and out onto a deserted King Street in the misty early morning fog. The adrenalin pumping through her veins rendered her judgment useless. She tried to focus her thoughts but was too terrified. She was confused. Her instincts said flee.

Battered and bruised, the two hoods lost no time regaining their senses. The taller, dis-bejeweled thug was usually the driver but was unable to manage anything other than his continued stream of profanities to various unnamed deities.

"I can't drive. Take me to hospital," he cried, still doubled over from the knee to the groin.

"How you so stupid to let her hurt you, Aristide?" Fidel Pinella chided. "I told you she could be dangerous. Get in the car."

Aristide pulled himself into the passenger side front seat, trying to maintain his fetal position. Pinella demanded the keys, stuffed the nine millimeter automatic in his belt, and with a notable limp from his fender thumping, climbed into the driver seat.

They sped from the parking lot and headed in the same direction as Codi. Pinella, an inexperienced driver, almost spun out on the slick street.

Codi was lost in the narrow short streets south of Broad Street downtown and was becoming more confused.

Her anxiety had muddled her sense of direction. She thought about calling 911 but reasoned she had too much cash on her and likely traces of cocaine.

Drive and run was all she could think as she rounded a corner onto Broad Street just as the thugs' Expedition approached from the opposite direction. The goons spun their Expedition around and gave chase. Codi sped up turning left at the first street she came to.

Gripped by paralyzing fear, Codi began to tremble. Fortunately, the streets were deserted as she weaved through the city, trying desperately to lose them. The night air hung like a foggy blanket as her vehicle sliced and swirled the fog in circles as she drove on.

Once, the hoodlums pulled side-by-side waving the pistol at Codi and motioning her to stop. She immediately turned left into their vehicle, forcing them onto the sidewalk and a collection of garbage cans. They skidded to a stop just before crashing into a light pole. Codi sped on.

Codi had now regained some of her wits and began thinking strategy. She needed out of the city. She observed, about half a block up, what seemed the only place in town open this time of the morning. It was the Meeting Street bus station, whose light emanated into the foggy mist, seemingly inviting her to safety.

She whipped by the station and decided to follow Meeting Street to its end, but just then, her pursuers crossed Meeting at Market and spotted her. The chase was on again, only this time Codi took a double left turn to south King Street, passing Arthur's and once again finding herself in the short narrow streets of the peninsula. She figured she could hide there.

She seemed to have lost them but Codi knew chances were good they would spot her again soon. She pulled onto a side street, turned off her headlights, and waited.

After about ten minutes, she crept onto East Bay Street. Seeing no one, she headed south. She knew at any minute they could find her. She and her pursuers seemed to be the only two vehicles on the city streets.

She turned onto a side street, once again passing within a block of the open bus station. That's when she knew she had to ditch her vehicle and seek the safety of other people, crowds of people if she could. She knew she had to find a hotel. She would be safe in the lobby.

She headed south down East Bay, following Charleston Harbor on her left. As she rounded a curve, she came upon a dimly lit park. She pulled over the sidewalk and parked with the rear of her vehicle still partially in the street. She opened the glove box and emptied all the papers, pulled her registration from the visor, and crammed everything into her small bag. She exited her Denali and ran across the park to

Meeting Street and up three blocks to the safety of the small well-lighted bus station.

Codi didn't know it, but her injured attacker was groaning in the front seat of the black Expedition, still begging to be taken to a hospital.

His partner warned him, "Sit up and watch for the girl."

They slowly cruised the Lower Peninsula. It had been fifteen or twenty minutes since they last saw her. The driver turned onto East Bay and announced his expansion of the search as his whimpering partner complained of his injury.

"Please, Fidel, take me to hospital. I need doctor now. Please!" Aristide begged.

"Shut up, Aristide. Watch for the girl!"

As the thugs approached Battery Park on East Battery Drive, they spotted Codi's SUV parked on the sidewalk. They arrived too late. Three Charleston City Police Cruisers had surrounded the abandoned vehicle. The officers had their spotlights trained on the interior of the black Denali as they attempted to unlock the doors.

The Haitian and Columbian hooligans drove by the scene and observed the bright police spot lights illuminating the SUV's interior. Seeing no one inside, they drove on, unnoticed by police.

9

CHARLESTON'S FINEST

Thomas could hear someone shouting, but whatever he was saying was slurred and garbled, like a recording playing lazily backwards.

At first, he thought he was dreaming one of those creepy wild ones where the body seems to turn to solid rock and, despite all attempts, won't come unstuck. Suddenly, he realized he couldn't open his eyes. They were glued shut. He tried to scream, but no sound would come from his moving lips. He was sure he was alive, but hopelessly trapped in a body of petrified stone.

By now, the jumbled noise had become uncontrolled shouting. He pleaded with the greater powers for mercy to open his eyes. They did not respond. He knew he had to run for his life, but he couldn't move a muscle.

Resolved he could not escape his fate, his eyelids snapped open. His netherworld terror was now visible. It seemed the sun itself had invaded the interior of the vehicle. The cruiser spotlights were so bright at first he thought he might be inside a light bulb. But he could feel no heat.

He was bewildered by his surroundings. They were unfamiliar. He tried to remember whose vehicle he was in. He couldn't recall last night. He had no memory of how he got into the back seat of this SUV.

Three police officers had been trying to unlock the doors. They soon discovered the burglar resistant technology of the latest electronic gadgetry was indeed thief proof.

After peering into the back passenger side window, Sergeant Kent Cooper, Charleston Police Department's long time night watch supervisor, yelled to the other two officers, "Hey, we got a guy laid out on the back seat."

Officer Jack Monck quickly replied, "Yeah, I saw him. He wasn't moving. Think he's dead? Is there any blood?"

Officers Monck and Courtney began knocking on the rear glass windows with their nightsticks while shining their flashlights into the backseat.

Sergeant Cooper tapped on the window and yelled again, "Are you hurt, sir? Unlock the door."

Thomas began to stir from his stupor.

Sergeant Monck cautioned, "Hey pal, make it easy on yourself. Okay?"

Thomas was still intoxicated. He tried to sit up and clumsily fumbled to unbuckle the middle seat belt. He was disoriented and his head was spinning.

Sergeant Monck yelled at the other officers. "Okay, we got a live white male in the back seat. Looks like he's coming to."

Thomas knocked on the inside of the window and yelled at the police. "Hey, cut the lights, man. Who are you guys?"

Sergeant Cooper shined his light into Thomas's face and knocked on the glass. "Are you hurt, sir? Please unlock the doors!"

Thomas tried to cover his eyes with his forearm. "You're blinding me, man. Where is this place? What time is it anyway?" His bladder clearly screaming morning, he announced, "I need to take a leak."

Sergeant Cooper placed his watch face against the glass and tapped his baton on the window. "5:50 a.m. Rise and shine, pal. We can help you. Just unlock the doors."

Thomas wrinkled an intoxicated smile. His slurred words angrily protested. "Yeah, like I'm really gonna believe that, dude."

He sat up with difficulty, hands on his throbbing brow. He tried to clear his mind and get a handle on where he was and how he got there. He leaned up and looked into the front seat. No keys in the ignition. No keys in the back seat.

He had no idea whose vehicle it was. He wondered if he'd been driving but quickly surmised without the keys, driving wasn't possible, which meant he wouldn't be charged with a DUI. That was good news. But whose wheels were these, he wondered.

Thomas looked out the window at the gathering crowd just off the sidewalk in Battery Park. Several early morning joggers were among the interested bystanders. Some of them just jogged in place watching his predicament unfold.

Still confused but beginning to come out of his daze, he wanted answers. He'd done some pretty dumb things in his life but sobering up in the back of someone's expensive SUV surrounded by Charleston's finest all lit up with fifty million candlepower of police cruiser spotlights was a new record even for him.

He sniffed his clothes. "180 proof all right, no doubt from a fifth or so of Jack Daniel's. But who was I with?"

Officer Courtney knocked on the window with his baton. "What are you saying, sir? Speak to us. Let us help you."

Thomas blurted a semi-coherent reply. "Cut me some slack, okay? Can't find myself, man. I think I'm gonna puke. Need some fresh air."

Daylight was beginning to break and the cruiser spotlights would soon have a less blinding effect. Thomas surveyed his situation and realized the vehicle was parked halfway on the sidewalk.

He leaned over the front seat and clicked the unlock switch on the door panel. All the locks snapped open in unison. He opened the passenger side rear door as the officers converged, weapons drawn and trained on him.

Unseen by law enforcement were the angel duo of JJ, quietly sitting in the front seat, and Tony B, next to Thomas in the back.

"I'm really surprised he's sobering so quickly," Tony B said to JJ as Thomas began trying to make his legs move.

"He stays pickled-brained most of the time," JJ replied, turning to Tony B in the back seat. "Those two hooligans must have bought him at least two fifths last night."

They watched Thomas throw his legs out the back door and struggle to exit. As Thomas stumbled out, Sergeant Cooper and the other officers shouted in unison. "Hands on your head! Hands on your head!"

"Hey, I'm lost, man. Don't shoot. Okay? Don't wanna die, man," Thomas slurred.

Sergeant Cooper and Officer Courtney holstered their weapons and moved in. They grabbed Thomas and pushed him securely against the side of the vehicle, twisting his arms behind his back. They cuffed him, searched him and moved him to a grassy area between the street and sidewalk. They slammed him down hard on the curb.

"You're hurting me, dude," Thomas complained loudly.

"Shut up, punk," Officer Courtney replied. "You wanted fresh air. You got fresh air."

By now, the crowd of onlookers, joggers accompanied by dog-walkers, had grown considerably. Most were dressed in fashionably shabby outfits and expensive Nike running shoes. They were gawking so seriously their expressions reminded Thomas of mythical Greek gods pondering the fate of their own navels: righteous, influential, important, at least unto themselves. They all seemed to be aiming their Nike Swooshes directly at Thomas, like razor-sharp boo-merang sickles slicing through the air, intent on cutting his throat.

The gawkers' silent attitudes seemed to accuse Thomas of murder and had already sentenced his drunken bum-ness to death by order of the Nike Swooshstika people's court. He didn't have a chance.

A dog began barking. Thomas looked up at a short obese lady with exposed thighs indiscernible from her oversized buttocks and multiple folds of corpulent flab rolling down layer over flabby layer. Her bulldog sniffed and barked loudly, pulling at its leash. Remarkably, her dog's layered folds had a striking resemblance to her portly embellishments. Their twin'ish resemblance was not a pretty sight.

The lady was allowing the dog to sniff closer and closer to Thomas, slobber dripping from its low hanging jowls. Soon the dog was growling and gnarling its teeth not more than three feet from Thomas. Officer Courtney stepped between the dog and Thomas, asking the lady to remove her animal immediately.

Sergeant Cooper interrupted the dog melee and spoke to Thomas. "Got a name, kid?"

Thomas looked up at Sgt. Cooper and fumbled slowly. "Yes, sir, sure do. Thomas, I think. Yeah, man, I remember—name's Thomas Houston Stirk." He confidently smiled an intoxicated grin.

Officer Courtney kneeled down in front of Thomas. "Nice rags, kid. Where were you last night?"

Thomas again slurred his response. "Totally sketchy, man. Arthur's maybe? Can't remember."

Thomas's head was throbbing from his excessive imbibing, a familiar sensation for him.

Sergeant Cooper returned, announcing loud enough for all to hear. "So you're Thomas Houston Stirk. RAP sheet as long as my arm. Twenty-eight year old white male, multiple possessions, multiple DUI's (one still pending), multiple petty thefts, larceny, public drunkenness, dealing, contributing. The list goes on and on."

Officer Monck interrupted, telling Sgt. Cooper, "Vehicle owner is Rachael Coedinger Joseph, Charlotte, North Carolina."

"So how'd you end up in Joseph's vehicle?" Officer Courtney asked. "Where are the keys?"

"Got no idea. Was just there. Never seen these wheels before. I swear."

Sergeant Cooper stood Thomas up. "Don't jack with us, Stirk. Where's Rachael Joseph? Where are the keys?"

Wobbly on his feet, Thomas emphatically slurred. "Told you I don't know any Rachael Joseph."

Sergeant Cooper turned to Officer Courtney. "He's still totally wasted. Take him in. Book him on suspicion of something! Anything! He's got to sober up."

As many times as he'd been arrested, Thomas never got used to being slammed into the back seat of a police cruiser. It was painful, his weight crushing his handcuffed wrists. He hated the drill. He'd endured it too many times. Thomas, his words clearly distinguishable, pleaded with Officer Courtney. "Can you ask them to put me in a regular cell? Please, Officer. Not the tank, man. Creepy crawlers in that tank!"

Courtney cut Thomas no slack. "Shut the punk up Stirk or we'll take you to county where you'll meet some of the real-men-love-real-men types. Over at faggot world, they'll dice you up and spit you out. So just zip it, punk. Understand?"

10

MORNING DEBRIEF

Lieutenant Kevin O'Reilly was a big man. He stood about six foot two sporting over two hundred forty pounds. His overweight belly drooped slightly over his belt. His stout build was almost unnoticeable when he was wearing his uniform, working attire that added integrity to his tough looks. He was a real cop. His degree was earned in the streets of Charleston. He couldn't afford to attend one of those institutions handing out degrees in criminal justice to guys only interested in applying to the FBI, DEA, or SLED. Serving anywhere except where a police officer really counted—in the trenches of a local neighborhood—had never interested O'Reilly.

O'Reilly's prematurely gray hair made him look much older than his actual forty-eight years. When he spoke, his gruff no-nonsense tone emphasized his take-charge style. As with most respected administrators, his subordinates clearly appreciated his honest, straightforward approach. They never doubted who was in command. O'Reilly's twenty-seven years on the force had given his officers a confidence in him that highlighted his character and integrity. They knew he could be trusted to cover their backs in inter-department skirmishes. It made navigating the bureaucracy easier and the job less stressful.

As an assistant chief and night shift commander, O'Reilly had an excellent reputation around headquarters. His officers gave him high marks for fairness and honesty. He was well liked and respected by everyone.

Charleston Police Chief Edward Newberg would quickly tell anyone who would listen, "O'Reilly's the best section chief I've ever had. He takes no prisoners. He's a 'do the crime, you'll do the time' kind of cop. Wish I had ten more like him."

O'Reilly had built a great reputation that served him well, but despite his popularity around the department, his mandatory 8:30 morning debrief with his officers would be no different today. He would, as usual, demand accurate answers to all questions regarding the night's bookings. He had to be tough since he was responsible for briefing the chief later the same morning. It was just the way O'Reilly did business.

As O'Reilly entered the squad briefing room, the casual conversation abruptly ended. Everyone turned toward the podium.

"Guys, I know you've had a long night," he began. "So sit. Let's get this started. Sergeant Brody, you're first, then Wilcox, Kent, and finally you, Cooper."

He flipped through the incident reports while Brody got started. Each team sergeant stood and reported the usual litany of offenses and incidents. The totals for the night: four DUI's; six minors in possession; eighteen simple possessions of marijuana, crack, coke, or drug paraphernalia; eleven public drunk arrests, mostly around the Market Street area;

several breaking and entering alarms; two assault charges from a couple of gay guys fighting with each other; two stolen vehicle reports; four domestic violence charges; three arrests for prostitution and pandering to the delinquency of a minor; and one firearms charge resulting from a minor traffic stop.

"All in all, it was a quiet night," Sgt. Cooper, whose report finished the briefing, concluded. "No shootings or major injuries last night. Maybe a new record, huh, Lieutenant?"

"Could be, Cooper. Good job, men. As always, you guys are on it. I appreciate it. The chief appreciates it. Thanks," O'Reilly said and continued thumbing through the stack of incident reports on his podium. He pulled one incident report aside.

"Sergeant Cooper, the only really unusual incident from last night is that public drunk you guys picked up early this morning. You know, the SUV with the drunk asleep or passed out in the back seat—the incident at Battery Park."

Sergeant Cooper stood as he replied, "Yes, sir. Punk kid. RAP has twenty-three arrests. You even arrested him about six years ago, sir. Nothing major—just mostly DUI's, drugs and public drunkenness. We really got nothing to hold him on, sir."

O'Reilly walked out from behind his podium and handed the incident report to Cooper. "SUV was clean. No booze. No drugs. No registration. No keys. Not reported stolen last night. Nothing! How many times have you see that, Cooper?"

"Never, sir. Really weird.

"Vehicle owner is Rachael C. Joseph, Charlotte, NC," O'Reilly said as he returned to the podium.

"Could be a missing person or worse. The scene is just too clean—seems really suspicious."

"Even though Stirk has twenty-three arrests, he's got no felonies," Sergeant Cooper said. "It's just petty stuff, except one vehicular homicide felony DUI, but the charges were dropped with no conviction. He's never served any time, Lieutenant."

"I know the vehicle was clean," Lt. O'Reilly said. "But just to be sure, I'm going to have the homicide guys scrub it for prints, hair—anything and everything. I'll have them run the VIN and see if we can find the owner's address and have the detectives check the local hotels and motels for Rachael C. Joseph. She's got to be somewhere. Good job, guys. Dismissed!"

11

GRAY JAIL CELLS

"Inside, Stirk," the officer commanded as he nudged Thomas inside the holding cell and banged the steel bar door shut with the unmistakable clang of steel on steel.

"Turn around and back up. Hands on the bars," the officer instructed. "Need to remove the cuffs."

Thomas obeyed. He was not totally sober, but having been through the routine enough times, his near incoherence didn't matter much.

His eight-by-six foot holding cell was bare of all but the essentials. Against the back wall was a round stainless-steel lavatory stacked on top a stainless-steel toilet bowl. A six-foot steel cot rested along the side wall.

Spartan was a gross overstatement. Drab and depressing was more accurate. The entire cell smelled of disinfectant. Everything except the toilet and lavatory was painted a dull battleship gray. In the center of the floor was a covered drain. Thomas tried not to think about the drain. The last thing he wanted to know was what had been washed away from the creepy crawler who was in here the night before.

At least he wasn't in the tank with dozens of drunks, psychopaths and weirdos. His gray cell was no five-star hotel, but at least it was single-occupancy. He knew he could survive anything for a few hours.

Thomas took a much-needed leak in the toilet only to discover the previous occupant had used the toilet, big time, and now it would not flush. It was officially out of order. He quickly moved away, trying to escape the assumed foul odor, but the strong disinfectant overwhelmed any stench.

The interwoven metal strap mattress scraped and creaked as he sat on the small cot. He rested his back uncomfortably against the steel cell bars. He shook his head, trying to clear away the fuzz. He was sobering up, but the alcohol still muddled his thinking.

He tried to recall how many times he'd been arrested, including his juvenile detentions. He guessed maybe twenty times in all. He quickly justified most of his bad behavior by assuring himself he'd never robbed or killed anyone. No one had ever gotten hurt, except once, and that wasn't his fault.

Thomas would never forget his first arrest. He had just turned fourteen and had lifted two six-packs of beer, one can at a time, from several local grocers over a period of about a week. He had accumulated a variety of brands, which was enough to have a real blowout. Thomas invited two kids from the neighborhood who were both younger than him, and the three had a huge beer blast behind his mom's garage. Unfortunately, the back-fence neighbor, a nosy wretched old lady, saw the festivities and called the cops.

By the time the police arrived, his nine-year-old neighbor, Jakie, from two houses down, had already chug-a-lugged three beers and was beginning to spin a bit out of control. Janice, a more sophisticated eleven-year-old friend from across the street, told the police she had only tasted the foam on the beer and hadn't actually consumed any.

It didn't matter. They were all guilty, according to the cops. Of course, Janice began to cry. The officer felt sorry for her and sent her home. Jakie, slightly tipsy, stood his ground like a champ. He wasn't about to cut and run. The cops blamed Thomas—he was the oldest and he not only admitted to drinking one or two but also stealing the beer and organizing the party.

Both Thomas and Jakie were taken to juvenile detention where the authorities called their parents. Thomas was formally charged with minor in possession of alcohol, underage drinking, shoplifting, and contributing to the delinquency of a minor.

Jakie was given a reprimand—just a slap on the wrist—by the juvenile detention folks because of his age. Thomas was sentenced to two years probation and had to make restitution to each grocery store where he'd stolen beer, which included a personal apology to each store manager. And as if that wasn't bad enough, Thomas had to report to a juvenile parole cop once a week for two years.

Thomas's mom was devastated. She restricted him for a month. Unfortunately, the incident was only the beginning of his rebellious misbehavior. He was destined to cause his mom much more grief and heartache during the next few years. He would run wild, out of control. The problem was, he enjoyed it. Underage drinking, distribution of illegal drugs, minor in possession, shoplifting several times over, petty theft, and even breaking and entering once to steal the stereo out of a car, were among his many convictions. He became known in the neighborhood as the juvenile Mafioso. When someone needed something under the table, they knew where to go. Thomas would do almost anything for money.

Thomas paid little attention to his mother's pleas and threats. The neighborhood cops knew him by name and knew where he lived.

He did, however, feel some belated remorse when he realized he actually had contributed to the delinquency of Jakie. Jakie's family had moved to Myrtle Beach about a year after that first arrest. He had recently been convicted of drug trafficking in Horry County and received a ten-year mandatory sentence in state prison.

Thomas was sad for Jakie and was sorry for whatever part he'd played in encouraging his illegal behavior. He wanted to put thoughts of Jakie out of his mind but couldn't. His entire life was just too sad to think about. And now, it had gotten much worse.

He was suddenly overwhelmed, drowning in a Tsunami of guilt and shame. Had he become the dad he vowed never to be? Just as surely as the sun will set tonight, he knew he wouldn't be able to pick up Little Thomas this morning for his weekend custody, and his mom would be without her beloved grandson. He was a dreadful father—a one-more-night-in-jail rotten excuse for a dad. He had the key. He knew what he had to do, but his lifestyle only guaranteed he could never be the father Little Thomas needed, the father Thomas himself needed as a child. He was a fraud. What would his son think if he was old enough and could see him in jail?

Thomas slammed his fist against the cement wall in his frustration and guilt. He wondered about Rachael Coedinger Joseph. He had no idea who she was or how he ended up in her back seat. He really had no memory of the night. He didn't even know anyone from North Carolina.

His throbbing headache relaxed some, but he desperately needed mouthwash or something to kill the awful taste in his mouth. "No Listerine in here, man," he quietly said to himself. "Nothing to do but wait and stare at these four walls."

Thomas lay back on the steel mesh cot and watched a huge cockroach, maybe a three-incher, crawl across the cement ceiling and then meander down the wall toward the toilet bowl. He wanted to ask someone how roaches defy gravity and walk upside down on concrete ceilings, but there was no one to ask.

And then unexpected knowledge, possibly stimulated by his still semi-inebriated brain cells, reminded Stirk of data he'd forgotten he possessed, stuff he'd learned in Biology 101. "Animal Kingdom, Phylum Arthropoda, you nasty crawling exoskeletal invertebrate. If the public knew you're a surviving relative of lobsters and shrimp, it might doom the seafood industry."

Sitting up now, Thomas watched the bug descend the wall, climb into the lavatory bowl, scale up and over the edge and down onto the lip of the bowl. Suddenly, the roach took the giant plunge and was gone. He wondered how he could endure the smell, but then he was a roach. Actually, Thomas couldn't recall if a cockroach was an "it," a "he" or a "she" but soon concluded only a "guy" roach would be dumb enough to crawl into a filthy toilet bowl.

Watching to see if the scum-diving creepy crawler would regain its wits and reappear, Thomas quietly said, "Come on, man. Losers never change."

The fact that he dropped out of college, barely passed high school and had a growing police record made it almost impossible for him to get a decent job. He was relegated to selling drugs on the street or hustling paid protesters for a shady community organizer and political hacks.

He shifted on the cot, trying to find some way to get comfortable on meshed steel straps. Thoughts of Rachael C. Joseph began to haunt him again as his mind sobered. He knew the cops would suspect him of kidnapping or murder or worse if they didn't find her soon. But who was this girl? Thomas panicked at the thought of arrest for kidnapping. He cringed at the thought of losing his son. He pined for the father he never had and detested the father he was becoming.

12

KIDNAPPED

Suddenly, Codi was alone. Her cuffs had been removed and her blindfold jerked off, but the bright light from the engine room blinded her eyes as the bulkhead door slammed behind her captors.

She was alone in total darkness. She could tell the door was heavy steel. The ring of steel on steel was unmistakable. The clang of the heavy metal latch grinding shut warned her escape was hopeless.

She wiggled her fingers in front of her nose but could see nothing. Soon, she thought, her eyes would adjust. But they never did. The black void enveloped her like a shroud.

"Escape?" she said to herself. "How?"

Codi remembered running from her vehicle to the bus station in the early morning darkness. She clearly recalled asking the attendant directions to the nearest hotel and leaving the bus station to walk downtown. She recollected starting to cross an intersection and being jerked backwards behind some tall shrubbery.

After that, her memory was fuzzy from her chemically induced unconsciousness by the cloth placed over her mouth and nose, but she did recall the repulsive scent of citrus cologne.

She'd been kidnapped. But she didn't know why. She was confused and frightened. Her captors' questions about Antonio Reyes rang loudly in her ears. They suspected she knew Reyes well.

"Tell us where is Antonio Reyes. We let you go. Okay, missy?" they had snarled as they slammed the door to the aft portside storage locker.

Everything was quiet now except for the faint lapping of water against the steel hull of the vessel. She no longer heard voices from the engine room. The blackness gripped Codi as her predicament crushed her spirit. She struggled to hold back tears. She was a captive, a prisoner.

Suddenly, her thoughts shifted to her family. Codi tried to remember for sure what day it was. She soon unscrambled her confusion and remembered it was Friday morning. At noon, her mother would be waiting for her at Oliver's in Raleigh. Her thoughts quickly screamed panic. When she didn't show up, her mother would immediately expect the worst, as she always did in a crisis.

Codi hadn't called her on Wednesday or Thursday, as she normally did each week, so her unexpected absence would cause her mother to mentally implode. Her anxiety would cripple her, and her condition could rocket out of control.

Codi's dad explained her mother's mental disorder last May when he picked her up at the end of the spring semester. Codi knew her mom, Elizabeth Jones Joseph, was high-strung and prone to serious anxiety attacks, but her father made clear that her illness had grown much more severe in the last year.

The family had tried to ignore her episodes, not wanting to acknowledge her progressively worsening bipolar condition since her case could be managed as long as she stayed on her meds. Aside from their family physician, Elizabeth Joseph's depressive occurrences were not known outside the family. Codi, her brothers, and her dad had always just blown it off to family friends by telling them she was just having a bad day.

But what now? Codi panicked.

Her dad knew better than anyone how precarious her mom's mental state was, and Codi's thoughts again went back to their conversation.

"Codi," her father had started, "your mom's problem goes way back. Back even before she and I knew each other. Your mom unexpectedly lost her parents in a tragic plane crash in Africa."

Her father sighed heavily. He cruised I-40 East, the heat of the afternoon sun rippling heat waves off the endless stretch of flat black asphalt.

"Your grandfather, who I wish I could have known, was a top official in the Department of State, and your mother had lived all over the world. She always attended the American School wherever they were stationed. Every two years, she had to adjust to a new embassy or consulate in a different country. She was never able to make many close friends.

"Your grandparents were stationed in DC for her junior and senior years in high school. When she was seventeen, she attended Friends Academy, a very prestigious private school in DC. Graduating from Friends Academy guaranteed acceptance to any college or university in the States.

"After your mom graduated high school, her father quickly took a new foreign assignment. She had been accepted at the University of Virginia for the fall semester. Her widowed grandmother, Rachael Jones, lived in Colthurst, Virginia, an upscale community just north of Charlottesville, and your mom decided to live with her grandmother during college. The arrangement would be convenient and pleasant. She would be with her grandmother whom she dearly loved.

"Her father and mother had been posted to a small United States consulate in Bamako, Mali, West Africa. It was a dirt-poor barren country bordered on the north by Algeria and the Sahara desert and in the south by Niger and Guinea. Ninety-nine percent of the population of Mali lived along the Niger River and made their living farming. Unfortunately, Malian agriculture had been unable to produce enough to feed its own population. Your grandfather, Charles Coedinger Jones, was tasked to insure United States agricultural aid was distributed fairly and was not pilfered or expropriated by local tribal chiefs."

"He traveled regularly between Bamako, the capital in the south on the Niger River and Timbuktu, an ancient and mysterious Muslim trading center in the north. Regrettably, on one of his trips, their small Malian airliner was caught in one of the infamous dust storms blown in from the Sahara and never landed at Timbuktu."

"After weeks of futile searching, the flight was presumed lost and all searches canceled. The wreckage was discovered about two years later only ten miles north of Timbuktu by indigenous nomads traveling in a camel caravan. Completely buried by one of the many shifting dunes in the Sahara, recent winds had uncovered part of the tail section that identified Malian Airlines Flight 002."

"Skeletal remains of your grandparents were returned in caskets draped in American Flags and accorded the highest honors. They were laid to rest in a diplomatic plot at Arlington National Cemetery in Virginia."

"Dad," Codi interjected, "I had no idea. How horrible! Mom never talks about her parents. When I would ask her, I could see it hurt since she always winced before telling me how wonderful they were. She said someday she would tell me about them. She would always begin to cry."

"Your great grandmother," Codi's dad continued, "was in her mid-seventies at the time of the crash. She pushed your mom relentlessly and told her she had to finish college and ignore her pain. It was weak to complain, she said, because everyone was hurting."

"How very agonizing it had to have been for Mom, not knowing for sure and all," Codi lamented as tears welled up in her eyes. "Had to be totally impossible having to study and take tests and … I hate to think about it. I couldn't have done it. It's all so very sad."

"Well, now you know the history behind your mom's bipolar condition. She can't help it. Her mood swings can be set off by most anything that reminds her of the painful loss of her parents." He paused, then added, "But it is fully treatable with medication." Codi recalled her father speaking compassionately.

Her thoughts returned to her reality and the salty damp stench of her prison. She felt very tired. Her muscles ached as her heavy eyelids fell shut. She drifted into slumber, her head pillowed on the oily brackish smelling rags piled behind her.

Codi awoke confused after a long slumber. Where was she? She noticed the shaft of dim light focused on the metal bulkhead. As she looked upward, she saw a round porthole some ten feet above. She was relieved she would not subsist in total darkness, like some upside down brown bat deep in a cave.

Suddenly, she was startled at the scraping of the metal bar of the lock, and the door was flung open, flooding her cell with the bright light from the engine room.

Her eyes again blinded, two men grabbed her. "Exito! Pronto!" one of them said. They pulled her into the engine room and cuffed her to the side rails of the stairwell steps.

"Momento, missy. You speak now," said one as he pointed to the two gunman she'd encountered at Arthur's. The two guys descended the stairwell steps as the unmistakable scent of citrus spice cologne began to blend with the diesel odor of the engine room.

The darker and taller of the two spoke with a winsome French Creole accent. His cunning, evil smile reminded Codi of her earlier placekick to his family jewels.

He directed his pent up anger at her as he spoke. "Missy, where you see Antonio Reyes? Tell me. We leave you. Okay?"

He leaned in toward Codi, dangling a lighted cigarette just inches from her face and blew smoke into her face.

"I've never met Antonio Reyes. I have no idea who you're talking about."

On the opposite side of the spotless white engine room, just behind the last cylinder of the starboard engine, Tony B, JJ, and Scribbee were gathered pondering the events as their wings flitted nervously. The worried looks on their faces hinted that an inevitable chain of unpleasant events was about to take place.

Ms. Scribbee said to Tony B and JJ, "The tall guy is the one we saw with Thomas Stirk at Arthur's, the nervous one who was constantly scoping the crowd. He's a Haitian national." She pointed to the thug standing directly in front of Codi. "Claude Pierre Aristide was named an undersecretary just last year by his cousin, the current Premier of Haiti."

"Do all these cartel gang types hang out together? Are they all in the drug business?" Tony B asked.

"Claude Aristide operates out of the Haitian Consulate in Atlanta. All these drug gangsters have full diplomatic immunity. Really convenient—cops can't touch them," Ms. Scribbee angrily retorted.

"He sounds French," JJ commented.

"Speaks a French Creole mix and broken Spanish," Ms. Scribbee noted. "He's also known as 'Anasi,' the spider. He's the cartel's muscle guy. He's the original definition of cruel and he lends merciless a whole new meaning."

"Is he the guy who was tried for the murder of two of his common law Haitian wives last year?" Tony B asked Ms. Scribbee.

"He's the guy. Been arrested for multiple killings. He's a certifiable murderer but never convicted," she said, folding her wings in tightly. "He would kill his mother if he knew he could make a buck from selling her body."

"What a creep. Really scary!" cried JJ.

"When the cartel wants someone to just disappear from the planet, they call the Spider," Scribbee explained.

"It's time to ask God for intervention. Maybe this is one of those visible angel moments," JJ proposed, although he knew if God wanted intervention, he would have already spoken.

"I agree, JJ," Tony B spoke up. "Scribbee, who's the other thug? The shorter guy who never says very much?"

"Fidel Rojas Pinella, the quiet one," Scribbee replied, "is a Colombian national and was appointed an undersecretary of some sort working out of the Colombia Consulate in Miami. He's the money and brains of the cartel. He has true Spanish ancestry. His Spanish pedigree goes back centuries. The family is wealthy aristocracy in Madrid. He still holds dual citizenship with Spain and Colombia. Usually lives in Cartagena but travels between cities."

Scribbee stopped. Anasi had pulled a long thin blade and was demonstrating its sharpness by shaving the hair on his arm.

"I say one more time, missy. Tell me Antonio Reyes or I burn you," he said as he pulled a drag, the tip of the cigarette glowing red hot just inches from her face. "Or maybe just cut your face. Your bonita disappear. Be all gone."

He rapidly stroked the long sharp blade close to her cheek. Codi flinched, almost causing him to slash her jaw.

"Tell us, missy," Fidel Pinella instructed, "or Anasi mess you face, girl."

"I told you, I don't know Antonio Reyes."

Aristide, without hesitation, pushed the red hot cigarette to her cheek. Codi screamed. She kicked at the Haitian just missing his jewels and caught her foot against his buckled knee. As he backed away, he slapped Codi twice hard across the face, gushing blood from her nose. Too tired to fight, she fell limp against the restraint of the cuffs, the black blotch on her right cheek already blistering from the burn.

JJ, his wings fully extended and skittering wildly, lunged toward Aristide, but Tony B and Scribbee restrained him.

"Let me take him," JJ yelled. "The cowardly bastard deserves instant retribution." But JJ's screams were heard only by Tony B, Scribbee and all the angels in Heaven above.

13

COURT SOBER

Around noon, an officer unlocked the holding cell. Thomas lay on the cot, his back to the door.

"Are you Thomas Houston Stirk?" he asked.

Thomas fully sober now with his clothes showing an overnight crumple, compliantly answered. "Yeah, that's me, man."

"Turn around, hands behind your back. Get cuffed. You're on your way to the city magistrate. Bond hearing and all."

The officer cuffed Thomas and led him into the dimly lit walkway between the cells along with two other men, both unshaven and disheveled. All three smelled like whiskey stills. After walking a short distance, they entered the Charleston municipal courtroom and were shown where to sit until called by the judge. Thomas noticed only one police officer in court and did not see the three officers who had arrested him.

The judge spoke to his clerk, who handed him a manila folder and briefed him on the case.

Continuing loudly, the clerk announced, "The honorable Quentin M. Gethers, magistrate of this Honorable Court. All be seated."

Judge Gethers quickly disposed the two public drunks with warnings and then motioned to the clerk, who quickly called, "Thomas Houston Stirk. Step up to the bar." As Thomas, a little bewildered, moved before Judge Gethers, the clerk began reading. "City of Charleston versus Thomas Houston Stirk. Please state your name to the judge."

"Thomas Houston Stirk," Thomas replied without looking up. He was determined not to acknowledge the judge or the clerk.

As the judge peered at the thick file of paperwork, he chided, "Drunk again last night, were you? Just one more time in a long list of alcohol and drug charges."

"I didn't drive drunk and I wasn't stealing anything," Thomas defiantly answered.

The judge sensed Thomas's belligerent tone. "Twenty-three arrests. I'd call that habitual, son."

"If passed out in the back seat is habitual ..."

Judge Gethers cut Thomas off mid-sentence. "Don't smart off to this court, Mr. Stirk. I don't put up with your kind. With twenty-three arrests, I could have you tried under the repeat offender statute."

Thomas winced at the judge's rebuke.

"Whose car were you in?" the judge continued.

Nervously fidgeting now and trying to move from directly in front of the judge, Thomas replied, "I got no idea, sir, but I wasn't drunk in public or nothing. I didn't destroy any property or hurt anyone or anything."

The judge pulled his reading glasses down on the bridge of his nose and looked over at the officer. "Lt. O'Reilly, what's he booked on?"

Lt. O'Reilly stood. "Vagrancy and public drunk, your honor," he said.

The judge again turned back to Thomas. "Your statement says you have no recollection of how you got into that Black Denali and have no idea who Rachael C. Joseph is? Are you telling this court that this is the truth?"

"No idea, sir," Thomas said.

"Why should I believe anyone with twenty-three arrests?" the judge asked skeptically. "Multiple arrests for possession, dealing, distribution, and a total of eleven priors just for drugs."

Thomas raised his hand and the judge nodded that he could speak. "I've never hurt anyone, sir."

The judge conceded a nod to Thomas and continued. "Multiple DUI arrests, your driver's license permanently revoked, and additionally, a felony vehicular homicide DUI."

Thomas grimaced in anguish and avoided eye contact with the judge.

Thomas's thoughts drifted back several years. He had just turned twenty-one and could legally partake of alcohol. No more false IDs—he was excited and thirsty. His coming out party had started around 11:00 p.m. at Creekside Bar on the Island. At 2:00 a.m. when the bar officially closed, he and his friends broke out their personal stashes. Around 4:00, the bar's owner told everyone he was closing and asked if anyone needed a ride home. Everyone declined, including Thomas.

Thomas figured if he was standing and able to function reasonably well, he could drive himself. Only twice while he was underage had he been stopped for a DUI. He was young and dumb. He had driven dozens of times after consuming more booze than he had that night. He felt safe enough as he walked to his car.

Thomas left Creekside and was driving west on the Isle of Palms Connector and had just crossed over the Intracoastal Waterway Bridge when suddenly he saw the headlights of two cars crossing the median and heading directly toward him. At the last second, he had to decide which of the two vehicles to avoid hitting and jerked the wheel sharply left.

The next thing Thomas recalled was the police opening his driver's door and asking if he was all right.

"Sir, you've been in a very serious accident," the officers explained.

"I'm fine guys," Thomas slurred as he stumbled out of the vehicle, He lurched forward, almost tripping over his feet.

"Sir, have you been drinking?"

"I had a couple glasses of wine with dinner." His words were garbled.

After EMS pronounced Thomas uninjured but drunk, the police informed Thomas the driver of the other vehicle had been killed in the collision.

"Sir, you're under arrest for vehicular homicide and felony DUI," the officers informed Thomas.

"Man, those two guys were coming at me. They crashed into me, dude," he said as his shaky legs almost gave way again.

As the police officer walked Thomas to the cruiser, he saw the extent of the damage in the accident. The entire passenger side of his vehicle was crushed into the back seat and the other vehicle was a mass of twisted steel. A bloody sheet partially hid the body of the dead driver who was impaled on the steering column. It was a sight Thomas would never forget.

Several days later, Thomas's attorney, Fred Harn, who had been retained by his mother, informed Thomas that his blood alcohol level the night of the accident was .0214 and the blood alcohol level of the deceased driver was .0289, almost three times the legal limit.

The Loye Harn Firm was the best in the city. Their talents could hang a jury of twelve church going members of Mothers Against Drunk Driving in any DUI case.

Fred Harn informed Thomas, "The driver killed in the accident crossed the centerline and median and crashed head-on into your vehicle. The police found an open and surprisingly unbroken fifth of vodka between his legs in the front seat."

Thomas gasped. He couldn't believe his luck.

"The really good news is," Harn continued with his reading glasses pulled down low on his nose, "the police have dismissed the vehicular homicide charge. The bad news is you're still charged with driving under the influence."

Harn advised Thomas never to drink and drive in the future because with a second conviction for DUI, the sentence could be very harsh. "If you should drink and drive and you are stopped, never, never, submit to any field sobriety tests," Harn said. "Immediately call me."

Thomas never listened to anyone, including Harn, about drinking and driving—but Thomas heard loud and clear Harn's warning about never submitting to sobriety testing. So by steadfastly refusing the sobriety drills at the scenes of his last three DUI arrests, Harn had been able to eventually get the charges reduced to reckless driving. Thomas knew how to game the system. It would be about the only thing he did well in his life.

Judge Gethers now looked at Thomas, snapping his thoughts back to the moment.

"So you finally killed someone and you weren't even scratched. Take a look at this photo from the scene," the judge said.

Thomas waived away the photos with his hand. He protested, "He was drunker than me and had an open container. My lawyer said he was .289. Three times the legal limit."

"You were lucky, son," Judge Gethers admonished, looking down at Thomas and then at the paperwork on his desk. "Mr. Stirk, are you aware Rachael C. Joseph is missing? Did you steal her car, son?"

Thomas replied, "No way, sir. Don't even know her."

Judge Gethers took off his reading glasses and leaned back in his chair. "So you're telling me you sobered up in the back of a vehicle that has no registration, no keys, nothing in the glove box. You're telling me you were locked inside and the owner of that vehicle is missing? Is that right?"

Thomas nodded his agreement to the judge. "Yes, sir."

Judge Gethers leaned forward and warned, "Stirk, if you're lying to me, I'll throw away the key. You understand?"

"Yes, sir!"

"I got nothing to hold him on, Lieutenant, but I would suggest placing him in your pre-trial intervention mentoring program. He's already attended the Alcohol Drug Safety Action Program three times and each time ADSAP evaluated him non-alcohol or drug dependent. He's never joined AA. He's one of our worst repeat offenders," Judge Gethers said.

"We'll make room, Judge," Lt. O'Reilly smiled as he turned toward Stirk. "We'll talk after court is dismissed, Mr. Stirk."

The judge firmly finished, "Listen to the lieutenant, Mr. Stirk. I don't want to see you in my court again. Next time, I promise you I will use the repeat offender statute to keep you off the street. Understand?"

"Yes, sir."

Lt. O'Reilly quickly motioned to Thomas to have a seat in the first row of seats behind the rail as he conferred with Judge Gethers briefly.

As the last spectator exited the courtroom, O'Reilly sat down with Thomas. "Well, let's see Thomas Stirk. I'm told even I had the pleasure to arrest you some years back. Is that true?"

"Could be, sir. I don't remember."

"Got any idea what pre-trial intervention is, son?"

"Heard of it."

"Well, the Judge hasn't sentenced you to anything yet, and if you complete the PTI course he won't, and he'll dismiss any charges against you."

"I don't have any charges against me now?"

"He can bring you up again on the repeat offender statute at any time. Ten years in state prison, son."

"So okay. I'm screwed again."

"Look at this as an opportunity, Stirk. It's not that bad."

"Yeah, heard that horse dookie before."

"What's got you so mad, son? You can tell me if you want or not. It's up to you, but I'm a really good listener."

"Nothing," Thomas said. He went silent and looked away from O'Reilly, tormented and overwhelmed by the guilt of his empty life.

"Okay, son. PTI meets at Our Lady of Saints Catholic Church, fellowship hall, every Thursday evening at 7:00 p.m. sharp. Tardiness is never allowed. Late is same as missing class."

"Miss a meeting, the judge you'll be greeting!"

"Understand?"

"You'll be the eighth in the class. Don't be late." Lt. O'Reilly stood and extended his hand to Thomas, who reluctantly responded with a lifeless grip.

"Everyone will welcome you, Thomas."

14

COLD TURKEY

As Thomas left the court and began walking the ten blocks to his mom's home, he tried to recall where he'd been last night. He clearly recalled beginning his evening at Arthur's. The rest was cloudy. Totally missing.

Who was Rachael C. Joseph? He knew the cops didn't believe him. The judge had as much as accused him of kidnapping. Actually, Thomas was even having difficulty believing his own story. How could he have ended up in her expensive Denali without knowing her? Nothing about last evening made sense. His memory was totally tanked out on empty.

He felt his usual shame as he approached his mom's house. He was almost twenty-eight and still living at home, unable to find employment to earn enough for his own place. He was working as a street organizer for a local media company and also pushing drugs on the side. He spent most of what he earned on his own addiction. Thomas knew he was living in loserville.

Even if he could have afforded wheels of his own, his DUI arrests had taken away his driver's license—probably permanently. Everyone in his neighborhood knew he was a complete loser with an extensive arrest record. The neighborhood cops knew him by name. His past haunted his present.

He had no direction or destination in life. He knew he was a lost loser wandering aimlessly down dead ends. He knew he was adrift but his anger clouded all that he did.

He wondered what O'Reilly's PTI class would be like. Authoritarian, very likely, and Thomas hated authority. It would probably be a boot camp deal like the Marine Corps or something with loud screaming and yelling of orders. He was certain it would be tough and demanding. Thomas hated compliance and this experience would be no different. He promised himself not to conform. He would protect his counterfeit freedom at all costs.

Tortured by thoughts of his inability to pick up his son, as he usually did each Friday morning, and knowing that the fresh lies he would have to tell his mother would challenge even his expert double-speak, Thomas accused, indicted and prosecuted himself for his bad behavior.

He quickly decided, as he unlocked the back door to his mom's house, that a shower and quick siesta would come first. Then, he would visit Solo at Arthur's on King. He was sure he could persuade Solo to fill him in on last night's scramble.

Solo, a burly rough-cut guy, about six two at maybe 240 pounds, had been the barkeep at Arthur's for more than three decades. His biceps bulged beneath the sleeves of his black tuxedo barkeep jacket. Under his jacket his white cotton

T-shirt had a black bow tie screen-printed at the neck and "Arthur's Pub Est. 1849" below and centered. His appearance was remarkably formal in a casual sort of way.

His soft, polite voice seemed to contradict his brawny nature. Arthur's hadn't needed a bouncer since Solo's unchallenged authority in any situation at the pub was notorious. He was adequate clout.

It was almost 6:00 when Thomas took a stool at Arthur's. The place was almost empty except for a couple of guys seated at a table in the back. Solo was tending bar as he had the night before. Thomas did remember that. This place would be hopping in couple of hours.

Solo draped his polishing cloth over the brass rail behind the bar and stepped toward Thomas. "Recovered from last night, pal?" he asked. "I've never seen you so plowed."

With a wry frown, Thomas shook his head. "Man, I was really pounded last night. I took the pledge today. No more booze. Gonna go it cold. Totally kick the habit, man."

Solo skeptically replied, "That's a loser, pal. A really tough gig."

"I got to, Solo. I gotta do it. I can't remember anything from last night."

"You were blitzed. Thought maybe those Latino thugs you were with spiked you. You were so wasted."

"Solo, I was seriously grossed out last night. Can't remember jack squat. Need some help. Can you fill in some blanks, man?"

Thomas knew bartenders had incredible memories and were able to recall the most insignificant details about their customers. Good ones could tell you how many times a customer left the bar to take a leak, but none of them ever remembered names. Names seemed to somehow totally escape them, a designed phenomenon well known to cops, respected bar flies and regular customers. After all, hammered patrons, coke blitzers, and ladies of the night needed anonymity. Thomas knew Solo would recall last night but he didn't expect to get any names.

Solo nodded with a hesitant look on his face. "You were drinking Jack with two guys," he said and pointed to the last three bar stools to the right. "Both guys had flashy sports coats. One guy was dressed real nice and the other was casual. One was very dark skinned, maybe from the Islands. Maybe from Jamaica or another island in the Caribbean. The other one was lighter. Maybe Hispanic."

Puzzled, Thomas flinched. "Dude, the problem is I don't know any Hispanic guys from the Islands or from anywhere."

"I thought it was weird," Solo continued. "Both guys looked like drug punks to me. I could tell they were big trouble just itching for a fight. I'd never seen you with street punks before, but you guys were talking seriously about something before you got so slammed."

"Was it crowded last night?"

"For a Thursday in February, it was really packed. Not even one open stool at the bar. Some girl was sitting next to you on your left. Newbie chick. Really good looking, wearing a raspberry red dress. She had long blonde hair to below her shoulders— Scandinavian looking. When she walked in, everyone in the place did a double take. How many times have you seen a really good looker come in alone? She was no skank."

"Got any names?"

"Now bro, you know I'm seriously bad for names." Solo turned away to look at two customers just sitting down at the far end of the bar. "Get paid to forget names, pal."

"Not even the girl's name?" Thomas pleaded. "I can almost remember her. She kept brushing my shoulder with her hair.

I recall turning around and seeing a triangular birthmark behind her ear. Really crazy, man—remember the birthmark but nothing else. I can't see her face and don't know her name."

"I got no name, but I will tell you she mostly had her back to you, spooning coke to two guys in pinstripes. Local attorneys, I think. They tried to stroke a line on the bar. Unbelievable. I thought I'd seen everything but stroking a blow line on my bar? Made me crazy. I sent them to the back."

"You passed out, smashed faced on the bar, around 2:00, and your Hispanic friends hauled you to their car to sleep it off. I saw the two guys and the chick leave around 4:30 or 5:00. As a matter of fact, your two acquaintances left about the same time. That's all I know, bro."

"Thanks, Solo. Owe you big time."

Thomas high-fived Solo as he stood to leave. Solo hadn't provided any names, but Thomas wasn't sure names would have helped much anyway. He was most concerned about the foreign thugs Solo said he was with at the bar. He had no memory of the two guys and that was frightening. Maybe they'd popped him a pill? He didn't know. Even though what happened last night was now a bit clearer, he wished he knew the name of the chick in the red dress.

Outside in the cool of the evening, Thomas's mind was now more lucid. He knew when he got home his mom would want to know why they didn't have Little Thomas for the weekend. He would have to explain. She would be disappointed. She loved Little Thomas. He would have to lie again. More deception stacked on top of lies and more lies—so much perjury in his life now it was impossible to reconstruct the truth about almost anything—too much to recall—which created a summit of deceit he could never climb.

15

EVENING AT HOME

As Thomas opened the screen door to the back porch, he could smell the wafting aroma of chicken fried steak. His mom was about the best cook in Charleston. Her cooking wasn't fancy, just good ole southern style fare using her own recipes. She loved to cook and her friends loved her cooking.

Mary Stirk, in her late fifties, was slim and neat. Always professional in demeanor and dress, she was the executive assistant to the President of the Freethinkers Society of Charleston, Grant Goldman. He would tell anyone and everyone Mary was indispensable, that the Society fellowship couldn't operate without her. Mary had been employed by the fellowship since coming to Charleston in the early eighties.

Over the years, Mary grew to love the Freethinkers Society and now considered it her fellowship—a gathering place to find companionship and friends. The Freethinkers met all her spiritual needs and she embraced their no-condemnation mantra. For Mary, it had become more than a job; it was her life and she cherished it.

Mary had never forced Thomas to attend Freethinkers meetings. She'd always told him that he needed to develop his own spiritual values. Over the years, Thomas had attended the Freethinkers a few times and his sporadic attendance always elicited the same response from his mom, "You've only heard enough to misunderstand the message, Thomas."

Thomas understood more than his mom knew. He'd taken two semesters of philosophy at the College of Charleston before dropping out and had already heard most of the humanist doctrine. A couple of professors tried unsuccessfully to indoctrinate Thomas with the same humanistic new age message preached at the Freethinkers Society.

"I mean, come on, people. You're all delusional," Thomas would say at Freethinkers meetings as they preached their "Okay'isms."

I'm okay, you're okay? If it feels good, do it. Total moral relevance. No boundaries. No absolutes. It was situational ethics to the infinite power. It was an invitation to write one's own Magna Carta, and Thomas had written his lengthy creed a long time ago.

Thomas was already living the *if it feels good do it* lifestyle, and he'd already perfected his own *no boundaries* concept, but Thomas somehow inherently knew he was not okay. He didn't feel okay. He knew the cops wouldn't say he was okay. Something was missing in his life but didn't bother to look for what it could be. He could feel the emptiness. He knew he was a loser. He never could buy into the Freethinkers enlightened philosophy. Somehow he suspected life was not just some giant crapshoot. There must be purpose somewhere, but his need to feel good always trumped his insecurity.

As Thomas opened the back door—surprise of all surprises—there sat Little Thomas at the table in his bright yellow high chair, his grandmother beside him feeding him mashed potatoes. His face and bib covered in potatoes, Little Thomas smiled and waved at his dad, slapping the high chair tray for some much needed fatherly attention.

"Mom, how...." She cut him off.

"Lestee brought him to my office around nine this morning. Said she could not wait for you to pick him up today since she had several appointments. I was delighted, of course."

"Oh wow!" Thomas was shocked but smiled in relief as he walked over to his son and caressed his head, avoiding most of the mashed potato mess.

"He got to know everyone in the office today and was well behaved. He played most of the time in the Day Care Nursery at the Society. Not a problem at all. I did so enjoy him today. He loved being at my desk and being held by everyone."

Demanding more of everything, Little Thomas began fussing as he slathered mashed potatoes over his bib, his bright blue eyes contrasting his blonde hair. He pushed his bits of chicken fried steak into a mountain on his tray and beamed a broad smile at his accomplishment.

"Okay my little one," Mary said as she spooned him another mouthful.

"Mom, I'm so grateful. Just slept over. No one awakened me. I thought I was too late to pick him up. I'm so delighted."

"Sit down, son. I'll put dinner on for you."

Mary placed the chicken fried steak on the table with a bowl of gravy. It looked sumptuous, but Thomas wasn't all that hungry.

His bender from the night before, his lack of sleep, and the beginnings of withdrawal from his alcohol itch had sapped his appetite, but he couldn't let his mom know. She had prepared this feast just for him.

He also anticipated his mom would have her standard barrage of questions about where he was last night. He didn't want to face the inquisition.

What he needed, he thought, was a good drink. Just one stiff triple shot of Jack Daniels, enough to relax so he could sleep. Think of it as a sleeping pill, he argued as he began to rationalize his abstinence vow. Could he really quit the booze? He'd never been able to quit before. Maybe fifteen days at the most. His past cold turkey attempts had never lasted very long.

Thomas sat down and helped himself to his mom's cooking. He praised her. "Mom, you need to write and publish your recipes. Write your own cookbook. I know it would sell." His stomach was queasy but he forced the food down, determined not to disappoint her.

"I mean, just look at Little Thomas. He loves your cooking."

"I know. I do love him so much son. I relish being his grandmother."

Thomas was waiting for her questions to begin but tried to sidetrack her. "Mom, the steak is really great and your spicy fried okra is always the very best." This provoked a measured smile from his mother.

"Your boss Chauncy Cloud called yesterday," she said, puzzlement spreading across her face. "He said he'd been trying to get you for two days and it was important and wanted to know why you're not calling him back."

"Yeah, CC called late this afternoon. We have a Saturday meeting for a Sunday trip. He just wanted to make sure of the meeting time, just wanted to be sure everyone was set to go."

"So I didn't know about this trip. Will Lestee come to pick up Little Thomas on Sunday?"

"Sorry, Mom, I've really been pushed this week—really running late. I'll find out from Lestee when she'll pick him up. Sorry. I should've told you. Just slipped my mind. CC's arranged an important gig in Atlanta at the state capitol next week."

"Well, Little Thomas is the light of my life. Wait till you see all the new outfits I bought him. He's my darling." She beamed with a huge smile. "I'm so delighted Lestee brought him over."

"Guaranteed, next weekend, too, Mom."

As Mary began clearing the table, she casually asked, "You and your friends have a good time last night?"

The inquisition was beginning. The questions would be probing now. "We had a great time."

"Was Lestee with you?"

"No, Mom. I keep telling you Lestee is ancient history. She's Little Thomas's mom and always will be, but she never had any intention of marrying. She just wanted Little Thomas, and in her game of father hide and seek, I was it."

"It's just little Thomas is almost two now, and I'd always hoped, I guess, that you and Celeste would marry. Just seemed right somehow," Mary said as she began wiping Little Thomas's face and cleaning the potato mess on the high chair tray.

"Not in the cards, Mom. Won't ever happen."

Thomas cringed inwardly a little but never allowed his mother to see his anxiety or his relief when he recalled the last time he'd been out with Celeste Warner. Lestee, as her close friends called her, was impulsive and brash. Their short relationship had derailed on something less than a high note. Thomas had been used and he knew it.

Thomas could not help but recall that fateful night over two years ago when he and Lestee returned from a local theater. They were home early and Mr. and Mrs. Warner were still up and enjoying a night-cap in their den.

Thomas was stunned when Lestee impulsively but matter-of-factly announced to her parents, "Mom and Dad, you're going to be grandparents. I'm pregnant with Thomas's love child."

Thomas had no idea Lestee was pregnant. His face went blank and his color drained as his life suddenly began sprinting south.

"I guess I should have told you first, Thomas," Lestee continued. "Sorry. But don't worry. I don't intend on demanding marriage, child support or anything else."

Jackson Warner, who didn't look up from his newspaper upon the couple's return, laid his paper aside. He smiled at his daughter.

Margaret Warner almost choked on the olive in her third martini of the evening, spilling her cocktail all over the small bar in their den.

"How could you, Celeste?" her mother screamed. "And with Thomas Stirk! For God's sake, he's never had a decent job his entire life."

Lestee was convinced marriage was an archaic ritual, totally out of style in the modern world. She wanted no part of it or traditional motherhood.

She had already explained to Thomas, "I'm free to love, laugh, and find my way to the stars. I'm not bound by tradition or society. I'm a liberated woman and in control of my own destiny."

Thomas had never bought into all of the Humanist philosophy of the Freethinkers Society. He was not a progressive. He certainly never shared Lestee's liberated beliefs, but marrying Lestee was way too scary a prospect. The fact was Thomas was greatly relieved at escaping any matrimonial commitment—truly a relief under the circumstances protecting his unbridled freedom.

Mary Stirk had been sure Thomas and Celeste would marry. What she didn't know was Lestee considered herself a true feminist.

At the time, Thomas had told his mom, "Lestee never wanted marriage. She was always too much the star-spangled-totally-liberated-female. She was all about single parenthood and herself."

Although Margaret Warner had squelched any legal battles for custody, Thomas had taken full responsibility for his offspring and his fatherhood. He was determined to pay some child support each month, which Lestee had finally agreed to accept providing there were no legal constraints tied to the money.

Further, Thomas was staunch that Little Thomas would not be the child of a nameless and faceless father as had been his experience. Thomas spent as much time as he could with Little Thomas. But he was always tormented by the facts of his existence. His record of bad behavior prevented him from holding a really good job. He knew he was an unfit father, always high or drunk, unable to find a stable, sober path to a real life. But he was determined his son would not have a nameless, faceless father.

When Lestee explained she was carrying her child to full term, Margaret Warner went ballistic, "This child deserves a real father, not some worthless, jobless, deadbeat loser with a police record a mile long. Thomas Stirk is a drunk, Celeste. What in God's name will we tell the family?"

"Frankly Mother, I don't care what you tell them. Just tell whatever. Make something up if you want," Lestee rudely answered, effectively blowing off her mom.

Thomas's thoughts then drifted back to the night Little Thomas was born. Mr. and Mrs. Warner were out of town. Lestee began having contractions around midnight, which she thought at first were not significant since the baby wasn't due for another two weeks.

Lestee became concerned when her water broke around 1:00 a.m. and she called Thomas. Thomas rushed her to the hospital in a taxi. The baby was born a few hours later about 5:00 in the morning with only Thomas and the medical team present at his birth.

Cutting the umbilical cord was more than perfunctory; it was a spiritual experience for Thomas and a determined aspiration come true for Lestee. Little Thomas cried loudly and healthily. He weighed 7 lbs 8 ounces and had thick black hair. Lestee and Thomas both agreed they'd created a beautiful baby boy.

Around 5:00 the same afternoon, as Thomas was gently stroking Little Thomas's tiny hand while Lestee breast-fed him, Margaret Warner, without knocking, erupted into the hospital room.

Facetiously confronting Lestee, without even a glance at the baby or Thomas, "Celeste dear, don't you think your little Jackson Warner could've waited till after our flight arrived this afternoon?"

Lestee disgustingly exclaimed without even looking up, "Mo-t-her!"

Thomas immediately spoke up, "I brought her here last night, Mrs. Warner. I've been with her all the time. I was with her all night."

Condescendingly, Margaret Warner cut her eyes at Thomas. She said, "Did you now?"

"Yes, ma'am. Our baby, Thomas Jackson Warner, makes us almost in-laws, right?" Thomas questioned with a huge smile.

Margaret Warner jerked around facing Thomas, the full force of her blazing green eyes sparking fire, her red hair dancing almost standing on end. She retorted, "Certainly not, young man. Despite being this child's biological father, son-in-law was never in your future!"

Thomas was crushed by Margaret Warner's degrading reply. He politely excused himself and left Lestee to be with her parents.

As Thomas left the hospital, standing alone on a street corner and waiting for the streetlight to change, he loudly exclaimed to the heavens, "Not tonight, not this week, not this year. Never! Not ever again. Margaret Warner, will never punk me again." He was entirely oblivious of anyone who might have overheard him.

Over the next six months, Margaret Warner and her attorneys forced Thomas to fight for custody in Charleston County Family Court. It had been a tough fight. Thomas had no attorney, but the battle was worth the effort when the judge granted joint custody.

Mary Stirk's voice jarred Thomas's thoughts back to reality as she continued to clear the table. Little Thomas jousted with his father, poking his finger at him as he sat rowdily ready for play time. "Where did you and your friends eat last night?"

"You're crowding me, Mom." Thomas was becoming exasperated. He looked up at the ceiling, pausing, perplexed. "I know what you're thinking. And NO, I wasn't out drinking last night. Okay?"

"I'm not prying, son. It's just I thought at least you would call. I was worried. You were out all night. I was concerned, like any mother would be." She lifted Little Thomas from the high chair, his legs kicking wildly.

"Get off my case, Mom!" he shouted, feeling guilty and irritated. He knew he'd lost control but couldn't help it. Once again, he snapped into denial mode and ran from the truth—his mendacity haunting his psyche. "Just totally leave me alone," he screamed at the top of his lungs as he left the kitchen and slammed the door to the living room.

Scribbee frowned at Thomas as he left the kitchen. The trio had been watching, unseen. "Boorish Rude 101," Scribbee said. "Somebody should have spanked that kid when he was a child."

"Tough being a single mom, Scribbee," Tony B said, his wings fluttering gently.

"Somebody needs to pop the kid up side the head a couple of times," JJ added. "He needs a couple of swift kicks to the butt and then he might think twice about being so rude to his mother." JJ took his normal retributive approach, his wings flashing and closing tightly against his arms.

Scribbee, JJ, and Tony B watched as Mary Stirk instinctively pulled Little Thomas close to her bosom, gently loving him as he began to cry. She turned away, gazing out the kitchen window at her garden. Years of anguish had used up all her tears as she sighed loudly, shaking her head in disbelief. She never knew when his anger would light off or what she should do when it did.

"There, there now, my beautiful grandson. Everything will be okay." She cuddled him. "You will grow up and everything will be fine. I love you so, Little Thomas Warner." Her upper lip stiffened against the furious outburst.

The angels raised their arms toward Heaven and spoke a silent prayer for Mary and her miscreant son.

16

O'REILLY'S ROUNDERS

Lt. Kevin Christopher O'Reilly's pre-trial intervention program was not the typical court ordered PTI program. As a member of Brothers and Sisters of Saint Paul, a layman's organization of the Catholic Church, O'Reilly had dedicated one night a week to mentoring young persons lost in the blunders of their teens and young adult years.

Local municipal judges and magistrates knew O'Reilly well and had seen first hand the positive outcomes Brothers and Sisters achieved with some of the worst offenders in Charleston County. The judges regularly sentenced guilty repeat offenders to Lt. O'Reilly's group. If the young offenders were able to successfully complete twelve weeks of O'Reilly's mentoring, the court would usually dismiss all charges. It was worth it to some, and for many, it was the only thing that saved them from serving hard prison time. O'Reilly was proud of his record and excited about the young lives he'd pointed straight. It wasn't exactly police work, but PTI did more to turn young lives around than jail time could ever hope to accomplish.

Of course, he'd seen his share of bad actors too. Some were too far astray, they were unrepentant and irredeemable. But even the most delinquent souls had some hope because at Brothers and Sisters, something good was bound to rub off.

As O'Reilly entered the fellowship hall and headed for the small semi-circle of seated young offenders, he began. "I want to congratulate all of you for choosing our pre-trial intervention program. I'm aware your first choice is probably not to be here in our church meeting hall tonight. I know that most of you just want to get this whole thing over with. And quickly!"

"I've been through this many times now and can assure each of you that if you can find a way to cooperate with the program and buy into our simple but effective recommendations, it can change your life. Most importantly, it will point you north and keep you out of the southbound repeat offender prison time you avoided during your last court appearance."

"Think of our time together as your date night out with the cops. Think of this as your *get out of jail free card.* Think about your situation and your future. That's all we ask," O'Reilly said.

He then asked the two girls and six guys to state their names and as much of their arrest history as they could recall.

"We have an open forum here. So speak up. I've got your rap sheets." He held up several manila folders. "Don't be shy, guys. Let it all hang out. Okay?"

As is almost always the case in a small group setting, everyone sat silent hoping someone else would be called on first. Thomas Stirk simply looked down, not wanting to make eye contact with anyone, especially O'Reilly. He wished he was anywhere but this church hall.

Fortunately for Thomas, O'Reilly called first on one of the two women, the shorter, heavier gal. It was obvious she had been somewhat more attractive when she was younger.

However, her orangey blond hair highlighted with a purple streak exposed not only the dark roots of a former brunette but also her rough rebellious nature and even darker past. She could have easily been a blocker and the taller girl a jammer in any women's roller derby league. Actually, they both looked rough enough for most any contact sport.

The other girl had a barbed wire lasso tattooed around her neck. She looked at O'Reilly and almost raised her hand to speak. She stopped and pulled her arm back. The barbed wire handcuffs tattooed around both wrists spoke of her evident *sado-masochistic* lifestyle. Everyone was no doubt wondering what other parts, if any, had been lassoed by barbed wire body art.

"Yes, miss," O'Reilly pointed to the tall girl. "You were going to say?"

"No, sir. Nothin," she meekly replied, not nearly as macho as her tattoos indicated.

"What's your name? We all got names. You know mine. Well, actually I know yours too, but it would be nice if you told us all. Okay?" He encouraged her with his look.

"It's spelled Joydie, but you say that like Jody, okay?"

"Okay, Joydie Jody. Did I get it right? What's your last name?"

"Brooks. Joydie Brooks."

"So, Joydie Brooks, what were you about to say?"

"Nothing important," she said and cowered her head, turning away as a maltreated dog might, cringing at someone's first act of kindness, mistaking the benevolence for another whelping. O'Reilly could hear the deep hurt in her voice. He was an expert at reading kids after his many years on the police force. He'd seen about all there was to see and nothing surprised him. He never had answers, but he did have the patience to listen. He knew all these kids needed was someone who would listen without condemnation. It was his ministry.

"Everything's important, Joydie Brooks. So please," O'Reilly gently coaxed her, "where do you work?"

"Don't work right now. Waitressed for a while but always got fired for being late or something. But it was really all my tattoos. They hated my tattoos. I'd get rid of them too if I could."

"Unique body art, Miss Brooks. Lots of folks, nowadays, sport body art. It's real popular. But what is it you were you going to say?"

"Okay, sir. It's about the pot, man. I mean I was totally busted four times for weed. Marijuana. The really good stuff! Everyone smokes weed. Everybody does it, so what's wrong with that? So how come I'm busted? I mean I'm just sayin, man, everyone does it."

"You got multiple possession arrests, right?" O'Reilly asked as the girl looked at the floor and brushed the hair out of her eyes.

"So? Didn't hurt anybody. Just hurt me, man. Couldn't make bond last time. Had just dropped my last $900.00 posting bond for my dad the night before. He punched his girlfriend and she reported him for domestic violence. Couldn't just let him sit in county. Was totally broke."

O'Reilly had no answer. He could have quoted the law, but the law was irrelevant. She knew the law, just as everyone there did.

"Joydie, you say the really good stuff? You grow it too? Growing pot takes some real talent," he said and smiled at her. "I understand the huge cash crop value. Can't hide that." O'Reilly moved on, slowly making his way around the circle and listening carefully to each offender. He gave each person an opportunity to share something they were proud of in their young lives. O'Reilly was good at compassionate listening. He tried to hear what their hearts were saying as they told their stories.

Finally, O'Reilly came to Thomas Stirk, whose head was half bowed. Thomas's black baseball cap was slightly cocked to the side, and his black T-shirt was stenciled in white with "F-Bomb," broadcasting his total revolt against society.

"Hey, dude, love that T-shirt," O'Reilly calmly noted. O'Reilly scratched his head, straining to make a joke, "That's a 'flea bomb' shirt? You know, the dog spray stuff? Or maybe 'fuzz bomb', like those dust balls under my desk? Right?"

"You got it, sir," Thomas sarcastically answered without lifting his head.

"Thomas Stirk, look at me, son." O'Reilly moved closer, looking directly at Stirk. "I don't bite. I promise." Thomas looked up briefly at Lt. O'Reilly. "Everyone here tonight is angry at something. You're not the only one, Stirk. So what's buggin you, pal?"

"None of your business. Whata'ya, my dad or something, man?"

"Could never replace your dad, pal. What's your dad do for a living? I'll bet he's important," O'Reilly said with sincerity.

"Never met the dude, man. Got no idea. He's never been important to me. Don't know who he is," Thomas looked at the ceiling, breaking eye contact with O'Reilly and fighting his resentment of the question.

Lt. O'Reilly instinctively knew he had pushed far enough for the session. He knew no one could replace a lifetime of fatherlessness. Immediately, he understood Stirk's rebellion. He'd seen too many lost young men forsaken by an absent, abusive, or derelict dad.

Fathers were necessary to young men. It was the way God made things, O'Reilly believed. Young men needed the discipline of a dad, the harsh strap of tough love, and the pain of obedience to authority. These were all necessary qualities for character building in young men.

Seated in folding chairs against the back wall of the fellowship hall, JJ, Tony B, and Scribbee, their wings folded, had been silently observing the two hour-long group session. They'd been very favorably impressed with Lt. Kevin O'Reilly.

"Kevin Christopher O'Reilly," Scribbee began reading from the upturned palms of her hands as JJ and Tony B listened intently, "born 1962 AD, Brooklyn, New York. Father started his own butcher shop near the old town in Brooklyn Heights. His mother was a stay-at-home mom with eight children. Kevin O'Reilly was the youngest. O'Reilly's father emigrated from Ireland 1927 AD and married a first generation American daughter of Irish descent. O'Reilly's dad was a taskmaster. Not a tough guy or tyrant but a loving disciplinarian. He spared not the rod. He appropriately stroked his son's backside with a leather razor strap and took no prisoners. He and his wife reared a fine Catholic family. All attended Mass every Sunday. Kevin's dad taught him the traits of honesty, truthfulness, and responsibility." Scribbee concluded.

"Kevin O'Reilly knows these kids and understands their lack of discipline and disdain for authority," Scribbee continued and warmly smiled at JJ and Tony B, her wings in sync with her enthusiasm.

"He's a living saint," JJ said. "I would never have the patience to take so much time to listen to each of them."

"More like a living and breathing angel on earth, I would say," Tony B added. "I don't know for sure, but it is possible, isn't it? I mean to have living angels on earth?"

"Could be, I suppose," Scribbee scratched her chin as she surmised. "Never heard of it before but looks like he fits the role well." She made a note on her palm to check into the question.

Tony B stood and began walking around the group seated in the semi-circle facing O'Reilly. "We know Thomas Stirk. We've been following him for some time now, but these others, especially Joydie pronounced Jody, she's been used and abused. She's just this side of mortally wounded." As he spoke, his wings flitted toward Heaven.

"I'd like to meet the guys who used her. They should have to pay," JJ said. He pointed up as he stood and walked over to the group.

"Retribution is no longer an acceptable notion," Scribbee reminded.

"I know," JJ lamented. "Still seems only right for the guys to get what they deserve. It's not like they kept her or comforted her, or made her life easier or anything. They used her then discarded her to a life of drugs and pain. Now she's damaged goods. Can we at least remove those tattoos? I mean someone needs to give the girl a break! She needs to get a start over free card. A real mulligan." His wings were energized as he thought about God helping Joydie.

"I love you, JJ," Tony B said. He and JJ sat down as O'Reilly stood. "Scribbee, can you check into that start-over-pass thing for Joydie?"

"Right away," Scribbee said smiling.

As Kevin O'Reilly stood, someone in the class under their breath sighed that it was about time. O'Reilly disregarded the veiled comment. He looked around the group as they all stood.

"Plan for next Thursday, guys and gals. Same time, same place. I only ask that you think about all we have discussed tonight and see if anything we've talked about applies in your life. You might be surprised," O'Reilly challenged them all.

Thomas Stirk already was racing for the door and said, unheard by all except the angels, "Not in my life, pal! You're not my dad, you fat ass jerk!"

17

MEDIA PRODUCTIONS

The next day Thomas rounded the corner at George and Meeting Streets just as irritated drivers honked their horns at a horse drawn tour buggy blocking the intersection. The anemic-looking workhorse's diaper had fallen loose from its leather harness, dumping its runny load onto the street. The smell of horse dung was overwhelming as the tour guide, totally unprepared for the emergency, innovated a shovel from a cardboard box lid in a nearby trashcan. Anyone could see the horse was sickly, and the cardboard lid did little to contain the semi-gelatinous load.

As his paying passengers began climbing down from the carriage, unable to take the smell or the incessant honking any longer, the embarrassed tour guide realized he needed a fire hose, not a cardboard box lid.

Charleston city ordinances were painfully strict. No manure on city pavement at any time. Thomas wondered where the innovative guide would deposit the load after cleaning the street but didn't have time to wait and see. He wasn't late yet, but he would be shortly.

He entered the walk up at 403 ½ Meeting under the small Media Productions sign. Chauncy Cloud owned the beautifully restored circa 1869 building. He rented the downstairs to a women's fashion boutique and converted the second floor to his apartment with the large living room serving as the office for his company. Media Productions was an event-organizing agency with a long list of well-known political activist clients to its credit.

Thomas topped the stairs and entered the very large front office. As he entered, he heard the doorbell chime in CC's apartment.

Central to the large office were the two comfortable leather sofas and three leather chairs arranged in a small rectangle. The corners of the area were appointed with antique marble topped Chippendale ball-and-claw end tables. The exquisite rectangular Turkish red and black silk rug and the furniture placement focused visitors' attention to a comfortable roll armed brown leather chair at the throne end of the rectangle.

When everyone was seated, the arrangement left no doubt who was in charge. CC had planned it that way. Even the priceless Turkish rug's 120-knot-per-square-inch design was meant to subliminally influence his guests. The rug was from artisan tribes in the south of Turkey. The pattern was appropriately named "Prevail," which CC usually did.

The walls of the office were covered with photos, framed letters, campaign posters, and banners from political action groups from all over the South and as far north as Washington, DC. Planned Parenthood, Right to Life groups, Christian Coalition, Pro Life Action League, NARAL Pro Choice

America, ACLU, Fair Tax Advocates, The National Council of La Raza, National Right to Life, Feminist Majority, Eagle Forum, The Gay Rights Victory Fund. All the major political players were there.

CC insisted that Media Productions had no viewpoint of its own. It was a 501 (C) (3) and often demonstrated on both sides of an issue at the same rally.

"Media Productions is flexible and non-partisan. We like to go with the flow. Pro or con, we'll be your Don," CC would famously say to interested clients.

Thomas turned as he heard CC open the door from the living quarters and enter the office. "Thomas, you never called me back Friday. Can't have my street organizer, my main guy, MIA," CC chided, his tone inflecting slight reproach.

Thomas walked from behind the sofa. "Sorry, CC. I got really tied up yesterday. I kept meaning to call you but just couldn't get time. Really sorry about that."

Chauncy Cloud was a small man, about five four or so. His lifestyle and appetite for fine food and vintage wine gave him one of those paunchy, ugly bellies that hung over his belt, like a partially deflated inner tube. He was about fifty or fifty-five and probably sixty pounds overweight.

Normal conversation with CC could be distracting. His face resembled the scrunched-up jowls of an English bulldog except his tongue didn't hang out one side of his mouth and he didn't drool.

He'd never married. He was a straight bachelor and would not hesitate to tell a curious individual just that at the first indication of doubt. He had a loud mouth and could be rude and crude. He shot from the hip in staccato half-sentences, splattering his words like buckshot. Blunt would be an understatement. But everyone who dealt with CC knew immediately where he stood, which was a bonus in today's politically correct world.

"You freakin had me worried, Thomas. Just where were you anyway that you couldn't answer your phone? I had some important stuff."

"Was helping my mom. One of her renters moved out and the place had to be cleaned. We had to steam clean the carpet. Sorry, just got too busy and lost track of time," he lied.

Thomas was never thrilled about meeting with his boss, but it was a necessary civility that came with the job. And although the pay was just slightly above slave wages by anyone's standards, it was work. In the current economy, some work was better than none, especially if one's police background check would turn up more hits than his resume had references. Thomas, as did all addicts, had to feed his expensive habits. His job was vital. His police record and confrontational attitude eliminated most job possibilities. Hustling for someone operating just over the legal edge was about all he could find—and they paid accordingly.

"We got that gig in Atlanta with La Raza on Monday. Remember, I told you last week?" CC sat in his divan chair and motioned Thomas to sit.

"I didn't forget, CC. I've already got the bodies lined up. Leave Sunday. Right?"

Thomas's job title did lend him a responsible manager's position without direct supervision, and Thomas enjoyed the freedom to organize the street demonstrators his way. Community organizing and street demonstrations were all he'd ever done. CC knew Stirk's street-smart organizing skills. He was good at what he did, so CC mostly overlooked his inclination for the juice.

"Yeah, Sunday about noon," CC replied. "I knew I shouldn't have worried. But you didn't call back and it got me concerned."

Everyone seemed to know Chauncy Cloud. Most folks who knew him well called him by his nickname, CC, and would say he was about as slippery as a used car salesman, greedier than a statehouse politician and about as honest as the last slick preacher anyone had mistakenly trusted.

CC graduated USC law school in 1979, near the bottom of his class, and had never actually practiced law in Charleston. He never passed the South Carolina Bar Exam, but his business acumen quickly earned him a PhD in "moxie." He knew when to hold'em and when to fold'em and had the financial balance sheet to prove it.

CC could be so cordial and believable, most folks realized too late how unwise it was to sign anything with him. He could squirm his way out of the most complicated contract.

The best deals done with CC were always verbal agreements. Deals done with a handshake. CC always felt more obliged that way. He was from the downright, upright southern school of shady wheeler-dealers. CC was perhaps the most notorious shyster in greater Charleston County.

CC, through many years of sit-ins, protest marches, demonstrations and rallies all over the Southeast, had set the standard for community organizing. He was politically ambivalent and the go-to guy in the South when someone needed to get out the vote or protest something big time.

His success at community organizing was no accident. He realized high achievement was basically all about advertising and marketing. He'd read Saul Alinsky's primer, *Rules for Radicals*, and was a dedicated ends and means guy. With every client, CC would pose a modified Alinsky axiom, "How important is achieving your end result? Consider your goal carefully and commit funding accordingly."

CC's strategy was amazing. Most of his clients revised their goals, embraced much grander expectations and increased their commitment to achieving them. It was always cash in CC's pocket.

Like most clever wheeler-dealers, CC made money on both ends. Customers paid for the demonstrators by the head. For $75 bucks down south, you could have a protester all day. Further north and in DC, the price could run three or four times that much.

Then, he gouged everyone on the placards, bumper stickers and signage. But it saved the clients the trouble of preparing the signs. CC enlisted college kids to paint the signs and even allowed some creative liberty in the message. They always looked original and handmade, without the look of being mass-produced.

In meetings with his part-time student artistic staff, CC was famous for coaching their creativity. He'd tell them, "Never forget what Mark Twain wrote, 'The difference between the almost right word and the right word is really a large matter—it's the difference between the lightning bug and lightning.'"

Media Productions was in fact an advertising marketing agency, which provided ample disguise for all sorts of community organizing. Thomas enjoyed the travel and the excitement of the events. He never knew where he would be or with whom he would meet week to week.

"Okay, we got the Georgia Legislature Monday," CC said. "La Raza has organized a huge rally on the steps of the capitol. They want three ten-hour days. They'll be pushing hard for driver's licenses for illegal aliens."

Thomas pulled out his list. He said, "I've got fifty demonstrators from the homeless shelter and crisis ministries. They're itching to go. Ready to leave town for a while. Looking forward to Atlanta."

CC walked to his roll top desk. "Open Borders is paying fifty grand for three ten-hour days plus giving the demonstrators free accommodations at the YMCA. I got ten thousand cash for you till we're paid," he said and handed Thomas a white envelope.

Thomas opened the envelope, unbuttoned his shirt, and stashed the cash in four of the many pockets in his money vest. "Give them the usual one hundred fifty for walking around money?" Thomas asked.

"Sounds good. Yeah. I'll deliver the protest signs to the bus tomorrow just before you leave." CC pointed to the signs neatly stacked in the corner of the office.

"Not too provocative," Thomas commented. He held up a couple of the signs; one read "GOT SPANISH WILL DRIVE" and another "ILLEGALS DRIVE CARS TOO!"

"We should net around thirty-five to forty thousand. Should be a good gig," Thomas said.

CC walked Thomas to the door and abruptly chastised him. "Stay off the booze, Stirk. Okay? Don't need you carrying around all that cash drunk up to your eyeballs. Understand?"

"Trust me, CC. Been totally on the wagon. No juice for over three weeks now," Thomas lied without the slightest indication of deceit. "I'll get the job done."

18

POLICE BUSINESS

Lt. O'Reilly looked exhausted as he dismissed the Monday morning debriefing. The spate of weekend DUI arrests had presented extraordinary challenges and denied him his usual weekend off. Totally spent, he felt as if he'd been on midnight shift since Saturday night.

The city normally booked five to ten DUIs on an average weekend, with spikes on holiday weekends or Saturdays after a Citadel game, but this weekend had no such events. So it was atypical when his guys booked twenty-three DUIs since Friday.

Chief Newberg had already warned O'Reilly that the mayor was not happy when a world famous travel journal recently bestowed the title "4th Drunkest City in America" on Charleston. He explained, "That kind of infamy draws the wrong crowd to Charleston. Brings troublemakers. The mayor is upset and insists the DUI problem must stop now before it injures the Holy City's reputation further."

Even worse than the numbers, two of the weekend's DUIs involved head-on collisions that resulted in three fatalities.

Neither of the intoxicated drivers had been injured in the accidents. O'Reilly knew the drill all too well. The outcome always seemed the same. The drunk drivers' intoxicated bodies seem to become elastic—malleable like spastic silly putty. Even without seatbelts, more often than not, drunk drivers survived with sometimes nothing more than minor abrasions.

Each of the drunks involved in the accidents had been charged with felony DUI homicide and tomorrow, O'Reilly would ask the judge to deny bail.

But O'Reilly knew justice would never be served for the families of those who died. The drunks would likely receive minimal sentences. The city prosecutors understood the local defense attorneys plied their trade well. O'Reilly was aware the public enjoyed booze and that would likely never change.

O'Reilly was all too conscious that it wouldn't be pretty when he briefed the chief. Chief Newburg was a staunch Baptist and a teetotaler who hated drunk drivers with a passion. He had already begun planning for what he was sure the chief would demand—revisit and revise his alcohol awareness program, prepare new Public Broadcast Announcements, set up random road checks, show more of a presence in downtown bars around closing time, all of which would cost lots of overtime. O'Reilly knew from years of experience that public awareness needed once again to be ignited in order to influence public conduct.

Seeing his guys leaving the meeting, O'Reilly tabled his thoughts and called to Sergeant Cooper, Officer Monck, and Officer Courtney to join him in his office.

Once they were seated, O'Reilly quickly began. "What's going on, guys? Were the bars giving away cases of Budweiser or fifths of Jim Beam this weekend? What's the deal?"

"Just a really weird weekend, sir. DUI madness," Cooper said.

"Weird? Is that all, Cooper? Try explaining weird to the families of the three dead victims. None of the fatalities had been drinking at all. Not a drop," O'Reilly quipped back with an apologetic look on his tired face. "Sorry, Cooper. No offense. It's just I'm gonna catch holy hell from the chief at this morning's briefing."

"Lieutenant," Courtney interrupted, "one of Sergeant Brody's guys was telling me their team had eleven DUIs just on the Cross-town over the weekend. They were all after midnight. Random road blocks on the Cross-town might help, sir."

"I'll point that out to the chief, Courtney. Thanks." He made a note on his briefing pad. O'Reilly relaxed and leaned back in his chair. "Cooper, your team busted the drunk kid in the SUV. Remember, no keys for the vehicle? Parked on the sidewalk at the Battery? The Stirk kid?"

Everyone nodded.

"Stirk's a really arrogant kid. Got him in my PTI class now. He was in the first session last Thursday. I'm not sure he knows anymore than he told us," O'Reilly said. "Have we heard anything on the case?"

"Nothing I know of, Lieutenant," Cooper replied.

"Well, it's been over a week now and we still don't have a stolen vehicle reported," O'Reilly said. "I have a bad feeling about this one. As I told you, maybe a missing person or worse. Our guys ran the VIN. Both the VIN and registration led to the same dead address in Mooresville, North Carolina. Apartment rented to a Codi Coedinger. Unfortunately, she's been gone from the address for over a year now. She left no forwarding and no one remembers her. Leasing agent said records showed she paid cash six months in advance and never used credit cards or checks. The vehicle was also never financed," O'Reilly explained as frustration tightened on his lips.

"Sounds like your suspicions were right," Sergeant Monck said. "Something's missing here."

"And how about this?" O'Reilly nodded. "There's no driver's license recorded in North Carolina for Codi Coedinger. The driver's license for Rachael C. Joseph lists the same dead end apartment in Mooresville. Obviously, Rachael C. Joseph is AKA Codi Coedinger. No record on either name. Nothing is adding up. No phone or Internet matches. Nothing."

"Man, I hate dead ends," Cooper said.

Lt. O'Reilly thumbed through his papers and pulled one page from the stack. "My guys ran several sets of prints from the vehicle but the only match was the kid in the SUV, Stirk. No other matches. Nothing but brick walls."

Sergeant Cooper quickly asked, "Has homicide finished the vehicle yet?"

"They're working on it as we speak. When I hear, I'll let you know. And please guys, don't discuss this case around the department. Don't want to muddy any waters."

"Count on it, Lieutenant. Not the first word," Cooper affirmed. "Maybe the Stirk kid will loosen up in your PTI program. Your class seems to have a positive effect on kids."

"Hope so, guys. We work hard at it."

19

HOT-LANTA

Thomas wanted to shout, "Shut the hell up, guys. Enough already!" But he didn't. He needed peace and quiet. His head was splitting with migraine intensity. They were singing so loudly, it was drowning out his iPod.

Thomas boarded his fifty demonstrators at the Meeting Street bus station about noon. Each of the guys and gals had received a brand new T-Shirt with the Mexican flag above "OPEN BORDERS" stenciled boldly in matching green, white and red letters. They were pumped. They were headed to Atlanta. For most, Atlanta was new territory and a break from the homeless monotony of their everyday lives.

CC had delivered about sixty protest signs, which were standing in the back of the bus. He had given all the demonstrators his usual motivational pep talk, trying to convince them about the worth of immigration to society. They politely listened and then gave CC a loud cheer when he finished. He'd gone on too long, as he always did.

The bus was headed for Atlanta, and the group had been singing at the top of their lungs ever since leaving Charleston.

"Forty-eight bottles of beer on the wall, forty-eight bottles of beer! You take one down and pass it around, forty-seven bottles of beer on the wall."

"No bottles of beer on the wall, No bottles of beer! You barf one up and bottle it up, one bottle of beer on the wall. You go to the store, buy ninety-eight more! Ninety-nine bottles of beer on the wall!"

They were relentless, singing one verse after another, over and over again. It was maddening to Thomas. However, they were having fun and the singing was arguably good preparation for tomorrow's protest demonstrations on the capitol steps.

Around 7:00 that evening, Thomas pointed out the Georgia State Capitol to everyone. The bus continued on its way to the YMCA, only three short blocks from the State House.

Before the protesters exited the bus, Thomas made each responsible for a sign or two.

He gave them his usual speech. "Remember, ten hour days. No misbehavior. Be polite and courteous. Remember you are representing La Raza and all good Hispanics. Don't let them down. They are paying your wages. Be on time. The demonstrations will begin at 9:00 a.m. sharp. Don't be late. Lose your sign and you lose your pay!"

Thomas motioned the driver to open the door as he warned them, "Drinking alcohol is prohibited. Anyone shows up drunk or stoned gets no pay. Everyone understand?"

The demonstrators timidly nodded. They were anxious to exit the bus.

"Now, that doesn't mean don't have fun," Thomas continued. "Have a good time. Enjoy Atlanta. No trouble. No bail bonds are included with your agreement, folks. Stay safe and out of jail."

As the demonstrators exited the bus, Thomas gave them each $150.00 and told them payday was Wednesday afternoon. He reminded them again no booze. Thomas made it crystal clear. La Raza would not pay for drunken protesters.

Thomas shouted at the group as the last of the demonstrators exited the bus. "Make me proud! 9:00 sharp."

20

STATEHOUSE PROTEST

The crowd around the Georgia State Capitol was much larger than Thomas anticipated. The weather was perfect. The forecast called for a pleasantly mild 80 degrees under overcast skies. His protesters had arrived on time.

Most of the bystanders seemed disorganized. The union folks from the AFL CIO were out in full force with about two hundred members in opposition to the Alien Rights Bill being debated on the floor of the legislature.

To union members, this bill was just a foot in the door for illegal aliens. It would trade American jobs for very low wages. The driver's license for illegal's campaign was just the first step in the process. Union membership could only see disappearing jobs, which added more pain to an already severe job shortage.

Some of the union members were on the steps of the capitol but without protest signs. Most of them were working behind the scenes, lobbying legislators to vote against the bill.

They wanted no publicity and there were no AFL CIO signs anywhere.

La Raza had rounded up about one-hundred and fifty Hispanics, most of them likely undocumented. They blended in with the Media Productions folks. Carrying their own protest signs, the La Raza marchers and the Media Production demonstrators greatly outnumbered those in opposition to the bill.

The area was crowded. Street traffic had backed up with drivers rubbernecking the demonstrations. Atlanta police were moving into the street to direct traffic.

Protest signs were everywhere: *"OPEN BORDERS NOW," "ILLEGAL IS NOT A RACE," "PROUD TO BE HISPANIC," "GOT SPANISH WILL DRIVE," "AMNESTY FOR ALL," "ALIENS DRIVE CARS TOO,"* and *"ALIEN NATION UNITED."* The message was clear.

Other demonstrators were shouting their messages over megaphones. Thomas had given his best two protesters megaphones.

"What do we want? Justice! When do we want it? Now!" the megaphones blasted.

"What do we want? Equality! When do we want it? Now!" others loudly shouted back.

The whole place seemed in total chaos, but it wasn't. Thomas had planned the chaotic anarchy in perfect harmony.

On Tuesday morning, State Congressman Kinlock Jefferson approached Thomas on the steps of the capitol. The noise was so loud, Jefferson could only get out a couple of words. "Need a word with you in my office, Mr. Stirk," he shouted.

Jefferson motioned Thomas up the steps. Once inside his office, Jefferson offered his thanks to Thomas. "Legislature wasn't expecting us to mount such a large crowd. This could have a huge influence."

"Pleasure to meet you, Congressman Jefferson. Glad we could be helpful," Thomas said as he reached to shake the congressman's hand.

"Most of the legislature was hoping this bill would just go away or die a quick death, but it looks like the vote might swing our way Wednesday."

"Great," Thomas replied.

"Mr. Cloud insisted I pay you in hundred dollar bills." He handed Thomas an envelope with five-hundred C-notes inside."

"Mr. Cloud and Media Productions thank you, Mr. Jefferson, and La Raza and whomever else. May I use your facility?"

Thomas excused himself to the nearby men's room, locked the door, and placed all the C-notes into his money vest. He then returned to Jefferson's office.

As Thomas opened the door to the Congressman's office, he found Jefferson speaking with several college kids.

Jefferson turned to Thomas and said, "Several of our senate pages have dropped by. They want to bend your ear if you don't mind. They've never met a real community street organizer. Hope you don't mind. Vote is coming up on the floor. I gotta run. Thanks." He headed for the house floor.

Thomas thanked Jefferson and turned toward the pages. "You guys aspiring politicians or what?"

The tallest of the guys stepped forward and extended his hand.

"Honored, sir," he said. "Thanks for talking with us. I'm Toby Harrell. Twenty-two. Majoring in journalism with a minor in political science. Completing my junior year at

Georgia Tech. I'm from Savannah. Work for Senator 'Dow' Covington, from the Sixteenth Coastal District of Georgia."

"Hey, you guys, just call me Thomas."

"Okay, Thomas," said another student, slightly older. "Baker Flack. Senior year at the University of Georgia. Majoring in American History. Headed for Washington to be US Congressional House page next year. Hope to eventually attend George Washington University for my Masters in Political Science." Thomas sized him up as the kind of a guy who could make things happen.

Flack turned to the only female in the group. "Hey, meet RaeAll, Thomas."

Allison Rae Baldwin had just turned twenty-one. RaeAll, as she was nicknamed, was a very bright young lady and a three-year senior at Georgia Southern. Her 4.0 GPA was only dampened by her average looks. She was leaning toward a postgraduate law degree from UVA where she'd already been accepted to the School of Law. She was a real blonde with a dated pageboy haircut. She made up for her lack of good looks with her bubbly personality.

With an elongated southern drawl, RaeAll smiled and said loudly, "Pleasure to meet you, Thomas. I'm in Poli-Sci and Pre-Law at Georgia Southern." She shook hands with Thomas, beaming a broad smile.

Toby Harrell interjected, "RaeAll only acts shy, Thomas, but she's hardly laid back. Senior senators fawn over her like she's really got the hots for them."

Baker Flack interrupted with his best impersonation of RaeAll's big southern drawl, "Now Senator, I would just love to, but what would that sweet wife of yours say? Why, y'all been married a lifetime, for goodness sake. I just couldn't break that up, Senator."

Everyone guffawed. Flack imitated her drawl and mannerisms perfectly.

RaeAll shyly looked away. "Come on, guys. I only flirt."

It was easy to see why RaeAll was just one of the guys. She fit in. She seemed fun. Blushing, RaeAll quickly changed the topic and introduced Paul Alex Jackson.

"Hey, Thomas," he said. "Paul Alex Jackson—everyone calls me Plex. Home is Valdosta. Majoring in Education at Valdosta State. Headed to South Georgia next year to teach in public schools. I'll miss Atlanta, but those rural school boards will pay my student loans.

"Thomas, why don't we all go to Poeff Huffingtons tonight? Say around 11:00? I guarantee you've never been anywhere like Poeff Huffingtons. The place is freakin unbelievable."

Toby, Baker, and RaeAll emphatically agreed. "Yeah, Thomas, come on. Join us?"

"Awesome, guys. Okay. Around 11:00, then."

21

MISSED CONNECTION

"I'm sorry. I didn't catch your name. Who did you say you were with, sir?" Lt. O'Reilly apologized to the caller as he motioned to the two homicide detectives who had just entered his office to take a seat.

O'Reilly had no choice but to continue the call he'd answered by mistake. He said to the caller, "I'm trying to shuffle two conversations. Impolite I know. I apologize. Please give me your name again."

"Michael Cox, Special Assistant to Vice President Walsh, the White House, sir," Cox impatiently replied. "If you're too busy, I can call back another time when it's more convenient."

Feeling really stupid that he'd once again thwarted Margie's excellent call screening, albeit accidentally this time, O'Reilly recognized Cox's impertinent tone of voice and pushy attitude.

"That won't be necessary," he curtly replied. "Now, just what is it I can do for Vice President Walsh's office today, Mr. Cox?"

"I'll get right to the point, Lieutenant. The vice president will be traveling to Kiawah Island next weekend, and we need an escort from the Air Force Base to the island on Friday night with a return escort Sunday evening. Air Force Two will arrive around midnight. May I count on you, Lieutenant, to arrange an appropriate escort for the vice president?"

"Can do, Mr. Cox," O'Reilly said. "It's the usual escort of six—two county, two city and two state. Right?"

"Correct, Lieutenant. Not so very complicated now, was it?" Cox condescendingly replied. He was clearly annoyed.

Angry now and visibly offended, O'Reilly calmly advised the impertinent assistant, "Okay, Mr. Cox, when you have the exact arrival time for the Vice President, please contact my secretary, Margie Knight, and give her all the details. We'll arrange the six-car escort. Not a problem. We'll be happy to assist. Anything else, Mr. Cox?" O'Reilly had arranged White House escorts for the Vice President several times in the past.

"Vice President Walsh thanks you, Lieutenant," Cox snapped and the phone line abruptly went silent.

Obviously aggravated at the extra duty and the blatant arrogance of White House staffers, O'Reilly looked at the dead receiver in his hand as if to say, "You pompous little creep; no one hangs up on me."

But it was too late. Cox was gone and even if O'Reilly could slap him up side the head, no White House staffer would ever understand the contempt felt toward them by those they regularly solicited for local support. O'Reilly knew all too well that even a brief encounter with one of them could ruin a person's entire day.

"So what else is going to piss me off today?" O'Reilly loudly announced to the two homicide detectives seated in his office.

"Nothing, sir," Sergeant Lewis piped up. "I can't believe that jerk hung up on you, Lieutenant. I mean what rock is he living under, anyway?"

"They're all delusional in DC. It's just the way it is. So what's got you guys in my office today?"

Sergeants Michael Lewis and Phillip Farley had been in the department more than fifteen years. They were seasoned veterans, experienced and meticulous. Little slipped by their investigations, especially when they worked together on a case. More than once, they'd come up with critical evidence that brought a murderer to justice or the overlooked clue that elicited a guilty plea. O'Reilly would tell anyone they were the best homicide detectives in the state. He relied on their expertise.

"Well, sir, we finished the sweep of that SUV owned by Rachael Joseph," Farley began.

O'Reilly sat up in his chair with interest. He said, "Yeah, I've been waiting to hear from you guys. What did you find?"

Lewis handed O'Reilly the written report as he began, "The guys at the scene did a really thorough job. The vehicle was basically clean. No evidence of any trauma, no blood, nothing under infrared. Some urine stains on the back seat and some puke on the floorboard. No drugs or drug residue. Was clean. Almost seemed scrubbed."

Farley handed O'Reilly a photo with a scribbled note on the back. He added, "Lieutenant, you need to see this. Found this stuck in between the pages of the owner's manual. Looks like Joseph wanted this concealed."

Lewis continued, "And what's really interesting, particularly after overhearing your last phone conversation, is that we believe this photo has a political connection, Lieutenant. Recognize the guy in the middle?"

O'Reilly looked at the photograph closely. "He looks familiar. Yeah, I know this guy. It's his hair. I've seen this guy on TV or somewhere. Can't recall his name. Who is he?"

Lewis stood and moved closer to O'Reilly's desk. "Well, sir, we can't be sure, but we think this is a photo of the young US Senator from North Carolina, Tobias Edwardson. The photo looks exactly like him and as you said, it's the hair."

Lewis motioned to O'Reilly. "Turn the photo over, sir. It's signed 'To Codi, All the best, Toby.' Seems pretty conclusive, Lieutenant. Codi would seem to be an obvious nickname for Coedinger."

"Photo's a little fuzzy but it's Edwardson all right. Got to be at a party somewhere. Do we have a clue who the other two guys are and the gal he has his arm around?"

"Not a clue, sir," Farley said. "But it does look like some high-class whoop-it-up somewhere."

"Okay guys, get me two sets of blow ups. 8 X 10's with good resolution. I'll speak with the chief and get permission to confront the good senator with this photo. Maybe he can help us identify Codi Coedinger. Maybe he'll cooperate."

"Wouldn't count on it, sir," Lewis blurted. "Not likely he'll volunteer anything without a subpoena. You know these self-serving politicos. Slim to none, I would say."

"Just get me the 8 X 10's and I'll follow up, I promise you. Who knows—we just might get his attention."

Farley handed O'Reilly a worn scrap of paper and said, "Sir, we also found this with the photo."

O'Reilly read the scrap of paper and exclaimed, "What the ....? S e y e r O i n o t n a?" He spelled the name scribbled on the scrap of paper and read the number 1382076404. "Sir-iree Eno-tona?" He mispronounced badly.

"Pretty sure it's Middle Eastern, sir," Lewis chimed in.

Margie Knight interrupted the conversation as she opened the office door. "Excuse me, sir, just wanted to remind you of your 10:30 with the chief."

O'Reilly stood at his desk and motioned Margie to come in. "Margie, need to ask you something."

"Of course, sir."

"Don't you do something with anagrams or word associations or something? You know, deciphering words?"

"Yes, sir, we have a Scrabble club. It's great fun if you like that kind of thing."

"Look at this note." O'Reilly handed her the scrap of paper. "Strange name and number I can't figure it out. What do you make of that? We think it's Middle Eastern," O'Reilly asked as Margie looked at the wrinkled paper.

After studying the note for about fifteen seconds, Margie pointed to the name, "Latino, sir. Hispanic name. Reading the name backwards, it's Antonio Reyes and the numbers are also backwards. Number's an Atlanta phone exchange, 404-670 2831. I'm sure of it, sir."

O'Reilly, Lewis and Farley were amazed as O'Reilly took the scrap from Margie. "Well, I'll just be damned ...," O'Reilly mumbled. He gave her a quick thumbs up.

"Not complicated, sir. Just backwards. Now don't forget your 10:30 with the chief." She closed the door and exited.

"Well, what are you waiting for?" O'Reilly quipped to Lewis and Farley, slightly embarrassed by the simplicity of it all. "Get on it. Run the name and the number, and let me know who's on the other end of that phone line."

22

POEFF HUFFINGTONS

Thomas declared a truce with his abstinence vow. He'd justified the juice for just one night and then promised to be on the wagon again tomorrow and was right on time to meet his newfound friends—Baker, Toby, RaeAll and, Plex. Everyone was excited for an entertaining evening at Poeff Huffingtons.

The maître d,' after collecting the fifty bucks a head cover charge, escorted them to a table near the side of the very large hall about half way to the stage. Thomas was amazed at the huge crowd—somewhere around four hundred, he estimated. The place was rockin' loud.

The main dance floor was shrouded in a misty-white blue gray haze, and the unmistakable sweet odor of burning cannabis mixed with cigarette smoke. The haze was highlighted by strobe lights reflecting their beams from spinning mirror globes hanging from the ceiling. It was hypnotic.

On stage, a heavy metal electro retro band blasted mind-pounding, eardrum-busting sounds. No one even recognized the music. No one even cared. To most, it was just loud noise. The raucous, throbbing sound provided a kind of psychedelic ambiguous rock beat that only heavy metal aficionados could appreciate.

Most of the patrons were orderly but very loud. There were several groups of four or five guys, dressed in business suits with ties loosened, all smoking pot from bongs at their tables. The scene was surreal. It was Arthur's on King on a larger scale and the marijuana and cocaine were brazenly public.

The waitresses took orders for drinks or whatever was desired. It cost $150 per line for the really good stuff. The wait staff told everyone Poeff Huffingtons served only the finest. A joint was $30 bucks and a bong at your table could be arranged for several hundred, depending on how many were smoking. It was wild.

Thomas, after paying the cover charges for everyone, agreed to pick up the tab for the evening. He'd ordered a fifth of Jack Daniels and five glasses of ice, from which RaeAll quickly pleaded retreat.

"Wow, Thomas, you're awfully kind and all," her face turning red as she blushed, "but could I have a virgin piña colada? I'm not a big drinker."

"Of course, a virgin piña colada for the lady," Thomas told the waitress.

The rest of the guys, not wanting to disrespect the very best bourbon whiskey on the face of the earth, as Thomas had described Jack Daniels, placed their glasses forward. Thomas poured each a drink straight up on the rocks.

Suddenly, the mind-pounding, eardrum-busting music stopped. The spotlights focused on a sophisticated-looking African man in a tails-length white tuxedo. "Welcome to Poeff Huffingtons," he boomed in a British accent.

His wide gray belt, adorned with an oversized round silver buckle, held back his enormous belly. The silver buckle sparkled from the strobe light flashes. He seemed larger than life, reminding Thomas of a well-dressed sumo wrestler. His appearance loudly broadcast his self-appointed importance.

"Huffington Charles Poeffers, here. Having a good time?" He turned toward the band and began clapping for the group as he continued, "Put your hands together for our band."

His long gray hair was swept back in a beautifully braided ponytail, which hung almost to his waist and was tightly secured with a bright, multicolored ring. "Just remember folks, huff and puff till you're bad enough. Don't forget we drive on the left side. So cheers to all and to all a good time!" He left the stage and began mingling with the patrons.

About 1:30, a wild-eyed Plex returned to the table from a visit to the men's room. "Man, you won't believe what I just saw," he said. "Guys and gals in this unisex restroom snorting coke big time. Everyone was blowin the stuff. Line after line. They even had mirrors on tabletops. Everything right out in the open." His eyes were excited from the discovery of forbidden fruit. "Someone offered me a snort. I told them I was smokin pot. Some really crazy wild dudes in there. Can you believe it?"

By now, Toby and Baker were feeling good. Thomas had ordered the second fifth of Jack Daniels, and everyone was pretty well sloshed, except of course RaeAll, who was enjoying the evening just watching the crowd. Plex was well on his way but was too excited at what was going on to realize how much alcohol he'd consumed.

No one in the group was expecting a floor show, but spontaneously, a very intoxicated young lady, dressed in a business suit, mounted one of the center tables just in front of the stage and began dancing to the beat. When the band saw her table-top performance, they immediately picked up on her bumps and grinds with the appropriate beat.

RaeAll turned her head away, claiming she couldn't watch, as the amateur stripper jerked off her suit coat and flung it into the crowd. Her sheer silk blouse exposed her rather large endowments that seemed to be bumping when they should have been grinding.

Plex stood up at the table to gain a better view, encouraging RaeAll to watch. "Man, what did I tell you? You can't see this kind of stuff for fifty bucks anywhere else on the planet."

The band played on with a faster and faster beat as the young lady began unbuttoning her blouse. Suddenly, some guy in the crowd stepped up to the table and encouraged her to come down. He covered her with his jacket. The excitement was over almost as quickly as it had begun.

Plex was disappointed. "RaeAll, you missed it. Freaking unbelievable!"

About 4:00 a.m., after the four guys had almost blown through two fifths of Jack Daniels, Thomas's young friends were sloshed out of their minds. Plex, especially, was totally stoned, feeling no pain from the combination of pot and booze. Surprisingly, the club was still rockin.

RaeAll still hadn't finished her piña colada. Thomas wasn't sure if she was having fun or had turned the evening into a psychological study of depraved adults blown out of their minds. Baker and Toby tried to nurse their drinks over the evening but had crashed and burned.

Then, out of the blue, some guy in a white jacket appeared at the table and began hitting on RaeAll. He'd placed himself between RaeAll and Plex. The guy was totally spaced out, eyes glazed, utterly stoned.

Then the guy in the white jacket grabbed RaeAll's hair and tried to pull her away from the table. His speech slurred as he ordered her to dance with him. She resisted and jerked free.

"I don't want to dance," RaeAll said, trying to regain her wits while suffering the pain of having her hair yanked so hard.

"What's with you, princess? Your friggin tiara bent out of shape or something?" the guy retorted. "You got some tight ass bitch thing or something?"

Plex came to life. He lunged at the guy in the white jacket, "Leave her alone you freakin' addict," he shouted with wild-eyed rage, his stupor obliterating any discretion.

The intruder reached under his white jacket and pulled a .038 caliber snub-nosed. He pointed the weapon at Plex and shot twice. Plex fell to the floor.

He then pointed the gun at Baker and pulled the trigger. The pistol jammed and misfired. He unsuccessfully pulled the trigger a few more times and then disappeared into the stampeding crowd.

Baker was petrified. Dazed and frightened, his sphincter flinched allowing his bloated bladder to let go down the inseam of his tan trousers. He groped, fumbled, and scanned his body, thinking he'd been hit, even though there were no shots.

Thomas stood up and saw Plex halfway under the table bleeding badly. What had just happened was no dream. Plex was hurt, blood spilling from his limp body.

Thomas leaned down as Plex tried to speak. He could only silently move his lips. "Help me, man."

Plex's lips continued to plead with Thomas as his eyes fluttered closed. Thomas's mind raced. His money belt contained five hundred plus C-notes, and Thomas knew when the police came, they would question everyone who couldn't leave before they arrived. He had to get out. The police would seize his cash and charge him with money laundering or trafficking. They would charge him with anything drug related just to confiscate the cash. He had no choice. He could not stay. Surely, someone would help Plex. He could not. He knew CC would kill him.

Since most of the patrons were running toward the front of the club, Thomas jumped over the booth and ran toward the back of the building. He grabbed a fifth of Jack Daniels from an abandoned wait cart and headed for the kitchen.

Inside the empty kitchen, Thomas discovered the back doors were padlocked shut. He grabbed a steel loading dolly, picked it up, and slammed its lip down hard on the lock. The padlock snapped. He opened the double doors and escaped into a very dark alley in underground Atlanta.

Thomas could hear the sirens, hopefully an ambulance on its way for Plex. He wondered where Toby, Baker and RaeAll had gone. Feeling guilty and cowardly, he cautiously exited the dark alley and spotted the gold dome of the capitol. His hotel was only three blocks away.

23

FACE THE MUSIC

Tony B, JJ, and Scribbee were clearly not happy with their latest assignment. Scribbee was not pleased with having to endure five hours of second-hand smoke, drunken perverted humans, and the insanity of some idiot kid, stoned out of his mind, wildly shooting at people. JJ grumbled about having to babysit a cowardly alcoholic.

Plex never knew Tony B escorted EMS to the hospital just to be sure he got the very best emergency care. Once Plex was out of surgery and stable, sometime around 7:00 a.m., Tony B rejoined Scribbee and JJ in Thomas Stirk's hotel room.

JJ and Scribbee told Tony B they'd watched as Thomas consumed an entire fifth of Jack Daniels in less than two hours. Thomas had drifted off to sweet inebriation about 6:30, once again temporarily suppressing his guilt, his fear and his cowardice with the help of whiskey spirits.

Morning became afternoon, then evening. The angels had been relegated to watching Thomas for the last twelve hours. They were bored and restless. The small hotel room was beginning to close in on them. They were well ready for their assignment to be finished. Over the years, they'd seen more than their share of selfish prodigal son types. Enough was enough, they all agreed.

"Jumpin' Jee-hosha-phat!" Tony B exclaimed loudly and as he stood up, his tiny wings flexing relief. "I wonder if old Noah had any idea what he wrought when he harvested those first fruits from his vineyard."

Scribbee quickly added, "Noah may have been the first drunk God had to deal with, but he was far from the last."

JJ snickered smugly. "Yeah, didn't take Noah very long to find out he liked new wine. They found him naked in his tent smashed out of his mind. That reminds me, we should thank God Stirk's not lying here naked."

They gazed at Thomas who held the empty Jack Daniel's bottle close to his mouth, much as a baby might guard a pacifier.

"Oh my, you do have a way of spinning things. I like that," Scribbee complimented JJ. "But I do wish you could be a little less graphic."

Tony B paced the room as he looked at Scribbee and JJ. "Noah was truly righteous before God," Tony B said. "When God spoke, Noah listened. He may have been God's first drunk, but Noah obeyed when God told him to build an ark. How crazy did that look to Noah? We probably ought to cut him some slack."

"What about Stirk here? Maybe we ought to nudge him a little," JJ suggested. "His bus leaves in about thirty minutes. What'da think?"

They all agreed as they watched Stirk begin to stir. Thomas rolled over on his side and opened his eyes. He focused on the bedside clock–5:30 p.m.

Thomas jerked up, sitting on the side of the bed, as the empty bottle tumbled to the floor. His head was throbbing. He quickly stood. He was a little uneasy on his feet and disheveled—his wrinkled shirt needed much more than a quick press and his beard sported two-day stubble.

Thomas looked in the mirror, splashed some cold water on his face, took a leak, packed his things and hurried from the room.

The angel trio sighed relief. They knew he had only three blocks to walk to the YMCA and would arrive just in time to beat his deadline of 6:00 p.m. They'd done their duty. Their assignment was completed. Relieved, they drifted slowly down the hall behind Thomas.

Out of breath, Thomas threw his black bag into the open bus door and pulled himself inside to the boisterous cheers of his demonstrators. His head was aching from the pounding pressure of his run to the bus.

"Man alive, me and these guys thought we'd lost you for sure," the bus driver began with a huge smile of relief. "We didn't know what happened. You look like you've been *bronco busted*, dude. These guys been talkin bout getting paid. Anyway, glad you're back."

As the bus slowly rumbled out of Atlanta amid heavy traffic on Interstate 20, Thomas pulled up the *Atlanta Constitution* on his phone and searched for a story of the shooting last night. There it was: GUNSHOT VICTIM CRITICAL. SHOOTER ESCAPES. No names were mentioned—not even the club. The brief story did say the victim was in critical condition in intensive care but would recover.

After twelve hours of solid, if not natural, alcohol-induced sleep, Thomas was still exhausted. The confines of his bus seat concentrated the foul scent of his body odor. He wanted to open the window but couldn't. The images of the white jacketed shooter firing at Plex played over and over again like a crawler at the bottom of a TV screen. They wouldn't go away.

The shooter had been direct. He'd shown no malice or hatred. He just pointed the gun and shot. He didn't even know Plex. How totally insane was that? It seemed like a dream but the splatters of blood on Thomas's pant cuff were real enough.

Thomas squirmed uncomfortably as he saw the replay of Plex's eyes and the plea for help on his lips. He could not black out what happened last night. All he could see was Plex, lying on the floor, bleeding and pleading for his help. Thomas thought Plex was on the verge of death.

Thomas, in his cowardice, had ignored Plex's pleas for help as he ran for the back of Poeff Huffingtons. He was sure Tony, Toby and RaeAll watched his escape.

He was deeply ashamed of himself. He closed his eyes, knowing he always stayed in the way of double trouble. His thoughts drifted. Where was Rachael Coedinger Joseph anyway? Had they found her? Would he be arrested as he exited the bus in Charleston? It was all too much. Maybe he would ask Lt. O'Reilly at the PTI meeting this week.

Thomas paid his demonstrators. Soon, most of them were asleep. He wondered if he would ever sleep again. His life, it seemed, was irreparably screwed up.

To Thomas's great relief, he wasn't arrested when the bus arrived shortly after 1:00 a.m. He walked home, comfortable the cops would not be waiting at his door. He immediately showered and crashed. Deep sleep came quickly.

CC had left Thomas several voice mail messages Wednesday, advising him of the 11:00 a.m. meeting on Thursday. CC said it was important and to be on time. Thomas set his alarm. He knew he would have to face the music.

Slightly rested after sleeping till 9:00 a.m., Thomas was up and out. He walked to Media Productions and was waiting for CC in the office. He was on time. CC was not.

Predictably, a few minutes later, CC came busting into the office, his voice raging fire. "Left six friggin messages yesterday on your cell phone. You never answered. I know you were sloshed."

Thomas, without even a slight flinch, fired back. "No way, CC. I was just very busy with the demonstrations. It was the last day, man. I was slammed. Sorry, I just didn't have time."

"You're lying. I know you were juiced. You had to be."

Thomas took off his money vest and handed it to CC. "Been on the wagon for weeks, CC. Just count the money. It's all there."

"Money won't lie," CC snapped as he began removing the C-notes from the vest pockets and counting them at his roll-top desk.

After what seemed like forever—CC had taken his sweet time counting all the cash then double checking each pocket to be certain he had all the bills—he calmly announced, "It's all there, even your pay receipts. We made a ton on this gig. Good job, Thomas. Take a seat. I have something important to discuss."

Thomas sat down on the leather sofa facing CC. CC began, the stern tone of his voice predicting something slightly ominous, "We have a very important meeting Friday with Grant Goldman. He's the president of the Universalist Freethinkers Society of Charleston. I know you know Goldman—he's your mom's boss. Anyway, he's bringing Rabbi Isaac Drazin, Chief Rabbi of the Talmudic Zionist Council of the Americas. Meeting's at 11:00." CC paused. "Apparently, the Rabbi wants to protest against Christian churches during Easter."

"Radical! Can we legally get away with that?"

"Free speech, Thomas. First Amendment rights and all. Zionist Council needs paid protesters. Be on time tomorrow. Okay?"

24

Thomas was still suffering the effects of Tuesday night's frightening bender at Poeff Huffingtons, which was aggravated by sleep deprivation and his somewhat dicey meeting with CC. His PTI meeting was this evening. The thought of that only added to his agony.

He was besieged by guilt-ridden thoughts of Plex. Was Plex recovering? What had he told police, and did it involve anything about him? He'd never given any of them his last name. State Congressman Jefferson knew his full name, but because of the cash deal, he would be too guarded to disclose additional info.

Thomas knew he would never be anything but a gutless coward. He imagined hearing Toby, Baker and RaeAll talking about his spinelessness. He couldn't blame them. They had every right. He ran out on Plex. That was reality, unadulterated truth. Thomas thought he'd accepted the fact of his weakness. He figured he would continue to run from himself and his fear. Denial and escape had always been easier than facing the truth.

It was Thursday and his body ached from abuse, but he would be expected to attend Lt. O'Reilly's PTI class. There was no way out. No excuses. O'Reilly's pre-trial intervention was better than having the judge sentence him under the repeat offender statute. That could lead to some seriously hard prison time.

Thomas arrived at Saint Paul's Catholic Church just as Lt. O'Reilly was beginning the session. He quickly took the last empty seat next to Joydie Brooks and regretted he had not arrived early enough to avoid sitting next to her.

"Okay, Mr. Stirk, glad to see you," Lt. O'Reilly said and smiled. "We were just discussing the possibility you'd dropped out."

"No, sir. I'd never drop out, Lieutenant. Couldn't do that, sir. I had to walk. No wheels. My mom's at her society meeting tonight," Thomas replied regretfully, nodding to the group.

"Yeah, Stirk, we thought you might be trying to make us all look bad, dude," Joydie chided Thomas.

The group chuckled and Thomas reddened.

"Hey, man, if you got a leather jacket, you can ride the back of my Harley next meeting. No trouble—just let me know," Joydie offered sincerely.

Thomas didn't know quite what to say. He stammered, "Hey, I like bikers and Harleys too, man. Thanks."

"Hey, you guys work it out on your own time," O'Reilly interrupted. "Tonight, Amber has agreed to share her story with us. Takes real courage so let's all support her." O'Reilly appreciatively nodded. He hoped that she wouldn't lose her nerve. Amber scoped everyone around the small circle, showing some hesitance. She nervously shifted her slightly rotund self in the folding chair, which was not quite large enough to accommodate her.

"I never had a real—like a total family or nothing," she began. "My mom was an addict. She OD'ed on crack when I was twelve. It was like one day she was just gone. Like I'd known her but couldn't remember her. I know I must've loved her but I can't remember when." She looked up at the ceiling, fighting off tears.

"When she said my name, it was like a waterfall washing all over me. She would say it real smooth. It was like the best thing all day since there wasn't nothing good about our neighborhood. We lived in LA on the south side with some really tough gangs. Had to fight your way in and out." She stopped, ashamedly looking down at the floor.

"Amber, we all got crap, girl. We all got tons of aches and pains stashed behind our smiles," one of the guys said. "Just livin lies, girl. I know your hurt."

"Please go on, Amber," Lt. O'Reilly encouraged. "What's your last name?"

"Never really had a last name. Never knew my dad. The guy living with my mom when she OD'ed was named Glenn. So when I left, I took his name. 'Amber Glenn' is on my driver's license."

"So Charleston from LA?" Lt. O'Reilly prompted, hoping Amber would continue to release her pent up anger and share her shame. She needed to release as much as possible.

His PTI classes were much more about liberating guilt and building character than about confession. Unfortunately, confession was the necessary beginning.

"I worked the street in south LA, pushin and dealin," Amber continued. "Got busted at least ten or twelve times. They always released me as a juvenile. After my mom died, her boyfriend got a new girlfriend. She was a real bitch. They kicked me out when I was thirteen. I caught a ride with a trucker to Reno. He raped me twice on the way.

"I always looked five or six years older than thirteen, so I easily got a job at a truck stop in Reno. I worked there for almost three years. I got straight. Kicked all the junk stuff. Had a real waitress job and made really good tips from those truckers." She proudly smiled.

"Then, I met this biker. He was a real nice guy. He was going east and asked me if I wanted to ride. I ended up in Myrtle Beach at Bikers Week. That's where I met my best friend here, Joydie." She pointed to Joydie with a huge smile.

"My ride tried to break up a fight at a beach bar between two other bikers, and one of the guys shot and killed him. I ended up with his Harley." She dropped her gaze to the floor again.

After a moment, she continued. "Then, I got busted in Charleston for smoking pot and the cops pulled my record from LA, and, well, here I am. Not proud of it. Hoping to get straight again. If I can complete this PTI, I've been promised a real job at WalMart. I guarantee I will finish this class, Lt. O'Reilly. Count on it!" She glanced at O'Reilly, beaming her determination.

Slowly, the group of eight PTI offenders began to clap. First one, then two, and then the rest, all clapping along with Lt. O'Reilly. One of the other guys in the semi-circle spoke up, his voice almost cracking, "Go Amber Glenn! Stay straight! You got guts, girl."

Soon O'Reilly had the entire group talking family and how important family is to staying straight. At the end of the evening, O'Reilly had each of them, even Thomas Stirk, who already knew the principle, believing that family was important and that they could be each other's substitute family if they chose to be. The group was softening, and everyone, except for Thomas, began sharing. The hard shells of pretense and charade were cracking.

Tony B, JJ and Scribbee were all three lamenting Amber's story, their wings somberly folded as they sat unseen in folding chairs along the bare wall behind the group.

"Repeatedly raped at thirteen! Mother dead. No family. That kind of pain is more than I can imagine," JJ spoke somberly.

"The shame of it is her biker boyfriend, murdered in Myrtle Beach, had treated her right. He'd taken care of her. They were falling in love. It was not his fight. He was trying to break up the fight. He just happened to be in the wrong place at the wrong time," Tony B lamented.

Ms. Scribbee, her wings flitting about, said, "Good news is God's got other plans for Amber Glenn and you've witnessed the beginning of His plan here tonight. Something tells me Amber Glenn and Joydie Brooks are going to get those 'get out of jail free' cards and a trip to a hair stylist. God sees the good in their hearts." JJ and Tony B nodded agreement with Scribbee.

"Lt. Kevin O'Reilly is doing God's work. He's one of the Father's champions. That's for sure," Ms. Scribbee added, her wings folding closed now. "He's building integrity and moral fiber. God loves what he's doing."

"Okay, everyone," O'Reilly said. "Great meeting tonight. I'm proud of each of you. Pre-Easter holidays next week at the church, so next meeting is Thursday evening after Easter. Okay?"

As the group got up to leave, O'Reilly motioned to Thomas. "Stirk, stick around a minute. I need to speak with you privately, son."

Everyone now gone, O'Reilly and Thomas sat down across from each other. O'Reilly pulled his chair up close. "You didn't have anything to say tonight, son. What's buggin' you? Still the father thing?"

"Not really. Just didn't have anything to add. That Amber girl had everyone almost in tears."

"Everyone has a ton of bad. Everyone has some real hurt. Me too. We all do. Anytime you want, you're welcome to bounce anything off of me. Just let me know." O'Reilly offered, smiling warmly.

"Yes, sir. Thanks." Thomas stopped short of allowing his true feelings for O'Reilly to be exposed.

"Thomas, there is one thing we need to talk about if you are willing. I need to let you know that we still haven't found Rachael Coedinger Joseph, the gal who owns the Denali."

"Hey, Lieutenant, not me, man. I did nothing to her. I got no idea. I know you all think I did something. I didn't, Lieutenant," Thomas pleaded convincingly to O'Reilly.

"I'm not accusing you of anything, son. Not suggesting anything. Just bringing you up to date."

"Sorry. Okay."

"Ever heard of Codi Coedinger?

"No, sir."

"Codi Coedinger is Rachael Coedinger Joseph's AKA. So you never heard either name?"

"No, sir. Never."

"Have you ever heard of Tobias Edwardson?"

"No, sir. Never heard of him. Who's that?"

"Edwardson is the Junior United States Senator from North Carolina up in Washington DC. There seems to be some connection with Codi Coedinger and Edwardson. Sure you've never heard of either of them?"

"Absolutely sure, sir."

"I'm just asking. Understand? It's my job. I'm not accusing you of anything. But still it's very strange to find you in her vehicle passed out and unable to recall how you got there. Wouldn't you agree?"

"I didn't do anything, sir. Absolutely nothing. Just was there. I would really like to know how I got there. I can't remember squat. Anyway, I did nothing to her. Don't even know her, Lieutenant."

"Well, Thomas Stirk, if you should recall anything—anything at all—please call me. The department would like to find Rachael Joseph AKA Codi Coedinger."

"Yes, sir. I will."

25

CAPTIVE

Codi was verging on total fatigue. Her muscles twitched and ached. She could no longer detect her foul body odor. She was constantly reminded of her fetid condition by the blood caked on her arms and dried brown stains on her filthy red dress. Although she'd used some of her drinking water each day to wash her hands, they were stained from the filth of her prison hole and the oily rags that served as her makeshift mattress.

The eight or ten festering blisters on her cheeks from the cigarette burns were beginning to scab over and no longer caused her any pain, but the dark bruises on her arms from fending off slaps to her face had only grown darker.

She was certain the little finger on her left hand was broken. She had no pain but the last joint was severely cocked to the left, the fingertip veering out and refusing to line up with the rest of the finger's bones. It was fortunate she had no mirror to see her black eyes and burns on her face.

Her captors gave her little food but kept her well supplied with water and provided a barely acceptable toilet in a connecting head. She was growing weaker by the day, but she was thankful she was still alive.

She'd been wise enough to keep track of her days in prison. As she reviewed her improvised calendar, she counted twenty-five days she'd been held hostage. It seemed a lifetime. It had become difficult for her to imagine she'd ever had a life outside her dank confines. She'd adapted as gutter rats do, fighting for every available scrap.

She knew her parents had to be in the final stages of total panic. She cried for them until she had no tears left. She could imagine her mother crumbling, her dad trying to hold her up

Thoughts of her big money drug dealing business, which so quickly paid off her student loans, now challenged her sanity, punished her relentlessly as she prayed to God each day for rescue. Although she tried to feel God's forgiveness, she did not. She'd asked for it, but she could not erase the enormous guilt. The shame overwhelmed her. Whatever pain she felt, it had to be much worse for her parents.

Codi had forsaken her faith when the fast money began rolling in. She'd forced God to take a back seat to the money. God, the Father, had been forgotten.

Now stripped of all but the ragged edges of life, she prayed for His mercy. "Please Father God, deliver me from the valley of the shadow of death." She begged, knowing full well that if she were God, she likely wouldn't give her request for forgiveness even passing interest. "Father, I had it all backwards. I was so wrong. Please forgive me."

The unmistakable grating of steel on steel once again announced the opening of her prison door. As the bright light of the engine room blinded her, she heard Aristide tell the guards to cuff her to the ladder well. She closed her eyes, already knowing the drill, as the guards jerked her from the cell and forced her against the side of the stairs.

"So, missy, you not tell us you know Edwardson. You know who I speak about, missy."

"Never met him," Codi lied as she opened her eyes just in time to turn her head away from Aristide's slap.

"We not want to hit you, missy, but you only lying. When you not lying, I not hit you. Comprende?"

Pinella interrupted, "We know you supply Edwardson cocaine, missy. We have photo at party on Virginia farm. We know many important people at party, missy. I know you know. We there too. We see you with Edwardson. So just say to us. Okay?"

Codi, weakly hanging in the cuffs, her head bent down, opened her eyes in time to wince as Aristide's black leather loafers shuffled toward her. She felt the slap of his left hand across her cheek, his large diamond ring slicing her. Strangely, it didn't seem to sting. She looked down again as drops of blood oozed onto the white engine room floor.

"Never met him. I told you. Don't know him," Codi slurred a feeble reply as her lower lip now exploded in pain.

"Missy, we know you know. Can't fool us, lady. We know Edwardson trying to control cartel's business. We know you help him. So just tell us, missy," Aristide declared as he lit a cigarette and exhaled smoke directly into Codi's face.

"Would tell you if I knew." Her head fell to the left side as she closed her eyes, blood slowly trickling from the corner of her mouth.

"You much crazy stupider lady, missy," Fidel Pinella brokenly said as he stepped in front of Codi and propped up her chin with his left hand and leaned in close. "Open you eyes, missy. You really not so dumb, lady? We no like to mess you face. So just tell us and we leave you alone." He turned away, letting go of Codi's chin as it dropped to her chest. Her eyes remained closed.

Pinella then swung around, furiously lashing his hand toward Codi's head but stopped just short of making contact; her eyes were closed and much of his satisfaction came from witnessing her terror.

The next sound Codi heard was a Smith and Wesson .38 revolver being cocked near her face. The unmistakable sound petrified Codi as she opened her eyes and jerked her head away from the barrel. She could smell burnt black powder. Aristide, pleased with the show, moved the tip of the barrel into her ear and pushed.

"Maybe I shoot you in ear, missy. How you like that?"

The Spider enjoyed her shock as he blew more cigarette smoke in her eyes.

"See, missy. We kill you if you not tell about Edwardson and Reyes," he said with sadistic anticipation. He dragged the barrel along her cheek, over her wounds, then tried to force it inside her mouth.

"Kill her. Pull trigger. Shoot her now," Fidel Pinella encouraged.

"See. Watch, missy. I pull trigger." The Spider slowly began squeezing the trigger. Terror flashed in Codi's eyes.

The firing pin clunked harmlessly against an empty cylinder, sounding like the crash of two freight trains to Codi. She screamed uncontrollably, her head slashing side to side, until she once again passed out. She hung limp as the cuffs pulled taut against her bleeding wrists.

"She is weak," Pinella said to Aristide. "Lock her up. Give her water. She no good dead!" He motioned for the two guards, both wearing black ski masks, to take her away.

"Missy difficult, but I break her. She breaks maybe not today but next day. But she break," Aristide assured Pinella.

Ms. Scribbee, standing with Tony B and JJ near the starboard engine, contorted her face with anguish and folded her wings solemnly.

"Anasi 'The Spider' Aristide is intoxicated with his power, but I'll tell you in a fair fight, he would beg for mercy like a cowering pup," she said as the guards returned Codi to the prison locker. The door swished shut, forcing the foul stench of the locker into the engine room.

"He is evil personified. Satan incarnate. They both are," JJ shrieked, his wings flailing wildly.

"JJ, no reason to be so bellicose. God isn't about to turn you loose for any self-gratifying celestial retribution like we did in the old days."

"I wish he would. I've never seen guys who deserve reprisal more," JJ retorted.

"Edwardson is up to his eyeballs in this cartel thing. Codi had no idea what she was getting into when she began supplying the good senator."

"Too late now. Codi's already suffered incredibly," Tony B looked upward. His wings cambered full spread, imploring God for mercy. "No question the cartel has started a fight they will lose."

"Pinella and Aristide are like so many other bullies with power," Scribbee added. "Their muscle just happens to grow on the coca plant."

"It doesn't seem to matter how men get power. Eventually, it corrupts them. Satan designed it that way and it's been so

since the beginning," JJ quietly declared, his wings set resolutely as the two guards removed their black ski masks, one of
them silently crying as he made the sign of the cross.

"God knows about power. He knew mortal men would mis-
use power. You could see the pattern in the Garden from the
very beginning," Scribbee added. "Cain slew Able and the whole
East of Eden thing happened—men and brothers began fighting each other. King David's son, Solomon, shrewdly wrote in
Proverbs, 'A friend loveth at all times and a brother is born for
adversity.'" Scribbee's wings danced briefly then folded tight.

"So that's where it all began. Eden corrupted. Eden corrupted has now become the way of the world," JJ said.

"King David had his mountaintop Goliath experience and
witnessed first hand the power of an Almighty God, and after
he'd gained absolute power, he met Bathsheba. David did what
he did because he could," Scribbee continued. Her wings flitted
briefly. "He did what he did because he lost his anointing. His
power corrupted his thinking. By the time the Prophet Nathan
rebuked King David for his duplicity and David repented, the
damage had been done. Uriah had been sent to die at the
front lines of Israel's army and David and Bathsheba's child,
born of their adulterous relationship, had died. Corruption
always seems to lead to death and suffering." Scribbee gestured
upward, her wings opening fully. "God is in control and never
condones fraudulent behavior, not from King David, not from
Tobias Edwardson, and not from drug cartel criminals."

"Power brings a sweet intoxication that feeds man's bas-
est needs. Men's egos naturally gravitate toward control and
power. It's inevitable," Tony B affirmed. JJ nodded too.

"Men like Nathan and Daniel seemed able to remain pure
and to gain their power from having none. Having no power
allowed them to rely on God's strength," Scribbee argued.

"Remember Nebuchadnezzar, King of Babylon? Now there was a King who was a real piece of work. Talk about corruption. Talk about misusing power," JJ said, shaking his head in disbelief.

Scribbee quickly referred to the historical record. "Nebuchadnezzar attacked and defeated Israel. He took the brightest of the bright from Israel back to Babylon and held them captive. He constructed a god in his own image. Under penalty of fiery death, he demanded Babylonians and the captive Jews alike bow down and worship his idolatrous god. He did all this because he could," Scribbee rattled off quickly. "Nebuchadnezzar was such an egotist he actually believed he built the golden idol for the benefit of his people. How's that for narcissistic chutzpah?"

"Yeah, but look at those three kidnapped bright young Jews, Meshach, Shadrach, and Abed Nego. They disobeyed Nebuchadnezzar and were tested. They were thrown into the king's fiery furnace and met Jesus, who protected them," JJ said and smiled enthusiastically as his wing remnants spread open toward heaven.

"Codi is being tested. She's in her fiery furnace. Her steel is being strengthened by man's illicit flames," Tony B said and smiled toward heaven.

26

STRICTLY BUSINESS

G rant Goldman and Rabbi Drazin were on time for the meeting. CC had them seated together on the sofa facing his leather divan chair. Thomas was seated to the right of CC. All were enjoying a special blend of Sumatran coffee, always freshly ground for occasions in CC's office.

Goldman was wearing a striped blue sports shirt with an open collar, khaki pants, and a brass-buttoned navy-blue blazer, all quite appropriate for a slightly balding tenured professor approaching the back side of fifty and struggling to appear young again.

Goldman, an avowed Humanist, was also the Chairman of the local Freethinkers Society. His secular views were well known, so the pairing of Goldman with the fundamentalist Hebrew Drazin created a number of questions that begged for answers.

Rabbi Drazin was smothered in black rabbinical robes and his head was covered with a black yarmulke; his full-length gray beard enveloped him from chin to waist. His flashing eyes defied his outwardly calm demeanor. They were nervous eyes. They pranced about CC's office as if taking inventory of everything in the room. The Rabbi was a senior gentleman for sure, but his actual age was cloaked behind his full gray beard.

After brief small talk about the weather, the spring dogwood blossoms, and historic Charleston, CC cut right to the chase. His haste embarrassed Thomas but then that was CC's "let's get it done" approach to everything.

CC was sitting in his throne and had the clout to kick things off on his terms.

"Grant, what kind of Easter demonstrations does Rabbi Drazin have in mind?"

Gulping his last swallow of coffee and quickly setting down his cup, Goldman, obviously caught off guard, tried to distance himself from any perceived collusion between himself and the good Rabbi. He said, "I'm less concerned about the so-called Christian Messiah or whether He is dead or alive—past or future or for that matter—or if a Messiah ever existed at all. I am, however, concerned that all the philosophies in the world have the opportunity to be heard in our great country," his scholarly tone epitomizing his tenured professorship.

Goldman paused, glanced at Rabbi Drazin, then continued. "The Zionist Council has demonstrated for decades in front of Christian Churches in New York City. They've never had any problems with New York authorities. They are free speech protected and have protested peacefully for many years. They need hired surrogates to demonstrate in their behalf in Charleston in the same peaceful way."

"Grant, why Charleston?" CC asked. "Why protest against Christians?"

"I'll let Rabbi Drazin explain," Goldman said, and he motioned to Drazin to begin.

With a heavy Slavic accent, broken but understandable, Drazin explained, "All Christian denominations take view that only absolute truth is Bible itself. Christian's claim Bible is inspired infallible Word of God and that God Himself gave words of Scripture without error. The Bible is said to be absolute truth because of divine inspiration, proven by multitudes of fulfilled prophecies. Biblical Christianity believes truth is not determined by circumstances or times in history or even culture, but only Bible determines truth. We Zionists do not agree."

Thomas squirmed about on the sofa, knowing the conversation was way over his head. He figured his pay scale never included ideological acrobatics. He didn't like taking part in philosophical discussion on any subject. Politically neutral was his standard gear. He'd always found debate to be a huge brain drain. "Just leave me out of it!" he wanted to scream. "This conversation's fryin the few brain cells I got left."

Drazin looked at everyone, apparently searching for some sign of disagreement, and then continued. "The Christian idea of Trinity contradicts most basic tenet of Orthodox Judaism that there is only one God with no other gods before Him. So how can there be Jesus who Christians say is also God in trinity? Jesus was no God. Jesus should have been real king of the Jews but would not accept crown from the people. Jesus cannot be God also. Jews have declared basic belief in a single God since the gift of Torah at Mt. Sinai almost two-thousand years before Jesus lived."

Seeing a restless concern flash across CC's face, Goldman interrupted Drazin. "CC, the good Rabbi speaks historic truth. I can't imagine anyone would deny the absolute truth of his theology. His group just wants to be heard. They have a right to be heard."

Rabbi Drazin stood and walked behind the leather sofa, his eyes again searching the room. With his voice raised and quivering slightly, he continued. "Christianity unfortunately denies eternal absolute truth of Torah Law, building concept of Christianity on New Testament only. It is clear God gave only the Torah to Moses. Torah can never be added to or changed and can never become obsolete in any way. This absolute truth is mentioned in Torah more than twenty-four times. It is for these reasons we have a sacred mandate to make Talmudic truth known to Christians and all peoples."

CC looked directly at the old Rabbi. "I understand about your demonstrations, Rabbi Drazin, but why Charleston?"

"Let me explain," Goldman quickly intervened. "The Talmudic Zionist Council has done their homework. Their research revealed some megachurches around the country, and as fate would have it, there's a considerable megachurch in the Charleston area. Maybe you've heard of Sea Island Fellowship. They have over 25,000 members. They've got more preachers on the payroll than most churches have members."

"I know Sea Island. They have an excellent reputation in Charleston for their food drives and helping the poor," CC responded.

Goldman continued, "The main reason they chose Sea Island Fellowship is every Easter they have a pageant that attracts tens of thousands of people. The Rabbi believes it would be a great opportunity to get the Council's Zionist beliefs known to the South."

"It is biggest. Very biggest in all South," proclaimed Drazin still pacing behind the sofa and now gesturing wildly with both his arms. "Very good place to get our message in the South for Christians to see." He stroked his long gray beard with his forefinger and thumb.

CC, eager for answers, pushed hard. "So, Rabbi, just what will your protest signs say?"

Grant Goldman quickly interceded, squirming to avoid any direct answers. "That will be up to the Talmudic Zionist Council and has not been decided yet, but I would expect they might include signs announcing, '*Only one God*' or '*King of the Jews*' or the like."

Thomas suspected Goldman intended to heavily influence, if not totally control, the protest signs for the demonstrations.

"What do you think, Stirk?" CC asked. "Can we handle something like this over Easter holidays with college kids?"

Thomas slowly sat up, perching on the edge of the sofa. Concern evident, he replied, "Okay, let me see if I got this straight. We're gonna protest in front of a upscale Christian megachurch, in the heart of the Bible Belt South, during their huge Easter pageant when they will have the largest crowds they have all year. Right?"

"Got a problem with that, Thomas?" CC inquired.

Thomas paused, then relaxed against the back of the sofa. "No! No problem, CC."

"Grant, we got a deal then," CC announced. "Welcome, Rabbi. We'll begin the week before Easter and continue until the pageant is over."

Thomas could see through the veil Goldman had thrown up to disguise the true nature of the demonstration.

Thomas sensed Goldman was up to something. He could feel it. He just didn't know what. But now he did know when. Thomas had seen Goldman in action before and had heard a few stories from his mom over the years.

But CC cut the deal. "So what. Forget it," Thomas thought. "It's strictly business. Money is money and fifteen or twenty protesters should be a piece of cake."

27

SMOKESCREENS

Lt. O'Reilly's morning briefing with Chief Newberg had been brutal. The chief had reminded O'Reilly that problem solving was a top-down exercise, and he wanted his best guy to have a solution to the DUI problem by the next day. Almost triple the usual number of DUI citations was intolerable and needed speedy resolution.

"Yes, sir. On it right away," O'Reilly replied as Newberg finally dismissed the hour-long briefing.

O'Reilly had just settled into his desk chair and pulled up the outline of his DUI Zero Tolerance proposal from last year when Margie interrupted him on the intercom.

"Sir, you have a call from Washington on line three. I think it's one you need to take. Wouldn't say who, but they sounded important."

O'Reilly immediately thought of that little arrogant twit White House staffer, Cox, who rudely hung up on him last week. He recalled specifically instructing Cox to contact

Margie directly with all information regarding the Vice President's upcoming visit.

O'Reilly thought about routing the call back to Margie or letting him hang on the line till he hung up, but in one of his more imprudent fits of rage, he picked up the receiver and blasted away.

"Cox, I thought I told you to speak directly with my secretary. The escort is arranged but we're still waiting on your instructions. You call Margie and give her all the details. Is that clear?"

"Oh my, Lt. O'Reilly. Looks like I caught you at a bad time. Would you like me to call back later?"

O'Reilly didn't recognize the voice. His emotions tanked south so fast he could feel his heart thumping in his toes. Who had he insulted?

But before he could begin to apologize to whomever was on the other end of his abusive comments, the caller continued. "Hey, Lieutenant, maybe the lines got crossed or something. I'm not Cox. I'm Tobias Edwardson, US Senator from North Carolina. Please call me Toby."

Queasy distress overwhelmed O'Reilly. "Sir, I sincerely apologize. Sorry about that. What can I do for you today, Senator?"

"Well, first let me say I'm glad I'm not on your bad-guy list today. Your Senator Tradd Gilliard tells me you're a top-notch officer. I'm sorry we've never had the pleasure, but I have met your fine boss, Ed Newberg. He's one of the best law enforcement guys I know. Always valuable to know guys like your chief."

"Yes, sir, we all think he's the best," O'Reilly said, remembering what Edwardson had likely called about. "What is it I can help you with?"

"It's Lieutenant Kevin O'Reilly, isn't it?"

"Yes, sir."

"Mind if I call you Kevin, Lieutenant?"

"Fine, Senator. Now how may I help you?"

"Well, Kevin, have you heard of the Coastal Law Enforcement Restoration Act, or CLERA, as we call it for short?"

"Yes, sir, I have."

Seeming a bit more comfortable now, the Senator continued. "Well, CLERA is one of those grant programs we do for certain organizations from time to time. Some people call the programs earmarks. CLERA is for your tri-county law enforcement team. Senator Gilliard and Chief Newberg have been instrumental in moving the legislation forward."

"Sounds impressive, Senator," O'Reilly responded.

"We can use everyone's help, Kevin. Tradd Gilliard has been bending my ear to vote for his package. I can be persuaded. That's what it's all about, isn't it, Kevin? Helping each other out."

O'Reilly knew where the conversation was headed but cleverly replied, "Well, Senator, you're talking way above my pay grade but that three million in grants would certainly help out the tri-county. That's for sure." He suspected he was being scammed by one of the best in DC.

"Does that mean I can put you in the 'yes' column, Kevin?" Edwardson asked.

"You can count me in, Senator."

"Great, I'll tell Tradd and Chief Newberg I spoke with you today. Glad to have you on board, Kevin."

Realizing the snow job had just begun, O'Reilly asked, "Anything else I can help you with today, Senator?"

"Well, yes, Kevin. Maybe you can help me with something else. Yesterday, the Capitol Police brought me a photo that Sergeant Michael Lewis faxed from your department. It was a photo apparently taken at one of my campaign events. They said it had to do with a missing person's case. They asked me if I knew the young lady I was embracing in the photo. They showed me my note on the back of the photo. Fact is, I wasn't really embracing her, you know. I had my arm around her shoulder like in all campaign photos. I trust you've seen this photo?"

"Yes, Senator, I've seen the photo."

"Kevin, sorry but I've no idea who she is. It's my campaign stuff. I sign hundreds every year."

"Recognize any others in the photo, Senator?"

Quickly, as if his answers were canned in advance, the senator continued. "Even asked my staff, Kevin. Sorry I can't help. What did this Codi do anyway?"

"Sorry we bothered you, Senator."

"Really wish I knew something to help. Where's Codi from, Kevin?" The senator was clearly fishing for information.

"Senator, I apologize for the inconvenience and we appreciate your cooperation."

"Not a problem, Kevin. I've enjoyed meeting one of Charleston's finest. Please tell Ed I've been talking with Gilliard about CLERA. Of course, everything depends on doing the right thing. I mean if Gilliard does the right thing up here, all the right things happen down your way. You know what I mean, Kevin?"

"I get the picture, Senator. Thanks for calling, sir."

O'Reilly knew he'd just been punked by one of the best. This guy was smooth, like drinking fine champagne; the bubbly left a good taste in the mouth but doomed a pounding headache the next morning. O'Reilly pushed down his intercom. "Margie, please ask Lewis and Farley to come in."

Lewis and Farley knocked before entering.

"What's up, Lieutenant?" asked Farley.

"Did you guys run that name and Atlanta phone number?"

"Yes, sir," Lewis began. "It's a cell phone for a guy named Antonio Reyes. Margie was right about the name. Phone is no longer in service. The name is clean in Interpol and stateside."

"Good job as usual, guys. I just got off the phone with Edwardson. He knows the girl all right, but he's lying."

"Capitol Police tell me the Senator is a real wild-ass," Farley said. "He has crazy wild parties with lots of women and tons of booze. They said some of his shindigs have gotten out of hand. Arrests involved—but not with the senator, of course. He has a total rounder reputation in DC but no arrests."

"He's a real pro," O'Reilly said with disdain on his face. "One of the best and he's got a really big set of brass ones. He knew that I knew that he knew."

28

THE EDWARDSON WAY

Washington DC was a minefield of unexploded IEDs, just waiting for a neophyte junior senator to trip and stumble. Senators from anywhere had lots of political enemies. Edwardson knew it. He had to be careful.

The last thing Senator Tobias Wiley Edwardson needed was his political enemies learning the real story behind his campaign for the US Senate. So far he'd been lucky, but political clout came with enormous risk. Now that he was in office, properly bought and paid for by his father's political shenanigans, the secret to his election needed to be closely guarded.

Somehow during his senatorial campaign, the deceitful practices used to gain victory were never reported. Edwardson liked to think it was providential or perhaps due to friendly media and the reach of his supporters, but he knew the family fortunes greased palms and promised instant access.

For better or worse, Toby Edwardson was now the junior senator from North Carolina and a politically savvy family's elitist, under-the-table stuff was fair game in big time politics. So was old family lore.

There was the disreputable back story of his great grandfather, Josiah Wiley Edwardson, who ran gallon jugs of whiskey by moonlight and slept next to his still while he cooked off his mash during the day near Asheville, North Carolina.

Around the turn of the century, Josiah had saved enough to buy a liquor license from the state revenuers. He built himself a rightfully proper plumbed single pot still and began distilling legal whiskey spirits.

Suddenly, Great Grandpa Edwardson found his distillery shut down, his mash pots drained, and his aging barrels of the really good stuff emptied into the swamp. The government revenuers and prohibition had finally put him out of business. Although old Josiah didn't know it, his career was just beginning.

Soon, Josiah had hooked up with a disreputable Scottish whiskey merchant and began smuggling scotch whiskey up the Cape Fear River to Southport where he would rendezvous with the Chicago mob. Cash on the barrelhead. He became a very wealthy man during the years of prohibition.

The rest was history. Old Josiah made the Edwardson family fortune smuggling booze and left the millions to his son who invested the family's wealth in real estate, furniture manufacturing and other legitimate enterprises around Thomasville, North Carolina, in the late twenties.

His son and the senator's father, Josiah Wiley Edwardson III, expanded the family holdings to The Furniture Mart, two and one half million square feet of commercial display space in downtown High Point. It was where anyone who manufactured furniture had to lease space to show their latest designs. They were the only game in town, and through this venture, the family's fortunes approached Ming Dynasty magnitude. The family bought, sold and traded political favors and owned most North Carolina politicians.

Senator Tobias Wiley Edwardson, his father's only son, had turned out to be something of a disappointment. He'd not married and had produced no male children to preserve the Edwardson name.

Toby Edwardson was never interested in the hum-de-dum of business despite the small fortune spent on his Bachelor of Arts degree in business, which had taken six long years of undergrad work to complete at North Carolina State University.

Taking six years to graduate would be embarrassing for most students, but North Carolina State was pretty much owned by the senator's dad, who had made millions in philanthropic donations over the years. Embarrassment had been permanently removed from Toby's transcript and resume.

After Toby finished college, his father felt he needed a law degree to be fully credentialed and ready to run the family businesses, so he was accepted to NC State School of Law over the heated objections of the dean. After two more years of fraternity nonsense, excessive tutoring, and very limited testing, Tobias Wiley Edwardson was awarded his Juris Doctor in 1995.

Toby spent ten years of mediocre efforts in the family furniture enterprises before his father encouraged and pushed him to run for the US Senate as a Democrat. Toby's election victory, of course, was, like everything else in his life, bought and paid for by his father. The billionaire family could afford to buy whatever was necessary to make it happen.

After being sworn into the US Senate, Edwardson was unexpectedly made Chairman of the Senate Subcommittee on Governmental Affairs as a political payoff by the Democrats to the new senator's father. The Governmental Affairs Subcommittee had total jurisdiction over the Capitol Police and Chief Larry Munday's position depended on knowing more than he should about each committee member and guarding it securely in the event he had to play defense.

Munday scrambled a bit and had to dig deep, but it didn't take long for him to discover that Edwardson's two serious opponents in the US Senate statewide primary races had dropped out of the contest early on, one stating personal health concerns and the other undisclosed family issues.

Josiah Wiley Edwardson III called it executive management. No headlines. No publicity—just quiet and discreet manipulations in the checkmates of business.

One of the former contenders now owned a ten-thousand acre ranch in Brazil worth millions and was exporting rare mahogany lumber to the furniture manufacturing industry in China, which then exported finished furniture to the United States and other countries. It was a goldmine, as rare mahoganies were long ago banned from import in the United States.

The other challenger now owned a hundred-square-mile island off the east coast of Belize—an elegant, invitation-only resort to the wealthiest jet setters. Touting a private landing strip with hangers and the finest luxury hotels in guaranteed seclusion, the resort offered deep sea fishing off the Belize Barrier Reef, great scuba diving and a widely acclaimed Trump golf course said to be the finest in Central America. They were always fully booked.

Both former opponents were now wealthy with off-shore millions totally unauditable by election officials and untouchable by the IRS. Munday considered it his job to uncover every politician's hidden baggage.

Munday had lobbied hard for Edwardson's confirmation and now they owed each other, even though the senator didn't know it yet. Larry Munday had first magnitude moxie. He was bright. He had no trouble figuring out what is known as "is is" in Washington, DC. As a matter of fact, Munday had "is is" filed away on just about anyone who was someone in DC. He called it blessed assurance.

Toby Edwardson had called the chief about 2:00 in the afternoon, and it was just before 3:00 when Munday arrived at Edwardson's Senate office. Edwardson walked from behind his desk. "How's the best DC Capitol Police Chief I ever got re-confirmed?"

As the Senator and Chief Munday shook hands, the latter deftly replied, "'Bout as good as the best Governmental Affairs Subcommittee Chairman the Senate's ever had."

The senator acted impressed and grateful, even though he wasn't. "Thanks for coming, Larry. How about the usual Scotch?"

"Can't, Senator, on duty. But thanks."

With a deceitful gleam in his eye, Edwardson replied, "I won't tell, Larry."

Disregarding the senator's remark, Chief Munday inquired, "What can I do for you today, Toby?"

Edwardson's brow wrinkled. "I need your help on something, Larry."

"Already seen the photo and read your cutesy note. Got to be careful what you write, Senator. Who is this Codi? They seem real interested in her."

Caught off guard, Edwardson hesitated, looked away. Then, he hurriedly said, "She's done some political events, parties, and social gatherings for me. You know, she organizes that sort of thing. I don't even really know her. My staff arranged her services."

"Is that all she does, Senator? I can't help you if I don't know the truth."

The senator, shocked by such bluntness, tried to disregard the comment. "Do you know this Charleston clown, Lieutenant Kevin O'Reilly?"

"Not yet. Give me a day or two, Senator."

"Can you imagine this podunk cop questioning a sitting US Senator? It's unbelievable!"

"I'll take care of it, Senator. Give me a few days. We'll make it go away. I promise you," Munday avowed, knowing he owned another even larger slice of Edwardson's soul.

"Thanks, Larry. I knew I could count on you. How about that Scotch now?"

29

GONE FISHING

The morning briefing was coming to an end and Lt. O'Reilly seemed a bit off his game, preoccupied. He was not his usual jovial self, and it had to be clear to every officer in the room. They'd all known O'Reilly far too long to be easily fooled.

Without looking up from the paperwork on his lectern and speaking casually as if he'd almost forgotten the briefing was over, he finally said, "Sorry, guys. You're dismissed." His officers got up to leave the briefing, no doubt delighted they could finally go home.

"Hey, Cooper, look here for a minute," O'Reilly called. Cooper turned around and walked toward the front of the room.

"Yes, sir. What's wrong, boss?"

"You told me yesterday that Monck and Courtney received a call from Senator Edwardson's office from a Rusty Keegan. I think you said he was a special staff assistant or something," O'Reilly said, a frown furrowed on his brow.

"Yes, sir, that guy Keegan was fishin' for whatever he could find out about you, Codi Joseph and our department. Strange call. My guys said he was real bold. Said he talked to them like he actually knew them. Called them by their first names. Telephoned them within ten minutes of each other. My guys told him nothing, of course." Cooper was proud that his men had followed orders so tightly and revealed nothing. "What's this all about, Lieutenant?"

"I don't exactly know, Cooper. I called Keegan's number, but it's no longer in service, so I called Edwardson's office and asked for Keegan and they said they have no one by that name," O'Reilly finished, shaking his head in disbelief. "So you know as much as I do. I got no idea what's going on. What's your take?"

Puzzled and pensive, Cooper set his jaw and stroked his chin. "I'd say we're being conned. The Keegan guy had to be from Edwardson's office. The guy knew too much about the photos, the Senator's note to Codi and you, Lieutenant. But why are they fishin around down here?"

"Calling Monck and Courtney had to be planned. Had to come from the top—the senator himself."

"I'd bet even money they're hoping to strike oil. They're betting on the chance one of our guys would slip up and disclose something they could use to get us off their backs. You told me yourself, Lieutenant. Edwardson knows a lot more than he's telling, including who Codi is. He knows you know he's not coming clean. That's why they're fishing for information."

"I know Edwardson would probably like our telephone conversation to just go away. I think you may be right, Cooper. Double down on Monck and Courtney just in case they get more calls," O'Reilly ordered.

"Sir, Jake Dooley, an old buddy of mine from college, used to be on the Capitol Police Force. He left about six months ago. He started his own security agency in DC, private investigators and protection strategies for business—all that kind of stuff."

"Go on."

"Anyway, he told me a couple of weeks ago when I was asking about Edwardson's reputation around town that he didn't know much, except Edwardson and Chief Munday at the Capitol Police were really tight."

"Why am I not surprised by that? Textbook politician. Of course—Munday's job depends on the Edwardson Senate Oversight Committee. I'll bet Munday has his guys digging for information for Edwardson or maybe Munday is fishing for himself. It's all political! I think you just rang the bell, big guy."

"How about I get Dooley to do some nosing around in DC? He offered last time I talked to him. Won't hurt, Lieutenant. Can check out Edwardson's wild parties and Munday too."

"Do that, Cooper. See what he can find."

30

PLAUSIBLE DENIABILITY

Ashlyn Jordan was mature well beyond her young twenty-five years, but her bouncy pony tail made her look much younger. She was the youngest assistant chief of staff serving any US Senator. Her youthful looks had become something of a detriment despite her impressive record.

She'd experienced reverse age discrimination. Certain unnamed staff members tittle-tattled she just didn't look old enough for the job. In fact, their observation was correct. She didn't look old enough. But Senator Tobias Edwardson had chosen Ashlyn from among thirty-five applicants and was well satisfied with her performance.

The fact that Franklin Seaman Jordan, Ashlyn's father, was a very successful real estate broker in Greensboro, NC, and a major contribution bundler for Edwardson's senate campaign, had stirred considerable jealous debate about the validity of Ashlyn's appointment among the old timers around the office. All the insider controversy hadn't mattered much over the last year since most North Carolinians had never heard of Ashlyn Jordan or known of her father's campaign connection to Edwardson.

Ashlyn Jordan was bright. She was beautiful in a snarky sort of way, her intelligence sometimes overwhelming her good looks. But typical of most college students, Ashlyn loved spring breaks, her besties, the beach, beer and boys, pretty much in that order.

Ashlyn completed her double major in Political Science and Pre Law in three years, just six months before Edwardson's election to the Senate.

After earning her undergraduate degree, Ashlyn was accepted to Georgetown School of Law. She had just finished her first semester when her father suggested she apply for Assistant Chief of Staff in Edwardson's office. She applied and got it.

She'd been with Edwardson just over a year and had become a valued staff member. Ashlyn was young enough to be totally relevant, smart enough to be effective, attractive enough to command everyone's attention, and trusted enough to have become an inner circle confidant.

Ashlyn was the senator's go-to person when he needed something stealthily arranged. She planned events that demanded total discretion and absolute privacy. She arranged the senator's notorious private parties, surreptitiously inviting the beautiful people of DC.

As those around the senator already knew (and Ashlyn soon discovered), the senator liked his babes, his booze, and his blow in private settings. He enjoyed the company of the DC celebrity movers and shakers and felt most comfortable around the eminently wealthy influential crowd—those with enough money to keep their mouths shut.

Ashlyn Jordan met Tracy Poole a couple of months after beginning her appointment with Senator Edwardson. Poole happened to be visiting Georgetown School of Law with other students from the University of North Carolina. All had come to hear the annual lecture series on human rights and social justice in America from prominent speakers, including one justice from the Supreme Court.

Ashlyn, by coincidence, was also at the lecture series. After the evening address, Poole introduced himself and put a polite move on Ashlyn. They'd gone for drinks together with mutual friends at a Georgetown watering hole.

Ashlyn overheard Poole boasting about his coke cash cow, and at the first opportunity, she pulled Poole aside for some private one-on-one rap. After confirming Poole's knowledge of the trade, Ashlyn let him know her need to feed her employer's thirsty party beast. Poole told Ashlyn about Rachael Codi Joseph. And so the saga began.

֎

Ashlyn knocked and entered Edwardson's office. He spun his chair toward his desk and welcomed her. "Right on time as usual. Thanks for coming, Ashlyn." He picked up a yellow-lined pad with his notes.

"Yes, sir, not a problem. Finished the staff meeting about fifteen minutes ago."

"Ashlyn, you're part of my trusted family. Actually, your parents and my family go way back. I just want you to know how much I appreciate that," the senator glibly said without making direct eye contact.

"Well, yes, sir. Of course, sir," Ashlyn replied, now a bit wary of what might be coming.

Then the senator looked at Ashlyn directly. "I want everything scrubbed. I mean medicinally scrubbed—so clean Rachael Codi Joseph was never born. She never existed. Understand, Ashlyn?" He pulled his chair close to his desk and faced Ashlyn straight on.

"Yes, sir," she replied. "Have we got some problem I don't know about, sir? Everyone knows Rachael Codi Joseph is missing, but no one can connect her to you, not even with that campaign photo."

"Not yet, but I'm concerned," the senator snapped back, reaching for his handkerchief and wiping perspiration from his brow. "My people have been calling Lt. O'Reilly's guys at the Charleston Police Department. They've been casting deep nets but keep coming up empty. O'Reilly's folks aren't talking and we need to know what they know. I'm beginning to worry. And you know I hate worrying."

"I understand, sir. But you spoke directly with Lt. O'Reilly. I assumed your conversation alleviated any potential problems."

"The problem is I'm not sure it did. So scrub everything— no email records, no phone records, no party photos—nothing. Destroy every hard drive. Wipe them clean. Rachael Joseph never existed. None of us ever knew her! Is that clear?"

"I'll get on it immediately, sir," Ashlyn answered with a confident know-what-to-do look on her face.

"Ashlyn, the Codi Joseph thing could go nuclear. It could blow up around us. No screw-ups, understand? Scrub this office. Wipe the servers in Raleigh, Greensboro, Charlotte. Not a file. Not a trace. Do it discreetly! Okay?" The senator squirmed, wallowing in his own embarrassing memories.

Edwardson pushed his chair back, stood and walked around to the front of his desk.

"And I've got to know where O'Reilly's going with this Joseph thing," he demanded. "This crap's driving me crazy."

"Sir, I worked one summer as an intern with the Charleston County Solicitor's office. I could be discreet. They had some really professional private investigators. I could easily arrange one of their best to look into things with O'Reilly and his staff," Ashlyn assured the senator.

"Do it. I just don't want to know about it. Okay? Plunder O'Reilly's closet. Shine daylight on some of his really sketchy stuff. Just don't tell me what you're doing!"

Ashlyn smiled as Edwardson turned away.

"Plausible deniability, sir. I understand."

31

SISSY SPAIN

When Ashlyn Jordan called her former co-worker Lynn Ward at the Charleston County Solicitor's office seeking advice in retaining a reputable private investigator, Ward unequivocally recommended Sylvia Spain.

"She's the best PI in Charleston," Ward responded. "Silvia 'Sissy' Spain is maybe the best in the Southeast and don't let her nickname fool you. She's one tough chick when it comes to developing hard evidence."

Many a jilted wife and most divorce attorneys in South Carolina could attest to the incredible detail captured by Spain's covert photo evidence. Plaintiffs' attorneys knew they could depend upon her explicit proof of adultery as legal grounds for custody, unusually generous child support and more than the customary fifty-fifty asset settlements. They almost always won.

That's how graphically compelling Spain's images were. Many a gentleman had suffered the shock of his most intimate dalliances exposed in open court from Spain's living color galleries. Spain contended her methods were legal. Divorce attorneys loved her when she was working with them. However, when they were on the other side, the very same firms, regularly introduced legal briefs to have her PI license revoked for introducing deviously obtained, deceitfully photographed images of such a scandalous nature they were, as some claimed, "downright pornographic."

The defense attorneys usually lost. The plaintiff's attorney would put Spain on the stand and eventually the defense would ask her how she obtained such private photographs, to which she would always reply, "With a camera." And before they could ask again, Spain would turn to the judge and say, "Judge, just let the pictures do the talking" to which the judge would consistently reply, "Let me remind the defense, Ms. Spain is not on trial here and is under no obligation in law to reveal her trade secrets. Motion denied!"

Ashlyn listened diligently as Lynn Ward concluded, "For women betrayed, abandoned, and wanting instant painful retribution, Sissy Spain is the best."

Convinced, Ashlyn called Spain the next day, introducing her position with Senator Edwardson's office and describing the tragic and yet unsolved disappearance of Rachael 'Codi' Joseph and the senator's alleged connection to her.

Ashlyn also carefully outlined the Capitol Police investigation into the matter. She was skillful to make no accusations but made it clear the senator had no knowledge of Joseph's disappearance.

Ashlyn tentatively asked, "We were wondering if we could solicit your help. Your reputation precedes you, Ms. Spain."

"Blarney will get you everywhere, Ms. Jordan," Spain jested. "Just what is it the senator's got in mind?"

"The Charleston PD is calling and questioning the senator and asking the same questions multiple times," Ashlyn said. "It's just so time consuming."

"I'm not sure I can help. It depends on what you need done."

"Just information," Ashlyn warily replied. "The senator needs to know - I'm sure you understand - some facts about O'Reilly and his officers. Got to be some trash in some closets somewhere."

"I understand. We're pretty good at developing that kind of tidy information. Sounds like something that would be interesting, but I'm really slammed. I'll have to see if I can work it in. I'd like to help. May I give you a call before the end of the week?"

"Perfect. Just call me directly. Don't go through the operator. I'll expect to hear before the end of the week, Ms. Spain, we look forward to doing business with you," Ashlyn finished the conversation, hoping she had covered everything.

Lt. O'Reilly had just returned from briefing the chief when his secretary interrupted on the intercom. "Sir, Sissy Spain is here to see you."

"A guardian angel from my past. Send her in," O'Reilly answered.

"Kevin, really sorry to bother you," she blurted as she moved to shake hands with O'Reilly. "But I think this stuff might be important."

"Take your time, Sissy. At our age, there's no need to rush things. Know what I mean? I haven't seen you in months. You look great. Still fleecing spurned spouses?"

"Yeah, you look great too, Kevin. Always did like your loose-lip-tight-ship routine," Spain scoffed back at O'Reilly, who motioned her to sit down.

"So what's the best PI in town got going on?" O'Reilly asked. "Must be important."

Sissy explained the call she'd received the day before from Edwardson's assistant chief of staff.

"The young lady never directly implied this, but it seemed clear Edwardson somehow feels implicated in Rachael Joseph's disappearance, whoever that is."

O'Reilly nodded his head, the hint of a wry smile curling on his face.

"I'm sure you know what she's talking about," Sissy mused, pausing briefly. "You already know I never had any intention of taking the Edwardson gig. I've still got to call them back, but I wanted to talk with you first, Kevin. Guess they've got no idea how far back we go or all the stuff we've knocked out together. If she'd realized, she'd never have called me."

O'Reilly leaned back in his chair, nodding his head as he considered Sissy's account. "Thank you for coming to me with this, Sissy. There is a young lady missing, and the only real clue is an autographed photo of the girl with Senator Edwardson. He says the photo was just campaign advertising and claims he signs hundreds every year. The call you received yesterday would seem to indicate there's much more to the story. I can't express my gratitude enough."

"Glad to help, Kevin," Sissy said and stood up. "I'll call them today and refuse the offer. I don't have to tell you they'll score the gig with another firm, so watch your backside."

O'Reilly walked around his desk and shook her hand again. "Keep in touch, Sissy. Don't stay away so long next time, okay?"

Spain quickly left his office, almost bumping into Sergeant Cooper entering.

"Hey, is that who I think that is?" Cooper asked O'Reilly.

"Yeah. Haven't seen Sissy Spain in forever around here," O'Reilly said. He scrunched his jaw, tilting his head as he sat down. "Cooper, I've got a hunch."

"Sir, you know hunches aren't worth wild goose crap."

"Just indulge me, Cooper, okay?" O'Reilly's frown was deadly serious. "The Joseph girl's been missing about four weeks now. I want you to call Charlotte PD. Get the missing person's guy on the phone and see if they've had any reports on Rachael C. Joseph AKA Codi Coedinger? I know it sounds stupid but just do it and see what they say. Soon as you finish, get back to me."

"Yes, sir, I'll be right on it," Cooper said as he rose to leave.

O'Reilly hadn't had time to finish rummaging through his desk when Cooper burst through the door. "Got a hit on Joseph, sir.

"I knew it," O'Reilly said, looking up and spinning his chair straightforward.

Cooper handed a file to O'Reilly. "Talked with Dean Taylor in missing persons Charlotte PD. Taylor said about three weeks ago Claude and Elizabeth Joseph from Raleigh reported their daughter, Rachael C. Joseph, missing. Taylor told me the case looked like a family squabble and didn't meet their missing person threshold. Anyway, the father's telephone number is in the file with the faxed copy of Taylor's report."

"Finally, we get a break." He motioned for Cooper to sit down, "I'll call Joseph now."

"Claude Joseph," the gentleman answered.

"Mr. Joseph, you don't know me, but I'm Lieutenant Kevin O'Reilly, Charleston, South Carolina Police Department. Sergeant Dean Taylor in Charlotte gave us your name and number." O'Reilly paused, giving Joseph time to digest what was likely a very disquieting call.

"What's going on?" Joseph sounded terrified. "Oh God, what's happened to Rachael?"

"Actually, Mr. Joseph, I don't know what's exactly happened. I know you're very upset about your missing daughter. We're doing our best to find out. About four weeks ago, we found your daughter's abandoned vehicle in Charleston. The vehicle was clean. There was no sign of a crime," O'Reilly tried to soften the news.

"Have you found Rachael? She's been missing almost four weeks now," Claude Joseph expectantly asked. "You say you found Rachael's car? Is Rachael in Charleston? Why would Rachael be in Charleston?"

"We don't know why she was in Charleston, Mr. Joseph. We would appreciate any information you might have that could help. A drunk kid was found passed out in the back seat of your daughter's SUV. Have you ever heard of Thomas Stirk, sir?"

"Never heard of him, Lieutenant. Rachael didn't know any Thomas Stirk. I'm sure of it. She had no reason to be in Charleston. She doesn't know anyone in Charleston."

"Did she use a nickname?"

"Yes, her friends call her Codi."

"Mr. Joseph, just for your information, our forensic team found no signs of crime or foul play from evidence in your daughter's vehicle. No blood or evidence of violence or a struggle. Nothing. The vehicle was really clean. Anything you could tell us would help," O'Reilly continued, hoping to calm Claude Joseph's anxiety and inspire some helpful information.

"Rachael's been missing so long now, Lieutenant. God knows I wish I could think of something to help," he said as his voice began to break. "Her mother and I are at our wit's end. We don't know where to turn next. Please help us, Lieutenant. Please find Rachael."

"Mr. Joseph, we're working on it. We'll find her. I'll call you with updates as I have more information. Please feel free to call me anytime. Thank you, sir. I'll be in touch soon," O'Reilly turned to Cooper as he hung up the phone.

"Cooper, it's time to get serious about Rachael Joseph."

Cooper nodded.

"Find out from Judge Gethers how we should proceed to arrange a hearing on the Rachael Joseph matter. We need to hear first hand from the Honorable Senator Edwardson, which no doubt will require an iron-clad subpoena. We can't let him off the hook. He knows what's going on with Codi Joseph. "

"Yes, Lieutenant. I will try to have something on it today, sir."

32

AN EASTER VOICE

Easter was fast approaching and Rachael Codi Joseph had been missing almost four weeks. From the time Liz and Claude had returned from Charlotte, unable to convince police authorities to place Codi's name on the missing persons register, Elizabeth Joseph had been unable to cope emotionally and was briefly hospitalized. Her doctor prescribed a stronger sedative, but nothing seemed to calm her anxiety.

Claude was reaching the end of his rope. He was grasping for the knot as he tried to hold his company's head above break-even in the local real estate market and figure out how to find Codi. He hoped their family doctor could keep Liz from crashing.

Claude had taken Sergeant Taylor's advice, retained a private investigator, and paid him a thousand dollars in advance. The guy had produced nothing. It was more than a week now, and the PI hadn't even called. Claude was totally dispirited. He didn't know where to turn next.

Finding out from O'Reilly that Codi's SUV was discovered in Charleston only added mystery to an already perplexing situation. The search always seemed to end up at a dead end. It was frustrating and with each day as Claude's worst suspicions grew. He struggled to avoid being overwhelmed. He had to be strong for his sons, for Liz, and mostly for himself to continue the search. Lt. O'Reilly's optimism that Codi would be found was encouraging but no brass ring. It was, however, the first glimmer of hope since Codi disappeared.

It was the Wednesday before Good Friday and Pastor Sara Willingham at First Presbyterian Church, the Josephs' family pastor, had arranged a prayer vigil for 8:00 p.m. Claude was worried Liz would be too stressed to attend, but she promised to try.

Liz struggled to pull herself together. She knew it would be difficult to sit through the service, but she'd taken an extra Valium and hoped to seem calm and normal to all their friends.

Her two sons encouraged her, reminding her that when they were lost at Disney World seven years ago, it was Rachael who searched and finally found them behind the entrance at Splash Mountain.

"Mom, we have to be strong for Rachael," they encouraged. "We've got to be there to pray for her."

As Claude, Liz, and the boys arrived at First Presbyterian, the brick-pilastered church directory and bulletin board announced the prayer service in honor of Rachael C. Joseph. Liz began to cry as they walked past the brightly-lighted directory and up the steps to the massive front doors.

The sanctuary was a sea of green and white. Mountains of Easter lilies silhouetted the chancel. It looked more like a spring meadow than a church, Liz thought, as her family walked to the second pew on the right, reserved with a yellow ribbon.

Sara Willingham was very close to the Joseph family. Codi was only ten when Sara became senior pastor. She'd watched Codi grow up. She'd been there as Codi matured and provided spiritual guidance during her formative years. Willingham had been more of a mentor than a pastor.

Pastor Sara was there when twelve-year-old Codi confessed Jesus as her lord and savior and requested to, "be baptized by immersion, just like Jesus," she'd said, not knowing Presbyterians only sprinkled from the font. Pastor Sara arranged for her and her like-minded teen friends to be immersed at First Baptist downtown.

Pastor Sara was there when Codi graduated from high school. She attended Codi's graduation from UNC Charlotte. Rachael Codi Joseph was more than a parishioner at First Presbyterian. She was part of the greater Willingham family.

Promptly at 8:00, a smaller than usual choir began their processional down the center aisle singing, "Praise God, Praise God, Praise God," in unbroken chorus until they were all standing in the choir loft.

First Presbyterian was packed. The only empty pews were the first two on each side of the main aisle in courtesy of the Joseph family. As Sara Willingham stood in high pulpit, wearing the classic Scottish black cassock, slightly trimmed in red, with a splendid stiff white ruff, she first turned to her left, acknowledging Rachael's family.

Pastor Sara began her liturgy with personal memories of Codi's younger years in church and school. She always used Rachael's familiar nickname, Codi. She explained Codi came from Coedinger, an old Scottish family name from her dad's side of the family. "Codi is talented, pretty, intelligent, witty, and most of all, she is committed to God. She is a God follower."

Pastor Sara's gentle, compassionate voice was reassuring to the congregation and to Claude and Liz.

"I know wherever she is tonight, as a strong Christian Codi's already talking with God. I know tonight she's likely not thinking about herself. She's thinking of her mom and dad and her brothers. God does know where she is and when she'll be home. God has her in His hands and God is protecting her.

"Before we kneel and pray tonight, please take the Bible from the pew rack and turn to Psalm 23. Let each of us read it silently. Verse four has always been most comforting to me."

After a moment of silence, Pastor Sara read, "Even though I walk through the valley of the shadow of death, I fear no evil; for You are with me."

She looked up at the congregation.

"When you are finished reading, shall we all kneel and pray for Rachael Codi Joseph, our daughter, our friend, and God's child."

The crowded sanctuary was quiet. It was quite extraordinary—the colossal power of fifteen hundred dedicated Christians praying, all in one accord. She glanced out at the kneeling congregation.

"God's power. His power," she quietly prayed.

There were still some in the congregation on their knees, but most had folded their kneeling benches and were again seated. Suddenly, without any warning, an older African lady finely, attired in a handsome all-white suit, boldly stood in the front left pew. Her stout frame was accentuated by her white, feathered, oversized fedora, which was cocked slightly to the right.

Scribbee, her wings hidden under her striking white suit, began almost shouting, "Do, Lord Jesus! Do Lord! We can feel the spirit here tonight."

Her head still bowed, Pastor Sara Willingham was a bit shocked at what she'd just heard. She opened her eyes to see the African lady standing in the front left pew. Pastor Sara immediately asked herself, where did this lady come from? Surely, I would have seen the hat earlier. She was certain the last time she looked the pew was empty. She silently prayed, "God, you move in mysterious ways. Your will be done tonight in this, your church, Father. Praise you, Lord."

Scribbee, standing tall and resolute, looked to her right at Tony B and JJ. Scribbee knew Tony B and JJ could not be seen or heard by the congregation, but she took great strength from their presence. They were all part of God's archangel multitudes, which gave Scribbee, now visibly exposed in an earthly venue, strength and fortitude.

"Oh, my! Oh, my, my!" a sophisticated Scribbee shouted as she seemed to sway, wobbly on her feet as if having just been smote with the rod of Moses gushing living water from her soul. "God's spirit is here tonight, friends. I can feel Him in this place; God's moving in our midst. Can you feel Him?"

She swayed back and forth. Several parishioners opened their eyes from their prayers.

"He's here tonight. God loves us all, brothers and sisters. He is here in this place tonight."

The congregation, not fully understanding what was happening, murmured in agreement. Scribbee was now standing fully erect. Her swaying had stopped. She was rock solid, sturdy as if anchored with steel pilings, her voice authoritative, loud, and clear for all to hear, as she continued, "Hear the word of the Lord for Codi. Oh yes, Lord. Thank you, Lord, for your word for our sister, Rachael Codi Joseph."

Claude had now turned toward the African lady. He was excited. He felt something stirring in his spirit. He couldn't explain the feeling, but he knew something special was happening. He knew God was among them.

Scribbee continued, "Offer to God a sacrifice of thanksgiving, And pay your vows to the Most High; And call upon Me in your day of trouble and I shall rescue you and you will honor Me."

Scribbee then turned toward the congregation with her countenance aglow, saying, "He who offers a sacrifice of thanksgiving honors me; and to him who orders his way aright I shall show the salvation of God."

The congregation was silent. All eyes were focused on the African lady.

Raising her arms in praise, Scribbee spoke directly to them. "Brothers and sisters, God has commanded us to offer our sacrifice of thanksgiving. Our hearts are broken tonight. It's difficult tonight to praise God because our sister Codi Joseph is missing. It's very difficult to think of our missing sister and be thankful for anything. But we must thank God tonight. To thank God for His everlasting goodness when things seem so hopeless and so impossible is a true sacrifice of thanksgiving."

Scribbee lowered her arms and pointed her hands at the congregation as she swept her arms from left to right. "So brothers and sisters, we must do what God commands, and He will rescue Codi in her and our day of trouble. Let each of us thank God for this circumstance just as it is."

She paused briefly.

"Are you with me?" Scribbee scoped the crowd again with her hand. "Brothers and sisters, if you are praying this prayer of praise and thanksgiving, say Amen."

The entire congregation was now standing, some swaying along with Scribbee and all feeling they had heard from God Himself. In unison, they shouted "Amen!" loud enough to rattle the age-old rafters of First Presbyterian.

Pastor Sara, now totally flabbergasted and amazed, nodded her enthusiastic approval.

Scribbee looked at Tony B and JJ as they both clapped, albeit silently, their wings fluttering from the excitement of hearing God speak through Scribbee.

Scribbee again turned to the congregation. "Brothers and sisters, hear the word of the Lord. Enter His gates with thanksgiving and His courts with praise. Give thanks to Him and bless His name. For the Lord is good."

Scribbee sat down in the pew, physically exhausted. She showed no expression. She showed no emotion. God had used her mightily to prophesy His message. She had been compliant and was now completely fulfilled.

Pastor Sara stood at the high pulpit and recited a brief benediction.

Afterward, the congregation milled about, many attempting to comfort the family. Claude pushed away trying to get to the right front pew. By the time he got there, the lady was gone. Claude immediately rushed to the foyer asking the ushers if they had seen her leave. They had not nor had they seen her enter the sanctuary. They were all sure they would have remembered her feathered hat.

Claude wondered where Codi was tonight. He felt comfort in hearing the strong words of the African lady. They were powerful, and he believed she delivered a message from God. He just wanted a brief word with her. But she was gone now.

33

UNORTHODOX DEMONSTRATION

It had been eighteen days since Thomas fell off the wagon in Atlanta. Surprisingly since then, he'd managed to remain respectably sober by ending his nightly outings at Arthur's before 1:00 a.m. He had concluded a good night's sleep was clearly more responsible behavior.

He'd promised himself to leave the coke alone and enjoy just enough Jack to get a good buzz on. He'd pledged to smoke only one joint a night to ward off the insomniac demon and purge his lingering anxiety about the missing Codi Joseph. Thomas continued to fear arrest and wondered if it might come at any moment. He knew if she'd been found, Lt. O'Reilly would have told him.

Thomas had always been a sucker for self-justification. He'd always tailored his personal ethics to fit his immediate situation. For a lush like him, strung out for as long as he could recall, semi-sobriety and not getting bombed out of his mind for almost three weeks was a monumental accomplishment.

Media Productions had applied for and received the necessary parade permits from the City of Charleston under the name of the Talmudic Zionist Council of the Americas. The permit allowed up to fourteen demonstrators on the sidewalk beside Sea Island Church. The demonstrators had to remain on the sidewalk and were not permitted to speak, shout, or communicate verbally with anyone. Loudspeakers were banned and passing out any printed literature was prohibited.

Thomas had easily recruited sixteen college kids, eight girls and eight guys. He had briefed them on their required behavior and their pay of $90.00 per day, cash and carry. The two alternates would rotate giving each recruit a couple of breaks. The times were set: 11:00 a.m. to 7:00 p.m. each day beginning the Monday before Easter Sunday and continuing till the Easter pageant at Sea Island was over.

The Media Productions van pulled up in the public parking lot directly across the street from Sea Island Church at 10:45 on the Monday before Easter. It was D-day and the kids were eagerly awaiting the action. Two squad cars from the Charleston PD were already parked in the church parking lot.

Thomas grabbed the clipboard with the names of his sixteen demonstrators from the front seat of the van.

"Charles Kincaid," he called, looking at his group of eighteen-to-twenty-something college kids. "Hey, man."

Thomas summoned the freckle faced slightly built red head and handed him a double-sided sign. The large placard was emblazoned on both sides with a black cross on a white background. A red circle surrounded the cross and a diagonal red line struck through it. The sizable edict was mounted on a six-foot wooden pole. The sign screamed *"NO CROSS."* Thomas could see the young man was upset by it.

"Mr. Thomas, sorry I don't know your last name, man," Kincaid explained after looking carefully at both sides of the poster. "I can't carry this sign. I'm a Christian. Why would I do this? I won't do this!"

"Kincaid, you were briefed on what was going down here today. So what's the problem? Just carry the freaking sign." Thomas demanded helplessly, but the young man already had laid down the sign.

"Ninety dollars a day's not worth it, dude. No amount would be worth it. You're asking me to deny my faith in God. That's the best thing I got goin, man. Anyway, Christians can't do that. I won't do it. Sorry, Thomas. Just can't."

He turned and walked away.

"You got to be psycho or something, dude," said another one of the guys. "Count me out too. You guys will all catch a lot of grief today when everyone sees these signs. Check me off that list. Name's Jacob Franklin." He jogged off and caught up with Kincaid. Both crossed the street and headed downtown.

With only fourteen demonstrators remaining, Thomas asked, "Anyone else with no balls? Come on, guys. This is only a demonstration. It's not some apocalyptic world-ending disaster or something. First amendment rights, for God's sake. So who's first? Who'll carry these signs?"

Thomas picked up both *"NO CROSS"* signs just as a stout young blond girl stepped forward.

"Name?" Thomas asked before anyone else could turn and run. "Got to check you off the list."

"Hillary Docktar," she replied. "I don't have a set but I'll do 'bout anything for ninety bucks a day." She grabbed the first *"NO CROSS"* sign, and then called to her roommate. "Come on, Sherri. I know you got balls, girl. So come on and take the other sign."

Sherri stepped forward and gave Thomas her last name. Thomas held up the next two signs: *"CELEBRATE LIFE NOT DEATH"* and *"IS GOD DEAD AGAIN?"* One of the taller guys came forward and took a sign.

"Name's Charlie Pullin, dude. Who's going to guarantee some nasty dookie won't happen out here today when we begin walking with all this anti-Christ stuff?"

He grabbed both signs and handed one to his friend.

"Raymond here will take one," he continued. "We both need the bread, dude. Any chance of crucifixion or being stoned to death?"

He laughed. The others didn't find his remark at all amusing. Thomas now realized his crisis might be over.

"You can be sure the cops will be out here all day every day," he assured the group. "There won't be any trouble. I guarantee! You guys carry the signs and just walk and don't talk. Okay?"

"All these signs are so vile and insulting," said a third young lady as she stepped forward. "They're totally disgusting. Can we be arrested for carrying them in public?" She picked up a sign reading *"BORN OK THE FIRST TIME"* on one side and *"ONLY ONE GOD"* on the other. "Somehow, it seems totally wicked, but I need the cash."

"Don't freak out, people!" Thomas cried. "Freedom of speech, guys! Protected freedom of speech!"

A blond kid with a buzz cut gave Thomas his name as he grabbed the tall oversized signboard reading *"IN DARWIN I TRUST"* on one side and *"WHAT WOULD DARWIN DO?"* on the other.

"Dude, what is this, Biology 101 and Philosophy 101?" the dweeby protester exclaimed to Thomas. "Totally nerdy but totally cool."

"Cho Shen Wong," announced the girl behind him. She picked up one of two controversial *"PRO CHILD AND PRO CHOICE"* billboards. In somewhat broken English, she said, "Only one child allowed in China each family. It very bad." She clearly misunderstood the meaning of the short epistle she would march with that day.

"Tamicka Yazmeen Cordray," the girl with Cho Shen said. "Everyone calls me 'Yaz.' Cho Shen and I are roommates." She picked up the second copy of *"PRO CHILD AND PRO CHOICE."*

The rest of the protesters checked off their names and took the rest of the offensive signs, including ones with such inflammatory messages as; *"GOD LOVES HUMANISTS TOO"; "TRUTH IS MY RELIGION"; "FREEDOM FROM RELIGION"; "EVOLVE"; "PEACEFUL UNIVERSALIST";* and *"KING OF THE JEWS."*

As in any crowd of impressionable young folks, the peer pressure exerted its intoxicating force until all but two had less than willingly complied for their ninety-dollars-a-day bag of silver shekels.

Even Thomas was shocked at how insulting the signs were, but he quickly realized Goldman had deceived the old Rabbi, who probably knew nothing of this brazen display of loathing against Christians.

CC had obviously prepared the signs at Grant Goldman's direction. When the press eventually requested the parade permit, it would show the Talmudic Zionist Council of the Americas as the demonstration organizers, and Goldman would not be implicated.

The traffic slowing was bad enough, but soon some of the drivers had their windows down and were harassing the demonstrators.

One irate driver exited his vehicle, abandoning it in the middle of the street. Before the police could get to him, he was screaming right up in the face of the young gal carrying the *NO CROSS* sign. "What are you guys, Communists or something? Where you guys from, anyway? You can't just get out here and spew out hatred, man. What are you guys, friggin crazy?"

The two Charleston police officers on scene had radioed for help, and soon several additional squad cars arrived and were able to get traffic moving again. But the demonstration had turned into mayhem.

Many drivers had now parked their vehicles in the Sea Island parking lot and were screaming indignations at the protesters. Stirk's demonstrators remained stoic. Several of the officers stood between the sidewalk and the demonstrators. Thomas realized without the extra police, this already chaotic situation would head south fast.

By 2:00, all three local television stations had crews on site. They had parked their large satellite dish vans on the opposite side of the street, additionally impeding the flow of traffic.

Thomas watched the reporters, like sharks circling fresh chum, as they probed the crowd hoping to capture overzealous reactions or angry replies. What they really wanted to capture was one of the pastors or protesters ranting or screaming or some bleepable four-letter profanity. The whole event had morphed to Circus Maximus in the Sea Island parking lot.

Shortly after 2:00, several of the Sea Island pastors brought bottled water to the protesters. The Media Productions activists silently and graciously accepted, but Thomas immediately thanked the pastors and told them the picketers were not allowed speak to anyone or accept anything from the crowd. The pastors acknowledged they understood.

Thomas hadn't seen it coming when a reporter and camera crew abruptly confronted him. "Sir, are you Chauncy Cloud?"

"No, sir, I'm not," Thomas politely replied.

"Are you in charge of this demonstration, sir?"

"No. My boss, Chauncy Cloud is, but he is not here at the moment. I'm just the street organizer," Thomas coolly replied.

"You're Thomas Stirk, right?"

"That's me."

"Do you think it's right for your demonstrators to tie up traffic in front of this church?" The reporter pointed to the snarled traffic.

"Looks to me like your TV vans have blocked the street as well."

"Do you consider your protests signs offensive?" the reporter asked, hoping to elicit an angry reply from Thomas.

"No comment."

"Well, Mr. Stirk, some of the observers in the crowd have told us the protest signs are insulting to Christians."

"No comment."

"Well, there you have it, folks. Thomas Stirk, one of the protest organizers, refuses to speak on camera. Back to you guys in the studio."

The media was persistent all afternoon. They didn't try to interview Thomas again, but the news coverage drew a huge crowd. It was approaching 5:00, and the street was totally blocked in front of Sea Island Church. Between the curious rubberneckers and the irritated commuters, things had gotten doubly congested. The police were having to re-route around the church on back streets. There were now twelve officers at the scene.

Despite the crowds and the boisterous anti-protesters screaming from the street and parking lot, the remaining fourteen protesters did a splendid job. Thomas was satisfied that the first day of demonstrations had been an overwhelming success.

34

DESPICABLE WORK

It was the Monday before Easter and over the weekend, O'Reilly hurriedly completed his proposal for dealing with the department's DUI crisis. He'd taken his DUI Zero Tolerance Plan from last year, re-titled some sections and rearranged the order. It was the exact same proposal, but this time around, it would be titled "Community DUI Awareness For Charleston's Future." It was a splendid re-do, in his opinion. He knew the chief would never recall the previous version. O'Reilly's presentation had consumed most of his morning with Chief Newberg, but it had been worth it. The chief praised his plan. "I really like the simplicity, Kevin. Why didn't we think of random Crosstown roadblocks last year? It all makes so much sense." O'Reilly smiled and accepted the praise as if some new and exciting idea had been presented. He'd seen about as much as any law enforcement officer could experience over the years. He regularly preached to his troops, "There's nothing new on the streets, guys, just bad stuff happening between midnight and 5:00 in the morning."

If the chief was pleased, O'Reilly was pleased. And at the end of the day, that was all that really mattered.

There was a knock at his door. Sgt. Cooper stuck his head in. "Lieutenant, need a minute, sir."

"Come on in, Cooper."

"Sir, you're not gonna believe this, but you gotta come see. We got this riot protest on the TV in the briefing room. You gotta see what's goin on."

O'Reilly followed Cooper to the briefing room where a crowd of about twenty officers was watching a live broadcast from the scene of the demonstrations at Sea Island Church.

O'Reilly asked how many officers were on scene.

"Two were originally assigned, but there are now twelve officers on site," Cooper said. "The protesters are paying for security, sir."

"Where are we here, guys? Where's this location?" O'Reilly inquired.

"Sea Island Church, Lieutenant," Sgt. Cooper replied. Lt. O'Reilly was amazed.

"What did this church do to deserve such bad behavior? Those signs are profane and disrespectful," O'Reilly cried. "How can anyone carry a sign asking *IS GOD DEAD AGAIN?*" or that black cross with the red strike-through? Don't we have some sort of ordinance against that kind of garbage? What about it, guys?"

"They got a parade permit, sir. Went through legal and everything," Sgt. Cooper answered. "I agree with you. It's repulsive, but it's within the First Amendment, sir. Unfortunately, they got rights."

"What a crock. Legal or not, it's sacrilegious. Blasphemous, I'd say. Sea Island does a lot of good things in this community."

The broadcast cut away from the protesters and began running the interview with Thomas Stirk recorded just moments earlier.

Sgt. Cooper quickly pointed out Stirk to O'Reilly. "Sir, remember the drunk kid in that SUV about three weeks ago? That's the kid. Thomas Stirk is the street organizer for this demonstration."

"Yeah, I can see. He's my PTI kid all right. Hard to believe he would do something totally reprehensible like this," O'Reilly said and shook his head in total disbelief.

"I checked the permit. Stirk works for Media Consultants," Cooper said.

"How disrespectful can a juicehead be? It's not just the SUV arrest or his rap sheet. Can you believe this kid is actually in my PTI class?"

"They're bottom feeders," Sgt. Cooper sympathized.

"Seeing is believing. I mean, I know this kid is a punk and a druggie booze head, but never would I have believed he could do something like this. He's just too quiet in my PTI class. I never had a clue."

As the TV station cut to commercial break, Lt. O'Reilly said, "Totally disgusting. Repulsive. I didn't know there were folks with enough audacity to protest so disrespectfully at Christian churches. I can't believe Stirk's in charge of this kind of rally.

Shows you what I know," O'Reilly quipped, shaking his head as he left the room. "The PTI class after Easter will be interesting. I can promise you that!"

Encouraged by an abundance of free publicity from the demonstrations, Sea Island Fellowship placed two tents in the parking lot on Tuesday morning and began selling tickets to extra performances of the church's upcoming Passion Play, *Gethsemane*. By late Wednesday, tickets for the added Monday and Tuesday night performances were almost sold out.

Thomas had advised CC of the extra days and told all his demonstrators they would be working Monday and Tuesday after Easter. They were delighted.

On Thursday afternoon, Simms Satcher, Senior Pastor at Sea Island Fellowship, cornered Thomas near the picketing sidewalk, offering him bottled water.

Thomas politely responded, "Thanks."

The pastor extended his hand to Thomas and introduced himself.

Simms W. Satcher was the founding pastor at Sea Island. He wasn't the average cleric and had never attended a formal seminary. He was reared in the Pentecostal faith where his pastor was his uncle. Cousin Jay Willard, as most called him, was one of the old school Pentecostal preachers shepherding a small church in Naches about fifty miles north of Nashville. Satcher often quoted Cousin Jay's homegrown ecclesiastical proverbs, "Son, don't ever let anybody purr-vert your beliefs. You make up your own mind. You gotta choose hot or cold, one way or the other. Can't survive in the middle. Just remember, son, there ain't nothin in the middle of the road 'ceptin yeller lines and dead dogs."

Satcher had started the fellowship in a rented movie theater some twenty-five years ago with only a handful of members and the unheard of perception that church shouldn't be so stuffy and formal. In the beginning Satcher proclaimed to his congregation, "Loosen up, guys, no coats and no ties."

His flip-flop dress code worked. Satcher was a conceptual mastermind and his clever and ingenious ideas had contributed to Sea Island's success. Among the most popular was the Sea Island drama group. The amateur actresses and actors were truly talented. Every Sunday, they performed a short skit that reinforced the sermon or exposed a moral axiom that fit the moment. The congregation never knew from one week to the next what bizarre event would take place during Sunday morning service.

Simms Satcher had built well at Sea Island. He strived not to preach down to his congregation. He jumped in the water with them and they swam through life's journey together.

As Thomas shook hands with Satcher, he backed off a bit, throwing up his arms in defense. "I hope this is not going to be a tongue lashing or something. We are following the parade permit and are on public property."

Satcher lit up a big smile. "Much to the contrary. You guys have done us an enormous favor."

Thomas looked perplexed as the Pastor continued. "When you began picketing, we'd planned six performances of *Gethsemane*. We've just about sold out two extra performances. Thanks to your demonstrations and the TV notoriety, we've almost doubled our ticket sales from last year. The church could never have afforded such incredible advertising. No, on the contrary, we need to thank you, Mr. Stirk."

Thomas painfully smiled, revealing his relief at not being castigated for the insulting comments on the signs.

"Well, I'm glad you're happy, pastor," he said. "Your staff has been very kind."

"And how about this," Pastor Satcher continued. "As you may know, *Gethsemane* is about the Jewish Rabbi, Jesus. Your client, another Jewish Rabbi, Isaac Drazin, has provided the extra excitement to nudge our Easter pageant over the top. We'll set new attendance records at Sea Island this year. How ironic is that?"

"Awesome, I'd say," Thomas replied, now feeling a little more comfortable in the conversation. "That's incredible. How could Rabbi Drazin have known?"

"I doubt the good Rabbi did," Pastor Satcher continued. "Since all this began, I've become a bit more familiar with the Talmudic Zionist Council of the Americas, and I'm pretty sure they weren't responsible for the tag lines on the picket signs. It's not their way. The message is much too New Age. They are Hebrew believers in our same God. The message is much too vile and evil for them. This view is a secular progressive worldview. The voice sounds more like some secular humanist group … Grant Goldman and the local Freethinkers Society possibly? Did Grant Goldman have anything to do with these protests?"

"I'm not sure, Pastor Satcher. I'm not in on all the planning stuff with CC. You know, I just do the street stuff," Thomas lied.

"The Talmudic Council of the Americas membership is only Orthodox Jews. They certainly don't believe in the deity of Jesus, but they're not anti-God. It's hard for me to believe they would have posted signs in favor of Darwin or asking if God is dead again. The Humanist theme could never come from the Zionist Council."

"Couldn't tell you, Pastor. I just organize in the community, round up the demonstrators and get them paid."

"Well, I'll have to admit, I don't know for sure and now it really doesn't matter much," Satcher explained. "We find the anti-Christ, the anti-Christian secular worldview everywhere. We don't exactly welcome the animosity of a demonstration, but we never let it sway our thinking or resolve."

Someone shouted from the ticket tent, "Hey, Pastor Satch—all sold out."

"Have you noticed the national press coverage, Mr. Stirk?" Pastor Satcher asked with a huge smile on his face.

"I haven't had time, sir," Stirk replied. There were no televisions at Arthur's and he never got home in time to watch the evening news.

"We're excited. Fox News covered the story last evening, and I was on 'Good Morning America' yesterday. This morning, I was on 'Fox and Friends.' That's heavy stuff for a church this size. It's phenomenal, actually. This whole week is hard to believe. All thanks to Rabbi Drazin. Please thank him for us," Satcher concluded, a huge smile on his face.

35

COMMAND PERFORMANCE

It was Tuesday at 7:00, the night of the last performance of *Gethsemane*, and Stirk's protesters were weary. The Sea Island parking lot was already full with the evening's patrons.

Except for a brief interval on Easter Sunday, over the last few days, there had been no TV crews, no jeering gawkers, no traffic jams, and no reporters asking insulting questions. The challenge was gone. These fourteen college kids had been one of the best crews Stirk had ever hired, but now they'd all grown tired of the tedium of the event.

Thomas had worn a hip new outfit hoping to dispel any suspicions of being uncool. His black fitted trousers, a tailored black sports jacket and a black T-shirt with "CIT SON GA" stenciled in white crazy letters on the front spoke volumes to the college crowd. That day, everyone had been asking him what it meant. No one figured it out and Thomas blew off questions by saying it was all about the primeval Shinto god, Kami-no-michi, from the ancient Japanese city of Kyoto.

On the last day, Thomas allowed his demonstrators to drive their own vehicles despite CC not having authorized the change. Stirk thanked his picketers, paid them and wished them well. They all insisted they would be available for the next local sit in or rally. Thomas promised he would call on them again.

He realized it had been over four weeks since the disappearance of Rachael Joseph. Had the police found her? Was she alive? Had she been murdered? Had she been kidnapped? He knew the police considered him a person of interest, if not the main suspect. They probably thought he knew more than he'd told them. Had they found her and not told him? Not knowing was the difficult part. How long would he have to wait? He was sure they would be coming after him. He just didn't know when or what was next.

He determined to ask Lt. O'Reilly the status at the PTI meeting on Thursday. He and O'Reilly had actually hit it off after the last meeting and Thomas felt a kinship—almost a connection. He wasn't sure what it was but it felt right.

One of the guys, after placing the last of the demonstration signs in the Media Productions van, turned to Thomas, who was leaning against the front driver's door deep in thought. "Hey, man. Can't believe we've been doin this for over a week."

Thomas looked up at the kid. "Yeah! Hard to believe it's Tuesday already."

The young kid, looking awkwardly at Thomas, said hesitantly, "Wanna burn some grass, dude? Got some premium weed—Spanish purple hash. Got two joints. How about it, man?"

To Thomas, the inquiry was a question demanding no answer. He never turned down an invitation for serious weed and found no reason to begin now.

The young picketer and Thomas sat on the back bed of the van, their feet hanging over the bumper, smoking the joints and drinking Jack Daniels from Thomas's pocket flask.

Thomas had no idea when his smoking partner left, but the joint was superior ganja—maybe some golden hash or some looney tunes. Along with the Jack Daniels, Thomas was soaring toward stoner's heaven. He took another swig from his pocket flask. He was totally relaxed but strangely energized.

Suddenly, Thomas saw Rabbi Drazin and Grant Goldman standing just behind the van. They were enshrouded in a murky fog made even more opaque by the evening twilight.

At first, Thomas was mystified by the images but then Rabbi Drazin, prompted by Grant Goldman, began speaking. "No need for Jesus to die again tonight, Thomas. He's King of the Jews. Jesus cannot be God. There can be only one God. Stop this crucifixion tonight. Be my messenger, Thomas. Stop the torture and killing."

Just as quickly as they appeared, they were gone. Thomas walked toward the misty haze, but saw no one. He swept his hand out through the foggy cloud as it swirled and vanished. There was only emptiness where they'd appeared.

His mind began to race. He felt dynamically animated somehow having seen them. What he had just seen was real. They were there. He should heed Rabbi Drazin.

Thomas thought back to the evening he and Lestee had seen *The Passion of the Christ*. The scenes of torture had made him wince. He was sure Rabbi Drazin was urging him to stop the pain and suffering—stop the torture before it began. Thomas closed the back doors of the Media Productions van and drove the vehicle across the street onto the Sea Island campus, parking the van in a loading zone nearby the main entrance. As he exited the van, he grabbed one of the demonstration signs, which read: "*CELEBRATE LIFE NOT DEATH.*"

Thomas was aware that he wasn't thinking clearly. His brain was on overload but all his inhibitions were gone. He was free. Everything seemed so right. Sea Island's audience needed to hear the truth about Jesus. His life had to be spared. Jesus had to be convinced to be the king of all the Jews. Thomas had to prevent Jesus from being painfully tormented, tortured, and crucified. He must stop them if he could.

Thomas entered the Sea Island lobby carrying his protest sign. The lobby was empty. He peered through the sanctuary doors and could see the Easter pageant just beginning. Jesus with Peter and three other disciples were in the Garden of Gethsemane. All the disciples were sleeping as Jesus fervently prayed to God the Father above. Hovering above Jesus was the archangel trio, Tony B, JJ, and Scribbee, with billowing white gowns flowing behind them hiding their wings. All three were clearly visible to Thomas and the audience.

Thomas was standing just inside the sanctuary doors at the back of the right aisle, holding his protest sign. He seemed confused and hesitant but instinctively knew that he was the messenger and must proclaim Rabbi Drazin's message. He felt new and free. He was fortified with a strange boldness as he stood at the back of the auditorium. He raised his sign and began marching down the right main aisle toward the stage.

Thomas was heavily under the influence, spaced out and wild eyed, but spoke loudly and clearly, with authority. His voice seemed to reverberate from wall to wall inside the sanctuary, as he carried his protest sign and loudly decreed, "People, celebrate life not death. Jesus didn't have to die. He could have been a real king. If God's alive, Jesus can't die."

Seeing the commotion in the audience, members of the *Gethsemane* cast began scattering from the stage. The suspended angel trio had disappeared. Some in the audience were standing, shouting their disapproval.

Thomas continued, undaunted by the uproar. "Every year, you celebrate Jesus' death as you watch Him nailed to a cross. You watch him suffer and die again. How cruel is that?"

Thomas paused as he quickly spun around and scoped out the audience. He then resumed his invective. "So-called religious Hollywood artists have made millions filming movies showing Jesus' torture, His suffering, His pain, His agony, and His blood. The scenes are so real you can smell the dying. You drown in His blood."

Thomas paused for a second. Then, he loudly continued. "The money's in the blood. If it bleeds, it leads."

Thomas had moved down the aisle and was now in front of the auditorium next to the stage. He mounted the short steps to stage left. All the actors were gone. The music had stopped. The stage was empty. He dropped his protest sign.

Thomas realized he was alone. He could see the audience standing in the aisles shrieking at him, but he couldn't hear their voices. He could see their lips miming words and their arms waving wildly. But to Thomas, all was silent and strangely peaceful in the midst of total chaos.

Some in the audience were motioning Thomas to come down off the stage and into the crowd where he imagined they would be happy to crucify him instead of Jesus. Soon the throngs seemed threatening—violent. They were out of control. Anarchical! They wanted blood. They wanted a crucifixion tonight, Thomas thought, and if it wasn't to be Jesus, then it had to be him. Somehow he was not afraid. Being on stage seemed to offer protection. He felt in no mortal danger.

Thomas waved his arms, motioning the crowd to settle down. "Okay! Okay!" he shouted. "Calm down, everyone. But hear me. Listen to the truth. Would you believe the torture, suffering, and the crucifixion done to your Jesus was encouraged and instigated by Jesus' own holy priests?"

Thomas crossed the stage with new boldness, looking and speaking down to the angry crowd. "Those Hebrew priests claimed they were protecting their God from blasphemy. How insane is that? It was man's inhumanity to man—on steroids."

Thomas walked to center stage front. He pleaded, "Please, people. Please don't celebrate Jesus' death."

36

GOD'S BUREAU OF
INTERVENTION (GBI)

As Thomas finished his tirade, he could see the *Gethsemane* audience milling about, gesturing wildly at him, but he could still hear nothing. They were out of control. The audience had obviously not heard his plea. The scene was bizarre. His sharp pang of fear was relieved some when he realized the crowd wasn't rushing the stage to lynch him.

Without warning, Tony B and JJ grabbed him from behind, stripped down his jacket to immobile his arms, and slammed him down onto a solid oak side chair that had been placed front center stage by Scribbee. It all happened so quickly Thomas had no time to react. Tony B and JJ pinned him tightly to the chair.

Thomas jerked and pulled against their grip as he screamed. "Hey! Easy, man. You guys can't grab me. I have a right to be here."

Tony B and JJ continued to restrain him. He cried out again. "I have rights, dudes. Peace, man. I only want peace. I'm like totally non-violent. No suffering, no pain, no death for anyone in my world. Everyone's peaceful. No fighting. Okay? Take your hands off me! Don't touch me, man!"

Tony B and JJ let go as Scribbee walked from behind Thomas. Now they were all squarely facing Thomas, and Tony B responded to Stirk's order. "Okay, pal, if you say so. We surrender." All three raised their hands, their mini wings folding shut.

Thomas was befuddled. His wits were whirling. He was still heavily under the influence. He shook his head, trying to clear his confused mind but everything only spun faster. What he was seeing made no sense. Standing in front of him were two white guys and a black lady all dressed in white—and they had small wings.

Each of the angel trio was wearing white trousers, elbow length knit white pullovers, and white sneakers. The pullovers had GBI embroidered in large black lettering front and back with SWAT below. Their mini wings were exposed through slits in the upper arms of their pullovers.

At first, Thomas thought the three were law enforcement officers and then guessed maybe they were volunteer Sea Island Church security guards.

He pushed up on the side of the chair trying to stand but could not. Something had him tied down tight. His legs were secured to the front of the chair. His arms were now cinched to his side. He looked but could see no ropes. He could see no restraints. Nothing!

"Hey, what's goin' on? I can't get up. Let me up, man!" Thomas shouted, panicked by his predicament as he struggled to free himself.

JJ casually responded, "You're juiced man. You're still totally wasted. Just relax."

Thomas, increasingly terrified, continued to tussle with his invisible restraints. "I can't get up. Okay, what's this all about? You've got me tied to this chair." He received no response from the angel SWAT team.

Thomas focused on the rows of small white feathers protruding through slits in their white pullovers.

"What's with tiny wings, man?" he asked.

The three angels were completely dismissive. "Don't worry about it, pal," JJ said, a hint of contempt in his tone. "How about we talk for a while and you try to listen? Okay?"

"You can't just march in here and disturb everyone," Tony B said. "Not in God's house. Understand, amigo? What's your name?"

"Hey, I'm not hurting anyone. You guys were going to show Jesus suffering, bleeding, and dying again. You were going to nail Him to a cross. He was going to be tortured. I was trying to explain to everyone how wrong that is. Torture, pain and killing are always wrong," Thomas replied. He thrashed about, testing his restraints.

"Just compose yourself, Mr. Stirk," Scribbee implored, pushing her palms toward the stage floor as she motioned Thomas to calm down.

Resting briefly at Scribbee's suggestion, Thomas asked, "What's with the dorky clip on mini-wings, ma'am?"

"Wings aren't important. They come with the job," JJ snapped.

"Okay. Oh, yeah, I get it. You guys are from the Angel Grass Posse. The AGP? You're that East Side Gang, correct? You're pullin a crazy on me? Come on, guys. What's going on?"

"How about JJ's suggestion that you should listen instead of talking so much? You never told us your name and I never like asking twice," Tony B demanded, displaying his authority as head of the SWAT team.

"Okay! Okay, take a chill pill, man. No need to be rude, dudes. Name is Thomas Stirk."

"That's it? You only got two names? Sophisticated dudes like you got at least three names," Tony B pressed in close to Thomas's face.

"Don't need a middle name. I never use one," Thomas insolently replied, glaring at Tony B.

"You need a middle name here, pal, and I'll just bet you got one. Right?"

Thomas pulled and jerked against his invisible bindings. "Hey amigo, let me up from this chair. Okay? Let me up and I'll tell you. Why the name thing? Like it really matters. I never use a middle name. Let me up. Okay?"

The stage lighting was so bright Thomas could no longer see the audience. Spotlights from the back of the auditorium blinded his sight. He wondered if those in the audience were watching his indignant cross-examination at the hand of his wardens.

"Give us the name. Spit it out, Stirk, and save yourself some grief," Tony B demanded in a much louder, unyielding tone, his wings flaring fully open then quickly flitting flat against his arm.

"It's Houston, okay? Thomas Houston Stirk. My mom told me it was my father's middle name. I hate the name. I never use it. It's a bastard's name, man."

Thomas's head rested on his chest, his voice reduced to faltering mumbling.

"He left me a bastard child," he continued raising his eyes to the angels. "He's never been my father. I've never even known him. I hate him. You understand? I hate him, man."

"We understand," all three angels spoke softly in unison.

Thomas looked up at the angels again just as the blinding stage lights went dark. Suddenly, just above audience level, an eerie three-dimensional cube about the size of a giant movie screen appeared out of the darkness. From a distance within the cube, Thomas watched as images of him and his mom sitting at the kitchen table filled the 3-D hologram.

Everything was so natural. The still three-dimensional image, hanging in thin air, was in full living color. Suddenly, action began as the still image played forward and it was as though past and present merged.

"Mom, just shut up about my fantasy father. You can't believe how I hate it. Just shut up about him. He hates both of us," Thomas watched himself scream as he smashed down the chair and left the kitchen, slamming the door so hard he could hear the china rattle in the kitchen cabinets.

His mother followed him to the living room, tears streaming down her cheeks, and took the wing-backed chair across from him, pleading with him to just listen.

Turning toward the angels to his left, Thomas yelled, "Stop this stuff, man. How do you have my private life on video or whatever? You can't show my life in front of all these people? It's private," he demanded but got no response. The angels were contented viewing his life as it unfolded before them in living color.

Thomas turned back to the hologram and watched again as his mother chided him. "Son, life's not perfect and certainly never fair, but I've tried. I know it's been difficult for you without a father. Over the years, we've talked some about your grandparents and my life growing up in Texas and now I think it's time I told you more."

"You can tell me whatever you want, but I'll still hate him." Thomas watched himself insolently reply to his mother.

For the next thirty minutes, the screen replayed his mom's explanations of some of his life's missing pieces. Tears steadily streamed down her cheeks as she spoke. She was Executive Assistant to the CEO of a very large international corporation, and she was duped to believe he really loved her. When she became pregnant, however, her true love had suggested an abortion.

"And that brings us to you, Thomas," Mary Stirk emphatically stated, her tears relenting briefly.

Thomas observed himself squirm on the sofa and then get up and begin pacing the living room. His mom's serious expression and terse tone warning him of stuff he might not want to hear—stuff that might hurt. Stuff that might be better left unsaid.

The angels viewed the hologram with great interest as Thomas informed his mom, "Wait! I mean, I want to know about my dad and all, but you don't have to tell me any more, okay? I can see it hurts you to talk about him, so just end the story now. You don't have to say another word. It's okay with me. It's okay, Mom."

"Thomas, sit back down. You need to hear everything. It's time. I can see this is making you nervous, but sit down and listen. We must have this conversation."

He watched as she motioned him to sit, her forefinger unmistakably signaling her insistence. He had no choice.

Thomas and the angels watched as his mom vindicated her decision to carry her child to term despite the fact that she knew it would end her career and her relationship.

"I was almost twelve weeks. Thomas, you were part of our life—my life. You were already part of my plans. I was angry and disappointed when he suggested an abortion. I was horrified at the thought.

"I screamed at him, 'I'll never have an abortion! Don't you understand? This baby is alive. This baby is our child. How could you ever suggest such a thing?'"

As Thomas watched the video of his mother struggle with words to explain, he realized for maybe the first time in his life that he felt compassion for her. Her courage told him more about her character than he'd ever known. She was brave and courageous. She was honest and rational. She refused to bend principle for expediency. Her compassionate feelings overflowed empathy for others. He knew above all else, she loved him despite his terrible behavior. She'd proved it. He was proud she was his mom.

"I was super naïve, Thomas, but now, looking at you, seeing my flesh and blood, I was never stupid. What would I do without you, Thomas? You are the light of my life, son," she continued as speaking the words eased her grimace.

As Thomas heard his mom's confession again, he recalled just how angry he'd been learning of his dad's suggested abortion. How could his dad suggest that he should not live! That he should never be born! That he should not be here today—alive in this place right now? How could his father demand he should have been scraped into a bloody pile of dying flesh, discarded, and incinerated in some medicinal waste bin? The bastard. How could he? Thomas watched himself in the hologram, seeing his rage boiling. He'd wished his father were dead.

The images projected in the hologram paused briefly, and Thomas's rage froze on his face. Scribbee turned to him as he squirmed in the oak chair. She said, "Thomas Stirk, you should understand your mother's bravery and courage. She saved your life. The ultimate sacrifice when she had no idea what the future held."

"My unnamed father battered her and hated me."

"Thomas, many centuries ago another very angry man writing to the Christian Church in Rome postulated, 'Vengeance is Mine, I will repay, says the Lord.' Free yourself from the need for retribution. Vengeance is not nearly as satisfying as is generally thought," Scribbee counseled with a gentle smile on her face, her wings set open and still.

Thomas watched as the holographic replay started again. His mother's face was sad and wrinkled as tears streamed down her cheeks. She looked very tired as she went to the bookshelf and selected a bound collector's edition of *Gone with the Wind* from the next to the top shelf. Opening the book, she removed a yellowed, worn envelope from the pages and handed it to Thomas.

"It's important you read this, son," she said and nodded to Thomas to open the faded plain envelope.

Thomas viewed himself, tears streaming down his cheeks as he finished reading the handwritten letter. He remembered the salutation was nothing but scribbled, unrecognizable initials.

Then, Thomas looked up at his mom. She was not crying anymore. Her eyes were brighter. Her furrowed brow relaxed its wrinkled grip. It was almost as if she'd been set free from something. A huge weight had been lifted from her shoulders. She was at last liberated.

"Mom, he preyed on you, he used you, and then threw you out like garbage! The bastard dumped you!"

Thomas stood, inserting the yellowed, musty two-page letter back into the envelope and handed it to his mom.

"Thomas, now you should understand why I felt just like that puppy. I was thrown out. I was lost and bewildered. My heart was completely shattered, but somehow I managed for you and for me—for us. I grabbed the only opportunity we had. I had no other choice. He was a powerful man. We—you and I, avoided the bloody splat in the middle of a highway. It has been the trust fund he provided that has kept us all these years, and someday it will be yours."

Watching and hearing the truth replayed was an unexpected revelation for Thomas. He could see his mom had told him all she intended, maybe a bit more. But she was finished now. She would say no more. She looked better. Her tears had dried up. She seemed relieved. Her story was not complete, but she had no intention of jeopardizing her long-term trust arrangement by revealing his name.

Seeing himself breathe in deeply, slowly exhaling as his eyes focused on his mother, he realized the truth hurt. That he would never know a dad was almost paralyzing. But the truth was redeeming for his mom. His spirit was trampled and she was strangely revived. Mary Stirk was almost joyful the truth was finally in the open, but her son's spirit was crushed.

Thomas understood the same spineless bastard who trampled his mother had severely wounded them both.

He wondered if his malice was in his genes? Was cruelty his destiny too? Was his rebellious behavior his natural instinct or an inherited personality flaw that would curse him forever? Or was it just totally providential?

The hologram abruptly ended. The rectangular cube disappeared into thin air. The stage lighting brightened again, blinding Thomas.

He lifted his head, more coherent now, and confronted the angel trio while wrestling against the invisible shackles. "Man how'd you get these video clips of all that stuff with my mom. Where'd you get that?" He squirmed, pulling against the restraints. "Let me up. You guys can't keep me tied to this chair."

Tony B, trying to be somewhat more temperate, gently advised Thomas, "None of us are going anywhere anytime soon, so how about you meet my archangel SWAT team?" Tony B turned toward Scribbee. "She's Esther Beulah Scribner, Heaven's Chief Scribe. We call her Scribbee." He glanced at JJ. "He's Jeremiah Jacob Israeli and we call him JJ. And you can call me Tony B. Okay, pal?"

Scribbee followed by JJ stepped forward and extended their hands to Thomas, but he refused their polite gestures.

JJ annoyed at Thomas's impolite behavior, pointed to the crazy white lettering on his black T-shirt, "What'da ya think you're fooling anyone with *CIT SON GA* on that shirt, pal? *AG NOS TIC* spelled backwards is still **AGNOSTIC,** Stirk."

37

GOD S.W.A.T.

Thomas opened his eyes. Had he dozed off? He raised his head and looked out toward the audience. The lighting was still so bright he could only see a dark emptiness where the spectators should have been. He could see his angel captors standing to the side quietly talking.

Tony B, noticing Thomas stirring turned and faced him, "Hey, pal, your space ship landed yet?"

"Come on, man. You're creepy insane. Let me up! What are you guys doing anyway?" Thomas tried to move but found his arms still restrained.

Scribbee and JJ joined Tony B in front of Thomas.

"Scribbee you got his profile?" Tony B asked.

Scribbee moved directly in front of Thomas, about two steps away and placed her hands together facing up as if her palms were the pages of a journal. She began speaking in a soft and gentle voice. "Born Thomas Houston Stirk, five May, AD one nine eight four, Charleston, South Carolina, USA. Single offspring of Mary Elizabeth Stirk. Living earth resident

5,501,224,175. Absentee father and single mom. Ex-girlfriend Celeste Warner, nickname Lestee. One out-of-wedlock son, Thomas Jackson Warner."

Incredulously, Thomas snapped at the angels, "You can't know all that stuff. Are you totally smacked on something, man?"

Scribbee never flinched. "One interesting side note in the Holy Journal: the raw definition for 'Stirk' is 'two-year-old bull.' Several sub-notes of interest: Mr. Stirk's AKA is 'strung-out perpetual street punk.' The vernacular meaning is not totally clear but can't be good. The local police know him well. He is currently enrolled in Pre Trial Intervention sessions with Lieutenant Kevin O'Reilly of the Charleston Police Department."

Scribbee continued reading from the Holy Chronicle, recalling relatives Thomas had never met or heard of. The information was mind-boggling. She turned the pages of her empty palms, recounting centuries of genealogy, including some relations he wished she hadn't mentioned, as she steadfastly avoided naming Thomas's biological father.

Thomas nodded his disdain, saying, "Okay, I admit you're very good, ma'am." Thomas turned toward Tony B. "But I'm no punk and you guys are liars. You already knew my middle name and all that other stuff."

He turned again to Scribbee. "But how'd you know my mom's name and birthday, and all that stuff about my family—and how'd you guys get that video? How'd you know about PTI? Come on, guys. You're messin with me, right? You guys are whacked on something, right? What'da been smokin'?"

JJ got nose to nose with Thomas as he angrily snapped, "Only punks do drugs, pal," his wings fluttering rapidly.

"Come on, you guys. You've got to be kidding. Angels? Archangels? You guys are wild. You guys are doin' it, man. Pop me some angel weed, dude. Is that chronic purple or what? Come on and donate some," Thomas said, as he jerked at his invisible restraints.

"You got a really filthy mouth, pal. Remember, I asked you to listen? How about give it a try?" Tony B admonished, but Thomas paid little attention as he strained at his invisible bindings.

JJ, wanting to slap some sense into Thomas, instead cautioned him, "You're still totally baked, pal, so just try and relax. We're not going anywhere."

Thomas turned toward Tony B. "I thought angels were respectful, you know, friendly and kind dudes. But you guys are sadistic and mean. You remind me of my mom's spinster aunts who were so angelic and sweet to my face but called me 'Sunday's child' behind my back. I mean how rude was that?"

JJ never gave Tony B or Scribbee a chance to answer. "You got no idea what rude is, pal. If you want to see rude, we got barrels of fully aged, majestic rude from all over God's universe. Stuff you wouldn't believe. You want some rude? Just let me know and we'll deliver as much rude as you want. Just give me the word, pal."

"I'll give you the word! What kind of sicko impersonates angels? What's up with the GBI thing and the clip on wings?" Thomas irately asked.

"Now, now, Jake," Scribbee intervened, her soft blue eyes and gentle tone somehow calming Thomas. "Try and go a little easy. Mr. Stirk just needs some convincing. He's not totally with us yet. This is all new to him."

"Yeah, man, go easy. Let me up from this chair," Thomas ordered JJ.

JJ's wings were flitting rapidly as he held his tongue. Scribbee continued, "JJ, show Mr. Stirk your wings. Really up close, Jake, so he can see they're real."

JJ bent down in front of Thomas, placing his motionless right wing close enough to be examined. Thomas realized his restraints had loosened and his arms were freed from his sides. He looked closely at the mini wing and hesitantly felt the ivory white feathers.

"Careful now," JJ cautioned Thomas. "I'd hate to have to break your arm, pal."

Thomas opened the slit in the upper arm of JJ's pullover, exclaiming, "You guys are freaking me out. His feathers are growing out of his arm. Those are real quills, man. Right out of your skin. They're real. What are you guys going Darwin on me? Who are you guys?"

JJ stood, satisfied Thomas had a close inspection. Scribbee answered Thomas, "How about angels, from God's archangel multitudes, Mr. Stirk. We're from God's Bureau of Intervention. Think of us as your FBI but with God's truth."

Thomas sat up looking at Scribbee and shaking his head, his restraints tighter now. "You're jerkin my chain, right? There is no God. There's never been a God. If there ever was, He's probably dead by now."

Tony B moved in close. "Don't you believe that garbage for one minute, Stirk. If you could see what we've seen, you'd know God's alive and well."

Thomas paused introspectively, now more puzzled and confused. He looked at the three angels, then said, "Intervention, angels with mini wings, SWAT teams, GBI? Okay, I'll admit I'm stretched pretty tight. But this is gotta be some really bad dream or I'm trippin on some seriously bad weed. So what's going on here?"

Tony B stepped in close and replied, "You may wish you were dreaming, but this ain't no dream, pal. We're God's Spiritual Warfare Angel Team. GOD S.W.A.T. to you. Might as well get used to the idea."

38

SOUTH OF THE BORDER

Thomas wondered if he'd fallen into a rabbit hole? He didn't see a Yellow Brick Road or Alice. So he wasn't sure. Maybe the Cheshire Cat was playing tricks with his mind? He was bewildered. He did know he was being held prisoner at the strangest tea party in town, and his invisible bindings wouldn't let go no matter how hard he struggled.

"Calm down, pal. Won't do for you to get all hot and sweaty pulling hard like that," Tony B said. "Just relax."

"You got me tied to this chair. How am I supposed to relax?"

"I don't see any ropes, Stirk," JJ responded. "Where are the ropes?"

"You guys are holding me prisoner, man. You couldn't be angels. You're jailers," Thomas complained as he struggled to free himself.

Tony B shrugged off his comment and looked Thomas in the eye. "You are your own worst prisoner. You're bound up by all the garbage in your life, Stirk. Think about it. You actually believe your lies. You're a certifiable alcoholic, an addict in total denial. You're a prisoner of real Spiritual Warfare, pal."

Thomas jerked his head away, sweat beaded on his forehead. "I'm no addict, man. Where'd you get off preaching to me? I got control of all my junk."

"Oh, sorry, I forgot you really don't need to blow that coke. It's just recreational, right? You never get strung-out, right?"

Thomas turned his head away, unable to look into the steely blue-eyed truth Tony B was speaking. Tony B followed Thomas's eyes as his mini wings began to flutter ever so slightly.

"And the Jack Daniels is just medicinal, right?" Tony B continued. "Just an over-the-counter sleep aid, I'd guess you'd say? No alcohol addiction, right? And what about the weed? You came in here all lit up like a Roman Candle. Maybe you were trippin on acid or hallucinating on angel dust. I've never seen anyone so stoned-out."

"You guys are trash smacking me," Thomas retorted. "You've got me tied down to this chair. Let me up. Not guilty, man! Okay?"

Scribbee moved to face Thomas. The stage was now quiet and she spoke softly. "Mr. Stirk, you're tied down by lies. You lie to everyone. Your whole life is a lie. Have you ever told the truth?"

JJ caught Thomas's gaze and added, "Truth will set you free, Thomas. Try it. You might like it. Truth is not nearly so complicated as a lie can get to be."

Scribbee smiled reassuringly as she spoke the hard truth to Thomas. "You fear living. You fear dying. You've got no friends. You fear relationships with anyone. You're always angry and you're way short on courage. Good news is all those things can change, Thomas Stirk."

"Face the truth for once in your life," Tony B said, raising his voice, forcing Thomas to hear. "You're an addict and a lush. Multiple DUIs. You've been strung-out so long, stoned cool is your new normal. You're a junkie and a pusher. You're hooked, Stirk. Admit it!"

"Get off my case. You got no right to trash talk me like that," Thomas angrily replied, pulling again against his restraints, perspiration dripping from his chin. "None of that was my fault anyway."

"Do you blame Sammie Sarmah? Isn't he the one who increased and nourished your addiction, Stirk?" Tony B demanded, already knowing the answer.

"I don't hustle for him anymore."

"Yeah, but you did. You'd still be hustling for him if you weren't such a spineless lily-livered punk. You found stoners for him. Sarmah put you in bondage, pal. He took you to a new level of limitless low—permanently trashed and addicted."

"Can't you see, Stirk? We've got no ropes holding you prisoner. It's just the sin in your life that has you all bound up," JJ added. He spoke tough love, hoping he would hear the truth, but Thomas never even looked up.

"Sammie Sarmah and Bhuta Gujarat almost got you killed, didn't they, Stirk? Big drug deal gone bad. Remember that night? Remember your old friends Sammie and Bhuta Rat?" Tony B persisted. All three of the angel trio were determined that Thomas would see the truth.

Thomas shuttered slightly as a clammy breeze cooled the heat on stage. He didn't want to remember what happened that night almost two years ago. He'd tried to forget but the images would never go away. They were indelibly etched on his brain's hard drive. Those horrible memories seemed able to randomly project themselves in living color, always reminding Thomas of his cowardice.

Sammie Sarmah and Bhuta Gujarat were East Indians from Bombay. They'd been mid-level hoodlums or "poxi mons," as the British branded the criminal element in India. They were heavy into gambling and drugs with the cartels of Southern India. They'd made a ton of money for themselves and millions more for their bosses. They would tell anyone interested they were the most feared "poxi mons" south of Bombay.

Sammie and Bhuta Rat, as their friends called them, were both suspected of double dipping certain fellow Tamil cartel members and were beginning to feel the heat. They had a price on their heads, and their enemies were closing in. Their skimming fraud had caught up with them and they had to leave the country fast.

They had none of the required skills to obtain work visas for the United States. Corrupt but entrepreneurial as they were, they forged Certification Certificates qualifying them for top-level technology positions in Silicon Valley. They then bribed an Indian clerk at the US Consulate in Bombay with 500,000 Rupees, about twice the money the clerk would earn working all year for the US State Department, to obtain their necessary visa and travel documents. Within days, these computer engineers, as their work permits proclaimed, were on a flight to New York.

Having no intention of traveling to California from New York, they changed their flights south to Charleston. After settling in the Holy City, they bought a fleabag motel with a convenience store attached in a blighted peninsula neck neighborhood.

The foreclosed real estate, long abandoned, was run down and in need of major renovations. The bank took ten cents on the dollar and was happy to be rid of the eyesore. The city provided the two new immigrants with a municipal tax moratorium for three years, guaranteed their very substantial bank loan, and the mayor publicly welcomed them to the city, touting their business savvy and thanking them for restoring a blighted area. The mayor attended their ribbon cutting ceremony and the story ended up on the front page of the *Post and Courier*.

Then Charleston's mayor went all-gooey about his multicultural triumph and crowned them with legitimacy. Sammie and Bhuta Rat couldn't have planned it better themselves.

Thomas would never forget the first time he met Sammie Sarmah. He'd just finished snorting a line of coke in the men's room at Arthur's on King and had returned to his bar stool when Sammie approached.

"You look like a nice guy, mon. Want to make some big money?" he asked. Thomas ignored his outstretched hand. "Name's Sammie Sarmah."

"What'da ya mean big money?"

"Dee-pends on you, mon."

"How much up front? What's the investment? What kind of scam you guys got goin on?" Thomas inquired.

Bhuta Gujarat reached to shake hands with Thomas, who ignored him as well, but that didn't stop him.

"I'm Bhuta Gujarat, Sammie's partner. No investment. Just give out markers. Just find new stoners."

"That's it?" Thomas asked, turning on his bar stool to face them.

Bhuta Gujarat immediately smiled. "Maybe a grand a month, mon, and big discounts on your stuff."

Over the next few months, as Sammie and Bhuta Rat promised, Thomas began knocking back some huge bucks and didn't have to sell a thing. All he had to do was furnish contacts. With three universities in town, business was good. His habit was much cheaper, but with the discounts, he used twice as much. Most of what they paid him went to support his growing habit.

In less than a year, Sammie and Bhuta Rat had captured the drug distribution in the Charleston area. No one smoked a joint, snorted a line, bought an ounce, or purchased a script without the transaction going through Sammie and Bhuta Rat.

Some of the drug dealers and pushers on the East side had been roughed up pretty badly the prior year. Several had ended up with cracked skulls, some had shattered kneecaps and some were just pummeled unconscious.

When questioned by police, none of the victims claimed to have seen their assailants. Amazingly, there had been no shootings or murders among the usual drug crowd in the past year. The local dealers got the message and courted friendship with the new drug bosses in town.

The police knew something had changed but they had little interest in investigating, as the drug-related murder rate had dropped to zero. There hadn't been a report of shots fired on the east side in over a year. Sammie and Bhuta Rat had cleaned up the drug business.

By working just evenings and weekends, Thomas had been making good money fronting for Sammie and Bhuta Rat, so when Bhuta Rat insisted he join them on their next merchandise pickup on I-95, he had little choice but to accept the invitation.

Suddenly, the stage lighting went dark again and the giant holographic cube appeared in the darkness with an image of Sammie Sarmah looking into the back seat of his minivan at Thomas.

As the image filled the screen, the action began as Sammie explained to Thomas, "My stuff is the finest from Colombia. Everything comes right up I-95, right off the boat from South America. Our Colombian Gold is organically grown indoors and we accept only pure refined coke. You can't get any better than that, mon."

Thomas was sitting in the left passenger seat just behind the driver's seat in Sammie's white Toyota Sienna minivan. Bhuta Rat was driving. The van was complete with a double drop down DVD player system. At night on the interstate, Sammie always had the DVD screens playing Disney cartoons. "You see, I got no tinted windows. At night, everyone can see we're a happy family with kids watching cartoons," Sammie said to Thomas. "Tinted widows tip off the cops. If you got heavy tinted windows, they'll stop you just for that when they can't find nothing else."

Bhuta Rat added, "Can't tell you how many times the Highway Patrol waves at night thinking we got a car full of tired kids watching cartoons."

As the images projected in the hologram fast forwarded, Thomas watched them race north on I-95 past the Florence exit. Then, the images slowed to normal speed again and Sammie explained to Thomas, "We're meeting our supplier around midnight at the South of the Border parking lot, just outside of Dillon. Ever been to South of the Border?"

"Yeah, when we'd go on vacation to North Carolina. Mom always loved the Pedro Signs up and down I-95. Food there was awful, but I loved the fireworks store. Haven't been there for years now."

Again, the hologram sped forward and then slowed again as Bhuta Rat pulled into South of the Border just before midnight and parked beside the closed Mexican restaurant, leaving the engine running and turning off the headlights.

Thomas and the angels watched the scene replay as just after midnight, a black Ford F-150 pickup pulled up parallel to the Sienna. Bhuta Rat opened the driver's window and passed a black leather bag to the driver of the pickup, who inspected the contents and then passed a large black duffel bag back to Bhuta Rat. Not one word was spoken and the entire transaction took less than a minute. The truck was gone in a flash, driving away without headlights.

Bhuta Rat turned on the headlights and pulled out of the parking area telling Sammie, "I'm taking Highway 301 back to Florence and then Highway 52 to Charleston." Sammie nodded his agreement.

Sammie turned toward Thomas in the back seat. "Now you see, Thomas. mon, no guns. No rough stuff. Just doing business like in Bombay. Guns get you killed, mon."

"Very civilized," Thomas nodded. "Very business-like."

Again, the image raced forward with a subtitle reading: "2:00 a.m. just north of Kingstree, South Carolina, Highway 52." Then, the replay slowed to normal speed again.

Thomas and the angels watched as the Sienna passed a convenience store and gas station at a major intersection. A vehicle pulled out of the shadows and followed them. It was pitch black. There was no moon and the vehicle was running without headlights.

"We're being followed," Bhuta Rat said. "He's staying back, trying not to be seen."

Sammie opened the glove box and retrieved his U.S. Army night-vision heat-imaging binoculars. He trained them on the highway behind. The twenty thousand dollars he'd paid on the black market for the "heanocs" would pay off tonight.

"For sure, we got someone who thinks we don't know he's there. He's on our arse, mon. So just keep driving like we don't know nothing. I'll tell you if he begins to move up," Sammie calmly advised Bhuta Rat, who was intently watching the rear view mirror.

Thomas's stomach churned as he watched the rerun. Sammie turned to him with a sense of urgency but with no panic in his voice. "Thomas, there are two baseball bats in the floor storage under the back deck. One is shorter than the other. Hand them to me, please."

Thomas observed himself fumble to lift the back deck cover. "Holy crap, Sammie. I didn't expect trouble," he winced loudly, his fear taking over. "You got no protection or anything." He handed the two bats to Sammie. "What if someone jumps us or something?"

After taking the bats and handing the shorter one to Bhuta Rat, Sammie calmly turned to Thomas again. "Stay calm, Thomas. Been here, done this many times. Smart poxi mons don't need guns. Guns get you killed, mon."

Just south of Kingstree, the black sedan begin to close the distance between them. The "heanocs" revealed a single person behind the wheel. No others in the sedan.

"He's moving up on us quickly now," Sammie said. "I'm guessing he'll try and take us at Highway 502 at Salters."

The holographic images sped forward rapidly now as Thomas and the angels watched intently.

Just after the 502 intersection, the headlights of the stealth vehicle came on and blue lights flashed. Bhuta Rat pulled the Sienna off the highway in front of an abandoned gas station. He turned off his headlights and the interior panel lights and rolled down the driver's side window.

The officer pulled up directly behind the Sienna, turned off his headlights and his flashing blue lights.

Thomas viewed the replay, feeling almost as much fear as when the incident happened. He saw the officer exit his unmarked cruiser. Dressed in all black, the officer approached the driver's side window, his flashlight sweeping side to side. He had drawn a large caliber pistol. Thomas remembered it looked like a small shiny cannon, and in the hologram, it seemed even larger somehow.

"Evening," the officer said. "Where you guys been tonight?"

"Just on our way home, sir," Bhuta Rat answered politely.

"On your way home from where?" the officer insisted.

"Been up to Florence earlier this evening, officer. Just headed back to Charleston."

"Now, I'll just bet," the officer continued, waving his huge revolver at Bhuta Rat. He shined his flashlight in Sammie's eyes first and then at Thomas. "I'll just bet you guys were at South of the Border. Would I be right?"

"South of the Border. Where's that, officer?" Bhuta Rat answered.

"Don't mess with me, you curry-sucking Punjabi retard. I know all about you guys. All you illegal migrants are the same. Where are your weapons?" the officer threatened, his putrid halitosis and alcohol stenched breath forced into the Sienna by his panting rage. Thomas remembered the wretched stench was intense, even from the back seat.

The angels observed as Bhuta Rat, Sammie and Thomas all sat silently.

"I've heard all about you Arab rag-head dealers. You got no guns. Don't believe in them, they tell me," he continued. "Well, you freakin aliens better believe this .357."

The officer gloated as he pointed the very large weapon directly at Bhuta Rat's head. Bhuta Rat never flinched and casually looked directly down the barrel of the shiny mini howitzer.

"What'da got in the bag, you friggin Osama terrorist," the officer demanded, shining his flashlight on the black duffle bag between the front seats. "Just hand over the bag real slow now."

He leaned in toward Bhuta Rat, his forehead touching the top edge of the driver's window frame.

Thomas knew what was coming in the replay and wanted to cover his eyes but did not as he and the angels continued to watch.

Bhuta Rat was holding the butt end of the short bat, which was resting business end up just inside the driver's door. With one smooth, swift and powerful stroke, he propelled the bat's fat end upward, striking the officer directly under the chin, driving his bottom jaw into his upper palate. The cop never saw what hit him. He crumpled unconscious to the pavement, dropping his flashlight and his weapon as blood gushed from his mouth.

Thomas watched himself as he sat trembling in the backseat. He was so frightened he couldn't speak. He watched the words form on his tongue as he tried to speak, but petrified the words would not come forth.

Somehow, the holographic images replayed Bhuta Rat's crushing blow to the rogue cop from various angles like instant replay in an NFL game. The bat had totally crushed his chin, which seemed to have completely disappeared into his nose. Blood spurted from his nostrils. It was not a pretty sight the second time around and Thomas thought he might be sick again.

Bhuta Rat calmly exited the Sienna. He stepped around the comatose cop, put on a pair of rubber gloves, dragged the rogue officer to his vehicle and propped him in the front seat.

The officer continued to bleed profusely. He placed the gun under the cruiser and kicked the flashlight to the side. Bhuta Rat returned to the Sienna and grabbed a plastic bag of pot from the duffle bag along with five one hundred dollar bills from his shoulder bag. He left the pot and the cash in the officer's lap.

Bhuta Rat returned to the Sienna, stripped off the rubber gloves and checked himself for spattered blood. Seeing none, he closed the driver's door, turned on the headlights and pulled calmly onto the highway.

The replay fast-forwarded and then slowed as a subtitle read "Fifteen minutes later."

Sammie turned to Thomas in the back seat and broke the silence. "I know you're scared, mon. You're real poxi mon now."

His voice trembling, Thomas blurted, "Scared? He could've freaking killed us, man." His voice was several octaves too shrill.

The hologram image ended, displaying the front-page headlines of the Charleston paper: "Drug deal gone bad. Williamsburg County officer involved."

The screen faded and was gone. The stage lighting again brightened to blinding intensity as JJ walked in front of Thomas. "So Braveheart you're not, Thomas Stirk. I'd have been scared, too. No honor in dumb courage. That's called insanity, pal."

Thomas hadn't forgotten that night. His cowardice haunted him. His career with Sammie and Bhuta Rat had ended with that encounter. The brutal incident on the highway was one of the most frightening experiences of his life.

Slowly, over the next two months, Thomas managed to convince Sammie that his work at Media Productions was taking too much of his time. He told them he'd still point stoners their way but would forgo the commission since he would be part-time. They believed him or at least said they did. Thomas would not realize until much later just how lucky his exit from the business had been.

"You're very fortunate, Stirk. Those guys were using you. They are smart. They never plan on taking the rap for anything. They would have laid it on you," JJ reminded Thomas as Scribbee lifted her hands toward heaven, thanking the Father for his mercy and grace. Her wings fluttered gently.

39

DIVINE RETRIBUTION

"Okay, pal, so much for scary huge drug deals gone bad. So Thomas, tell us about your father," Tony B asked as the trio gathered facing Thomas.

"Told you. I hate him. I never talk about him," Thomas said, refusing to look up at Tony B.

"Why do you hate him so much?" Tony B responded. "Have you bought into what you told us your mother's spinster friends called you? Sunday's child never made you a bastard child, Stirk. An out-of-wedlock child of God, but no bastard."

Tony B moved beside Thomas and continued. "Or maybe you think you're some kind of biological mistake. God never makes mistakes, Stirk. God knows each of his lambs by name. Don't forget Scribbee's reading of the Holy Book of Records."

Thomas looked up. Tony B paused for a moment, his wings fluttering. He was a bit thrilled that Thomas showed interest in hearing more.

"You're no random selection either. You're not some haphazard accident. We can all verify that God picks the seed and the egg for each of His lambs. God placed enormous trust in your parents, married or not. He can't control what parents do with their lives but you can be absolutely certain there was no mistake about who your parents are."

Thomas looked up at Tony B, wanting to believe what he'd heard, but he was only able to respond belligerently. "No God picked my dad. My dad never meant for me to live. My dad is all anyone needs to prove there is no God."

"Unfortunately, Mr. Stirk," Scribbee said, her mini wings stirring the warm air, "delinquent parents are much more common that you may think. God weeps over them every day. God would like to change things, but His no-retribution plan for salvation gives everyone free will. So from time to time, God intercedes with the parent accepting the responsibility for the child and provides them an extra measure of chutzpah. Admittedly, it doesn't always work but God tries."

Tony B sighed deeply as he looked at Thomas. "Actually, God has been dealing with errant parents from the beginning of creation. At one time, God's celestial analysts concluded certain errors had been made in the DNA regarding testosterone levels in the male of the species. Turned out not to be true. God later explained the absentee dad deal had more to do with a rebellious spirit, excessive wanderlust and a particular mutant cluster of chromosomes identified as *irresponsibilitis totalitus* than it did anything else."

"Not too much God can do with bucking bronc cowboys, Stirk," JJ piped in. "Those dads have been around forever, causing a world of hurt."

"Know what you need to do to turn this around, Mr. Thomas Stirk?" Scribbee asked. "God promises long life for all those who honor their father and mother. And God means honor them even if they don't deserve it. Anthony's right about parents' behavior. God's been dealing with some really bad ones from the beginning."

Thomas warily looked at Tony B. "Why'd she call you Anthony, tough guy? Anthony's such a wussy pansy name, man."

JJ pushed in front of Thomas, shaking his fist, as Thomas's restraints tightened. "Watch your mouth, punk. I told you before; you got a really smutty mouth. Show some respect for your elders. Tony B would never tell you, but I will. Anthony Cloutus Bartholomew is God's chief celestial law enforcement guy. He's God's—what you guys call today—Attorney General. He goes all the way back to Adam and Eve. He prosecuted the Cain and Able murder case and arranged that famous East of Eden exile plea bargain deal. So watch what you say. Okay, pal?"

"So what?" retorted Thomas. "So he goes way back. How was I supposed to know? This place is psycho crazy. This conversation is bangin off the walls. I'm freakin out. Turn off the bright lights. Turn down the heat." Thomas twisted and turned, trying to free himself. "Let me loose! You're all lunatics."

Scribbee placed her hand on Thomas's shoulder as the stage began cooling again from a gentle breeze.

"Just calm down, Mr. Stirk," she said. "We're not going any-where yet. So don't fight it. You've got to discover the secret of the knots so you can untie yourself. All in good time, Mr. Stirk. All in good time." Her wings flitted compassionately.

"Remember, Stirk," JJ began firmly, "obedience under God's new covenant is voluntary. Cooperation is your choice in God's Kingdom. Under God's new covenant, an angel's job changed drastically. We don't do enforced retribution stuff any more. Today we're more about guardian angel missions."

"Anthony, tell Mr. Stirk about our final three enforcement gigs," Scribbee continued.

Tony B's expression turned serious. "Stirk, you came in here protesting Jesus' suffering and crucifixion, so you should understand the day Jesus was murdered was not a good day for God. It was not pleasurable to Him to watch his own flesh and blood suffer and die."

Thomas was bewildered by what Tony B said. He agreed cautiously. "That's what I was saying. Jesus didn't have to die. He could have been a real king. He could have been King of the Jews."

Tony B looked toward Heaven and paused prayerfully. "To be honest, that decision was way above my pay grade. The day Christ died was the worst day of my career, and I've seen some heavy stuff over the years."

"Thomas," Scribbee continued as somberly as a theology professor lecturing on the ancient Roman church, "we've all seen God command justice, demand sacrifice, and even proclaim scorched earth. But on that day, watching His son die a slow and horrible death, God wanted to taste some real retribution, some eye-for-an-eye vindication, but he knew he couldn't. God had proclaimed a radical new covenant. A free will relationship without enforced retribution. The new covenant was a voluntary relationship with men who loved and believed in Him."

"Scribbee's right, Stirk," Tony B spoke up, the tears in his eyes confirming his first-hand knowledge. "We were all there. At the exact moment Christ died, God ordered an earthquake. Not a total wipeout, but a shaker that would get everyone's attention. Medium intensity—I guess by today's standards a magnitude five or six. It was just enough to split the veil of the temple and get the undivided attention of the Pharisees. It was incredible. God told me to just point my finger and the whole earth shook. That's power only God can give, pal." Tony B pointed his index finger upward. "Glory to God. Hallelujah!"

"I'm not believin this," Thomas eagerly began. "I saw that stuff happen in that bloody, gory *Passion* movie. My ex-girl-friend and I could feel His torment. We were drowning in His blood."

"Least you've got some feelings," JJ quickly replied. "I like that, Stirk."

Tony B picked up the story again. "After the earthquake, God ordered an extended total solar eclipse. It was simple but very effective. There was total darkness stretching over three hours in the middle of the day. Had a great visual effect."

"Yeah, that was in the movie too," Thomas interjected. "It should've been X-rated with so much blood and torture. Should have been called '*Murder for Beginners*' or '*Crucifixion 101*' or something even more brutal."

Tony B nodded and continued. "Our final and last gig, three days later, was our best, when we rolled away the stone from the tomb and Jesus rose from the dead. Afterward, Scribbee and I sat on that stone. We watched as the two Marys attended the very first Easter Sunrise Service. It was truly a humbling experience. Every time I think about it, I tear up."

In her best scholarly tone, her tiny wings fluttering with a touch of excitement, Scribbee added, "It was God's ultimate satisfaction. Divine retribution. Death and the grave defeated for all mankind to see. God is alive, Mr. Stirk."

"There is no God," Thomas sharply responded. "If there was a God, He wouldn't let you hold me prisoner. Let me out of this chair. You guys aren't for real." Thomas struggled to pull free.

Tony B, impatient and fed up with Thomas's total disregard for the truth, got in his face, just inches away. He startled Thomas.

"Doesn't matter if you think we're for real," he said to Thomas. "Fact is you're here. We're here. You're in that chair and we're in your face—and you're almost sober now. That's some serious reality, pal."

"Yeah, Stirk, you just don't get it, do you?" JJ added. "Can't you see Jesus died for you and for all mankind?" JJ's wings flapped wildly, trying angrily to thrust him forward toward Thomas.

Tony B interceded, restraining JJ and quickly changed the subject. "Got anything in your life worth dying for, Stirk?"

Thomas, irritated by the question, attempted to shift his weight to his feet and stand up but was quickly thwarted by the tightening of the restraints. He screamed at the angels, "What kind of totally moronic wall-banger question is that?"

40

THE QUESTION

To Thomas, Tony B's question sounded insane. Why would anyone try to figure out what was worth dying for?

As weird as the question appeared and as much as Thomas tried to disregard its implications, it would not leave his thoughts. It was a question that demanded an answer. But Thomas had no answers. Nothing. Not even a clue.

To Thomas Stirk, death was *the end*. It was the end of today, tomorrow, and yesterday—all days forever. Death was the beginning of endless nothingness, blank and void. Death was a place of murky emptiness where black and white images were screened silently, endlessly repeating, looping again and again. He'd seen the darkness many times in his dreams. Thomas was certain there was only abyss after death. So why would there ever be anything worth dying for?

Thomas closed his eyes, his restraints more tolerable now. His thoughts drifted back several years to when he, his mom, Lestee and her parents attended the Universalist Freethinkers

Society annual Spring Renaissance Festival at Society Hall on lower King Street. The event was memorable for Thomas because it was one of the few times he'd ever attended a Freethinkers Festival. It was especially worth remembering because it was the spring before Little Thomas was born. And those were happy times when he and Lestee had been seriously dating. Thomas particularly recalled Lestee's dad's embarrassing behavior that evening and his profound comments about death.

A crowd of about one hundred Humanist Society members and their families had gathered as they did in April each year to celebrate nature's springtime wonders, Darwin's birthday and the coming Summer Solstice.

Dinner was finished, the introductions made and the evening's program began with several members reading their self-published spring enlightenment poetry. It had been received with polite if less than thunderous applause.

The program speaker for the evening had been some guy with the *International Humanist Ethical Union* from Detroit whose speech was titled *Social Justice and Human Rights in Amerika*. Thomas found his remarks irrelevant, somewhat offensive and dismissed them outright. He resented the way the printed announcement of the evening's program spelled America.

Coffee had been served and after dinner conversations filled the room with a subdued tumult as everyone awaited closing remarks.

Mr. Warner had been particularly sociable, which was very unusual since his grapes had soured years ago. Thomas always thought of Warner as the type who had trouble enjoying anything. His customary demeanor was extremely detached—classical elitist.

Warner was in his mid-to-late sixties. He was some years older than his wife, Margaret. He was trim and fit, but his gray hair added ten years to his looks. Thomas could never recall him actually smiling. It seemed he'd been born with a permanent scowl. He was intellectual, opinionated, loudly overbearing and very articulate.

Jackson Warner was also a first-magnitude secular humanist, although he rarely attended the Freethinkers Society. Warner was from the Ayn Rand-*Atlas Shrugged* School of enlightened minds and if given the opportunity could ramble on for hours promoting Rand and her philosophy of objectivism.

Thomas recalled Warner's doctrine from a brief lecture he'd forced Thomas to endure about a year ago while waiting for Lestee to primp for their date.

"I am absolutely certain Rand's objectivism is the only true form of humanism," Warner began. "You must understand, Thomas, true reality exists independently from consciousness and individual persons are in contact with reality through sensory perception."

Thomas simply nodded his agreement, but the actual understanding of Warner's diatribe was well beyond his grasp.

"The moral purpose of life is the pursuit of your own happiness and your own self-interest," Warner continued. "Transform your best ideas—your best metaphysical thoughts—into some physical form or work of art so you can comprehend life in everyday living."

To Thomas, Warner's theories were incomprehensible, but he was polite and listened thoughtfully. Fortunately for Thomas, Warner enjoyed hearing his own oratory more than anything else, which left little time for him to ask Thomas any questions.

Warner was a pacifist. His antiwar sentiments had become clear to Thomas over the months. Lestee had told him that her dad was a third year senior at East Lansing University in October 1967 when the dreaded Vietnam draft letter from the Department of Defense arrived at his parents' home.

He had been competing for valedictorian in his class. He was very bright, majoring in mechanical engineering. He would have graduated in December 1968, had already done two summer internships at Ford and had been promised a design engineering job when he graduated.

Warner felt he could never kill anyone and could not be part of any war where innocent civilians and others were being slaughtered. So he packed his bags and fled to Canada. The Vietnam War ended in 1975 and after President Carter pardoned all evaders and deserters in 1977, he returned home to a hateful family and a scornful nation.

At the dinner that evening, Thomas sat beside Lestee. Next to Lestee was her mother Margaret Warner, then Mary Stirk, and completing the circle was Lestee's dad. They had all enjoyed the evening.

Jackson Warner finished his conversation with Mary Stirk and turned to Thomas. He asked, "Thomas, where are you and Celeste off to tonight?"

Thomas, caught somewhat off guard, glanced at Lestee first. She nodded, and Thomas quickly said, "We're going to see Mel Gibson's *Passion* film."

Sarcastically, Jackson responded, "Ah, yes. Jesus King of the Jews. The movie is nothing but bloody death and suffering, I hear. I've never understood the mentality of folks attracted to blood and torment. Have you, Thomas?"

Thomas was at a loss for words, but Lestee immediately came to his rescue. She replied, "It's history, Dad. Thomas and I enjoy historically accurate films."

Scornfully, Jackson looked around the table, determining if he'd offended anyone. He continued, "It's crucifixion. It's a slow, painful, agonizing death. The Jews killed their own Rabbi by suffocating him on a cross."

Thomas, his courage renewed by Lestee, said, "Mr. Warner, its reality sir. The reality of what actually happened. It's reliving history."

"Reality? Wake up, son," Jackson raised his voice. "Iraq is today's reality, Thomas. More than four thousand dead! The entire Middle East isn't worth the sacrifice of one American life let alone over four thousand. America has no business there!"

"It's not the same, Dad," Lestee tried to reason with her aggravated father, but his face angrily contorted.

Even louder now, Jackson exploded at Thomas. "Death is death, Thomas! Jihadist terrorists killing innocents around the world or Muslims killing Jews or Jews killing Palestinians or Muslims killing Muslims or Shia killing Sunni or Americans dying attempting to impose peace and stop the killing and death all over the Middle East. It's all death and suffering—and very wrong."

"Seems inevitable, sir," Thomas meekly replied. "The world has always known war and pestilence."

Jackson, now enraged at Thomas, pushed his chair back from the table. Mary Stirk viewed the growing conflict in disbelief.

"Inevitable, you say?" he cried. "Just killing fields? Why must we always have a world full of killing, hate, and death? Nothing ever changes!"

Lestee observed the room becoming quieter as several members took notice of the loud argument. "Dad, chill out," Lestee said quietly to her father.

Agitated and totally undeterred, Jackson spoke loud enough now to be clearly heard by everyone in the hall. "Some in this world love killing the People of the Book and the Great Satan."

"Really enough, Dad. You're much too loud. Okay?" Lestee pleaded with her father.

"World wide insanity! Global madness," Jackson screamed.

Margaret Warner yanked on his jacket sleeve as she admonished her husband, "Jackson, you're making a scene. Please?"

Unperturbed by the crowd or his family, a crimson glow now on his face, Jackson pulled the napkin from his belt and tossed it on the table.

Speaking loudly enough for all to hear clearly, he continued his tirade. "In my day, there was another war. It was called Vietnam. Gutless politicians and a president never willing to win the victory perpetrated the Vietnam War. It was no more than a political game to them. But it was no game to the 58,000 young dead American soldiers."

He lowered his head in reverence and paused for a moment. When he lifted his bowed head, tears were streaming down his face.

"Those soldiers were just kids, now dead kids," he continued. "They were never-to-marry—dead! Never-to-have-children—dead! Never-coming-back-home—dead! I ask you unto what purpose did they die? What gain was it to our country or to Vietnam? Nothing I tell you. Absolutely nothing!"

Warner picked up his napkin and wiped his tears. "They were America's blood treasure. Their lives were squandered senselessly. American blood spilled on politically barren soil.

Imagine! 58,000 young men dead! 58,000 mothers' sons gone from this earth, their lives wasted for nothing."

His harangue was over. His voice dropped some but was still loud enough that everyone could hear. Warner looked around the room and concluded, "Nothing in this world is worth dying for! Nothing."

41

GOOD ENOUGH TO DIE FOR

Thomas's eyes fell open. His chin was heavy on his chest. The back of his neck pinched painfully as he slowly raised his head. His eyes were drowsy, but he forced his lids fully open. The bright lights blinded him. He turned and saw his angel captors standing nearby.

Sleep had been a relief. He felt rested some, but his awareness returned and reminded him of his prisoner status.

"Let me up," Thomas insisted. The angels paid little attention to his frail plea.

JJ walked from behind Stirk and once again leaned in close to his face. "So we took a little snooze, did we? Hope you got some rest. You're gonna need it, pal."

"Get off my case, man. Let me go!" Thomas grumbled.

"So what about it, pal," JJ continued. "You got anything worth dying for?"

"Stupid question," Thomas responded, glowering at JJ.

"God didn't think it was stupid. God thought you were important enough to die for, Stirk. That's why he sent his only son, Jesus, as a Passover sacrifice. He was the perfect unblemished lamb. God sent Him to die just for you, Stirk, and all of mankind," JJ concluded with a tender smile on his face. He folded his arms across his chest and used his hands to restrain his wings from fluttering.

Tony B continued the conversation, posing an equally demanding question. "If it's not worth dying for, can it be worth living for, Stirk?"

Thomas looked at the angel trio and shook his head. He argued, "I'm not fighting anyone. In my world, no one has to die. Everyone lives and lets live."

Tony B challenged again. "If there's nothing you're willing to die for, you won't understand the sacrifice worse than death. Ever heard of Abraham?"

"Lincoln?" Thomas queried, looking up at the angels.

"Aah, America's sixteenth president? Lincoln fought the war against the secessionist Confederate States of America and saved the Union. How's my history, Stirk?" Tony B mused.

"Yeah, that's the guy," Thomas quickly confirmed. "President Lincoln."

"Not quite, Stirk. Abraham was President Lincoln's namesake all right, but my Abraham was the father of the Jewish nation. He was God's covenant partner and lived about 2200 BC."

"Mr. Stirk," Scribbee attempted to answer the puzzled look on Thomas's face, "I understand you may not think we look that old, but we've been around well over four millennia now. We've been with God from the very beginning."

"Ma'am, that's a joke, right?" Thomas, still befuddled, questioned Scribbee.

"When I first met Abraham, he was well over a hundred and his wife, Sarah, was 90. Just after my watch began, God saw to it Sarah conceived in her old age. Nine months later, she gave birth to their first born son," Scribbee told Thomas.

Thomas shook his head.

Scribbee raised her arms toward heaven and shouted, "Praise God! Praise God! I recorded that birth. A beautiful boy child he was. Sarah even nursed the infant. Boy's name was Isaac."

JJ picked up Abraham's story. "God had a covenant with Abraham. They had a devoted, trusting relationship. Abraham loved God and trusted Him without reservation. One day, God spoke to Abraham and told him to take his son, Isaac, who was by then a young lad, to a stone altar on Mt. Moriah and offer him as a blood sacrifice."

Thomas strained against his invisible bindings, shaking his head in disbelief and shouted angrily, "Christians are so bloodthirsty! That's what I was trying to tell you guys. If it bleeds, it leads with Christians. Crucifixion is totally insane. Bloody death—it's always wrong. That's what I was trying to say."

"I'll admit it sounds barbaric," Tony B agreed with Thomas. "No doubt Abraham wondered if he could actually do what God had commanded. But his overpowering love and trust of God guaranteed his obedience. Just as Abraham started to plunge the curved saif into his son, God spoke to Abraham in an audible and loud voice, '*Abraham, do not harm your son, for I know you fear God since you have not withheld your only son from me.*'"

Confused, Thomas asked, "Then, the boy wasn't killed?"

"Well, actually no," Tony B sighed loudly in relief. "In fact, Isaac was never in any real danger. Those of us who were there had been briefed by God and knew the Mt. Moriah altar thing was only a test."

Tony B paused, looking up toward heaven, his small wings quivering slightly.

"Of course," he continued, "Abraham didn't know it was a test. God always looks for faithful obedience and total allegiance. God found commitment in Abraham and made him the father of the Jewish nation."

Thomas asked Tony B, "What was Abraham's last name?"

Scribbee, pleasantly surprised at Stirk's interest, replied, "Back then, Mr. Stirk, there were not too many inhabitants on God's planet. Most folks didn't have a last name. It wasn't till later when God's people multiplied and increased that last names became necessary."

JJ stepped in front of Thomas and asked, "How old is your son, Stirk?"

Thomas, a bit startled, looked up. "He's almost two." "Do you love him?" JJ asked.

"You know I do. I love him more than anything in the whole world. I'd do anything for him. He's my only son. Of course, I love him."

"I understand the feeling, Stirk. Now imagine, Thomas, you're laying your son on a slab of stone and about to plunge a knife into his heart."

JJ mimed the actions of Abraham laying his son on the altar and plunging the knife toward Isaac's heart.

Thomas was dumbfounded and stunned at the suggestion. He was at first speechless. He wanted to tell the angel trio they'd finally gone too far. They were cruel and heartless.

His anger boiled up and he let go his barrage. "Oh no! No no. Okay! Okay, just shut up. No way could I kill my own son. No one could do that. Killing your own son is worse than dying. If there was a God, He would never make anyone do that."

As he spoke, Thomas violently pulled against his restraints. JJ, excited by Stirk's reply, gave him a thumbs up.

Then, he replied, "So there is something in your life worth dying for?"

Thomas, his voice quivering with anxiety, looked JJ down. "You're psycho insane! Brutal! Totally cruel! No one could kill his own son. Yes, if I had to, I'd die first."

Tony B stepped in front of Stirk. "Remember Stirk, you're God's son, too. You're His one of a kind unique creation. God loves you just as much as you love Little Thomas and even more."

Scribbee waved off Tony B and JJ. "I suggest we change the subject." She looked toward Heaven for a moment of divine inspiration. "Ever heard of Moses and the Promised Land, Mr. Stirk?"

"Lestee and I saw the Moses movie. He wrote the Ten Commandments and did all those bloody Nile illusion tricks. Right?" Thomas answered proudly, feeling good about knowing something about Moses.

"They weren't tricks or illusions," Tony B reminded him. "They were all the real deal, pal. My enforcement guys worked for months on those plagues. Really complicated stuff— locusts, boils, snakes, hail, and the bloody Nile. Wasn't some carnival sideshow magic, Stirk—it was all real."

"Come on, you're lying, man. Just illusions. Cheap magic tricks."

JJ pointed his finger angrily at Thomas. "Illusions, you say? Cheap magic tricks, are they? How about this, pal? Get up off that cheap illusion you're sitting on if you can. Okay?"

Abruptly and dramatically, Thomas was jolted hard upright. His back slammed against the back of the chair. His neck almost whip lashed. His head violently jerked taught. His arms were yanked so tightly against his body he could hardly breathe. His legs were drawn forcefully against the base of the chair. He couldn't move.

For a moment, Thomas was unable to speak. He whispered a hushed squeal at JJ. "Easy, JJ. I get it, dude. Don't jerk any more knots. Can't breathe. Loosen up. Let me breathe, man."

Just a quickly as his bindings squeezed his breath away, they loosened and his head pitched forward from the quick release of pressure.

"So now you're saying you get it, huh, Stirk?" JJ bragged as Thomas wearily looked up. "Still believe everything is just an illusion? Still believe there is no God?"

"You guys all the time keep talking about God, but no one's ever seen God. None of you can prove there is a God. Everyone says God is dead. If He were alive, everyone would see him. Why would He hide?"

Very gently, Scribbee entered the conversation. "I'll admit, Mr. Stirk, that it is rare for God to be seen in public. He's not big on crowds. God's always wanted to meet each person individually. He wants to get to know you one-on-one. God's always been up close and personal with folks. He's never pushy or demanding and He's always available and really easy to get to know."

Her reassuring smile and gentle eyes almost melted Thomas's icy skepticism.

The calm of the moment was quickly interrupted by Tony B. "So Stirk, you want to see God? You want some face time with God Almighty? Is that it?"

"Seeing is believing," Thomas curtly replied.

"Abraham never saw God face to face; he only heard God's loud, clear voice, but try telling Abraham God didn't exist. Or try telling Joshua that God was not leading that final charge on Jericho on their way to the Promised Land. Many of the great saints never saw God's face but they knew Him well. The saints saw God with the eyes of their heart," Tony B said, his wings fluttering a bit. He hoped Thomas could hear the truth.

"Remember, Stirk, those people who knew and followed Jesus saw God on earth," JJ said. "Jesus' face is close enough to what God looks like, don't you think?"

Thomas bowed his head, pressed his hands against his temples and then sat straight up, looking at the angel trio.

"So, say there is a God, like you guys say. You say Jesus looked like God. No one really knows what Jesus looked like, but in pictures I've seen, Jesus always looks like some bearded WASP-y white American guy. No way can that be. For real, Jesus was from over there—you know, camels and desert, some kinda Middle-Eastern Ahab man. So is that what God looks like?" Thomas reasoned with the trio.

Scribbee gently but authoritatively continued, "Mr. Stirk, God fits in wherever he goes. He wears whatever fits comfortably and is most appropriate for the occasion. God looks like God, Mr. Stirk. To know God is to see God. When you meet Him, you'll know Him."

42

THE MOSES GUY

Thomas was still uncomfortable, but his bindings were not as tight. He was now able to move his arms, legs and head freely. The inner turmoil he felt had nothing to do with his restraints. He was suddenly perplexed by strange feelings. He wondered why he should care what God or Jesus looked like since in his entire life, he'd never believed God existed.

Discerning Thomas's thoughts and sensing a possible opening, JJ interrupted with an unusual, peaceful reflection. "So, Stirk, what about it? Do you believe in God? Or still believe God is dead?"

Thomas opened his eyes and looked up at JJ.

"How should I know? I suppose there must be someone or something in charge out there. Someone's got to be pushing some buttons out there somewhere, I guess."

JJ sighed and nodded as he moved closer to Thomas. "Just level with us, Stirk. Tell us what you really think. Just saying *'there must be someone or something out there'* doesn't really tell us very much."

Thomas shook his head. He was surprised the angel trio was interested.

"What can I say? I'm an invisible tiny speck on this planet, and the earth is a beautiful tiny blue speck of an oasis in the universe. When I see pictures from the Hubble telescope of other galaxies or our Milky Way, I wonder where all that ends?

"When I see the symmetry and order in the universe, it's like there's got to be someone who planned and arranged all that. Otherwise, it makes no sense. It's hard for me to believe the engineering of Earth and the universe was just some giant stroke of luck—some crapshoot."

The angels looked on as Thomas spoke, their wings fluttering.

Thomas looked up at them. "I know I'm right. I just can't explain very well."

"Please, Stirk, go on," Tony B encouraged. "Tell us more of what you really think."

"When I see the balance and proportion on earth among all living things, it's mind-blowingly incredible. Or how about when I watched my son being born—witnessed a new life beginning? Seeing the birth of a new human is truly awesome. Absolutely unbelievable!"

Thomas paused, reflecting on the birth of Little Thomas.

"Go on," JJ coaxed.

"No one knows exactly how that happens. Some say they do, but the very best scientist has never created one new life in a test tube. Only a man and a woman can create new life. It's indescribable to watch your child being born. It's a marvel each time new life begins."

Thomas paused again and the angels' wings fluttered in agreement.

"Just watch a sunset," Thomas continued as the angels intently listened, "or look beyond the ocean. How awesome is our beautiful blue planet? You say it's God. Who knows? One thing I do know: Our Earth and the universe were absolutely not some gigantic explosion. There's total order in the universe, complete harmony—the big bang thing has never made sense to me. It's really perplexing stuff but Earth's not just some random accident. Someone somewhere has got to be controlling this. It's all just too perfect!"

"Stirk, you're on a roll, pal. Tell us more," JJ assured.

"When I see pictures of space and the universe, I wonder where it all begins and where it all ends. What does infinity mean? Everything's got to end somewhere. Everything I see and understand has a beginning and an end. It makes me crazy to think about what infinity means. I mean contemplate—an endless universe? Someone has got to know where infinity begins and infinity ends."

"Listen, Stirk," Tony B interrupted. "I can absolutely tell you someone is in control. He's the Almighty One. His name is Yahweh, the God of the universe. Only He can make a tree, light the stars, part the seas, create human life, and know where infinity begins and ends. We know because we work for the Big Man."

Tony B backed off several steps and as he raised his arms to heaven in praise, his wings fluttered rapidly. In a deep and resounding voice he bellowed, "He is the great I AM."

JJ nodded his approval, a wry smile on his lips.

"Did I hear you right, Stirk?" asked JJ. "No big bang? Maybe there's hope for you yet, pal."

"I'm impressed with your understanding of God's universe," Scribbee said. "I couldn't have described it better myself, Mr. Stirk."

JJ changed the subject. "Stirk, remember we were talking about Moses and the plagues?"

"Yeah, man, but no jerkin me around about the magic tricks. Okay?" Thomas raised his arms in defense.

Scribbee took over the story from JJ "The Chronicles of Moses are a kind of perpetual everyman's story of God's relationships with His people, both ageless and enduring. Moses knew God. So to know Moses allows you to see God. Actually, it's exciting ecclesiastical history, edited by yours truly, of course."

Scribbee proudly announced this last detail to Thomas, her wings excited.

"I think I might like hearing that history if you wrote it, ma'am," Thomas quickly replied.

Tony B's eyes flashed as he rebuked Thomas. "Unbelievable! You're a class 'A' certified suck-up. Just need to point out, Stirk, that God abhors suck-ups."

He motioned to Scribbee to continue.

Scribbee began, "The Hebrew people were slaves for more than 350 years in bondage to the Egyptian Pharaohs. More correctly, they should be termed indentured servants. They were paid. They were cared for and had become totally compliant to the Pharaoh. They were bound with invisible chains of fear, intimidation, servitude, but most of all, daily dependence. They'd been slaves so long they no longer had any concept of freedom. Their dependence had robbed them not only of their self-esteem but of their desire to be independent as well. They no longer had any understanding of liberty. They were compliant prisoners, unable and unwilling to set themselves free. They needed courage and fortitude to untie their knots of bondage and to once again trust in God."

Moving directly in front of Stirk, Scribbee pointed to his chair.

"Your bondage to that chair is no different than the Hebrew's bondage in Egypt. You're still your own prisoner. We're not your jailers. We're not holding you prisoner. Remember, courage is not the absence of fear. Courage is overcoming fear, Mr. Stirk."

Thomas knew Ms. Scribbee was speaking the truth. He had no idea how strong the links in his chain were, and he really didn't want to find out. He didn't want to hear any more. He wanted to run but couldn't. The truth hurt and he had no choice but to listen.

"It's time for you to begin untying your knots of self doubt, of low self-esteem, of fear and cowardice, of dependence on alcohol and drugs, and of anger. You must choose to be free. You must choose liberty, Mr. Stirk," Ms. Scribbee said firmly. She smiled at Thomas.

"Freedom is never easy, Stirk," JJ continued. "It was hard for the Jews in Egypt to believe they could be free. Moses had a very difficult time convincing his own people let alone the Pharaoh."

"I must admit," continued Scribbee, "persuading Pharaoh was difficult. Moses' smiting staff and Tony B's many plagues were truly works of art, but it wasn't until the last of the plagues, the great Passover plague, that Pharaoh finally relented and allowed the Hebrews to leave Egypt."

"Remember Passover, Stirk," Tony B interjected. "It will be important."

Thomas nodded his agreement. "Okay, Tony B."

Scribbee turned to JJ. "JJ, your special operations group handled the pestilence plan and war strategy. Tell Mr. Stirk what happened that night."

"Stirk, listen up. It was to be a terrible night. God told Moses He was going to visit a plague of death on the land and kill all the firstborn sons of Egypt in order to convince Pharaoh to let God's people go. But to protect the Hebrews, God instructed each Jewish family to slay a perfect lamb, one without spot or blemish, and spread the blood of the lamb on their doorposts so that the plague of death would pass over them."

Thomas grimaced. "More blood and death. It's like I said, always more killing and dying. Why does everything have to be so Rocky Horror bloody scary? Why does someone always have to die?"

JJ, undeterred by Thomas's charges, persisted with the account. "I'll admit it was scary and bloody, but it was necessary to save God's people. After midnight, the angel of death passed over Egypt and every firstborn Egyptian son died, including Pharaoh's oldest son. But all the Hebrew children were safe and unharmed. Pharaoh had finally been convinced and he let God's people go. Since that day, the Passover has been the most sacred of all celebrated Jewish holidays."

"Pharaoh not only let the Hebrew people go, but he demanded they leave Egypt immediately," Scribbee said. "Unfortunately, some hours later he changed his mind and sent his army after the Jews. God requisitioned 600,000 angels to blow non-stop, parting the Red Sea until the Hebrew people crossed. Once safely on the other side, God ordered the angels to halt. The wind lay down and the Red Sea engulfed the entire Egyptian Army. It was a very long night."

"I saw all that stuff in that Moses movie. You guys were really there? For real, you were there? Come on, are you guys lying again?"

"On the scene big time, Mr. Stirk," Scribbee replied. "It was the largest single army of angels God ever assembled. We created a very tight, well-aimed category ten hurricane that night. God can do anything."

Scribbee proudly beamed, pointing her index finger to the heavens. Her wings gently twittered her delight.

"After crossing the Red Sea," Tony B resumed the story, "Moses led his people to the land of Canaan, God's Promised Land, but the Hebrew people argued and complained. They were quickly learning freedom was frightening and not free at all. They were not listening to God. The strife became so bad that the Hebrews could never agree to go in and possess the Promised Land. Their defiant behavior kept them in the wilderness for forty years."

"Stirk, Moses was the man," JJ added. "He was God's man, and it was during those wilderness years that God gave Moses the Ten Commandments and the Israelites built the first great Tabernacle and the Ark of the Covenant to hold the tablets on which the Ten Commandments were inscribed."

"I saw that Tabernacle Ark Covenant thing at the Indiana Jones show at Disney World," Thomas said. "Did Hitler actually get the Ark?"

Tony B angrily waved his hand in Thomas's face. The other two angels shrugged.

"What ya think—this is MGM or something?" Tony B asked. This ain't the movies, pal. Didn't you hear anything we've been saying?"

Scribbee quickly intervened. "You're too hard on Mr. Stirk, Anthony."

"Yeah! Cut me some slack, Anthony Cloutus," Thomas sarcastically jibed.

"Someone needs to jerk a knot in your suck-up chain, pal," Tony B said, moving in front of Thomas his wings flapping rapidly.

"Come on, guys. Loosen up," Scribbee said. "Mr. Stirk has discovered something worth dying for."

Tony B and JJ backed away, acknowledging Scribbee's point.

So the next big question, Mr. Stirk," Scribbee continued, "is whether there is anything in your life worth living for?"

43

SEMPER FI

The stage lighting dimmed and went dark. The holographic cube once again appeared in the darkness, this time with a 3-D image of Stacy Howard. Thomas and the angels watched as the scenes began to unfold.

Stacy's dress blue uniform was strikingly handsome. The splendor of the midnight blue blouse and sky blue trousers, trimmed with red and gold command braid said a great deal about the pride and professionalism of the United States Marine Corps. A marine's "dress blues" spoke volumes about the fearless warriors who wore them. The left breast of his jacket displayed the many medals and ribbons from his foreign campaigns. His right jacket breast displayed his Navy Seal Unit emblem and his Marine Airborne medal. His sword was holstered and attached to the white belt around his waist. His white-peaked hat saluted smartly while his short-cropped hair and cleanly shaven face made him look a bit younger than he was.

Stacy Howard didn't look dead, but he was. His young life had ended heroically eight days earlier on a dusty roadside in Iraq. He was only twenty-eight. As the hologram rolled on, Thomas watched himself peering down into the casket at his friend Stacy. Thomas had never seen a dead person before. He recalled how surreal it seemed the first time he peered down at Stacy in the casket.

Challenged by Scribbee's last question, Thomas recalled the funeral of his best friend, who lived his short life serving in the US Marine Corps that he loved. Being a Marine was all Stacy had ever wanted. It was his calling. The Marine Corps completed his life … yes, it made his life worth living. Stacy had something to live for, but now he was dead. Thomas couldn't help but weigh the irony of Stacy's fulfilling yet short life and tragic death.

The images on the holographic screen began fast forwarding as Thomas and the angels watched his sorrow turn to reality. He stood next to the casket, his hand resting on Stacy's left shoulder epaulet.

"Stacy, I miss you, man," Thomas whispered out loud.

Stacy looked so alive Thomas expected any moment he would answer. He didn't.

Thomas wanted to rouse Stacy and say, "Wake up, man, we've got to talk. It's important you know how I feel about you. You're the best friend I ever had. I've got things to say. Things I should've said before and didn't."

Tears filled his eyes and he walked away from the casket. Thomas had never been inside a funeral home before. He'd never given much thought to dying. As he mournfully looked at Stacy, he wondered just where Stacy was now. If he was not in his body in this casket, where did he go? Thomas had no answers. Death and dying were difficult for Thomas to comprehend. He watched himself walk away and recalled his effort to stifle his uncertainty.

Thomas observed the profound sorrow of Stacy's parents as he spoke with them in the viewing parlor. He'd only met them a few times when he and Stacy were in high school. Stacy and Thomas mostly hung out at Thomas's house after school. Thomas had always been pretty sure Stacy's folks never wanted Stacy to spend much time with him because of his well-known reputation for drugs and alcohol.

Stacy's parents were completely destroyed by their son's death. Stacy was their only child and now he was gone. Thomas paid his respects politely to Mr. and Mrs. Howard. He hurt for Stacy's folks, especially because there were only eight persons in the viewing parlor and six of them were the USMC Honor Guard. Where were all his classmates? It was only ten years since they'd both graduated. At least a few of them should be here.

Thomas had been frustrated. He had wanted to go onto the street and scream loud enough for everyone in town to hear. "Wake up! Stacy Howard's lying dead in here. Remember him? Remember Stacy? Come say goodbye. He gave his life for you. Show some respect, you jerks!"

The hologram sped forward a few minutes. Once again, Thomas approached the casket and quietly whispered, "You're my very best friend, Stacy. You're my brother. I'll never have another friend like you." Tears rolled down his cheeks as he quietly sobbed.

Scribbee, JJ, and Tony B watched as a lady in the Honor Guard approached Thomas.

"You were very close to Sergeant Howard?" she asked Thomas. "I was his Gunnery Sergeant. He's an American War Hero." She added emphatically, "He was like my brother, too."

"I'm Thomas Stirk, ma'am. Were you with him in Iraq?"

"I was. Wish you'd call me Gunny, like he did," she invited Thomas.

"He was my very best friend in the whole world, Gunny."

"Copy that, Thomas," Gunny nodded.

"What happened in Iraq, Gunny? I mean, I know he loved the Marines," Thomas asked, wiping the tears from his cheeks. "Was it dangerous duty?"

"Not usually. Sergeant Howard was the US Embassy escort platoon leader. They worked the airport corridor to Baghdad and the Green Zone. That particular day was notable because several bigwig US Congressman were visiting Baghdad. We always worried that if they ran their mouths at the airport before we traveled to the Green Zone, the trip could become dangerous."

"VIP targets, right?"

"Yes, apparently they had mouthed off or let their schedules get out. Somebody screwed up. Anyway, some Jihadists ambushed the convoy about half way to Baghdad. It wasn't pretty. My Humvee took a hit from an IED. All of us were thrown from the vehicle. Stacy dismounted his Browning M2 .50 caliber machine gun, jumping from the safety of his APC and began sweeping the area with covering fire."

She flinched, fighting back her tears.

Gaining control, Gunny continued. "Bad guys seemed to be everywhere in the nearby trees. Stacy popped at least twenty-two enemy and held them down until the rest of the convoy could begin spraying the area with defensive fire. Saved my ass and all my guys. Firefight lasted about five minutes. There were forty dead enemy and not even one of my guys was lost in the battle. The fight was over."

"Stacy was always brave like that. He was never a coward about anything," Thomas confirmed.

"We all were standing at the side of the road checking on the VIPs when, from out of nowhere—without even a sound—came a .50-caliber round that hit Stacy in the neck. Damn near decapitated him. He never knew what hit him." Gunny paused briefly. "All we saw was a puff of smoke from the edge of a rooftop. My guys took out the sniper. The medics air evacuated Stacy immediately. Just no hope."

Gunny looked at Stacy resting peacefully in his casket.

"So he never suffered?" Thomas inquired.

"Never," Gunny quickly responded. "He was at med central in the Green Zone in five minutes. He's in for the Medal of Honor. He'll get the Silver Star for sure. Stacy Howard's a real American Hero."

It didn't seem right. Only eight or ten people at Stacy's laying out. It was unforgivable. Where was the appreciation? He had given the ultimate. He had given his life.

At least the local newspaper should run Stacy's story above the fold in tomorrow's paper, but Thomas knew that would not happen. Tomorrow, the front page would no doubt be dominated by the annual Wine Tasting Festival or the Southeastern Birds of Prey fundraiser or some other irrelevant story about some local fluffy, feel good organization the newspaper could thoughtlessly print because of freedoms secured by sacrifices of heroes like Stacy Howard. Tomorrow, Charlestonians would continue their lives unaware that one of the country's bravest heroes had paid the ultimate price for freedom and was being laid to rest.

The video fast-forwarded a few minutes showing scenes from the next day at the graveside. Twelve people aside from

Stacy's parents showed up for the service. Seven of them were the Marine Honor guard and some of the others may have been from the funeral home. It was disgraceful.

Thomas and the angels watched as the Marine Honor Guard Commander accepted the folded American flag from the six Marine pallbearers and handed it to Stacy's parents. One of the Marine Honor Guard played taps as the rest saluted their fallen comrade. The Gunny Sergeant presented Stacy's sword and a beautifully framed mahogany shadow box case with all of his awards and medals to Stacy's mom. The Honor Guard re-grouped and fired a 21-gun salute. The service was beautiful with due military honors shown to Sergeant Howard.

Thomas stood as the Marine Honor guard thanked Mr. and Mrs. Howard for their son's sacrifice. Gunny told Stacy's parents they would each never forget Stacy. She asked God to bless Stacy's family. Then, backing off several steps, they all saluted and loudly proclaimed in unison, "Semper Fi! Forever our brother."

Thomas was alone at the graveside as the gravediggers lowered the vault into the ground and began shoveling dirt. He sat down on one of the green covered folding chairs under the tent with his coat draped over his shoulder, shading himself from the hot sun.

The civilian pastor who had preached the short message of hope and prayed at the graveside service was leaving the cemetery. As he drove past the funeral plot, he noticed Thomas sitting alone under the green tent. The pastor parked his car and joined Thomas.

"Son, would you like me to pray with you?" the pastor gently offered as Thomas looked up at him.

"Life is totally insane, pastor," Thomas replied, shaking his head in disbelief.

"Can really seem that way at times," the pastor softly countered as he sat down beside Thomas.

"Stacy was meant to live." Thomas looked at the pastor, his eyes flooded with questions for which he had no answers. "Stacy found something worth living for. He loved being a Marine. Stacy was a winner."

"He was a real hero," the pastor agreed, "a Medal of Honor nomination. Doesn't happen that often."

"So why didn't he live?" Thomas asked the pastor, who really had no answers, only questions just like Thomas.

"Only God the Father knows, son."

"So pastor, if winners die, do losers have any chance at all?" Thomas buried his face in his hands and sobbed softly.

The hologram faded to darkness and the stage lighting came up.

44

GOOD ENOUGH TO LIVE FOR

Stacy had been dead for over a year now, but Thomas's memories of his best friend still haunted him. He was a winner and he was gone. Stacy's death only worsened the hopeless irony of searching for anything in his life worth living for. Thomas wished he could forget.

Fully awake now, Thomas wondered how long he'd been sleeping. He looked around. Where was everyone? His angel interrogators were gone. Unexpectedly, Thomas felt a twinge of fear in his gut. Where were the angels, he wondered. He struggled against his restraints. He was still tied down, but now he was totally alone on the stage. He could hear nothing and could see only empty darkness beyond the foot lights.

Thomas actually missed the angels. How could he miss their interrogations? They were freaking hammering him from all sides. They were ripping his life apart and exposing all his garbage, so why should he miss them? He was perplexed.

"Ms. Scribbee, ma'am?" Thomas called out, but got no reply. Then, he yelled louder again. Still, he received no answer. His voice echoed off the walls as if he were in a deep canyon. Anxiety enveloped him. Was he alone in this giant auditorium? Was he abandoned?

"Tony B, JJ?" Thomas shouted. "Where are you guys?" No answer. Thomas tried to fight off his panic and stay calm. He realized he was most concerned because he didn't have the angels to talk with. Even though they were his jailers, his interrogators, somehow that didn't matter. Thomas wanted their company.

Thomas tried to relax. He occupied himself thinking of all he and the angels had discussed. After what seemed like hours, Thomas glanced off to his right and saw three persons approaching from what appeared to be a very long distance. It was as if they were miles away, tiny specks on the horizon. Strange, Thomas thought, they should seem so far away yet still be inside this building.

Then, all of a sudden, the three angels were much closer and Thomas recognized them. This gave him a deep satisfaction, which surprised him a little.

"You're awake now?" Tony B asked as the angels approached Thomas. "It's been a long night. We thought you might appreciate some shut eye."

"So, Stirk," JJ quickly upped the dialogue, "find anything in your life worth living for? Find your Promised Land?"

"I've got no Promised Land. I got nothing," Thomas dejectedly answered, lowering his head to his chest.

"Everyone should have a Promised Land," Tony B insisted as Thomas lifted his chin, looking up at Tony B. "You've just got to go in and take it. You've got to conquer it."

Thomas looked up. He felt lost and worthless. "Not me, I'm a total loser. I'm kinda floating, going from one gig to the next, always roaming in someone else's wilderness, throwing rocks at other people's stuff, smoking other people's grass. I got nothing. I got no life. I can't remember what feeling good feels like. Remember that feeling when you're all happy inside, like on Christmas Eve when you were a kid? Where did that kind of happy-feel-good go?"

Scribbee quickly encouraged Thomas, "You don't have to stay that way, Mr. Stirk. You can have a life. You can find your Promised Land. Happy-feel-good is not lost. Get to know God, Mr. Stirk." Her wings danced.

"Speaking of throwing rocks," JJ said, nudging in front of Scribbee, "ever heard of King David, Stirk?"

"Never," Thomas replied, his lack of biblical knowledge oddly causing him some shame.

"King David was one of the famous Kings of Israel and lived about 350 years after the Hebrews took their Promised Land," JJ said.

Thomas could hear JJ talking about King David, but suddenly a strange feeling came over him. JJ's voice faded but his lips were still moving. Thomas felt free. He felt his bindings had come loose. He was sitting in his chair but his body seemed totally unbound. At first, he was afraid to test the bindings but knew he had to try. He inched his body to his right and felt no restraint. He lifted his legs and found them loose and free at the ankles.

Thomas knew he had to try to stand. He moved forward in the seat, braced his legs, placed his hands on the side of the chair and boosted himself. Suddenly, he was standing. His legs were wobbly but he could walk. He was free!

Exuberantly, Thomas yelled at the angels as if they couldn't see for themselves. "Hey, you guys! I'm standing. I'm free. I'm walking around with you guys. Is this for real? What happened to the ropes or whatever? How'd you guys tie me up, anyway?"

Tony B shrugged, muffled his tone, and said, "What can I say, Stirk? Your ecclesiastical time out is over. It's in the secret of the knots, pal, and you can see you're freed up now."

"Hey man, don't jerk any knots on me, okay?"

JJ chuckled. "Wish I could, Stirk. Would love nothing better than to see you trip over your suck-up chain. But I can't, pal."

"Okay, whatever." Thomas said.

Thomas picked up the oak chair and turned the back toward the audience. Then, he sat backwards in the chair, resting his elbows on the back splat. He faced the angel trio.

Turning quickly toward JJ, Thomas asked, "So, okay, what were you saying about King David? I'm guessin King David must've had a Promised Land or something. Right?"

"Welcome aboard, Stirk. Glad to have you with us, pal," JJ assured Thomas with a big smile. "You're right. King David lived in God's Promised Land. He was a covenant man, a relationship guy, a God-follower and a brave warrior."

"When David was a teenage shepherd boy, Israel was at war with the Philistines. This 10-foot-tall Philistine giant, Goliath, lived in the valley. Goliath challenged Israel to a kind of a duel. You know, a one-on-one fight to the death. Winner takes all. The prize was Israel, God's Promised Land."

"The guy was that tall? Unbelievable!" Thomas exclaimed, gesturing widely with his arms. "That's ginormous. Winner takes all? You mean like the whole country of Israel?"

Scribbee nodded. "Correct, Thomas. Whoever won took Israel. But God had assigned JJ to the Elah Valley that day. So, JJ, tell Mr. Stirk about the battle with Goliath and about David's courage."

"Stirk, as hard as it is to believe, none of Israel's brave warriors would fight Goliath," JJ began, his eyes reflecting intense eyewitness knowledge of the battle scene. "For more than forty days, Goliath mocked and taunted the Israeli camp while King Saul and his army trembled, cowering from the fight."

"Like anyone could win that one. Going one on one with a 10-foot Titanic man? I'd be outta there too,"

"David, the shepherd boy, didn't run. All David could see was his land, his way of life, his people, and his family threatened by the ungodly Philistines. David stepped up and faced off against Goliath in the name of the Lord of Hosts, the God of the Israelites," JJ excitedly recounted, his wings beginning to flutter.

JJ's arms were animated and pointed toward the imagined giant as he spoke. "David used no sword. He declined the battle shield and body armor he was offered. His only weapon was his leather sling and a stone." JJ swung his arms as though he were rotating a sling. "And with the powerful speed of his whirling sling, David let go his stone and struck Goliath directly between the eyes, killing him instantly. Amazingly, the little shepherd boy had slain the Philistine giant and saved Israel."

Thomas was spellbound by JJ's first-hand account.

"That shepherd boy was good and he loved God," Tony B said, "but I've got to tell you, Stirk, JJ had made certain the boy's stones were perfectly balanced and smooth and insured the wind was calm so David's trajectory would be true. By angelic standards, Goliath had no chance, but David didn't know that."

"Mr. Stirk," Scribbee picked up the story, "David had something worth living for, God's Promised Land, God's gift to David's people, his family's inheritance. David was determined that no uncircumcised heathen Philistine, no matter how big, was going to take from him and his people all the magnificent blessings God had given Israel."

"So, Ms. Scribbee, ma'am," Thomas said as he stood and stepped in front of the oak chair facing Scribbee. "So it was worth fighting for and maybe worth dying for because it was worth living for?"

"Halleluiah, Praise God!" Tony B shouted, his arms lifted toward heaven. "I believe he gets it, guys. Score a big one for Stirk."

Thomas quickly paced a dozen or so steps then came back to the oak chair and sat down. He buried his head in his hands.

"I'm confused," Thomas said as he covered his eyes. He let out a sob.

"Crying is good for the soul, Thomas. Don't be ashamed. Let go! Let the cleansing tears flow," Scribbee said and rested her hand on his shoulder.

Continuing to sob, Thomas removed his hands from his face. Tears flowed down his cheeks. He looked up at Scribbee. "Hey, I'm losing it. Jesus-God, death-dying, life-living? It's all so confusing. How do you rise from the dead? I mean, death is the scary end, the final finito."

Scribbee gently assured Thomas, "If you know God, there's only a wispy little skip between life and death and absolutely nothing to fear."

He covered his face, which concealed his tears but didn't silence his whimpering. The finality of death had always plagued Thomas. He was terrified of the unknown, of nothingness. The haunting thought of endlessly drifting alone in nothingness, a black void, sent him over his mental cliff.

"But Ms. Scribbee, ma'am," Thomas blurted, his tears blurring her soft features. "Death is all there is. It's totally like the last verse of everything. Is there really for real a Heaven? Like a paradise where hurt-never-is and happy-feel-good-lives?"

"Well, aside from the fact that Tony B, JJ and I live and work in Heaven," Scribbee quickly affirmed, "consider the fact that Heaven is cited 691 times in God's Sacred Book. I can tell you God would never allow such creative liberty if it wasn't true."

"Even if there is a Heaven, I've never known God. I've never even read His Sacred Book. No way God wants to know me," Thomas confessed to the angels, continuing to sob softly.

"Just let the cleansing tears flow, Mr. Stirk," Scribbee repeated, placing her hand on his shoulder.

Abruptly, Thomas sat up, wiping the tears from his face. He pleaded with the angel trio. "Please, you guys, listen! I'm nobody. I'm totally worthless. I'm a total loser. I got nowhere to go and I can't get there."

JJ quickly repeated Stirk's admission. "You got nowhere to go and you can't get there? Sounds like you're totally cashed in, pal."

Slowly, Thomas's sobbing stopped. He wiped his cheeks dry with the back of his hand. Thomas felt a freedom. He felt somehow less burdened. It seemed the weight and guilt of all his garbage was suddenly gone. Wiped clean. He was new and different but didn't understand why or how exactly. He stood and turned to Scribbee, Tony B and JJ. Each of them smiled at him, not condemning smirks, but the warmest, most radiant welcome home greetings.

Tony B picked up the protest sign Thomas had carried down the aisle earlier that evening and pointed to the 'CELEBRATE LIFE' message.

"Easter's not about Jesus' death, Thomas Stirk," he said. "Oh, for sure Jesus died on the cross, the perfect Passover lamb on Passover weekend. Was that perfect timing or what? God's perfect dramatic moment."

"His blood is available for your doorpost too, Thomas—to save you like God saved the Jews in Egypt," JJ interjected, his wings fluttering excitedly. "Jesus died for you and all mankind."

Tony B continued, his gaze fixed on Thomas. "Jesus' crucifixion was all about the stone, Thomas—the rolling away of the stone and the empty sepulcher. His crucifixion was about the resurrection of life. It's all about His living—not about his dying."

Thomas looked questioningly at the angel trio. "The stone? What stone?"

"The stone that sealed Jesus' tomb. Remember, we told you? We rolled away that stone the very first Easter Sunday morning over two thousand years ago," Scribbee reminded Thomas, her wings quivering briefly.

JJ promptly reminded Thomas, "Rolling away the sepulcher stone was the most exciting day of our careers."

"Thomas Houston Stirk," Scribbee said, motioning for him to stand. She removed a replica sepulcher stone pendant from around her neck, hewn in an exact copy of the round milling stone that sealed Jesus' tomb. "God followers sometimes wear a cross around their necks. Instead, I wear this sepulcher stone replica. It always reminds me the stone was rolled away and Jesus walked out of the tomb alive. He still lives. Please take it." She placed the pendant around his neck.

"I can't accept this Ms. Scribbee, ma'am. It's yours."

"I insist. I have many more," Ms. Scribbee implored Thomas. "This will remind you that God lives."

"God is not dead, Thomas Stirk. He's alive. He lives," Tony B encouraged. His wings fluttered with the excitement of the Easter message.

Thomas, only partially convinced, questioned Tony B again. "So He's alive? Why can't I see him? I've heard all those TV preachers scream, 'Have faith. Just believe.' They want everyone to believe in stuff they can't see and stuff those preachers can't show anyone. That's some serious brain strain, Tony B."

Scribbee jumped in. "Might help if we explain that during the forty days Jesus was on earth after His resurrection more than 500 of his followers, the first believers, saw Him and were with Him. Believing was easy for them because they saw Him."

Tony B followed Scribbee's insight. "Thomas, never forget Jesus said, 'Blessed are they that did not see and yet believed.'"

"Find your promised land, Thomas Stirk," Scribbee gently encouraged. "Let this sepulcher stone pendant always remind you He Lives, and find your life worth living. God's blessings are promised to all his people. Just ask."

She closed the pendant clasp, assuring the stone was fastened around Thomas's neck. Her tiny wings quivered flat against her arms.

45

THE ROOKIES NEST

Thomas was feeling much better. His fears relaxed and his anguish waned as he stood with the angel trio around the oak chair on the stage. Earlier, he'd stripped off his black T-shirt and turned it backwards. The *CIT SON GA* insult was now across his back, hidden under his black sports jacket.

Tony B rested his hands on the back splat of the chair as he looked at Thomas. He said, "We've all done a lot of talking around this chair tonight. You've got to be tired of sitting, Stirk. What if we all take a little walk? I'll bet you could use some exercise."

"I think I'd like that," Thomas agreed.

"Well, everyone, come along and follow me. I think we'll all enjoy a trip to the Rookies Nest." Tony B waved his hand to follow.

Thomas didn't ask about the Rookies Nest. He was certain he would find out soon enough. As he was about to descend the stage steps, he saw the protest sign he'd dropped when his

Sea Island encounter began. Now the *"Celebrate Life-Not Death"* message had real meaning. Thomas was beginning to understand *seeing with the eyes of your heart.* He saw the value in a *life worth living.*

He was still having some difficulty understanding why his life was worth dying for. Why Jesus would pay the ultimate price for such a lost and worthless soul as Thomas Stirk belied all human logic.

Thomas felt almost happy inside. He loved his angel friends. They'd made him a part of their family. The angels loved him enough to tell him the hard truth, even though it hurt. He still had trouble believing they loved him despite knowing all the garbage in his life. Being loved as he was, unconditionally, was a new concept for him.

Thomas was beginning to see his angel friends with the *eyes of his heart.* He could feel it, the value of real love. He felt free and honest, clean and fresh, for the first time in his life. Everything around him smelled better, like being in a country meadow after a spring shower.

As Thomas and the angels moved toward the back of the auditorium, he could see no one in the audience on either side of the dimly lit aisle, but he sensed they were quietly watching as he and the angels passed. Somehow that didn't concern him, despite the fact they had watched his soul stripped naked as his life was exposed for all to see. That didn't matter now. His life was an open book, and his journey was just beginning.

Thomas listened to the angels' affable conversation as they walked up the aisle. The distance to the exit doors seemed endless. Each time Thomas looked, the doors seemed a little farther away. It was odd but Thomas didn't mind. He enjoyed just sauntering along, listening to the trio's rich memories from past millennia. He liked the whole love and trust concept; it was a totally new awareness for him. He'd never felt so much a part of any group before. He liked the feeling.

When the dialogue finally began to wane, Thomas and the angel trio reached the elusive sanctuary doors.

They stood in front of two massive mahogany doors. The doors were intricately carved, embellished with Seraphim and Cherubim surrounded by mighty archangels.

The archangels were authoritative, almighty, loving, and not the least bit vengeful. The archangels were ecclesiastical yet ecumenical and eclectic. One look at this barrier would give anyone the impression that behind the doors had to be a holy place.

The doors had no doorknobs or locks. There was no keyhole. There were no hinges. There were no handle pulls. Their massive size and height seemed hostile at a distance, like a moated fortress. However, Thomas sensed the doors were not to keep people out but to welcome everyone in.

Tony B gave the colossal doors a gentle nudge. They opened outward, inviting the group into the vast space. The walls, rising from the light gray floor, never seemed to reach a ceiling. Thomas thought it odd, but everything in the room seemed far away but at the same time easily accessible. The room was lighted with soft white light, subtle illumination that softly shimmered from above; there were no visible light fixtures or lamps.

The room was so gigantic and endless that Thomas exclaimed to Tony B, "Awesome! Is this infinity?"

"Not exactly," Tony B replied, knowing Thomas would understand soon enough.

The room was filled with thousands of folks all dressed in white pullovers, white trousers, and white sneakers. Their outfits matched the angel trio, except none had wings or SWAT printed on their pullovers.

Everyone was milling about and seemed to be moving deeper into the immense room, randomly stopping to talk with others in small groups.

There were no windows or other doors in the room. The temperature was comfortable, cool but not cold. There were no loud noises, just a gentle murmur of low voices. There were some young folks, but most were seniors. All ethnicities seemed present. Thomas assumed they were from various nationalities from all over the world. Everyone was in mixed groups. Skin color seemed to disappear. Everyone was happily chatting with each other and language wasn't a barrier.

Thomas felt torrents of joy flooding every corner of the space. Joy and love cascaded over him, enveloping him; he felt embraced but without constraint.

Suddenly, Thomas realized he saw no children or infants in the crowd. Just as the thought crossed his mind, he caught a glimpse of a pair of tall golden arches. There must be a heavenly kid's nursery and playground with unlimited happy meals and ice cream with sprinkles, all supplied by some very special guardian angels. Thomas spread his arms, gesturing the room's vastness to Tony B.

"What is this place? This is about the most ginormous, humongous place I've ever seen," he excitedly asked Ms. Scribbee.

"Transition, Mr. Stirk," she answered. "We thought it would be good for you to see the transition place. We call it the Rookies Nest, because it's where newly transitioned believers and God-followers come to begin their *life after living*—their evolution to Heaven." Scribbee's wings fluttered rapidly. "From here, they go on to the Heavenlies of their choice. Many choose family reunions, others choose contented solitude, and some are pleased to stay with their new friends. By the time they reach the end of this room, their decisions have been made and they travel onward to their chosen Heavenlies."

"Everyone seems so happy, so joyful, ma'am. They're so contented and peaceful," Thomas observed.

"All the folks in the Rookies Nest are naturally happy and joyful," Scribbee continued. "They're happy because during their *life worth living*, they were God followers and trusted God while living on earth, so in their *life after living*, they are happy and contented as well. It's God's natural order of things, Thomas."

Tony B turned to Thomas, placing a firm hand on his shoulder. He said, "Stirk, we have another reason for bringing you here today. There's someone we want you to meet. She recently arrived from your hometown, Charleston. Would you like to meet her?"

"Yeah! Totally. Completely cool. Anything I shouldn't say?" Thomas asked.

"Say anything you like. Just remember everyone in the Rookies Nest is happy to be here and would never go back to the *life worth living*," Tony B cautioned. Before he'd even finished, a young lady began moving toward them from a very long distance away.

As Thomas squinted to see her, he was surprised to find the young lady was almost upon them. Tears were streaming down her cheeks. She walked passed Thomas to greet Tony B, Scribbee and JJ. They each embraced her warmly.

"My life is so incredibly wonderful now," she cried tears of joy. "How can I ever thank you for saving me? For giving me new life and bringing me here?"

She was beautiful—a total knockout. Thomas guessed she was in her mid-to-late twenties. She had shoulder length blond hair. Her face was Scandinavian. She was fresh and wholesome looking. Thomas had no time to think. He had always been klutzy around women, and especially good-looking women totally freaked him out.

"Codi, there's someone we'd like you to meet," JJ comforted her, his hand on her shoulder. They turned toward Thomas, and she wiped the tears from her cheeks.

"Codi, this is Thomas Houston Stirk. He's from Charleston, where we discovered you."

As they shook hands, she said, "Pleasure, Thomas Stirk, I'm Codi."

The moment was electric. She was so sensationally gorgeous. Thomas was completely blown away. Her eyes seemed to gently beckon Thomas. He was sure he'd never met anyone as beautiful. Where had she been? She was the girl Thomas had always dreamed of.

Codi smiled and announced before Thomas could speak, "Actually, Thomas, you probably don't remember, but we met once before."

Surprised and shocked, Thomas blurted, "I apologize, Codi. I should know—I mean should remember—someone as pretty as you. I mean how could anyone forget you? I mean how could I have forgotten," he paused.

"Maybe you'll recall I was wearing a red dress and sitting next to you at Arthur's on King in Charleston just last month," Codi said. "But I think you may have been too smashed to notice." She pummeled Thomas.

Embarrassed and blushing now, Thomas attempted to recover, "Oh yes Codi. Okay! Wow. Okay, Solo told me. You're the girl in the red dress?"

"I am," Codi answered, a smile on her face.

"I apologize for being such a lush that night. Was totally uncool. Really. Should never have behaved so badly."

"You were completely smashed," Codi said.

"Some of that evening is coming back to me," Thomas anxiously began. "I don't mean to be rude, but do you have a triangular birth mark behind you right ear?"

"You mean this?"

Codi brushed her hair back, turning so Thomas could observe the small mark.

"Yes. Of course. That's it. What is your full name, Codi?" Thomas asked.

"Rachael Codi Joseph, the one and only."

"Are you *THE* Rachael Codi Joseph, who owns a black Denali SUV, with North Carolina plates?"

"I am."

"The Charleston Police and everyone are looking for you. Do you know you're missing? We've all been trying to find you. I've been hoping to find you."

"I know I'm missing. But now you've found me, Thomas. I know I've caused everyone tons of trouble."

As Thomas began to understand, he was stunned and confused. He'd found Rachael C. Joseph. He was relieved. She was here, alive and in person. The search was over.

But then Thomas quickly realized she wasn't on earth. She was in Heaven. Thomas's heart sank. But she didn't feel dead. Her touch was warm and firm. Her eyes sparkled. Her tears were real. More desperately than anything he'd ever felt in his life, Thomas wanted her to be alive.

46

SCUMBAGS & ANGELS

Thomas noticed Ms. Scribbee, Tony B and JJ off to the side, politely listening to his conversation with Codi as if they were hearing her story for the first time.

Now that Thomas had found Rachael Codi Joseph, he was even more confounded. Thomas wanted to ask Scribbee how Codi could be so alive in the Rookies Nest. He wanted to scream out loud at the top of his lungs: "Codi's been found! She's alive! Like totally fully alive! Like seriously touching, speaking, walking around alive." Thomas needed Scribbee to explain.

"Codi, it was like no one could find you the next day," Thomas eagerly explained. "You were missing like you'd never been there. The police found your SUV with me locked in the back seat, but no keys, no registration, nothing. You just totally vanished."

Thomas paused as Codi's smile seemed to fade a bit. Her eyes urged him on.

"I've been so stressed. I've been expecting to be arrested any day for kidnapping because you were missing. But now you're found and I'm so thankful. You're so lucky to be here. I don't know what to tell everyone looking for you."

Thomas paused again, shifting closer to Codi. He grasped her hand, restoring her slight smile.

"Codi, I know you probably don't want to talk about it, but I've got to know what happened at Arthur's Pub that night."

"It's a long story," she began, releasing her grip. "You'll think shamefully of me."

She contritely smiled, as they both glanced at the angels, who quickly avoided their gaze and pretended to be indisposed.

"Codi, nothing you've ever done would come anywhere close to the grief I've caused people with the garbage in my life. Solo told me about those coke heads you were with at Arthur's."

"You've got to understand, Thomas, I never used. I was never a junkie," Codi insisted, hoping Thomas would understand. "Those guys were just clients. It was only business. That was my business. I arranged private parties, drug parties, coke, pot, and scripts—whatever. I paid off seventy thousand in student loans in less than a year. I never used. I don't even drink." Codi looked at the angels, hoping for some confirmation.

"How can I fault you, Codi? I pushed on the street for a couple of years. Only difference is I never made squat and was my own most expensive junkie. You never used, made tons of cash and spent it wisely."

"My two clients at Arthur's were high rollers—attorneys. They paid me six grand to furnish the coke. They demanded only the best blow. It was a service and I was paid well. I only dealt with fat cats, carefully vetted clients with deep pockets. Most were well connected," she explained.

"Wow, Codi, I'm impressed. Paid off all your student loans—how totally impressive."

Thomas looked at the angels, who had non-reproachful, gentle smiles on their faces. Their wings gently fluttered.

"I was lucky, Thomas, and I promise you I never used. My biggest and best client was a senator from North Carolina. Met him through a mutual friend of one of his assistants. The senator was hooked on the stuff and needed someone to supply his addiction. I did a poolside party every two months at his gorgeous country estate, just outside of DC. He'd invite all the beautiful people. I furnished the scripts, coke and pot. His people furnished the alcohol and other entertainment. His parties were totally insane, but he paid thirty grand cash for my stuff six times a year."

"Amazing! You were careful and smart. I can tell you never used. I believe you, Codi, but what happened at Arthur's that night?" Thomas asked.

"I put my clients in a cab around 4:30 a.m. and headed for my car. I was going to drive back to Raleigh, except those two goons you were with jumped me in the parking lot. They pulled a gun."

"Codi, I swear, I didn't even know them. I'd never seen them before. You've got to believe me. They just showed up and sat next to me at the bar and began buying me drinks."

"I managed to get away from them in the parking lot then tried to outrun them. I finally lost them. I knew they'd find me if I stayed with my SUV. I had to ditch it and run." Codi paused and Thomas listened anxiously when she continued, "I drove up on the sidewalk in a park near the water. I took the keys, insurance papers, registration, everything from the glove box. As I got out, I saw you totally passed out in the back seat."

Thomas shrugged and lowered his eyes.

"Since those foreign punks and I both had black SUV's parked side by side," Codi continued, "I guess they dumped you in my back seat by mistake after they carried you out of Arthur's. I looked into the back seat and saw two angels sitting with you." She turned to Tony B and JJ. "I didn't know them at the time, but I do now."

"Wow! Really?"

"I could tell you were safe. Anyway, I locked the SUV and ran for the bus station, which was the only establishment open at 5:30 in the morning. I rented lock box 321, knowing I could never forget the box number. I placed all my valuables, my purse, wallet with fourteen thousand in cash, insurance, and registration documents in the locker. I flushed the key down the toilet in the women's room. I wanted no ID if they caught me."

"Where'd you go when you left the bus station?"

"I started toward downtown. I was trying to find a big hotel so I could hang out in the lobby, but I never found one."

JJ gently interrupted. "The two thugs spotted Codi walking down lower King Street toward town and parked their vehicle around a corner, waiting for her at the next intersection. From behind some tall shrubbery in front of one of the row houses, they stealthily waited as she approached."

Codi continued. "I was just starting across the street when suddenly I was grabbed and pulled behind some bushes. They cuffed and blindfolded me and taped my mouth shut," Codi recalled, beginning to sob. "They loaded me into their SUV, saying, 'We not hurt you, missy.'"

"I heard one of them say 'up East Bay.' They drove about five or six minutes. I remember it smelled like the ocean when they took me out of the back seat."

JJ filled in some more gaps. "Two crew members escorted Codi up a gangway and onto the deck of the large yacht. Then, they led her down two flights of steps to the engine room."

"It hurt when they jerked the tape off my mouth. I could see I was in a clean white room with two very large engines. They wanted to know where to find Anthony Reyes. I told them I'd never heard of him before."

"Actually, Thomas, I never met up with Anthony Reyes, my supplier. I had never met him in person. We were supposed to have met that night at Arthur's. I had eight grand for him. Reyes knew I would be at the bar in a red dress, but he never showed.

"They kept me prisoner in that locker until yesterday. The only light was from a single small porthole about nine feet above the floor. There was nothing I could stand on to look out.

"The ship's nameplate on the bulkhead of my prison locker revealed I was aboard the Hocus Pocus from Columbia, South America."

"South American drug thugs, probably the cartel. How perilous is that?" Thomas angrily said.

"Absolutely, they were dangerous. No doubt about it. They were looking for Antonio Reyes.

"About noon on my first day in the prison locker, I found a long brass screw in a shallow crevice. I knew I needed to keep track of the time. I had no idea how long they would hold me, so I scratched a line on the orange bulk head under the ship's nameplate at around noon the first day and then scratched another at noon each day thereafter. I scratched a straight line for weekdays and Saturdays, and a crooked S for Sundays," Codi recalled with a pained look on her face.

"How moxie is that, Codi? Incredible. Really smart and so cool in such a scary situation. Not many people would think of that."

"Wasn't really cool. I was always so frightened. They were merciless mobsters and killers. They would take me out of the locker two or three times a week. Each time, they would cuff me to the stair ladder, slap me around, and threaten me with their guns. One time, they put a gun to my head and pulled the trigger two times. I just about never recovered from that little charade."

She flinched, bowing her head and looking down. Scribbee, JJ and Tony B watched from a short distance. They heard all Codi was saying and their wings twitched nervously at the horrid tales they had witnessed first hand.

"Solid courageous, Codi," Thomas added.

"I had no choice. I was a prisoner. I didn't realize what I'd lost till I didn't have it at all."

"No one would, Codi."

"They were the meanest people I've ever seen. I could never have imagined in my worst dreams. They burned my face with cigarettes at least six or seven times." She rubbed her cheeks feeling for the scabs. "The scabs have fallen off, I guess, but I know my face will be scarred forever."

Thomas said nothing. He was standing close enough to her that he could see the smooth unblemished skin of her cheeks. There were no scars, only many tiny areas that were slightly rosier.

"Some in the crew brought me food and water," Codi continued. "After about a week, those same guys began bringing me extra water and asking me if I had enough to eat. It wasn't great but even little things were encouraging.

"I felt so guilty. I had abandoned God. I prayed to God every day and attended church regularly until I began the drug thing. I let big drug money ruin my life. When the money began rolling in, I didn't need God anymore. I just drifted away and forgot Him. I knew I was very wrong."

Codi looked over at Scribbee, Tony B and JJ repentantly. Their wings shuttered curtly as if to acknowledge Codi's confession.

"I began to seek God again. I prayed every day. I told God I was lost and had forsaken Him and deserved nothing. I confessed my sins. I asked him to forgive me for turning away from Him. I begged for his mercy. I told him it was fast money, easy drug money that pulled me away. I confessed my shame and asked God to please take care of my family. I knew I had hurt them badly," Codi finished as tears streamed down her face.

"I understand," Thomas said.

"Then, totally amazingly, Thomas, God spoke to me as I was praying one night. It was like an audible, clear voice and God told me He would rescue me. It was truly awesome. I knew it was God."

"Really? Wow. Awesome!"

"When the crew took me out of my prison locker, my stickman calendar showed the fourth day after the fourth Sunday."

"You'd been in that steel storage locker for about a month," Thomas calculated.

"Yes, actually maybe just over a month. I recall thinking how fast the time passed. I don't recall much after that thought. It all seems blurry, almost like waking from an exciting dream before it ended and trying to remember the finale. I remember they took me onto the stern deck. It was cold and dark. I was so frightened my whole body was trembling, but I never forgot God told me He would rescue me."

She paused.

"Go on," Thomas said encouragingly.

"Everything else is fuzzy. I think I remember a Mexican guy with a ski mask telling me in very broken English, 'Missy lady, please, I sorry. We no choice you see for us. They kill us, missy. Dios cuida de usted,' I was so terrified I blanked out."

JJ and Tony B, listening off to the side, moved a little closer.

JJ enlightened Codi and Thomas. "She was thrown overboard. Tony B and I grabbed Codi about the time she reached the bottom of the shipping channel. We loosed the chained cement parking lot bumper from her ankles and with Tony B under one arm and me under the other, we propelled her to the surface and beyond to the Rookies Nest."

"Everything is misty, totally hazy," Codi said. "I can't recall anything except I'm certain there was an explosion in the harbor—everything else is fuzzy. But it was very loud with bright orange flashes. Next thing I knew, I was changing into fresh clothes in the Rookies Nest."

She hugged Tony B and JJ.

"So how did you guys know?" Thomas anxiously questioned the angel trio.

"Angels always got your back. It's our job. Codi here was a real catch, like landing a yellow fin tuna," JJ said.

"And hey, underwater is not an angel's most comfortable venue," Tony B emphasized, stroking his left wing gently.

"You, on the other hand, Stirk, were a bottom feeding mullet. You just flopped up on the beach," JJ said, laughing loudly.

Ms. Scribbee moved closer to Thomas and reluctantly advised, "Might want to say your goodbyes to Codi. She has to catch up with the others."

Thomas turned to Codi and grasped her warm hand. "Codi, I just got to know you. I need more time with you. I've never met anyone like you before. I've missed you all my life."

Tears began to glisten on his cheeks. Codi slowly pulled her hand away from Thomas, wiping the tears from his cheeks with her forefinger.

"Thomas, I know we'll meet again someday in the *life after living*," she said.

She turned and began walking away. Thomas watched her disappear into the Rookies Nest crowd.

47

THE NEW LIFE

As he watched Codi disappear, Thomas realized she was the one. He was in love. It happened so quickly, in a matter of minutes, he hadn't seen it coming. His heart told him Codi was the one, the only one—and now she was gone. He would never see her again.

When he and Lestee were dating, Thomas recalled asking his mom how he would know when he was in love. "When it's right, you'll know it, son," she'd told him.

Thomas had never felt really right with Lestee. He'd never experienced that knock-me-over-fall-on-my-knees feeling, even after Lestee was pregnant. It was just never there. He knew what he felt for Codi was real and honest. It wasn't going away.

The thought of never seeing Codi again crushed his spirit. Thomas wondered if God was allowing him to see what he could not have? Was he in the midst of some kind of God "gotcha game" about what his life might have been?

Ms. Scribbee, perceiving Thomas's ache, placed her hand on his shoulder as they all walked toward the doors.

"I know how you feel," she said. "True love is always that way, Thomas. It grabs you, spins you around and won't let go. Honest, committed love is God's most treasured of all relationships. You're very lucky. Few ever really experience it."

Thomas and the trio exited through the massive doors into a small, lush garden just outside the Rookies Nest. Every conceivable flower was blooming in dazzling multi-colored splendor astride a short winding pathway bordered by an ivy covered brick wall. Spring fragrances wafted about, stirred by the wings of white doves feeding among the blossoms. Everything was ordered in perfect harmony.

Thomas sat down on a park bench just off the path. Scribbee sat next to him and was beginning to speak when Thomas interrupted, "I don't even really know Codi, Ms. Scribbee. I just met her. My friend Solo's description wasn't even close. She's the most incredible and beautiful person I've ever known. Why couldn't I have met her before? I'm so ashamed. I was so drunk that night I didn't remember I'd met her. I might have saved her—rescued her. I'm a total loser. Nothing but a coward."

Scribbee listened empathetically. She put her hand on Thomas's shoulder.

"How can I ever change my life without her?" he asked, softly sobbing. "I can see she's my reason for living."

"Just let the tears flow out," Scribbee leaned down and whispered.

"I don't know about God, except what you guys have told me," Thomas continued. "I never even once read God's Sacred Book, not even one time in my whole life. I never cared about God. He was dead for all I knew. God's always been nothing to me. I never wanted Him. I never even thought about Him.

I've hardly ever been in a church—not even once till now. If it was illegal and felt good, I did it."

Thomas wept, covering his face with his hands again. He paused for a long time.

"No way God wants a total loser like me!" he suddenly exclaimed.

"Don't get too down on yourself, Thomas," Tony B suggested. "The bad stuff always feels really good. Makes you feel super ripped. No boundaries, livin' in the zone—the demon zone. Instant happy high—then you crash and die."

JJ quickly continued, "Satan invented the counter culture lifestyle and made up that stuff about *if it feels good just do it*," JJ said. "He knows the rebellious nature of man and what tickles his desires." JJ paused briefly and then continued once he caught Thomas's eye. "And, Thomas, don't be too hard on yourself about not going to church. Remember, God's church is in your heart."

JJ's wings jounced smartly. He stood in front of Thomas, motioned for him to stand then pulled him into an embrace.

"Stirk, man, I love you," JJ said to a surprised Thomas. "You pass my test anytime. And lots of folks never take the time to meet their creator. Good news is you don't have to be one of them."

As JJ released his clutch, Thomas smiled gratefully. Again, he felt fully accepted and loved. Tony B reached out, took Thomas by the hand and drew him into a hug.

"We all love you, Thomas," he said. "Let God into your life and begin taking out those giant Goliaths, pal. Rise up from Satan's death word and walk out of the tomb. Find your promised land as a born again child of God."

As Tony B let go his embrace, Scribbee moved in front of Thomas with a warm smile as she fluffed the collar on Thomas's wrinkled jacket.

"I've acquired some wisdom with my age, Thomas Stirk. Would you listen to some maternal counsel?"

"You know I will, Ms. Scribbee, ma'am."

Her voice gentle but commanding, Ms. Scribbee began, "When you know God and His promises, there is no fear of death. Transitioning to the *life after living* is a seamless experience and holds no fear. Once you know him, the *life worth living* on God's earth will be so much happier. *Happy-feel-good* was never lost, Thomas. Invite God to come and live in your heart. Enjoy his abundant blessings on His earth. God wants to live with you and dwell in your heart. He is absolutely always faithful to those who seek Him."

Scribbee spoke with Godly authority as she motioned to Thomas to sit on the park bench.

"Please take a seat here, Thomas," she said. "Talk to God. He's here right now. Ask him to come into your life."

Thomas sat. He bowed his head and rested his face in his opened palms. Tony B, JJ and Scribbee gathered behind Thomas, each of them placing a hand on his head, their other arm lifted toward heaven. They interceded in prayer with God the Father. Thomas continued to weep softly.

For the first time in his life, Thomas let go his inhibitions and his fears. Everything was quiet and peaceful. Somehow, even with his eyes closed, he could see the myriad of flowers in the garden. Time seemed to stop and allow him just to hang out for a while and tell God in his own way about all his hang-ups, his alcoholism, his drug addiction, his fears, his sins and his wasted years. He confessed everything, telling God he'd never read His Holy Book and how ashamed he was of his useless life. Confession swept clean the dark corners of his heart. He began feeling scoured and fresh. Everything just spilled out. Finally, Thomas asked God to come live in his heart.

As he sat on the park bench, deep in prayerful solitude, he heard someone speak, "I truly am the I AM, my son."

The voice startled Thomas and he sat up. He stood and wiped the tears from his eyes and searched for the angel trio.

"Who is that?" he asked. "Who said that? Ms. Scribbee, Tony B, JJ? Where are you guys? You can't leave me now. I talked to God. I asked him to come into my heart."

Thomas turned his head toward the corner of the small garden. Silhouetted against the ivy-covered wall, stood Jesus.

Astounded, Thomas blurted out, "Jesus! Father God!"

Jesus walked toward Thomas. He said, "To know me is to see me. Here am I, Thomas."

"Please forgive me," Thomas stuttered.

"I once knew another doubting Thomas. He became my disciple," Jesus replied as He exposed His arms, and Thomas felt the nail scars on His wrists. "I heard the pain of your heart. I felt your cross, Thomas. Celebrate abundant life, knowing death is but a window to *life after living*. I will never leave you."

Jesus embraced Thomas. The phenomenal experience was over as suddenly as it had begun. Thomas fell back on the park bench. He was peacefully smiling and overwhelmed with joy.

"Thank you God for loving a loser," he repeated joyfully.

Abruptly, Thomas's cell phone disturbed his solitude. Startled, he sat up, confused and bewildered. He fumbled for his phone in his pocket. It was CC.

"Thomas here," he casually answered, not wanting CC to feel too stoked about his actually taking the call.

"Where you been, Stirk? Been calling you all day. You wasted again? On the juice again, Stirk?"

"No way, CC. Absolutely not!"

CC exploded into the phone, "You left the van in the loading zone at Sea Island Church last night. They had it towed today. Have you lost it, Stirk? Cost me a bundle to get it back, and you've got the only set of keys."

"Owe you, CC. Sorry about that. I'll pay you back, I promise," Thomas contritely replied as he felt the van key in his coat pocket.

"You're headed to DC on Monday. This one's a really big deal, Stirk. We have over five hundred demonstrators for Planned Parenthood. The organizational meeting is at 11:00 on Friday. Be on time, okay?" CC said as he hung up.

Thomas clutched the stone pendant around his neck as torrents of memories began gushing from his mind. He realized God had changed him. He could actually feel God in his heart. He felt completely exhausted but somehow renewed. He felt as if he had a brand new body and had just run a marathon. It was exhilarating and exciting.

Thomas felt no thirst for booze. The gnawing itch was gone. He couldn't recall a single day before when he didn't have a craving for the juice. His unquenchable thirst had always driven his habit. But it was gone.

His thoughts quickly changed to the Rookies Nest and Codi Joseph. His heart ached for her, but he knew she had ultimate joy in Heaven.

He imagined what JJ and Tony B would tell him: "Suck it up, pal. Just get over it. Codi is blissfully happy in Heaven."

They were right. He prayed peace and joy for her. Thomas slowly stood from the park bench and focused his view on the ivy covered brick wall in the back of the small garden. He recognized the lush perennials and unmistakable white Calla Lilies planted so carefully and nurtured so lovingly by his mother.

He turned to his left and headed up the short path dividing his mom's garden, past the garage and up the steps to the back porch. God had brought him full circle. Thomas was home now. And for the first time in his life, he knew he had a Father.

48

UNBELIEVABLE DISCOVERY

Thomas was exhausted as he sat down at the kitchen table and read the short note from his mom:

*"Won't ask where you've been. Sandwich
in the fridge. Late meeting Freethinkers
Tonight. Love, Mom."*

As Thomas read the note, he smiled, appreciating his mother's effort. Appreciation she'd always deserved, but he'd never offered. He vowed never to make that mistake again.

Thomas grabbed his sandwich from the fridge, some chips from the pantry, and clicked on the television in the kitchen just in time for the 7:00 p.m. local news.

The news led with a breaking story about a professor who taught a popular class on entrepreneurship and served as dean of an MBA program at a local university. He'd just been arrested for embezzling millions from local investors in a Ponzi scheme.

Thomas ate his sandwich while expecting to see the story of an exploding yacht in the harbor, but there was no mention of an explosion during the broadcast.

Thomas finished his sandwich, flipped off the TV and booted up his mom's laptop on the kitchen counter. He did a Google news search for "explosions in Charleston harbor" but came up with no hits. The story of an exploding boat in the harbor should have been big news. Thomas was puzzled.

"You've got to be kidding me! I heard what Codi said— boat explosion in the harbor. Media loves that stuff. Where's the story?" Thomas said to himself as he rubbed the sepulcher stone pendant around his neck.

Exhausted, he attributed his confusion to sleep deprivation. He vowed to investigate the confounding lack of information about the explosion after a good night's sleep.

❧

Thomas awoke, rousing slowly, and looked at his bedside clock – 9:31 AM, THURSDAY, MARCH 28.

He lay back on his pillow. He'd totally crashed and couldn't believe he'd slept for over twelve hours. He sat up feeling happy inside, even joyful. He was just like a little kid on Christmas Eve. Happy-feel-good was back. He relished the new feeling.

Thomas searched himself, trying to sense the craving, the itch for the juice, the lust for coke. The gnawing habit was gone.

"Thank you, dear Father," Thomas said loudly as waves of inner happiness overwhelmed him.

Thomas wished his life could have been different with Codi Joseph. Even so, he was grateful to God for letting him meet her. He certainly would never forget her. Memories of Codi would always be with him. Forever.

As Thomas showered, he wondered why the local news had no story of the exploding Hocus Pocus. Suddenly, it came to him. Ask the Coast Guard. If anyone would know of a boat explosion in the harbor, it would be the US Coast Guard.

Thomas sat down at the kitchen table with a fresh cup of coffee. His mom had left him a note:

> *"Glad you're home. Glad you slept in.*
> *Will be late again tonight. Freethinkers*
> *Fellowship conference. Love, Mom."*

Thomas decided to contact the local newspaper before calling the Coast Guard. He looked up the number for Charleston Publishing and dialed.

"Charleston Publishing," the polite receptionist answered.

"May I speak to the local desk, please?" Thomas asked.

"One moment, sir."

"City desk, Tompkins," a voice abruptly demanded.

"Mr. Tompkins, there was no story in the paper yesterday about a boat explosion," Thomas said. "What about the yacht explosion in the harbor? I thought you guys covered stuff like that."

"We do. But we've got to have an explosion first," Tompkins dryly responded.

"You're saying there was no explosion?"

"I wish. But nothing that exciting around here in months."

"Thanks. Wow! Okay, thanks!" Thomas hung up the phone, baffled at what he'd heard.

Thomas repeated the process with a very polite seaman at the US Coast Guard station. The seaman reported no explosions or incidents in the Southeastern Sector in the last seventy-two hours.

Thomas was totally confounded. He knew what Codi said. He'd heard her story. He wondered if Codi was some sort of dream, just in his imagination. Thomas reached for his sepulcher stone pendant and was again assured it was no dream. The Rookies Nest was real. Codi was real. He'd touched her. He'd held her hand. She'd cried wet tears.

And then out of the blue, Thomas had a flash. He remembered Codi saying something about the four-four thing. It was like receiving a text message from God. Codi said that when the guards took her from her prison locker, her makeshift calendar was marked the fourth day after the fourth Sunday. What day in March is the fourth day after the fourth Sunday? He had to find out.

Thomas quickly went to the refrigerator where his mom kept her "Yemassee Home for Funerals" calendar. The calendar was unopened. His mom only used it to display its beautiful floral print on the cover.

Thomas laid the calendar on the table, broke the seal, and turned to the month of February. He began counting forward from that fateful final Thursday in February when he and Codi were together at Arthur's on King. Codi said she made her first stickman mark Friday around noon.

Thomas carefully counted forward and finally placed the pencil point on the fourth day after the fourth Sunday. It was Thursday, March 28th.

"But that's today!" Thomas cried, looking the date on his cell phone to be sure.

Thomas was certain he'd made a mistake and counted again. He arrived at the same day. He checked his watch and confirmed the date, Thursday, March 28th.

"Can't be today," Thomas exclaimed to an empty kitchen as he checked his counting a third time.

"Got to be right!" he shouted. "Codi will mark her fourth day after the fourth Sunday around noon today."

He pounded his fist on the table, wanting to believe what he'd just discovered.

"Incredible! That's got to be it. Explosion hasn't happened yet. The Hocus Pocus is still docked somewhere in Charleston," Thomas exclaimed.

He could hear his heart pounding. His heart accepted the good news but his brain told him he must be confused. And then he reasoned again out loud as if the sound gave credibility to his deductions, "Of course, that had to be it. If she were taken from her prison locker tomorrow morning early, then the she would have seen her calendar showing the fourth day after the fourth Sunday." No wonder there wasn't any record of an explosion—it hadn't happened yet. He wondered how he could have met Codi in the Rookies Nest if she weren't deceased. How is it March again? Maybe this all was a fantasy. Maybe he was dreaming. Could it be wishful thinking? Maybe his hope was shouting or his love for Codi was screaming so loud he could hear nothing else.

Confused or not, Thomas grabbed the phone book and began calling every marina in town, asking each of them if the Hocus Pocus was berthed at their docks. None of the marinas along Lockwood Boulevard had any record of the Hocus Pocus.

He sat down again at the kitchen table, still a bit mystified. It was now 11:30 a.m., and he was not coming up with anything. He closed his eyes, trying to remember everything Codi said in the Rookies Nest. What was he missing, he wondered?

Suddenly, it came to him. Codi said after she was abducted, she heard one of them say "Up East Bay." She said they drove

about five or six minutes. Thomas reasoned that would place the
boat at about the foot of Market Street at the Passenger Terminal.

Maybe the Hocus Pocus was anchored at the Passenger
Terminal dock? Thomas had no time for phone calls now. He
grabbed his mom's bike and raced across to King Street then
south to Market. As he reached the end of Market Street, he
could see a huge cruise ship docked at Passenger Terminal.
He locked the bike to the South Carolina States Port Authority
Passenger Terminal sign and took the walkway to the passenger dock. Once Thomas was on the dock, he looked beyond
the cruise ship and saw a large vessel docked at the northwest
end of the pier.

Thomas walked quickly, almost running. The yacht was
massive, gaudy, definitely looked a ship a drug boss wouldn't
mind tooling around in.. There was a black Ford Expedition
parked near the gangway leading to the stern of the vessel.
Had he found the Hocus Pocus?

He slowed his pace as several crewmembers came onto the
stern deck. He continued casually toward the high-rise apartment complex at the end of the dock. As he passed the stern,
he turned and looked back: HOCUS POCUS, CARTAGENA,
COLOMBIA, SA.

Thomas nearly shouted. He restrained himself as he
walked up the pier toward the entrance to the apartment high
rise. Hidden from sight of the Hocus Pocus, he fist pumped
his joy. He was right. The Hocus Pocus and Codi Joseph were
still in Charleston.

"Unbelievable!" Thomas cried. Codi had to be in her
prison locker. Thomas knew that if he could just look through
that small porthole near the stern of the vessel, he would see
Codi. He was overcome. Tears streamed down his cheeks as he
ran up Concord Street to Market where he left his mom's bike.

Thomas repeated over and over, "Thank you Lord for saving me and showing me where to find Codi."

Reality quickly gripped Thomas. He didn't have much time. Codi was the prisoner of dangerous gangsters—ruthless, violent criminals who would stop at nothing to do their drug deals. He was up against a South American drug cartel. He needed help.

Thomas's fingers were trembling with excitement as he sat on the bike and considered his options. He glanced at his watch. It was just after 1:00. What could he do? Who could he find to help him? His mind raced, searching for the perfect plan. There could be no mistakes, not even one!

Rescuing Codi had given Thomas something worth living for. Somehow he knew it was his destiny.

Thomas thought of his best friend, Stacy. He wished Stacy were alive and could enlist his navy seal friends to mount a rescue. He knew they could do it perfectly. If Stacy were here, he would have the answers to all these questions.

Thomas wondered if Stacy had gone through the Rookies Nest and selected one of the many beautiful Heavenlies. But knowing Stacy, it was more likely he was working at the golden arches, serving up happy meals to little kids.

Thomas thought briefly about contacting Sammie Sarmah and Bhuta Rat, but it had been over three years since he'd had contact with them. He knew they could gather a small army of baseball bat goons on a moment's notice. Bhuta Rat could plan the whole thing. He would know exactly what to do, and no one would get killed.

But it was possible Sammie knew these cartel thugs, Thomas reasoned. Maybe they were customers of the cartel. It seemed too risky. Thomas knew he could not take the chance.

As Thomas rode the bike down Market Street toward Lockwood Boulevard, he decided to report everything to Lt. O'Reilly and hope to enlist the help of the Charleston Police Department.

Thomas sped to the Police Department, and breathlessly told the duty sergeant he needed to speak with Lt. O'Reilly.

The duty sergeant told Thomas the lieutenant was busy and was not seeing anyone.

"Tell Lt. O'Reilly Thomas Stirk is downstairs and knows where to find Rachael Joseph," Thomas panted.

The duty sergeant's phone rang back in less than two minutes, the electronic door buzzed open, and the sergeant motioned Thomas inside."Take the elevator, second floor, take a left, third door on the right," the sergeant said.

As Thomas entered the office, O'Reilly stood behind his desk. "So have you finished your anti-church, anti-God demonstrations?" he asked. "Hard for me to believe anyone would protest in public against God and especially against Sea Island Church, knowing all the good they do in our community."

"Not proud of that, sir. Actually, I'm ashamed of it," Thomas apologized as he lowered his eyes.

"Ashamed? Save that story for PTI session tonight. We all can listen at the same time," as O'Reilly motioned for Thomas to take a seat.

"The desk sergeant said you have information on Joseph?" O'Reilly said, looking quizzically at Thomas. "That's interesting since we haven't found as much as a hair from her head after we found you in her SUV. Just yesterday, we located her parents in Raleigh and filed a missing persons report. We still got nothing to go on. So what gives, Stirk?"

Thomas began, his voice a little weak but sincere. "I know for a fact Rachael C. Joseph is being held on a large yacht, the Hocus Pocus, which is docked at the north end of the Passenger Terminal Pier."

"We know the boat," O'Reilly replied, showing interest. "It's registered out of Colombia, South America. Among others on board are two real yahoos, a black national from Haiti, assigned to the Haitian Consulate in Atlanta, and another guy who is a minor undersecretary in the Colombian Consulate in Miami. They've been here over a month now. Caused us all sorts of problems around the city. They both have diplomatic passports. Can't bust them or we would. We know them real well," O'Reilly paused, seriously eyeing Thomas.

"So tell me how you know Rachael Joseph is being held on board that boat? Last time I talked to you, I believe you told me you didn't know any Rachael Joseph. You also told the judge you didn't know her and had never heard of her," O'Reilly concluded, a glowering demand for proof written on his face.

"Lieutenant, I know her now. Met her two days ago," Thomas said and squirmed uncomfortably in the chair. "Well, actually what I mean is, I can tell you for certain she's on board that boat."

He was stumbling over his words, knowing he had not one shred of hard proof to offer Lt. O'Reilly.

Searching for something convincing to say, Thomas continued. "Can't you just swear out a warrant or something against those guys and go in and get her? I know she's on that boat. She's being held in a storage locker in the engine room. I can't explain how I know, but she's been on board the Hocus Pocus since the morning you found me drunk in the back seat of her SUV."

Thomas grasped the sepulcher stone pendant around his neck, reinforcing the truth he knew so well.

"What do ya take me for, a complete idiot? Where do you get off, Stirk?" O'Reilly blasted back at Thomas.

"Rachael Joseph's on that boat, Lieutenant," Thomas insisted.

Lt. O'Reilly paused, a bit perplexed as he contemplated Thomas's remarks. "Come on, Thomas. I mean, I know you, kid, and I like you, but the truth is the truth. First, you said you don't know who she is. Now, you're telling me you know she's been held on that boat since the morning we found you in her vehicle? You told the officers and the judge you didn't know her, had never met her, and had no idea who she was. How can you come in here and tell me that while she's been held prisoner on that boat you've suddenly, magically, gotten to know her two days ago? What kind of a cockamamie tale is that?"

Knowing he could provide no proof that O'Reilly would believe, Thomas simply replied, "I know it sounds bizarre, but it's true."

"Why didn't you tell me this sooner? We could have talked any evening after PTI. You never mentioned anything. Now you expect me to believe you when you can't provide any hard proof? If I went to the chief and got permission to seek a search warrant from the Feds based on what you've told me, I'd be laughed out of court. These guys are diplomatically protected. Envoy status, diplomatic passports—only the feds can intervene."

"I appreciate your listening," Thomas reached to shake hands with O'Reilly.

"Tell you what, Stirk, the chief's out this afternoon. I'll try to speak with him about presenting your story to the Feds tomorrow morning. Wouldn't hold out much hope if I were you, though. I mean, with your record and their diplomatic immunity, it makes it tough. But I'll let him know."

"Thanks, Lieutenant. See you tonight at PTI. Seven sharp, right?" Thomas stood to leave.

"Yeah, seven sharp. See you there." O'Reilly shook his head. He wanted to help but was confused about what to believe.

He turned around and called at Thomas. "Hey, kid, tell you what I'll do. When those guys juke around tonight, I'll put a black and white on the scene. We'll give it a watch. Best I can do, son."

Thomas left the office. He knew what he had to do. By the time Lt. O'Reilly spoke to the chief, Codi had to be free!

49

UNFORESEEN COURAGE

When Thomas returned to his mom's house, it was 2:00. He had to come up with a plan. He sat down at the kitchen table to sort his thoughts. Rescuing Codi would likely be the most difficult and daunting challenge of his life.

A twinge of fear gripped him. He recalled Ms. Scribbee saying, "Courage is not the absence of fear. Courage is overcoming fear." He prayed for the strength to overcome his fear.

Thomas considered purchasing a pistol—maybe a small cannon like the .357 magnum the Lake City cop flaunted. But he might not pass the background check with his multiple DUI arrests and no permanent driver's license. Anyway, he'd never shot a pistol. He'd never been to the shooting range, and he would have to attend classes. He had no time for that. And then Sammie Sarmah's words rang loud and clear, "Guns get you killed, mon." Thomas agreed. Guns were definitely out. They were far too dangerous, especially for a novice.

Thomas was running out of time. The next morning would arrive quickly. He felt totally inadequate. The lined legal pad in front of him proved his inability to create alternative plans. His mind was as blank as the pad, but he had to come up with something. He had to rescue Codi without slip-ups or he would get them both killed. It was a daunting mission, and his mind raced for a fail-safe strategy.

Suddenly, the foggy muddle cleared. He needed no legal pad. The only possible strategy was to be in a position to save Codi when they pushed her overboard. It was up to him to execute the rescue without any blunders.

Thomas felt anxious. Some of his old fears began to haunt him, but each time doubt threatened, he realized God had already provided a preview. He already knew what was going to happen. God intended to free Codi and was going to use him to facilitate the rescue. God was in control. The fear and cowardice that plagued him all his life had been replaced with a brave new confidence that came only from God.

Thomas hurriedly changed into a dark black pullover and blue jeans. He tucked the sepulcher pendant snugly under the pullover. He left his cell phone on the kitchen table with a note to his mom:

> *"I love you, Mom. You're the best*
> *God Bless You. Thomas."*

On his way out, Thomas grabbed his mother's 15 x 70 mm binoculars. His mom used the powerful glasses to watch birds perched at the feeder in the garden. He slung the thick leather strap around his neck. He then went to the storage shed behind the garage and found what he was looking for: his mom's bolt cutters. His mom kept the twelve-inch pair of heavy duty bolt cutters in the shed, using them when renters left padlocks on doors or abandoned bikes chained to the porch. Thomas would use them to cut Codi's chains. He secured the bolt cutters with an eight-foot length of nylon rope that he wrapped around his waist and tied off in a tight square knot. He pocketed a small flashlight and a jack knife then shut the shed, grabbed his mom's bike, and set off for the apartment complex adjacent to the Passenger Terminal Pier. It was 3:30 in the afternoon. Thomas nervously anticipated the danger ahead, knowing there would be no cut and run this time.

The developers of the apartment complex had built a public pier into the Cooper River just past the north end of the Passenger Terminal wharf. Thomas sauntered onto the pier, just past the end of Terminal dock. From his vantage, he was only about 150 yards from the stern of the Hocus Pocus. It was a perfect location to observe the action. Thomas dropped his shirt like he was catching some rays and sat down with his back to the pier railing. He wanted to remain totally anonymous, even if others from the complex ventured onto the dock for a stroll.

All was quiet aboard the Hocus Pocus. No activity at all. He whipped out the binoculars and could see everything. He could even make out the design on the brass hardware on the stern deck cabin doors. Thomas studied every inch of the yacht, observing two lockers marked "Recro Equipo" on the outboard side on the lower stern deck. He took note of the swim platform about six feet below the stern deck and two feet above the water line. Six angled metal braces under the swim deck supported the meshed metal platform.

As Thomas sat against the railing in the warm afternoon sun, he realized for the first time in his life he'd made a total commitment—a pledge from which he could never turn back, no matter the consequences. His and Codi's lives depended on his success. He regretted his cowardice in the past. He'd always done whatever necessary to avoid conflict or controversy—to stay ahead of his fear and panic. Not this time, he promised.

He was determined never to cut and run again. He pledged he wouldn't leave Plex bleeding under the table this time. At the same time, Thomas worried he wouldn't have the courage to carry out the plan. He was freaked out by the thought of the incredible danger he was facing. He tried not to think about it, but the clock was ticking toward zero hour.

He longed for Ms. Scribbee, Tony B and JJ. He was alone but enveloped by God. God would supply his missing courage and show him the way.

The sun was beginning to set. It was almost 7:30 and there had been no activity all afternoon on the Hocus Pocus. The crew and the cartel goons seemed to be hibernating. Over the last few hours, Thomas had gradually tweaked his plan. He would lower himself into the water around 4:00 a.m. and swim quietly to the stern swim deck, where it looked like he could hide safely. He'd rest on the metal support braces and stay there until they dumped Codi overboard. His plan was terrifying, but he had no choice now. He was committed.

He wondered briefly about missing tonight's PTI class and what Lt. O'Reilly would do. Missing a class was the same as a parole violation, and a parole violation always resulted in a jail sentence. But now wasn't the time to think about that, Thomas quickly concluded.. Not this Thursday night. Tonight, Codi's survival was all that was important.

Just after dark, as Lt. O'Reilly had promised, a Charleston PD cruiser drove onto the dock and parked about seventy-five yards from the gangway. The officer left the engine running and turned off the headlights. Thomas could see two officers inside through his field glasses. He wished he could tell them to draw their weapons and go get Codi, but he knew that wouldn't happen. Around 10:30, after observing for about three hours, the black and white exited the pier. Thomas wasn't surprised.

Around 11:00, the floodlights near the stern deck came on, almost blinding Thomas as he observed through his powerful lenses. The Haitian thug and the Colombian with the open shirt and hairy chest walked down the gangway followed by one of the crewmembers. They all piled into the black Ford Expedition and drove off. The floodlights over the gangway went dark.

Except the three who had left in the Expedition, Thomas had only seen one other crewmember since he arrived that morning. He knew there had to be others on board. He just didn't have any idea how many. A night chill was settling in and Thomas pulled on his long sleeved black shirt. It was almost midnight, and the lights along the railing on the pier had remained off. Thomas knew he'd caught a break.

About 3:30 a.m., the Expedition returned and parked at the stern gangway. The two Hispanic cartel goons exited the vehicle and stumbled aboard the Hocus Pocus. They looked pretty much sloshed.

The driver motioned to another crewmember who had been helping the cartel bosses up the gangway. The driver and the second crewmember opened the back doors of the

Expedition and slowly removed a heavy cement parking lot bumper, tied a yellow nylon rope to it and dragged it across the pier to the edge of the dock. They then threw the end of the rope onto the stern deck and boarded the vessel. With much difficulty, they hoisted the cement bumper on board then disappeared below deck.

Thomas was certain now. The bumper was exactly as JJ had described. His confidence swelled. It was 3:45 and he knew exactly what was going to happen.

Thomas quietly lowered his body into the murky cold water of the Cooper River and swam away from the pier. There was no moon. The darkness engulfed him, but his eyes adjusted with the help of scant illumination from a few lighted windows in the high-rise apartment building. The dim light was enough to zero in on his target.

After twenty minutes of slow breast strokes, he reached the stern of the Hocus Pocus. Thomas eased himself up on the angled swim deck supports. He found he could lie between the six pair of supports easily. However, the angled stainless steel bit into his back, making it impossible to stay in one position very long. He could see up through the steel mesh of the swim deck, but it would be impossible for anyone on board to see him because of his dark shirt and pants.

The deck of the Hocus Pocus was dark and deserted. All he could see was a faint glow from inside the lounge glass doors. There wasn't a person in sight.

Discovering some unforeseen God-given courage, Thomas dropped quietly into the water and quickly hoisted up onto the swim platform. He stood just high enough to peer over the stern railing—still no one on deck. He was certain everyone was sleeping. Thomas climbed the ladder and rolled over the railing, dropping gently onto the stern deck. Quickly, he slinked to the outboard side of the recro equipment bin. There was just enough room between the locker and the starboard deck rail for him to hide. Thomas peered over the top of the locker. The dim glow in the main stern salon left no doubt the space was empty.

Thomas slowly raised the right locker lid. The hinges creaked loudly, salt air having long since displaced the necessary lubricant. As his eyes began to adjust to the black shadows inside the bin, he saw swim fins, water skis, wet suits, and all sorts of other stuff. Then, he found what he knew he would need. He grabbed four life vests. They were black with "Hocus Pocus" monogrammed in small white letters.

Without any warning, a crewmember clambered down the stair ladder from an upper deck on the port side of the vessel. He rounded the portside corner to the stern deck as Thomas crouched hidden behind the locker. The crewmember sat in one of the deck chairs and lit a cigarette. The flame from his lighter illuminated the deck as if the sun had unpredictably risen.

Thomas realized the lid to the locker was open but he could not attempt to close it. The pungent odor of sweet foreign tobacco settled across the deck in the still night air.

Suddenly, Thomas heard the guy get out of his chair and quietly utter some profanity in Spanish. Before Thomas could think about what the guy was doing, he'd pushed the locker lid shut. Thomas peered from the end of the outboard side of the locker. The crewmember was only inches away from Thomas but hadn't seen him. The guy paced about, continuing to drag on his cigarette. Thomas's heart was pounding as loud as a giant bass drum in a fourth of July parade. He was certain the guy could hear his every heart beat.

Suddenly, the guy walked back over to the locker and flicked his cigarette butt over Thomas into the Cooper River. He then rapidly walked around the corner of the stern deck salon and went up the portside deck stairs.

Thomas was relieved but had no time to think. He immediately grabbed the four life vests, rolled over the stern railing to the swim platform and quietly slid into the water. The four life vests cushioned the sharp edges of the deck supports, making it more comfortable to lie in wait.

Thomas looked at his watch. It was 4:15 a.m. His heart rate slowed. The immediate excitement was over, but Thomas was pumped. His adrenalin was flowing. He'd actually enjoyed his close encounter on the stern deck. This stunned him. He'd never felt so jacked without having popped a pill or snorted some coke. He thanked God for the unexpected courage and for showing him the way.

50

HOCUS POCUS

Thomas was resting uncomfortably. The life jackets had cushioned the sharp edges of the swim platform supports but provided only partial relief from his discomfort as he waited in his makeshift lair.

He abruptly heard voices on board. He looked up through the mesh steel deck but saw no one. Then, he caught sight of a guy standing dockside at the stern of the Hocus Pocus.

The crewman walked to the edge of the dock, not two feet from the swim platform. He did his thing, streaming warm piss that splashed down on the swim deck and into the river. Thomas remained motionless in the dark shadows. He avoided most of the splatter as the warm urine condensed short columns of steam upward from the cold steel.

No doubt bloated from multiple pitchers of beer, the guy finally finished. He then spoke to crewmembers on the stern deck. The angle was too severe to see anything except the crewman's knees, but Thomas saw him release the mooring line from the stern. One of the crew yelled something in

Spanish and the guy heaved the rope onto the stern deck. It was too dark for any of them to see Thomas. He felt confident. He checked his watch – 5:05 a.m.

Shortly after the deck hand heaved the mooring line on board and disappeared, Thomas heard a deafening roar. The water under the swim platform began belching thick exhaust as the giant engines of the Hocus Pocus fired up. The choking smoke boiled from the stern water line, and the engine roar became so loud that it would be impossible to hear any voices eight feet above from anyone on deck. He knew now there would be no verbal warning. He wouldn't know what was happening until they lowered Codi to the swim deck to dump her overboard. He had to be alert.

Soon the Hocus Pocus began pulling away from the dock. It slowly drifted out into the Cooper River. The roar of the engines and clouds of exhaust almost overcame Thomas as he struggled to find fresh air while choking on the fumes.

The water from under the stern of the vessel changed from boiling clouds of exhaust to a frenzied swirl of sea water as the two large marine screws got the Hocus Pocus underway, thrusting her away from the docks and out into the dark waters of the river.

Thomas reviewed his plan. He was concerned something unexpected would happen. Something he couldn't deal with. He had to be sharp. He had to be ready for anything. Codi's life depended on it! His life depended on it!

The engines increased their forward speed. The vessel was cutting a clean wake now. The air flow began drawing away some of the choking exhaust. Thomas had fresh air as he watched the Passenger Terminal Pier fade into the darkness.

Thomas searched the night, trying to maintain his sense of direction but could see no lights. Nothing.

Soon the whine of the engines increased as the Hocus Pocus picked up speed. To Thomas, hanging only inches above the water's surface, the speed was grossly exaggerated. He couldn't be sure but judged they might be making ten or fifteen miles per hour.

The higher speed helped smooth the stern wash, freeing Thomas of any seawater spray. He could see much better now. He searched the night for lights he might identify, but no landmark was in sight. Only darkness shrouded the thunderous noise of the engines.

Codi had been awakened by the loud whine of the engines. She'd felt the Hocus Pocus as it got underway. She'd had no time to consider anything when the locker door swung open and three guys in black ski masks stormed in.

This time, they didn't blindfold her or tape her mouth. They cuffed her hands but not behind her back. They led her up the two flights of ladder-well steps and onto the deck where, for the first time in weeks, she breathed fresh air. The crew pushed her ahead, making their way along the port side walkway to the stern deck.

When Codi arrived at the stern deck, her red dress wrinkled and torn, the two vile mobsters were sitting in deck chairs waiting for her. The three masked guys forced her down on the carpeted deck just in front of the cartel thugs. Codi, weak and tired, crumpled compliantly. She was unable to fight, her tangled wisps of blond hair covering her bowed head as she silently prayed to God for strength.

"Missy, just we want again. Por favor Missy, tell us where is Anthony Reyes and say Edwardson's drug plot. We let you go.

Okay? Just say to us where is and what is, por favor," said the greasy dark Haitian in broken English, his open shirt exposing his black, wiry chest hair.

Codi looked up at the Haitian through her tousled blond strands. Her face was bruised and blemished. Black scabs covered the burns on her cheeks.

With her eyes pooling tears, she replied, "I don't know him. I never met him. Please. I have no idea where he is or who he is. I don't know any plot. Just let me go, please."

The Haitian, again wearing his gaudy floral Tommy Bahama print and smelling of sticky sweet citrus cologne, stood up from his deck chair. He was somewhat wobbly on his feet as he loomed directly over Codi.

"You no help us, missy? We no help you. Comprende?"

He pushed her hip hard with the sole of his shoe, knocking Codi flat on the deck.

Codi slowly pulled her shoulders up, swishing her hair away from her pock-marked face with her cuffed hands. She turned, looking directly at her two evil captors.

"I told you. I don't know him and never met him. I would help you if I could. But I can't. Just let me go," Codi pleaded, her voice breaking.

The two Hispanics scoffed at her appeals and motioned to the three guys in black ski masks.

The Colombian national then condemned Codi. "You not say. We not help."

The pair left the deck and climbed the stairs to the upper lounge. The masked deck hands moved quickly, chaining the concrete bumper to Codi's ankles as she watched in horror. She was paralyzed by fear, too frightened to scream, too exhausted to fight.

The Hocus Pocus increased speed again. It was all Thomas could do to remain calm and hang on. The wind and fine salt spray stung his face as the speed pushed his body hard against the swim platform braces.

"Father God, take away my fear and give me courage," Thomas prayed.

He looked north and saw the lights of Patriot's Point and the Yorktown. They were in the shipping channel, speeding out of the harbor with the lights of Sullivan's Island soon to come into view. His arms ached as he struggled to reposition his body to withstand the crushing pain.

Thomas closed his eyes briefly to avoid the stinging spray, but he opened them immediately when he felt the thud of one of the masked deckhands jumping onto the swim platform from the stern deck. The guy was motioning to his accomplices on the main deck.

Then he saw Codi in her rumpled red dress. One of the deckhands was pushing her down the ladder to the swim deck. She stumbled down the last two rungs and fell onto her back. It was still too dark to see, but it didn't matter. Thomas knew what was happening. Codi was exhausted and unable to fight.

Thomas watched as the guy on the swim platform climbed the ladder to the stern deck. What Thomas didn't see were the other two deckhands struggling to throw the concrete bumper overboard from the stern deck. Its chain was fastened around Codi's ankles, ready to jerk her from the swim platform and drag her to the bottom of the shipping channel.

Thomas never saw it coming. As the bumper was finally shoved over the deck rail, it struck the outboard corner of the swim platform. With pile diver force, the bumper bent the steel deck, pinning Thomas's right arm between the jagged steel and the support bracket. His arm was trapped, the sharp, ribbed steel cutting into his flesh. He could feel the stinging pressure.

His fear of something unexpected confounding the rescue was happening and he had no time. He saw Codi dragged from the platform and into the murky water.

With his left arm, he quickly tried to force the mesh deck upward to release his forearm. He didn't have enough strength. He increased the force to his left arm by pushing with his feet against the angled support bracket. The swim deck wouldn't give. He pressed even harder, but his right foot slipped its grip on the wet angled brace. The swift wake water snatched his leg and jerked his body from the snare of mangled steel, spinning him like a boogie board riding a speedboat's wake.

Violently wrenched free but dazed, he bobbed in the dark water. His confused thoughts flashed rapidly. The Hocus Pocus motored on toward the Atlantic. Things were moving much too fast. He immediately dropped the four life vests. And then there it was like a bright ribbon from Heaven. The yellow rope the deckhands ineptly failed to remove from the concrete bumper was floating nearby. He hurriedly grabbed the line as it snaked and writhed as Codi was dragged to the bottom of the shipping channel.

As he gripped the line tightly, he noticed the severe ten-inch cut to his outside forearm and the large wound on the back of his hand. He was bleeding profusely, but there was no sting or pain. He inhaled a huge breath, and pulled hard down on the yellow rope that seemed to glow in the dark water.

"Thank you, God, for yellow rope," Thomas prayed as he pulled himself downward toward Codi, the briny taste of seawater in his mouth.

The water somehow felt warm. He pulled faster, harder and deeper. The seawater was murky green, but somehow there was enough luminosity for him to see the yellow rope. The salt water didn't burn his unprotected eyes.

Thomas reached the cement bumper only seconds after it hit bottom. Amazingly, in the darkness, there was just enough illumination to see Codi's red silhouette. Thomas wrapped his leg with the rope and braced his other foot against the bumper. He took the bolt cutters from his waist, opened the blades and felt for Codi's legs. Finding her ankles, he searched for the lightweight chain links and placed the bolt cutters square on a link. He quickly snapped a link and unwrapped the chain. Codi was released. She burst toward the surface as if she were jet propelled. Thomas swam behind her, pushing her ever faster.

As they raced to the surface, it seemed to Thomas they were being sucked upward in a dimly lit upside down funnel. Every time they churned the water with their feet or hands, it left a bright luminescent glow. God was lighting their way.

Thomas could barely see Codi. She pushed hard against the water with her cuffed wrists, swimming with all her strength toward the surface. She was totally out of air. He was too. His lungs were burning.

Codi broke the surface first, gasping for air, coughing up salt water and purging phlegm from her lungs. Thomas was a half second behind her. He found the four life preservers floating nearby. He swam the short distance to Codi and strapped a life vest under each of her arms. She continued to cough and choke. He strapped the third vest to her back, providing extra buoyancy to her head and neck. Thomas donned the other vest and tied Codi's vests to his.

"You're safe now, Codi. You're safe. You're okay now. Just try and breathe," Thomas yelled.

Codi, her lips blue and her eyes panicked, continued to gasp for air. The bright beam of the Sullivan's Island Light House rotated over them, flashing its welcome. Thomas knew where they were now and once Codi caught her breath, they could swim for South Beach on Sullivan's Island.

Hiding in the darkness of the pre-dawn, the angel trio had been following the rescue in their inflatable raft. JJ and Tony B were at the oars and Scribbee sat astride the boatswain's seat at the bow. They were each wearing black rubber wet suits without the headgear, their white mini-wings protruding through slits in their sleeves.

"Condition red resolved!" Tony B yelled to Scribbee as they watched Thomas secure the life vests to Codi.

Tony B pumped the oar to align the raft, and JJ pulled in the very long and very yellow nylon rope, winding a perfect round coil on the slatted wood floor of the raft.

Scribbee, watching and evaluating the situation, warned, "Codi's breathing is rapidly improving; still, I think it would be best if we stay on station for a while. Just to be sure they get to the beach."

"I'm already soaked," JJ quickly snapped and quivered his waterlogged wings in an attempt to flutter them dry. "This rubber suit didn't help much. Frankly, these aquatic operations are becoming a little too complex, don't you think?"

51

TO THE BEACH

As Thomas turned toward Codi, he watched the Hocus Pocus speeding off in the distance. The powerful beam from the Sullivan's Island lighthouse rotated overhead, overwhelming the first faint light of dawn on the horizon.

"Codi, just relax. Let the life vests hold you up," Thomas urged. Her breathing was more stable now. She was still coughing but was no longer choking. She nodded to Thomas. As she relaxed on her back, her head was buoyed high by the black vests.

"Try to breathe deeply. I'll swim us to the beach on the south end of Sullivan's Island. Stay calm. Let me do the work. Everything's going to be okay. You're safe now."

Swimming toward the beach, he saw his right arm clearly for the first time. Strangely, there was no pain, but his arm was filleted from just below his elbow to just above his wrist. The gash was deep and the flesh was laid open, but amazingly, the massive wound was not bleeding. It must have been the salt water, Thomas reasoned. He noticed the cut to his hand. The skin was laid back as if someone had begun to skin the back of his hand, a flap of about two inches folded toward his wrist. It was not bleeding either.

Thomas felt fortunate. The crushed swim deck could have permanently entrapped him. He shivered at the thought of the close encounter and thanked God for watching over him.

As Thomas pulled Codi toward the beach, the dark dawn sky lit up with huge orange and white balls of fire. The silent dawn reverberated with thunderous explosions, one after the other in rapid succession. Thomas turned Codi toward the incredible sight as they both watched the Hocus Pocus exploding into flames.

Suddenly, concussions from the explosions slammed them as waves of sonic pressure rippled the calm water. After several more loud explosions, the Hocus Pocus was left a mass of burning wreckage adrift in the shipping channel. Plumes of black smoke illuminated by orange balls of fire shot high into the dark night sky raining down shards of flaming debris.

Thomas and Codi were spellbound as they rested for a moment. They were about a third of the way to the beach.

"We're safe now, Codi," Thomas said. He began towing her again toward the beach.

What an awesome God, Thomas thought, as he pulled hard toward the island. A God who could so precisely arrange Codi's rescue is a God who could do anything. A God who would use an alcoholic, cokehead, cowardly, spineless wuss of a loser to rescue Codi was a God beyond amazing.

"Lord God Almighty, you're totally indescribable!" Thomas wanted to scream when he realized the courage God had supplied. He was overwhelmed, recalling all that had happened over the past two days.

Thomas pulled Codi faster now. The Hocus Pocus was burning intensely, casting an eerie orange reflection on the water as balls of flame erupted within the dense black smoke.

Surprisingly, the beach was closer than Thomas originally estimated. His feet caught firm sand in four feet of water about 50 yards out. Thomas began walking and pulling Codi more easily now. As they reached shallow water, Thomas lifted Codi to her feet. Her color was pink now and her lips were no longer blue. She was breathing easier. Walking and stumbling toward the shore, Thomas carried Codi. After reaching the beach, they continued about twenty yards and collapsed on the dry white sand.

Codi was bleeding from her ankles where the chain had ripped her skin. She buckled to her knees as Thomas tried to make her comfortable with the life vests. Her hands were still cuffed in front of her, but Thomas lost the bolt cutters in the underwater melee.

Codi trembled from both the chill in the morning air and the joy of miraculous deliverance. She didn't mind being cold. She was free. They watched as the Hocus Pocus continued to burn, razing columns of sooty smoke aloft as the early morning seemed to capture the image permanently against the grayish blue dawn canvas.

Thomas lost his watch when his arm was jerked free, but he knew sunrise was soon. "Codi, it's gotta be around 6:00. Sunrise soon. Once the sun is up, we'll both warm up."

Codi had recovered enough to roll up on her elbows. Her tangled, matted hair covered her face as she looked up at Thomas. "Who are you?"

Before Thomas could answer, Codi continued. "Wait! I know you. Hold on, let me think." She brushed her hair from her face with her cuffed hands. "Of course, I know you. How could I ever forget? You were the jerk sitting next to me at Arthur's on King the night my kidnapping nightmare began." She paused, perplexed. "You're the stumbling drunk those Colombians hauled out of Arthur's and accidentally parked in the backseat of my Denali."

Thomas grimaced—Codi only knew the old Thomas Stirk. "Codi, I'm not proud of the guy I was that night at Arthur's. It's got to be hard for you to believe, but I've made a lot of changes in my life."

"How'd you know my name? I never told you my name at Arthur's that night. And what's yours?"

Thomas was baffled. "Thomas Stirk. We met less than two days ago. Remember? We met in the Rookies Nest. Ms. Scribbee, Tony B, and JJ introduced us."

"What's the Rookies Nest? Anyway, I never heard of Ms. Scribbee or Tony B or whoever, but I owe you my life. That's for sure. I'm not ungrateful, I promise. God told me I would be rescued. God spoke it to me in an audible voice while I was a prisoner on the Hocus Pocus. I'm so blessed to be alive, to be saved. I'm so thankful to God and you, but I've never been to the Rookies Nest or met any of your friends."

Thomas was totally bewildered. How could she deny the obvious? It was less than forty-eight hours since they'd properly been introduced. He needed time to unravel Codi's response as he looked toward Charleston Harbor and saw flashing blue lights on the water.

Thomas watched as Codi again swished her hair from her face and stroked her cheeks with her hands. "Hey, I have burns all over my face but I can't feel them. Can you see the burns on my face?"

"When you told your story in the Rookies ... I mean the Rookies Nest where you've never been ... or whatever. Anyway, you told us those drug thugs burned you with cigarettes. I couldn't see any burns in the Rookies Nest and you sure don't have any burns on your face now. Not even one. If I had a mirror, I would show you."

Thomas pointed to the harbor. "See the lights? In a while, this place will be crawling with rescue folks. We'll be picked up."

Codi totally confused nodded and then turned her attention to the burning hulk of the Hocus Pocus, still blazing fiercely and pumping clouds of dense black smoke high into the dawn sky as dozens of flashing blue lights dotted the harbor.

With Codi distracted briefly, Thomas had to think fast. He reasoned that this moment was real time for Codi. And then it came to him. He wondered why he hadn't realized sooner. The Hocus Pocus left port today and exploded today. Codi was thrown overboard today. Everything was real time. Everything just happened. Thomas realized Codi never died. She'd never transitioned. She'd never left the *life worth living*, and she'd never been in the Rookies Nest. All these events happened just a few minutes ago, not almost two days ago.

Thomas reached for his sepulcher stone pendant and grasped it with his forefinger and thumb. He was thankful it was securely around his neck, providing proof of marvelous things unseen and reassuring him that God lives, just as Scribbee had promised. He wondered how the angels arranged for him to meet Codi so she could reveal her future.

Thomas turned back to Codi, who was resting more comfortably on the stacked life preservers. "Codi, Jesus saved me two days ago. I'm not the same guy you saw at Arthur's. God's angels, Ms. Scribbee, Tony B and JJ, brought me to the Lord. I'd like to tell you about it, if you'd like to hear?"

Codi nodded her approval. Thomas moved closer to her, both of them facing the harbor as the flashing blue lights on the rescue boats had now been joined with the flashing red beacons of helicopters headed toward the burning Hocus Pocus.

Thomas began his story, telling her first of Little Thomas and his ex-girlfriend and how much he loved his son. He related all his sinful past with alcohol, all his DUIs, his drug addiction, his work with Sammie Sarmah and his days pushing drugs on the street. Finally, he told Codi of his anti-Christian disruption of the Easter Pageant at Sea Island Church and his experiences with Ms. Scribbee, Tony B and JJ. He related his unbelievable experience of meeting Jesus in the garden. Thomas left out nothing, feeling God was prompting him to tell Codi everything.

"And Codi," Thomas concluded his testimony, "we actually met in the Rookies Nest two days ago but in the future somehow. The Rookies nest is a place of transition for persons who have died and gone to Heaven. It was spectacular. That's how I knew you were aboard the Hocus Pocus. You told me, Codi. You told us all about that night at Arthur's, your kidnapping, your locker prison cell, everything. You told us about the bus station, renting lock box 321, and placing your purse with fourteen thousand dollars inside, then flushing the key."

Codi was totally astounded, a look of amazement on her face as she began her shocked reply. "Thomas, only God could have revealed that to you. I am the only person who knew about that." She began crying, confirming again that God had arranged her rescue. "Only God could have shown you all those things, Thomas Stirk."

Codi looked back toward the Hocus Pocus, now clearly visible in the bright dawn light. The fire had burned it almost to the waterline.

Still crying, she said to Thomas, "I'm so ashamed. I'm so thankful to God and to you for rescuing me. You saved my life. I'd sold out to big drug money. I ran completely away from God. I ignored everything I'd ever been taught by my parents. I had forsaken God. After I was kidnapped, I was terrified. I was lost. I begged God for mercy. I asked God to forgive me. I told Him I deserved to die, but He saved me." She was smiling through her tears of joy.

"Codi, look," Thomas interrupted, pointing to the orange and white Coast Guard boat headed directly for them. "I told you they'd come for us."

52

RELIEF AT HOME

As the Coast Guard rescue craft beached in the shallow water, several of the Coasties jumped off and ran toward Codi and Thomas. After initial evaluation for injuries, the two medics in the crew bandaged the deep laceration on Thomas's arm and the gash on his hand. The other medic wrapped the deep cuts on Codi's ankles in protective gauze.

After the wounds were treated, two of the crew carried Codi to the thirty-foot rescue craft and helped her aboard. Thomas and the other two Coasties waded to the boat and climbed the short rope ladder at the stern.

As they backed into open water, Codi and Thomas caught a final look at the burning Hocus Pocus. Its dark plume reached hundreds of feet into the morning sky. It was a sight they would never forget.

The crew wrapped Codi and Thomas in blankets and placed them in the back of the small cabin as the vessel sped to the US Coast Guard Tradd Street Station in Charleston.

The Master Chief in command of the vessel knelt in front of Thomas and Codi and advised them what would happen once they arrived at the Coast Guard Station. "The medics will be at the dock when we arrive. Our small clinic will conduct your medical exam and treat your wounds. Then, you will be able to clean up, shower, put on some dry clothes, and share our mess for breakfast. There will be some debriefings after that. Since this incident occurred in the shipping channel leading to international waters, the investigation is under the jurisdiction of the US Coast Guard and other federal authorities. DEA will certainly become involved since preliminary inspection reveals a record stash of cocaine floating in the water. We'll do our best to make you comfortable."

The chief stood and turned toward the small wheelhouse. He pointed to the seaman to steer the vessel around Drum Island toward the Battery.

Codi asked Thomas, "Are you sure there are no burns on my face? There must be scars. They burned me over and over again." She was still in disbelief and rubbed her hands across her cheeks.

"None, Codi. You're good. You'll soon see. We'll get you a mirror."

The engine noise on the small rescue craft was loud enough to make normal conversation difficult. It had been a very long night, so Thomas and Codi rested and didn't attempt to talk.

Thomas felt alive. They were safe now. For the first time in his life, he felt a sense of worth. He had a Father. There were no scary challenges left to conquer today. God had already completed the mission and all his fears had been vanquished. Mission accomplished. His anxiety was at rest, but he was exhausted.

Thomas was amazed at all God had done. He had over-come his cowardice; he had not cut and run. He was proud that he had fulfilled his commitment.

When they arrived at the Tradd Street Coast Guard Station, there were swarms of reporters on the dock. There were TV crews everywhere. Thomas suggested to Codi that they make no comments to anyone until after their debrief-ings. Codi, still shivering, nodded from beneath the blanket.

Codi and Thomas shook hands with everyone in the crew as they disembarked the vessel, thanking them for all they had done. The crew helped Codi into a wheelchair and Thomas pushed her as they were escorted off the dock. At the end of the pier, dozens of media folks were asking different ques-tions simultaneously. Thomas and Codi smiled, giving them thumbs up.

The medical team first photographed Codi's injuries to her ankles. They removed her handcuffs, which had cut deeply into the skin of her outer wrists. They cleaned and bandaged her gouges and scrapes and gave her a Tetanus shot. They also photographed Thomas's wounds. The doctor advised stitches for his arm and for the back of his hand. He would also need a Tetanus shot.

Novocaine-numbed and forty-eight moderately painful staples later, Thomas's forearm laceration looked more like a zipper on a fighter pilot's leather jacket than a splayed fish filet. The doctor took a little more care with the back of his hand, using silk sutures, which he told Thomas would leave practically no scar.

After the medics finished, it was off to the male barracks for Thomas and the female watch officer's facility for Codi. They were both anxious to clean up, especially Codi. One of the female deck seamen volunteered to help Codi with her hair. Codi was appreciative. Her hair, a mess of knots and tangles, hadn't been brushed in over a month.

Dressed in fresh blue US Coast Guard overalls and white sneakers, Codi and Thomas joined each other in the small mess kitchen. The aroma was overwhelming. Facing each other at the bench table, Codi savored her coffee. "I'd almost forgotten what coffee tasted like." She smiled as Thomas consumed a large helping of scrambled eggs, greasy sausage and slightly burned toast.

"Well, it's not Starbucks, but for right now, it'll have to do," Thomas said. He smiled back. "Codi we are both so blessed. God has done such wonders how can we ever thank Him? It blows my mind."

Codi and Thomas agreed to disclose in the debriefings exactly what happened. There was nothing to be gained from hiding any detail about what God had done.

"After all," Codi declared, "God was there with us. He orchestrated the rescue. So what if the skeptics or the media don't believe us. We know what God did today. And I for one want to let everyone know God saved me."

Codi and Thomas were whisked away for their separate debriefings around 9:30. Thomas's interview lasted until just after noon and when he left the debriefing room, he caught a snippet of the local news on a television in the reception area. The clip showed Thomas pushing Codi in the wheelchair with the high plume of black smoke from the Hocus Pocus in the background. Then the camera zeroed in on Codi's bandaged ankles. The next clip was an aerial of the burned-out, smoking hull of the Hocus Pocus surrounded by floating bodies, burning debris and hundreds of packets of cocaine.

"Mr. Stirk," a voice summoned from behind. Thomas turned to see his assigned escort. "Ms. Joseph is not through with her debriefing yet. She will be some while longer, I suspect. The media is waiting to speak with Ms. Joseph and you. Would you like to talk with them alone or wait for Ms. Joseph?"

"I'll wait for Ms. Joseph to finish," he said. "Got a place where I can wait? Some place where I might be able to make a call to my mom?"

"Sure. You can stay in here.. When Miss Joseph is finished, I'll let her know where you are. You'll find three lines. Just dial "9" for an outside."

"What's your name?" Thomas asked.

"Murphrees, sir, Petty Officer First Class. I'm public relations Coast Guard Charleston, Southeastern Sector, sir," he proudly proclaimed.

"Mr. Murphrees, I want to thank you and the Coast Guard for the kindness you've given Ms. Joseph and myself. We thank you, sir." Murphrees nodded his appreciation and disappeared into his office.

Thomas picked up the phone and dialed his mother. He assumed she'd be home eating lunch and watching the local news.

"Hello," his mom answered anxiously.

"Mom, it's Thomas."

"Thomas! I just saw you on television. That was you, wasn't it? I've been frantic. You didn't come home last night. I was so worried I hardly slept. I knew something was wrong. I knew something had happened. Where are you? How did you get on that boat? Thank God you weren't hurt. You're not hurt, are you? Are you coming home now, son?" she hysterically questioned Thomas.

"Mom, calm down. I'm fine. I'm not hurt. I don't have much time to talk right now, but I'll be home later today. All morning we've been debriefing with the Coast Guard. We should be finished later this afternoon and then I'll be home."

"Thomas, I'm just so glad you're okay," she said, more calmly..

"Mom, I need your help. I'm probably going to bring a friend home with me. She will need a place to stay tonight, and I told her you wouldn't mind. Her parents will probably come from North Carolina and pick her up tomorrow. Anyway, can you fix a bedroom for her and get her some jeans and a shirt and stuff? She's about your size. All her clothes were pretty much trashed in the accident. Will that be okay?"

"Of course, Thomas. Of course! Just leave everything to me. I'll take care of everything."

"Thanks. You're the best. See you later today."

Thomas hung up the phone, knowing his mother would have enough questions to keep him tied up all afternoon.. He would tell her everything, but not now and not over the phone.

It was after 2:00 when Codi finally finished her debriefing. When Murphrees brought her to the reception area, she looked tired. Murphrees had gotten her another cup of coffee and a blueberry muffin.

Codi sipped her coffee then set her cup down, perching her chin on her palms pensively.

"Thomas," she said, "they gave me time to call my dad in Raleigh."

"Everything good, I hope?"

"My mom's in the hospital. Severe anxiety, dad said. He thinks she'll be fine when she hears I'm okay. They'll try and drive down tomorrow," Codi said, tears welling up in her eyes. "I promised I'd call him back later."

"Codi, you can stay with my mom tonight. She has plenty of room."

"Thanks. Are you sure your mom won't mind?"

"No way. You'll like her, Codi." Thomas paused looking at Codi's tears. "You're sad, Codi. I can see you're sad. What's wrong?"

"I just realize how deeply I've hurt my parents. I've hurt too many people." Codi bowed her head and began to sob.

"Thomas," Codi could barely speak through her tears. "Oh, Thomas, when I called, my dad's assistant answered. I told her it was me, and she dropped the phone and began screaming, 'Mr. Claude, Mr. Claude. She's alive! She's alive! She's not missing anymore. She's on the phone, Mr. Claude. It's really her, Mr. Claude. She's alive! Praise God.'"

Thomas rested his hands on Codi's shoulders. Finally, she looked up.

"What have I done, Thomas?"

"Codi, your mom and dad will be here tomorrow. Everything will be okay. You'll see."

53

ANSWERED PRAYERS

Petty Officer Murphrees opened the door to the reception day room, allowing Lt. O'Reilly and two of his staff from the Charleston PD to enter. Thomas and Codi politely stood.

"Mr. Stirk, I believe you already know Lieutenant Kevin O'Reilly from the Charleston PD," Murphrees said, moving aside. O'Reilly and Stirk shook hands. O'Reilly nodded at Thomas and said, "I knew something was up when you didn't show for PTI last night. I should have figured it out."

"Sir, I'd like to talk with you about making up the missed class from last night."

"We'll talk, Mr. Stirk. I'm just glad you're okay, kid. No exaggeration about what you told me yesterday. I was shocked when I saw the TV coverage today. I'm sorry I couldn't—I mean, sorry I didn't help yesterday. Even now, I'm not sure what I could have done. Anyway, you're safe now, thank God."

Thomas quickly introduced Codi to Lt. O'Reilly. "Sir, meet Rachael Coedinger Joseph."

"Talked to your dad just a few minutes ago," O'Reilly told Codi. "He and your mom are coming down tomorrow. They're in high spirits knowing you're okay. We all are relieved this turned out so well for you both. So many times the results are tragic."

The lieutenant grabbed a folder from one of his assistants.

"God watched over us, Lieutenant," Codi asserted, "and He sent Thomas to rescue me."

"I'm just glad you're both safe," O'Reilly continued. "Would you believe we've already fished out nineteen bodies? Some are well known South American drug thugs. We've also recovered about 800 one-kilo plastic-sealed packets of cocaine. Street value is huge. Well over twenty-five million, I suspect. This may be the biggest East Coast drug bust—or should I say discovery—in history."

Codi shuttered. "God truly protected me."

"The Hocus Pocus is still smoldering," O'Reilly continued. "Burned down to the water line. They're preparing to tow the hull out of the shipping channel and clear the wreckage. I understand the port has three container ships waiting off shore."

He paused and turned toward Thomas.

"Listen, I'm really proud of you, son. I've read part of your debrief. I guess you're one of those certifiable hero types now. You'll have to tell me the complete story sometime. Okay?"

"Certainly, sir," Thomas faltered.

"Miss Joseph, we're sure glad you're no longer missing. I know you've been through hell and back, but we've got to get your statement. So Thomas, if you will excuse us, we shouldn't be too long."

O'Reilly and his assistants escorted Codi out of the room. O'Reilly had no idea, but his praise meant everything to Thomas. For a former loser, a well-known public drunk,

and a habitually arrested punk, to be praised by the lieutenant sparked a charge to his self-worth. Thomas knew now he
could walk proudly. He could be a productive citizen. He also
had a Father and renewed purpose to his life.

After about an hour and a half, one of O'Reilly's assistants
returned and invited Thomas on a trip to the bus station.
As they left the Coast Guard Station, they drove past a mass
of reporters gathered in a tent on the lawn in front of the
Headquarters Building. TV cameras were set up and ready to
roll.

Inside the bus station, Lt. O'Reilly presented the bus station manager with a search warrant for the contents of lock
box 321. The manager produced a master key and opened the
lock box.

Lt. O'Reilly removed one item at a time. His assistant photographed each as they recorded O'Reilly on a small hand held
video camera. First, he logged Codi's purse, noting her North
Carolina driver's license, vehicle registration, cell phone, car
keys, and a slip of paper with SCV 404 scribbled on it. O'Reilly
already knew who owned the scribbled tag number. "The tag
goes to a Hertz plate," O'Reilly pointed out. "SCV is for South
Carolina Visitor. That's the standard plate for rental vehicles.
Those yahoos kidnapped you in a vehicle rented from Hertz,
Ms. Joseph," as he handed all Codi's belongings to her without looking inside her wallet.

Later, Codi told Thomas she'd gone over everything with
O'Reilly. He knew how much cash was in her wallet, how she
got it and what she was doing at Arthur's that night. For whatever reason, O'Reilly chose not to confiscate the money or her
vehicle.

When they arrived back at the Coast Guard Station, the
black body bags were lined up on the dock, a horrific sight

and grim reminder of all that had happened this fifth day after the fourth Sunday in March.

As Codi and Thomas waited in the conference room, Lt. O'Reilly and his two detective assistants conferred at the other end of the long conference table. O'Reilly sifted through the paperwork with the detectives nodding their approval. He then approached Thomas and Codi from the far end of the room.

"Ms. Joseph," he began, a smile on his face, "I don't think I can find anyone alive to charge with your kidnapping. Looks to me like they've all gone to their eternal reward in the fiery furnace of hell. And as far as your missing persons file? Well, you've been found. File closed." O'Reilly closed and handed the manila folder to one of the detectives. Codi and Thomas smiled at each other.

"I'll make the necessary arrangements for you to pick up your vehicle from the impound lot," O'Reilly said. "I'm waiving all impoundment charges."

"Thank you, Lieutenant. That's kind of you," Codi replied.

A serious concern furrowed on O'Reilly's brow. "I've found no evidence of cocaine or any other illegal drug in your possession or in your vehicle. I've run a background check and am unable to find any arrests, not even a minor traffic violation. I can find no trace of you in the federal snitch files, not even a mention."

Codi silently sighed her relief.

O'Reilly continued, his demeanor more grim. "However, you did tell me about your drug services and your anonymous clients, including your relationship with Senator Edwardson. Since you were never arrested or charged with any crime, a good attorney would insure your statement could never be used against you.

"What I'm saying, Ms. Joseph, is I've got no charges to hold you on." O'Reilly paused pensively. "But I would like to offer some fatherly advice if I may? Don't do the drug stuff again. Do the drug thing and you die. You almost lost it this time. Let there be no next time. Don't end up in one of those black body bags." O'Reilly's face blossomed to a huge smile, relaxing his wrinkled brow. Codi's solemn concern melted to relief.

"You guys are free to go. When you're ready, I'd be happy to drive you wherever you need to get to," O'Reilly happily offered.

"Thank you, Lieutenant," Codi said. "We'll need that ride, but first I would like to talk with the media and express my gratitude to everyone."

"Reporters can be a little rough. I would suggest you just make a short statement and take no questions," Thomas suggested.

"Thomas is right. Spare the details and keep it short."

Thomas escorted Codi from the Headquarters Building to the podium under the tent and addressed the assembled. "Everyone, I would like you to meet Rachael Codi Joseph. She's had a long and difficult day, but she does have something she would like to say." Thomas moved aside as Codi took the podium.

"Hi, I'm Codi Joseph and I want everyone to know I'm here today because God answered my prayers. God saved me from certain death today. God is always faithful. I want to first thank God. He's so awesome! God sent Thomas Stirk to rescue me," Codi concluded with a weary but confident smile on her face. She thanked the crowd for listening and told them she had no time for questions.

Two officers escorted Thomas and Codi through the crowd to O'Reilly's waiting squad car, and they sped away from the crowd at the Tradd Street Station.

A short time later, Lt. O'Reilly pulled up in front of Thomas's mom's house. As Thomas and Codi got out, O'Reilly let Codi know if she needed anything to let him know. Codi thanked him, especially for the fatherly advice, and promised him she would live up to all his wise counsel. She gave him a kiss on the cheek.

Wearing a huge smile, Mary Stirk was waiting at the top of the steps.

As Codi and Thomas climbed the steps, Mary Stirk began, "I'm so glad to see you both. I've been so worried. I can't begin to tell you."

She hesitated. Codi took her hand.

"How nice to meet you, Miss Joseph," Mary continued, not allowing Thomas time for a formal introduction or even commenting on his heavily bandaged arm. "Oh, you're so much prettier in person than on the television, my dear. From North Carolina, I understand?" She opened the front door and nudged Codi inside.

"Yes, ma'am, Raleigh."

"Oh, my, my, my," Mary persisted as she scoped out Codi with her third-degree probing eye and escorted her to the sofa. "Please come and sit down, my dear. We've just got to get you into something other than those dreadful blue overalls. Thomas, why have you never told me about your friend, Miss Joseph?"

Thomas nodded in astonishment, smiling contritely at Codi.

54

THE BEST OF TIMES

Claude and Elizabeth Joseph and Codi's two brothers drove to Charleston on Saturday morning. The Joseph family reunion was joyous. Going from lost to found in less than twenty-four hours was overwhelming and difficult to comprehend. Tears of joy and happy laughter were sensations none of the family had felt in weeks.

Mary Stirk prepared lunch for everyone and invited Codi's family to stay overnight, which they gratefully accepted.

Codi and Thomas recounted unedited editions of their merging stories. No detail was left out. Codi's pre-teen brothers made sure nothing went unanswered.

Claude Joseph described the prayer service for Codi at First Presbyterian in Raleigh. "The sanctuary was packed with folks that came out to pray for you, Codi." He paused, wrinkling his brow, somewhat puzzled as he continued. "The most amazing thing was this black lady, whom nobody saw come or go, who was suddenly standing and praying for you in the front pew, Codi. She told all of us we needed to make a sacrifice of thanksgiving."

Elizabeth Joseph added, "'Pray a prayer of thanksgiving and God will be with you in your time of need,' she said. It sounded weird. She said we had to thank God for your situation just like it was. It was very hard to pray that prayer, but everyone did."

"That had to be Ms. Scribbee," Thomas said. "She's God's Chief Scribe. She keeps the eternal heavenly record."

Mr. Joseph interrupted, "Ms. Scribbee's an angel? All I can say is she was surely encouraging when I had nothing else to be encouraged about. And now I sit here and look at you, Codi, understanding for the first time in my life what praying a prayer of thanksgiving is all about. The angels were truly watching over you."

All the glory was given to God. Not one miracle was omitted, even as Codi pointed in a mirror to the very slight redness in seven or eight spots on her otherwise unblemished cheeks where the cruel Haitian had repeatedly burned her with cigarettes.

"Yesterday, I promise you, there were these huge raised scabs," Codi said. She brushed her cheeks with her fingers, more amazed than anyone listening. "I just knew I would be permanently scarred but I'm not. Not one scar. Only God could protect me like that!"

As the Josephs left for Raleigh on Sunday, Codi made Thomas promise to stay in touch."No need to ask, Codi," he said. "How could I ever do anything else?"

A huge smile spread across his face as he held Codi's hand. Her brothers snickered from the back seat, "Codi's got a boyfriend, na na na, Codi's got a..." Codi cut them off, grabbing for their shirt collars.

"I promise for sure, Codi. I'll call every day. Absolutely, totally for sure."

As the Josephs' car pulled out of sight, Mary Stirk beamed at Thomas. "Well, son, Rachael—I mean Codi—is certainly a beautiful girl ... such a sweet young lady. I'm amazed at how brave and courageous too! Hard to believe she experienced all that awful treatment on that boat. I don't know how she did it. I would have buckled under all that torture and pain."

"She's incredible, Mom. Her courage takes second only to her brains. She's so bright and intelligent. She's a totally spectacular person," he said, a prophetic smile all over his face.

The following Monday, Thomas quit his job at Media Productions. He told CC he was going back to college. CC was upset he hadn't shown for the job in DC but wished Thomas well.

Thomas called and made an appointment to see Lt. O'Reilly, who gladly set aside time to meet over a cup of coffee.

"Sir, may I be forgiven for missing the required PTI session last Thursday? It's important. I need to finish the course. I'm going back to college."

"I think we can arrange that, Thomas."

"I promise to attend all the meetings in the future. I won't miss even one."

"Something tells me things have definitely changed in your life, Thomas Stirk."

"Yes, sir."

"I can see it all over you, son."

"May I ask a big favor?"

"Go ahead, Thomas."

"I need to make sure I have a legal driver's license so I can get to work."

"We can probably fix that," O'Reilly said, a huge smile on his face.

That afternoon, O'Reilly took Thomas to see Judge Gathers, who told Thomas that with good behavior and no more DUIs, he could earn back his permanent license in six months. Until then, the Judge told him he would issue a work-only driver's permit.

"You still attending Pre Trial Intervention, Mr. Stirk?"

"Yes, sir. I intend to finish the required classes."

"I'm glad to hear it."

"Your honor, I'm stone cold sober. I have no desire for alcohol and I'm totally drug free. I thank God every day," he proclaimed. "God gave me supernatural deliverance from my addictions, a spiritual relationship with Him and most of all, a completely new life."

As Thomas entered St. Paul's Catholic Church the following Thursday, he was filled with anticipation. He was actually eager to see everyone, especially Lt. O'Reilly. He arrived fifteen minutes early and hoped to have time to chat with Lt. O'Reilly before the meeting began.

As he entered the fellowship hall, he saw everyone was already there and waiting for him. O'Reilly and the seven others rose and began clapping thunderously when they saw Thomas.

Joydie Brooks ran to Thomas with outstretched arms and hugged him. "We all actually prayed for you, man, when you weren't here last Thursday. I never prayed to God for anyone before. It's totally wild, but you're safe now."

Thomas hugged back as tears came to his eyes. He felt love in his heart for Joydie and all the others. He felt connected. It was warm and wonderful.

"Hey, I know all about lost and scared with nowhere to go," Amber Glenn said. "I know what no-clue-what-to-do-next is like. I saw all your stuff on TV. You're a hero! You're superman saving that chick from that explosion and from drowning and stuff. How'd you do it, man?"

Amber was crying too as she hugged Thomas. He loved this group and wanted them to feel and to know what God had done for Codi and him. He wanted them to know about meeting Jesus. He wanted them to know that God could take them wherever they dreamed if they only surrendered and let Him live in their hearts.

"I met three of God's angels last week," Thomas said. "And it changed my life forever."

Thomas gave his testimony about God's power and intervention. Everyone was spellbound. They asked endless questions and Thomas answered each of them from his heart. That PTI meeting, the first after Thomas's resurrection and new life, lasted more than three hours.

After the meeting, Lt. O'Reilly and Thomas went to the Waffle House for coffee.

"Lt. O'Reilly, you told me once that if I ever needed to talk to just let you know."

"I did, Thomas, and I meant it."

"Did you mean, like maybe—like possibly when I have a question, something I need to ask someone—like a real dad. You know, when I need to make a really important decision about something?"

"Exactly, Thomas. You can ask me anything. Whatever you need. Whenever you need. Anytime. Yes, you can. I would like that, son. Always just between you and me."

"Yes, sir, I would like that too."

"Thomas, I know you never had a relationship with your father. You told me you've never even met him. I can never fill those shoes, but I'll try. I'll fill in if you want."

That evening at the Waffle House, a new era began in the life of Thomas Houston Stirk. The father figure and mentor he needed soon became his best friend. Thomas respected and loved Lt. O'Reilly. The feeling was mutual.

55

CONSEQUENCES

October had come and gone and Charleston finally found relief from one of the hottest summers on record.

Repercussions from the explosion of the Hocus Pocus, Charleston's most exciting news event of the year, precipitated discussions between the United States and the Colombian government. The negotiations became embroiled in serious disagreements over culpability, a usual occurrence when billions in drug profits were at stake.

Lieutenant O'Reilly acted as spokesperson for the enormous drug discovery. He'd become the custodian of the contraband cocaine and was planning its disposal. Almost 800 sealed plastic packets of cocaine had been recovered. At 2.2 lbs each, the total weight amounted to more than 1,760 lbs with an estimated street value of over twenty-seven million dollars. It was by far the largest single domestic drug discovery by any local law enforcement agency in US history.

Late in October, Congress passed a resolution condemning Colombia for its lack of responsibility in dealing decisively with the international drug trade. The Department of Health and Human Services and the Coast Guard demanded more direct cooperation from Colombian law enforcement authorities to eliminate drug trafficking from South America.

Despite US Government demands and intervention, the cocaine train never even slowed down. The stuff was as easy to snort at Arthur's as ever.

Among those who died on the Hocus Pocus was a Colombian national, Antonio Reyes, who was found chained to a heavy decorative column floating in the shipping channel. The ship's builder identified the mahogany pilaster as having been part of the main dining salon aboard the Hocus Pocus.

Statements given to the local police and investigation records from the Coast Guard were finally released to the public. The records disclosed most of Codi's harrowing tale and the details of her rescue. Newspaper and television reporters interviewed Codi and Thomas, and the local newspaper published a serialized feature story every Wednesday and Sunday over a four-week period.

In early November, Federal Authorities arrested Jose Molina Vargus, the owner of the Hocus Pocus. He was charged with nineteen counts of murder for each person who died aboard his yacht. His trial began in late February.

The real back story of the Vargus trial had much more to do with prosecutor Fred Houghton's ambitions to expose and embarrass those in Congress who were complicit, if not directly culpable, in their blatant disregard of the lawless behavior and grief perpetrated by the South American drug trade. He was determined.

Houghton had effectively used former United States Senator Tobias Edwardson to fabricate multiple Washington headlines and build upon his prosecutorial reputation. Houghton, along with the majority of Washington insiders, knew Edwardson was guilty of major crimes and misdemeanors, but the Department of Justice couldn't prove it.

Codi and Thomas were in the courtroom the day Houghton began his examination of Edwardson.

"Mr. Houghton, please call the prosecution's next witness," Judge Falcon calmly directed, never looking up from the papers he was perusing.

"Prosecution calls Senator Tobias Edwardson," Houghton loudly announced. He had eagerly awaited his opportunity to examine Edwardson on the stand.

With his hand on the Bible, Edwardson was prompted, "Do you swear to tell the truth, the whole truth, and nothing but the truth so help you God?"

"Yes," Edwardson answered, glaring at Houghton. He had already agreed to cooperate with the prosecutor in a plea bargain deal that spared him from prison but necessitated his resignation from the United States Senate. Edwardson's hatred for Houghton was palpable in the courtroom.

Evidence indicated the former North Carolina Senator knew the two diplomats on board the Hocus Pocus, and it was well known around Capitol Hill that Edwardson enjoyed his blow with certain less than credible diplomats who ran freely up and down the East Coast, bribing politicians with big bucks to blindly ignore the so called "recreational" drug trade.

Edwardson's friendships had not served him well, including the fact that Jose Molina Vargus was a close friend of his father and had made substantial campaign contributions to the senator's election campaign.

The former senator knew if Houghton had been able to put together all the pieces of the puzzle, he would also be facing prosecution before a federal jury and would never have been allowed by his political peers to resign so quietly from the Senate.

But providentially for Edwardson, the prosecution's major witnesses died in the explosion, diplomatic passports and all.

"Please take your seat," the bailiff offered.

Edwardson turned toward the judge as if he wanted to speak but then thought better of his inclination. He took his seat, his eyes never connecting with Houghton's.

"Mr. Edwardson, are you the infamous former United States Senator from the State of North Carolina, *the* Tobias Wiley Edwardson?" Houghton's condescending inflection was unmistakable as he relished the moment.

"Objection, your honor. There is no need for the prosecutor to demean my client, to patronize Senator Edwardson so callously, your honor," Beau Ravenel firmly protested.

"Just stating the facts, your honor," Houghton quipped.

"Gentleman, I'll have no more theatrics. Is that understood?" Judge Falcon cut in. "Mr. Houghton, reign in your fork-id tongue or you'll both be in my chambers. Is that clear?"

"Yes, your honor," Houghton replied. "Mr. Edwardson, did you know the late Haitian National, Claude Pierre Aristide?"

"I'm not sure to whom you are referring, sir."

"Oh, I think you do, Mr. Edwardson. I think you remember Claude Aristide, a Haitian National and Haitian Undersecretary, assigned to the Haitian Consulate in Atlanta, otherwise know as 'Anasi,' the Spider?"

"I only knew him as Secretary Aristide and never knew him as the Spider," Edwardson answered.

"Where did you meet him?"

"At a party in Washington."

"Where was that party, sir?"

"Aboard a yacht moored at the Navy Shipyard on the Anacostia River, just south of the Capital."

"Do you recall the name of the yacht?"

"Not sure about that."

"Does Hocus Pocus ring any bells?"

"Yes, I think that could be the name."

"Senator, who else was at that party?"

"Objection, your honor," Beau Ravenel intervened. "The senator cannot be expected to recall guests at some party almost three years ago."

"Overruled. The senator will please answer the question," Judge Falcon said, never glancing up from his comfortable repose in his high-back tufted brown leather chair.

"I can't recall."

"Oh, I think you do, Senator. Did you meet Fidel Rojas Pinella?"

"I think, maybe. But I'm not sure. Probably."

"Is that a yes, Senator?"

"Yes, damn it! I met him."

"Fidel Rojas Pinella, a Colombian National and minor Undersecretary, Colombian Consulate, Miami, Florida, originally from Cartagena, Colombia. Is that the gentleman you met, sir?"

"Yes! I met him."

"How many times were you at parties aboard the Hocus Pocus?"

"Several times. Don't recall exactly. Every time Pinella sailed up the Potomac to DC. He would always throw parties for members of Congress and others."

"Were you aware, Senator, that the Hocus Pocus was sailing under the flag of Colombia with the protection of Diplomatic Immunity?"

"Yes, I think I was aware of their diplomatic status."

"Senator, do you know Jose Molina Vargus, owner of World Quest Ltd. and former owner of the Hocus Pocus yacht?"

"Yes, I've met him."

"Is Jose Molina Vargus is in this courtroom? And if so, please point to him."

Slowly and with obvious reluctance, Tobias Edwardson turned toward his friend and significant financial contributor.

"Yes, he's here," Edwardson said. He pointed and quickly continued. "Jose Molina Vargus is my good and close friend and I've never known him to have any connection to any drug cartel from South America. He's an upstanding businessman and was citizen of the year in 2009, in Cartagena, Colombia. You'll find no finer man than Jose Vargus," Edwardson rattled off, looking directly at the jury, all before Houghton could object or the judge could stop him.

"Objection, your honor." Houghton was too late to cut off Edwardson.

"The jury will disregard the outburst from the senator. Strike his remarks from the record," Judge Falcon spoke directly to the eight women and four men.

"Your honor, the good senator was just sharing his heart-felt friendship with and admiration for Mr. Vargus," Ravenel retorted, a sly grin on his face as he directed his comments to the judge but looked directly at Houghton.

"Isn't it true, Senator?" Houghton continued. "Mr. Vargus was operating or allowing to be operated from his vessel, the Hocus Pocus, a cartel of drug smuggling and drug dealing criminals passing themselves off as diplomats while they distributed cocaine up and down the East Coast?"

"Objection, your honor!" Ravenel cut in. "Mr. Houghton's conjecture has no place in this court and my client cannot be required to answer such speculation."

"Sustained! Need I warn you again, Mr. Houghton?" Falcon casually stated without even looking at Houghton.

"Isn't is true, Senator, that Mr. Vargus, through his operatives, Fidel Rojas Pinella and Claude Pierre, AKA the Spider, implemented and sustained the cartel with the help of certain legislators in Washington, DC, who looked the other way because of their so-called diplomatic status?"

"Objection, your honor," Ravenel again interrupted, now standing and raging toward the prosecutor. "Outrageous! Total speculation. The prosecutor has no proof, your honor. This prosecutor is once again asking my client to hypothesize with him. The senator has never stated he had any information regarding this matter. I must instruct my client not to answer the question."

"Sustained, Mr. Ravenel. Please calm yourself. I must ask you, Mr. Houghton, to be more specific. Just the facts."

"Judge, I don't apologize. Nineteen people are dead. Over 1700 pounds of cocaine have been seized. The people of the United States deserve answers."

"Not at the jeopardy of my client, Mr. Houghton," Ravenel insisted, his anger obvious but perhaps overdramatized. He jerked his large white handkerchief from his vest pocket and began wiping invisible beads of sweat from his brow.

"Isn't it true, Senator Edwardson, the Hocus Pocus exploded in Charleston harbor twelve months ago, exposing Mr. Vargus and his cartel's drug business?"

"Objection, your honor. Once again, I must instruct my client not to answer the prosecution's speculations."

Houghton continued, moving very close to the senator. "Senator Edwardson, I think you're aware of the testimony earlier this week by a Mr. Terrell Boydon. Mr. Boydon is a defendant in this matter and is charged with nineteen counts of murder. He testified in open court that he was paid some $10,000 to drop a stainless steel GPS tracking device down the diesel fuel tank as he delivered fuel to the Hocus Pocus the day before the yacht sailed from Charleston. Are you aware of his testimony?"

"I read something in the paper. I was not present for his appearance in court and cannot verify anything he said," Edwardson stoically replied.

"Mr. Boydon worked for a local Bunker Oil Company and says he was approached by a Hispanic gentleman about a week before fueling the Hocus Pocus. Boydon said the gentleman claimed to own the yacht. He told Boydon there were irregular activities on board and he needed to know the ship's position at all times."

"I read that in the paper. I have no first-hand knowledge."

"Objection, your honor. Anyone can see where the prosecutor is headed with this misstatement of facts. Mr. Houghton is misleading the jury. The testimony shows that Mr. Boydon was unable to pick the alleged perpetrator from a lineup of photos, which included photos of Mr. Jose Molina Vargus from several different views."

"Sustained! Watch your step, Mr. Houghton."

"To continue, Mr. Edwardson, the investigation of the explosion discovered the cylindrical device was actually a red phosphorus signal flare with an attached waterproof cell phone fuse inside an eight-inch stainless steel tube. As it turns out, the device was quite an effective and lethal bomb. Do you recall Mr. Boydon testifying that that gentleman was Hispanic?"

"Damn it. I already told you I read the paper," Edwardson blurted loudly as Ravenel once again objected to Houghton's line of questioning.

Jose Vargus was eventually found guilty of gross complicity and negligence in the matter of the explosion aboard the Hocus Pocus but not guilty of the nineteen counts of murder. They were eventually dropped. The jury was hung by the somewhat sketchy testimony of two hotel witnesses from Nevada, who swore they'd seen Vargus at least a week before the explosion of the Hocus Pocus at a Lake Tahoe resort.

Judge Falcon sentenced Vargus to twelve years in the Federal Prison at Salters, South Carolina. Falcon then suspended six years of the sentence. Federal sentencing guidelines allowed Vargus to be eligible for parole in less than one year.

Tobias Edwardson, having been damned by the persistent examination of Houghton and having surrendered his US Senate seat to save his culpable skin, returned to his family's business in North Carolina.

Edwardson was possibly a bit reformed, certainly more cautious, but nonetheless remained totally narcissistic. His desire for lost political power would haunt him the rest of his life.

56

THE SWEET LIFE

In August, Rabbi Isaac Drazin and the Talmudic Zionist Council of the Americas filed a civil action suit against Chauncy Cloud and Media Productions LLC, also naming Grant C. Goldman individually for fraud and misrepresentation while engaged in a legitimate business contract. Additionally, Rabbi Drazin claimed defamation of the Zionist Council's reputation and good standing. The newspaper reported the suit claimed $37,000 in actual damages for the monies paid under the breached contract and $2,000,000 in punitive damages.

CC had recently told some of his associates that operating a small business had become much too complicated, and he would soon announce the closing of Media Productions. Word was he was leaving the Charleston area.

In June, Thomas enrolled at the College of Charleston as a full-time student majoring in Computer Engineering and Business. He was still living at home with his mom. Thomas had taken a part-time job with a local health food grocery chain that paid him well and flexed his hours so he could attend school. Thomas had purchased a used car. It was no BMW, but it was the best he could do on his limited pay.

After Thomas completed PTI classes, he appeared before Judge Gethers to present his PTI completion certificate. The pending repeat offender charges were dropped by the court.

Since April, Codi and Thomas had been dating regularly. Codi usually drove down from North Carolina on the weekend and stayed at Mary Stirk's home. According to Mary, Codi was just part of the family now. Codi adored Little Thomas.

In August, Codi took a job teaching World History at one of the local high schools and moved to Charleston permanently. She rented an apartment from Thomas's mom, just upstairs.

Thomas and Codi restricted their dates to weekends because of Codi's daily lesson prep and Thomas's studies, but Wednesday, September 17th was Codi's birthday and Thomas made an exception. He'd secretly made reservations at Sweet Magnolias, an upscale southern bistro where reservations had to be made at least a month in advance and everyone lusted after their shrimp and grits.

On the corner of East Bay and Queen Streets, Sweet Magnolias seated only thirty-six at ten tables. Rated five-star by Conde Nast, Charleston's most famous restaurant was lavishly exclusive, nine-star expensive and ten-star delicious.

Codi was excited and surprised when Thomas told her the day before they'd be celebrating her birthday at Magnolias. Thomas had guarded the secret tryst well.

"Right this way, sir," the Maître d' directed as he pulled out the chair for Codi, seating them in the rear corner of the small dining room.

"Happy birthday, Codi," Thomas said and smiled broadly across the table as Codi scoped out the room.

"I feel so special. How will you ever afford this?" she whispered to Thomas. "Look at the prices." She smiled. "Really incredibly special. I don't think I've ever had a birthday so amazing."

Dinner began with the shrimp and grits appetizer. Thomas ordered pecan crusted salmon and Codi's main course was sweet chili rubbed ahi tuna. For dessert, they shared the vanilla bean crème brule. It was a delicious evening.

Soon after they finished dessert, the wait staff, singing happy birthday to Codi, gathered around an individual birthday cake with one sparkling candle.

When they finished singing and the other patrons stopped clapping, Thomas boldly stood then kneeled beside Codi's chair. In a voice loud enough to be heard by everyone in the dining room, he proclaimed to Codi, "Rachael Codi Joseph, you know I love you. You know God brought us together. Will you be my wife for life?"

Codi loudly effused, "Yes. Oh yes! Definitely! Yes, I will." Thomas opened the ring box and slipped a small diamond engagement band on Codi's finger as she began to cry. Everyone in the room stood and began clapping and cheering even louder.

Unseen and unheard by the patrons at Sweet Magnolias, and seated at their own table near the kitchen door, were the angels. JJ's small wings pulsated wildly, mostly from the delicious smells coming from the kitchen and the sumptuous meals he'd watched Thomas and Codi consume. His mouth was watering for shrimp and grits. He turned to look at Scribbee and Tony B, who were both gazing heavenly, arms uplifted in praise to God as their tiny wings swayed gently.

"Thank you, Father, for this heavenly union brought together under your divine authority," Scribbee said.

Tony B looked over at JJ, sensing his craving. "Shrimp and grits isn't all it's cracked up to be. Just take a cold gluttony pill and sleep it off, JJ."

Codi and Thomas planned the ceremony for the Saturday after Thanksgiving. Codi's apartment became the hub of wedding activity and she included Mary Stirk in all the planning, sometimes calling Mary, Mom. Mary Stirk was thrilled.

Over the summer, Lestee Warner won a permanent position with the National Organization for Women (NOW) as an International Foreign Director. NOW stationed Lestee in Kibungo, Rwanda where she would teach both married and single women hygiene, birth control, civil rights, and social justice while organizing them into militant women's activist groups. Her goal for some of these enlightened women was for them to take their rightful place in Rwandan society as political opportunities allowed.

Lestee recently wrote her mother she hoped to stage a qualified female candidate in the next local council elections in Kibungo later that year. Lestee loved her work and considered her professional calling a great contribution to the world and all womankind.

In October, Lestee's mother took a full-time job and no longer could care for Little Thomas during the day. Lestee suggested to Thomas in an email that she would consent to Little Thomas's adoption.

Codi loved Little Thomas as much as Thomas did, and they agreed to adopt him after the wedding. In the meantime, Little Thomas moved in with Thomas and his mom. Mary Stirk was ecstatic. She rearranged her position and schedule at the Freethinkers Society and quickly assumed full responsibility for Little Thomas.

Codi and Thomas's wedding was beautiful. Classic Charleston. Little Thomas was the ring bearer and Lieutenant Kevin O'Reilly the best man. Codi and Thomas had invited only close friends and family. The wedding wasn't expensive or extravagant. It was simple and meaningful. The wedding vows, which Codi and Thomas wrote, were eloquent and taken from Scripture.

During the ceremony, just before the rings were exchanged, Thomas removed his sepulcher stone pendant and fastened it around Codi's neck. Codi and Thomas, along with the three invisible but completely conspicuous angels sitting on the front row, understood the true meaning of the exchange.

Scribbee, splendidly elegant, was wearing her classy white suit and feathered over-sized fedora with a large white plume cocked slightly to the side. JJ and Tony B were handsomely attired in pinstriped navy blue suits and red ties. Several times during the ceremony, their angel wings danced, especially when Thomas transferred the sepulcher stone pendant to Codi.

Just as Thomas and Lt. O'Reilly turned to face the bride coming down the aisle, Tony B, his wings convulsing in a boogie, could not restrain his feelings. Totally unheard except by his Archangel companions, he exclaimed, "Unbelievable! Look who's the best man! And would you look at Codi? Is she a total drop dead knockout or what?"

When Claude Joseph gave away the bride, the guests could have heard a pin drop in the sanctuary, but that didn't stop JJ from continuing loudly to Tony B and Scribbee, "Mr. Joseph looks so proud."

As Little Thomas came down the aisle with the wedding rings on a small silk pillow, JJ, his wing's rhythm unable to decide between tango or rumba, commented to Scribbee and Tony B, "Little Thomas looks just like his dad. Thomas has got to be proud."

As the rings were exchanged, Ms. Scribbee, her wings waltzing gently, reminded JJ and Tony B, "God's infinite circle of eternity is completed." Thomas slipped the plain gold band on Codi's finger and she did likewise as the angel trio and everyone watched.

"He's my kind of guy," JJ added, fist pumping the young couple with tears welling in his eyes.

"My, my, Jeremiah, are those tears?" Scribbee chided JJ as Thomas and Codi turned to exit down the aisle.

"They are two of our most rewarding assignments," Tony B added.

"God is so good," Scribbee said and raised her hands toward Heaven in praise to God.

Everyone in attendance knew Codi and Thomas invited the Lord and could feel His presence.

After the wedding and a short honeymoon, Codi, Thomas and Thomas Jr. set up house in Codi's apartment.

Codi continued teaching history while Thomas completed his academic requirements for his degree in three years and graduated mid-term in January. Immediately after graduation, he was hired by an international software engineering firm with offices in Charleston.

Thomas, Codi and Thomas Jr., as Little Thomas was now legally renamed, bought their first home in a new West Ashley subdivision.

They joined Sea Island Church, where they had been attending for some time, and were baptized as a family.

Mary Stirk soon began attending Sea Island with them. About a year after joining the Sea Island Fellowship, she gave up her secular membership at Freethinkers and was also baptized a Christian.

"For the first time in my life," Mary would tell anyone close enough to hear, "the emptiness in my soul is gone. I am complete. I know who I am and to whom I belong. Jesus came into my heart, held me and told me I can never be thrown out!"

EPILOGUE

Dancing Angel Wings

Over the next few years, Thomas and Codi had three children.

About the time Thomas Jr. turned ten, on a bright sunny spring day, Codi, Thomas, Thomas Jr., Anthony Barclays Stirk, then six, Jeremiah Joseph Stirk, then five, and Mary Scribner Stirk, not yet four, were playing in the back yard.

Off to the side, next to a large oak in the corner of the lot, the invisible angel trio looked on. Scribbee was wearing a sleeveless white spring dress and a large natural straw sunbonnet adorned with white ribbon, her wings catching the cool afternoon breeze as she watched the children play. JJ and Tony B were outfitted in white sport coats, white trousers and open necked light blue sports shirts. They marveled at the happy family.

"Did I tell you guys Thomas and Codi legally adopted Little Thomas?" Ms. Scribbee said to JJ and Tony B.

Tony B quickly acknowledged that she had. "I hear everyone calls him Thomas Jr. now. He looks just like his dad." His wings flitted for a moment.

As Anthony Barclays ran nearby, Scribbee pointed him out to Tony B. "Your namesake is six. He took his middle name from Barclays Coedinger, an old British family name, and they call him Tony B."

Tony B beamed his delight. He had trouble keeping his fluttering wings in check.

Jeremiah Joseph followed closely behind his bigger brother. Scribbee pointed to him and to JJ. "And your namesake is five and took his middle name in honor of Codi's family. They call him JJ." JJ fist pumped at little JJ, his wings flapping coolly.

Then, little Mary Scribner, chasing after her brothers but unable to catch them, scampered passed. Scribbee, tears welling up in her eyes, looked at JJ and Tony B just as Thomas Jr., teasing his sister, dared her to catch. "Scribbee, you can't catch me. Scribbee, you can't catch me." Tears of joy flooded Scribbee's cheeks.

"No one's ever been able to pronounce Scribner, including me and JJ," Tony B confessed to Scribbee.

"What a beautiful family," Scribbee proclaimed, her wings still while tears washed down her cheeks.

Scribbee wiped her tears and asked JJ and Tony B to pray with her. The trio lifted their hands toward Heaven and spoke together. "Father God, may Thomas Jr., Tony B, JJ and Scribbee grow in wisdom and stature and in favor with God and man according to the prayers of their parents and the abundant blessings of God."

"AMEN"

ABOUT THE AUTHOR

James White grew up in South Texas. After graduation from high school, he attended Texas Christian University, where he earned his Bachelor of Science Degree in Petroleum Geology. It was at TCU he met his wife to be, Charlotte Lynn Johnson. After graduation, he was commissioned a Second Lieutenant in the United States Air Force and he and Charlotte married. They were soon off to US Air Force Pilot Training and after almost two years of challenging training, long days on the flight line and endless academic classes, he and Charlotte earned his wings. Permanently stationed at Charleston Air Force Base, he flew with the 17th Airlift Squadron on MAC missions all over the world, including many trips to Vietnam, the Far East, Africa and US Embassy support around the globe. His worldwide travel in the US Air Force spawned his second career in international business, and he built a successful multi-million dollar furniture, lamp and accessory enterprise, with manufacturers throughout the Far East and India while maintaining wholesale showrooms in High Point, North Carolina, Atlanta, Dallas and New York. In 1999, he sold the second manufacturing company he founded and attempted to retire. His desire to remain productive cut short his admittedly tedious try at retirement and today he stays busy with part time obligations as an independent security investigator and writing Christian fiction and short stories. The father of three daughters, the grandfather of nine, a committed Christian and longtime resident of Charleston, South Carolina, his background and experiences contributed to the exciting exploits in his first Christian Adventure Fiction novel.